KING OF PAIN

PIPER STONE

Published by Stormy Night Publications and Design, LLC.
www.StormyNightPublications.com

Stone, Piper
King of Pain

Cover Design by Korey Mae Johnson
Images by Romance Novel Covers and Shutterstock/Image Craft

CHAPTER 1

Carina

Betrayal had a bitter taste, a caustic bile slithering through my system. The acid burned as it slid through my veins, infecting my blood with its heavy treachery. My legs felt heavy as I moved toward the vestibule, my father waiting with an extended arm. He smiled as if this day meant something other than what it was. He'd told me I was his shining star, proud of me in everything I did.

Then he'd sold me off like a cow waiting for slaughter. I was disgusted by the sight of him, his fake smile adorning his look of contentment, an effect of the contract signing away my life. In my mind, he deserved to be gutted like the pig he was. All respect for him and his empire had been lost, my innocence traded for millions of dollars and the welcome thought of inheriting additional power from the unholy union.

My father had been stupid enough to believe that I wouldn't make good on the threat I'd made, the dutiful daughter being led around by a strong sense of family. But I wasn't interested in remaining in a noose that would only get tighter.

I would honor the promise I made.

To myself.

Destroying both families.

And I'd enjoy every moment of doing so.

I'd put my armor on, showing him how strong I was, but the bastard had broken through my defenses, using the single thing against me he knew I wouldn't be able to tolerate: tossing my younger sister to the wolves. Still, he had no idea my level of strength or the lengths I was willing to go to in order to regain my freedom.

And to rid the earth of vermin.

And in my mind, I was unstoppable.

If only I could be wearing red, my favorite color. That was more fitting for an act of vengeance, the hue exactly as I imagined Diego Santos' blood would be the moment the blade tore through his neck.

Despite anger simmering in my veins, I slipped my arm around my father's, providing a practiced gaze of admiration. Yet the anger remained a raging inferno ready to explode. As he pulled me to the entrance of the church, I took a deep breath, rubbing my fingers across the knife I'd purchased only days before. My father had underestimated me, which would ultimately lead to his death. I'd start with my intended husband first, a man I loathed with every fraction of my being. Then I'd go after Diego's father before ending my killing spree by cutting my father's heart out and shoving it down his throat.

Only then would I feel vindicated from the atrocity that my life had become.

"Are you ready?" he asked as he patted my hand, unaware of my plans.

"Absolutely. Let's get this party started."

As the traditional music began playing, I scanned the crowd of three hundred people; celebrities and musicians, politicians and heads of state who wouldn't miss the wedding of the year for anything. Little did they know they'd be witnessing a bloodbath.

And I couldn't be more excited to see their horrified reactions.

My beautiful baby sister stood at the altar, her face beaming from happiness. She had no idea I'd saved her life in more ways than one. She would be leaving town soon, her dream of living and playing music in Paris coming true. I hadn't regretted my decision. I would do anything in my power to protect her against the evil running through our family.

My pulse was racing, my heart thudding rapidly as I took my first steps toward the monster waiting feet away from the priest. While I knew my soul would be damned for all eternity for what I was about to do, I'd lost any ability to care. No longer was I the special princess. I'd become a woman expected to accept a crown of blood and thorns.

Perhaps my father had also considered me weak, choosing me to marry the son of a cartel kingpin. However, he had no idea just strong I'd become. The crowd rose to their feet, most looking at me admiringly as I walked down the soft red carpet, white rose petals already adorning the path. At least Diego's blood wouldn't stain the precious tile hand selected from Italy.

As we approached, my intended remained where he was, facing the thick pane of stained glass, the image of Christ a symbol of good, in contradiction to the blasphemous ceremony about to occur. He didn't flinch nor did he bother watching my approach, his air of arrogance creating another wild thrumming of my pulse. When we passed my mother and sister, I turned my head, noticing my mother was crying. She'd been under my father's thumb for so long she hadn't said a word to me about the atrocity or asked what she could do to help. She'd been a willing participant, but she would remain alive because I knew she had no other choice.

My father would have beaten her for disagreeing with him.

At least the beatings I'd received as a child had allowed me to become resilient, hardening the shell and in a town like Los Angeles, that had become a benefit. What my father also didn't know is that his anger had given me the courage to become cunning in everything I did.

He handed me off, squeezing my arm and lowering his head to kiss my cheek through the veil. As my stomach recoiled, I flicked open the knife, exposing the blade.

After the guests had returned to their seats, the priest began his sermon. I wasn't a woman who had patience, but I'd learned to do so over the years. It was just a matter of minutes now before I'd begin my revenge.

As I inhaled, I was surprised he wore a different scent than I was used to, the richness of timber, citrus, and exotic spices assaulting my senses. Then as we turned toward each other, I allowed Diego the gesture of lifting my veil as I controlled my rapidly beating heart. I wanted the monster to look me in the eyes and know that I was sending him off to the fires of hell.

I took a deep breath, prepared to slice his jugular when I lifted my gaze, his eyes piercing mine.

And in those few seconds there was no one else inside the church, no sound other than that of my beating heart. When his nostrils flared and he parted his ruby lips, I returned the knife back to its original position. A jolt of powerful electricity tore through me, causing my legs to tremble. I'd never felt this way around the brutal man before. Not once. But as I stood here in the hallowed location, my core began to heat, the inferno of rage turning into a wave of desire unlike anything I'd ever felt.

I took shallow breaths, blinking several times to try to regain control of my resolve, but something was very wrong.

The man standing in front me was gorgeous, tall, and muscular with a stunning carved physique. Thick dark hair framed his chiseled face, his jaw clenched as if irritated by the proceedings. He exuded power in his presence, his eyes commanding, peering down at me like a wolf whose hunger knew no bounds. But as I stared into them, the same ones I'd gazed at on several occasions, I concentrated on the flecks of violet surrounding his steel gray eyes. And I knew without a shadow of a doubt I couldn't carry out my act of retaliation.

Because the man standing in front of me was an imposter.

But that was only the beginning of the nightmare.

CHAPTER 2

 iego

I'd never intended on getting married, but as I took the hand of my bride, I was struck my how small her fingers were, her skin soft and smooth. I was in awe of her beauty and touching her shot arrows of lust straight through me, my cock already pushing against my zipper. While I'd seen her before, I hadn't taken the time to indulge in just how insanely gorgeous she really was.

Carina's cheeks were flushed, the light shade of pink pulling on every filthy desire that had ever entered my mind. Soon, she would be all mine to taste and touch, tease and fuck. I should feel elation, even a stronger sense of power, but with great dominance came concern. By accepting my hand in marriage, she'd just become my greatest weakness, a tool to be used by every Santos enemy.

She was trembling, but more so out of desire. I'd never experienced true animal attraction until now, but the amount of electricity soaring through us both was significant. As I took a deep breath, her luscious scent floated into my nostrils. She was as aroused as I'd become, her breath rapid and scattered. I sensed she hated the pompous ceremony as much as she did the man standing beside her, but there was no denying our intense connection just as there'd been when we'd sparred.

The alliance between our families would create a powerful combined empire, which would rock the entire Western region, as well as various global locations. Our respective fathers were celebrating our union, but she'd been coerced into the arrangement, forced to realize she was nothing more than a rich man's possession. Now she was shifting from one gilded cage to another.

The air of tension between us was understandable, her desire to end my life in order to save hers written all over her lovely face. It was the intense burn of her heated gaze that intrigued me. She was a formidable woman for her age, only agreeing to an unholy marriage to save the life of her sister.

And I was the monster who would take full advantage of the difficult situation.

As the priest stepped forward, the congregation standing, so began the sanctimonious ceremony of our unholy matrimony. To feel such desire burning through me was unusual, especially given the circumstances.

Her hand was trembling in mine, but not out of fear. Only rage. We were enemies in a sea of sharks and piranhas, the blood-infested waters of Los Angeles not for the faint of heart. But she was strong.

Only I was stronger.

But I would remember that Carina DeMill was a force to be reckoned with.

I would need to break her to make her mine. The thought was riveting but complicated the situation. However, I had to stay focused, or the last months of preparation would mean nothing.

Throughout the ceremony, she kept her head down except when required. And when she lifted her chin, her deep green eyes piercing mine, I gathered a sense she wouldn't be easy to break. The challenge kept my balls tight.

Thirty minutes later, the pomp and circumstances were nearly concluded, the vows already stated, hers through clenched teeth. As she turned to me, tilting her head, the amount of venom in her eyes was both understandable as well as enticing. As I lowered my head for the kiss, I sensed everyone was holding their breath. Carina squeezed my hand as she slid the other around my shoulder, rising onto her tiptoes.

As she nuzzled against my neck, I smiled, hearing her whispered words.

"One day I will kill you, my husband."

I wrapped my arm around her waist, jerking her against my chest. "I can't wait to see you try." I sensed her heart racing, the pulse in her neck increasing. As I brushed my lips across hers, I heard her audible shudder. Soon, she would cry out my name in throes of passion.

The level of silence in the church was deafening.

Then I heard a noise.

Snapping my head toward the front of the church, I sensed exactly what was happening, but my reflexes weren't fast enough.

Gunshots from automatic rifles rang out, the peppering of dozens of rounds coming from several locations inside the church. Screams erupted, guests trying to flee the pews. Carina immediately reacted, trying to race toward her family, but I jerked her back and yanked out my weapon. Within seconds, an asshole in a mask rushed from the side, coming within a few feet of us. I fired off two bullets, hitting him directly in the face. He tumbled forward, blood splattering across Carina's face and dress.

I pushed her down, searching for the soldiers assigned to the location. Popping noises continued to occur, bodies flailing as they were struck, a mass stampede of confusion adding to the melee.

Carina struggled to get from under me, whimpering as she fought.

"Stay down," I hissed. "Do not move. Do you hear me?"

"Yes. What is happening?"

An attempted massacre. My father had laughed at the thought, his arrogance refusing to accept that with all the pomp and circumstance of the high-powered union, both families had placed targets on their backs. He'd believed none of our enemies would dare have the gall to attempt an assassination.

Xavier Santos was a fool.

Carina's voice was smaller than I was used to, the fear crippling. I shifted away by a few inches, taking aim as one of the masked assailants bounded close to the altar. As soon as he dropped, two others appeared. I remained crouched, shifting and taking aim, striking one between the eyes. Before I had a chance to twist my arm toward the other, he lunged forward, tackling me onto the floor.

Carina screamed from behind me as I rolled with the assassin, yanking my arm free. The asshole was larger, but I was stronger and even as he tried to force the barrel I held toward my chest, I snapped my other fist against the side of his neck, wasting no time before firing two shots. Several of my men were headed in our direction, jumping over fallen guests.

As another assassin came at us, I was shocked when Carina kicked out, catching him in the stomach. That allowed me fire to off two shots in rapid succession.

It would seem my bride wasn't a wilted flower.

As he started to go down, I grabbed her around the waist, keeping us both as low to the floor as possible, heading for the side door leading to the church offices.

"No!" Carina screamed, trying to get away from me. "My family!" I was shocked when she slipped through my hands, grabbing one of the rifles from the dead assassin.

"We don't have time, Carina. You're coming with me." Yanking her backward, I barreled her through the door as another series of shots rang out, the wall and doorjamb punctured with bullet holes.

Sergio Ivanoff was my second in command, the Russian considered brutal under anyone's terms. He tossed and dragged furniture in front of the door, even though that would only hold off the perpetrators for so long.

"Get them out of here," he called to the other men. "We have the SUV waiting in the back. We need to get out of here now!"

Our departure route had been preplanned, the alleyway behind the church the perfect location to keep away from the press. Our impending nuptials had been a top news story for days, reporters unable to get enough of our fairy-tale romance. They'd camped outside both our houses in their attempt to obtain an exclusive, the alliance of two of Los Angeles' most powerful families boosted to national news.

Only our lives weren't beautiful like the make believe of the movies. Instead, they were raw and dangerous.

"No. Please. I need to see them." Carina managed to break free, smashing her way through three of the soldiers. She pointed the weapon in her hand, somehow able to get off a few wild shots.

Hissing, I fisted her hair, yanking her back with enough force she yelped. Then I tossed her against the wall, wrenching the weapon from her hand and keeping my eye on the door. I tossed it to one of the soldiers, taking several ragged breaths. It was only a matter of time before another line of assailants burst through. I kept the full weight of my body against hers, cupping her jaw. "Listen to me. We have about thirty seconds before the assailants come through that door. Do you understand me?"

She nodded as best she could, her eyes wide and glistening from tears. "Save them. Save my family. Please."

"First, I save you. This is going to be dicey so when I put you in the vehicle, you're staying all the way down. Do not look back, Carina. No matter what you do."

"We need to get the fuck out of here!" Sergio hissed, firing off a full round at the door.

I wrapped my arm around her, holding her tightly against me as several of my soldiers surrounded us. I gave the nod to throw open the door, able to shove her inside the back-seat but only seconds before assailants rushed down the alley heading for us.

Sergio pushed me, halfway tossing me inside then jumping in the passenger seat. "Go. Go. Go!" he barked.

The driver took off, slamming his foot down on the acceler-ator, the popping sounds continuing. Carina yelped as at least two bullets hit the rear of the SUV, the sound echoing. I kept my body straddling hers, cringing when the back window was cracked. The damn thing was supposed to be bulletproof.

"Get us out of here," I snarled, wrapping both hands around the Glock, prepared to shoot out the back window if necessary.

Sergio threw his arm back, cursing in Russian. "Stay down, *El Jefe*. We need you."

Huffing, I crouched lower, hating the way she was trembling in my arms.

When the driver swung to the right, hitting the street with a brutal jolt, I scanned the area around us.

"How the hell did they get through our defenses?" I demanded.

"They were in the crowd of reporters outside," the driver answered, Sergio giving him a harsh look.

"And I thought you checked for weapons," I retorted.

"We did," Sergio answered. "They must have hidden them."

"Fuck," I hissed. Who the hell would dare do this now? The list of Santos enemies was long, but only one organization would have the balls to do something so egregious. "Get us to the goddamn plane."

The next few minutes continued to be harrowing, the driver skidding through several traffic lights, gunning the engine to bypass every vehicle in the way.

Carina continued trembling, but she remained quiet.

I waited until it was obvious that we weren't being followed before gathering my bride into my arms, lifting her chin when she refused to look at me. Blood had marred her lovely face, strings of it caked on the side of her neck, her dress ruined.

Her eyes were wild, full of fear. At least at first.

Then she seemed to have a razor-sharp focus, jerking out of my hold. Then she issued a hard slap across my face as tears slipped down her face.

"You did this. You killed my family."

CHAPTER 3

 arina

Numb.

My arms and legs remained numb, but my stomach was churning, my mind a foggy mess. How had this happened? I folded my arms, struggling to breathe, the weight on my chest unlike anything I'd ever felt before. "Find out if they're alive. If they're not…" Unable to finish the threat, I made the statement as if anything I said to the man would matter. I couldn't stand to look at the man I'd agreed to marry.

"I will find out, Carina. That I promise you," Diego said, his voice softer than it had been before.

I'd seen the look of horror in my sister's eyes just after all hell had broken loose. Her terror was mine. If I lost her, I wouldn't hesitate to use the knife on the man I didn't even know. I twisted my head, studying him carefully.

Something wasn't right. Or maybe I was losing my mind. "Where are we going?"

"To my house in San Diego. For now." He yanked out another magazine of ammunition, tossing the old one onto the floor. I wondered whether he had to take a weapon with him everywhere. To the bathroom. Out to dinner. To a family gathering.

My thoughts were all over the place, my head aching.

"That's not wise, *El Jefe*," the man with the Russian accent said. I almost laughed at the term he used, my mind churning from trying to remember what I'd seen. A sea of men in dark clothes. And blood. So much blood.

I finally held up my hands. They were stained with crimson and suddenly they started to itch. A tremor from deep inside rushed through my system with such force I couldn't stop shaking.

"Get every available man to stand guard. Have them sweep the place before we get there," Diego answered.

"Why don't we go to the safehouse in North Coast?"

"Maybe, but not now. Whoever did this will pay and I'm not going to hide some like terrified asshole. We go to San Diego," Diego snarled.

"You did it. Your enemies. Your friends. Everyone wants you dead," I half whispered.

"That may be the case, princess, but you could be the target as well."

His tone had changed, the sultry sound lacing every syllable making me sick to my stomach. I turned my head, glaring at him as I'd done so many times before. He was splattered with specks of blood, but it didn't mar his handsome face. He was far too debonair, acting as if the violence was an everyday occurrence. I'd never been faced with that kind of nightmare. Never.

You should have killed him.

Would that have changed anything? No. I'd likely be dead. However, the fact he'd saved my life didn't calm the rage.

Or the hatred.

I took several deep breaths, rubbing my hands together. Then I started scratching, digging my nails into my palms. I had to get the blood off. I couldn't stand it. God, oh, God. Were they alive? As a whimper escaped my lips, he took my hands into his, just like he'd done at the ceremony.

"You can wash your hands on the plane."

"I'm not going with you," I snapped.

"Yes, you are. You're my wife, which placed a target over your head even before you said 'I do.'"

I finally broke into laughter. "And you think this is going to be a happy marriage?"

Sighing, he glanced at the man up front. "Find out about her family."

18

The Russian snorted. "I'll see what I can do."

"I'm going to protect you, Carina, but you'll need to do everything I say."

"Not a chance."

"Then you'll learn the hard way."

"Are you threatening me?"

"Would I threaten my wife? That would make me a terrible man."

There was strange sense of sincerity in him. I took a deep breath, trying to keep my shit together. The horrible visions would remain in my mind forever.

"We're almost at the airport, boss," the driver said. "There are several men stationed there."

"Good. Get us as close as possible," Diego told him.

"Yes, sir."

"Sir. You must think you're an important man." I told him, still staring at my hands.

"No more than most, Carina. I'm just a man attempting to do his job. Now, that includes protecting his wife. I'm curious. Where did you learn to shoot?"

"It was one thing my father didn't mind teaching me." What did Diego care? I refused to look at him as the driver swung through a series of gates, heading onto a private airstrip.

The driver jerked the SUV to a stop, immediately getting out.

"I don't have any clothes. Nothing." I don't know why I even made the comment.

"Take a look. Your suitcases are in the back."

I barely glanced over my shoulder. My life had been sorted out, altered in less than two weeks. "Of course they are."

"The church is swarmed with police officers. I can't get any definitive answers," the Russian said. "But there are several fatalities."

I lifted my gaze, and I felt the heat of Diego's. I couldn't panic. There was a good chance they were okay. But what if they weren't?

The driver climbed out, immediately yanking the suitcases from the back, heading toward the person standing by the plane. Then another haze formed over my eyes.

Diego pressed his fingers against my arm, and I wanted to pull it away so badly, but his touch made me shiver in a good way. I hadn't been anticipating the instant connection or the way my nipples had hardened.

"It's all clear, boss," the driver said as he opened Diego's door.

And it was until it wasn't.

We were only a few feet away from the steps when additional shots rang out. This time, the adrenaline rush I'd felt before was long gone. I was incapable of fighting, only clinging to Diego as he jumped in front of me, using his body to block mine. This wasn't behavior I expected from a man nicknamed 'the Butcher.'

"Get her on the plane," he hissed to the Russian, firing off several shots.

The Russian grabbed my arm, tugging me up the metal stairs. I almost stumbled given the long train on my dress, the man cursing when he was forced to catch me. He shoved me inside, immediately returning to the open door.

"Get ready to take off," the Russian barked at the pilot then snapped his head in my direction. "Sit down."

The asshole didn't like me very much. The feeling was mutual. I eased into a seat, holding my head in my hands. I had no idea if my purse or phone was with the suitcases. What did it matter if I had no one to call? I could sense I was becoming hysterical, which wasn't my personality. The only comfort I had was the fact I still had the knife with me. After throwing a quick glance toward the door, I pulled the switchblade from the holder I'd fashioned into the sleeve, still furious with myself for not using it. Everything was such a mess, including my thoughts on him being an imposter. His actions certainly didn't corroborate my strange thoughts.

I heard another series of popping sounds and moaned. Then I felt a presence beside me and took a deep breath before lifting my head.

"It's over. We're safe," Diego said in a hushed voice.

As the plane lurched forward, rolling down the runway, I lifted my head but couldn't look at him. The stench of blood was everywhere, the coppery odor sickening.

He placed his hand under my chin, forcing me to look at him. "I will find out about your family."

I wanted to believe him but at this point, I wasn't certain what to believe. "Yes, you will."

As he inhaled, I was startled by the sensations tearing through me, the white-hot heat that occurred every time I was close to the man. When he brushed his thumb back and forth across my cheek, I found myself wanting to nuzzle into his hand. That was ridiculous.

Swallowing, I pulled away and he curled his fingers. "Please find out, Diego. I might not like my father very much, but I don't want anyone in my family hurt."

"I understand. I keep my promises."

He never blinked as we studied each other and I was mesmerized by the flecks of gold, trying to remember if I'd seen them inside the courtroom. I was possible with the ugly fluorescent lighting that I would have missed the intense shimmer, especially when he was angry. At this point, I wasn't certain of anything.

As the plane ascended into the air, he breathed a sigh of relief. "Do you want a drink? I certainly need one."

"Yes but is there a bathroom I can use? I'd like to try and get the blood off." I needed time to myself to process everything or I was certain I'd go mad.

"Of course. Behind me."

I glanced toward the door and nodded. When I tried to stand, the ugliness of everything that had happened rushed into me, my legs shaking.

"Whoa. I've got you." He jerked to a standing position, wrapping his arm around me. I wanted to shove him away, but I wasn't certain I had the strength or agility to take the few steps needed. After guiding me down the corridor and opening the door, he turned me around.

"What are you doing?" I heard the biting tone in my voice and sighed.

"You'll need help getting out of your dress."

"Oh. Thank you."

He brushed my hair over my shoulder, his hot breath skipping across the back of my neck. Another quiver trickled down my spine and I bit back a moan. I didn't want to enjoy his touch. I couldn't stand the thought of being close to him. Now all I wanted was to have his arms wrapped around me and it felt wrong.

Unholy.

Sinful.

But I needed his touch.

As I gripped the doorjamb, my once beautifully polished nails digging into the synthetic material, he slowly unfastened the three dozen small satin buttons. He was deliberate with his actions, treating the dress as if it hadn't been ruined. I heard his deep breath from seeing my naked back, the sound ragged and full of desire. I closed my eyes, trying to slow my breathing, biting my lower lip until I tasted blood as he brushed his fingers all the way down my spine.

"I shouldn't have allowed that to happen," he muttered.

No, you shouldn't have. But I didn't say it. I couldn't blame him, at least not entirely. "Thank you for helping me." I had no idea what else to say.

"I'll bring your suitcase. Just take your time. There are fresh towels and toiletries. We won't land for an hour."

An awkward silence settled in.

"Diego. I'm sorry. I didn't ask about your family. That was heartless of me. Do you know anything about them?"

"Not yet, my beautiful bride."

There was a sadness in his voice I had yet to hear, and it surprised me.

"I'll pray for them." I had no idea why I'd made the comment. I hadn't prayed since I was a child, but there was nothing else I could do at this point. When he didn't say anything, I turned sightly, crossing my arm over my chest. He seemed to be a million miles away, his eyes not focusing on anything.

Maybe I was still in shock, the anguish of not knowing as horrible as the shooting. I closed the door behind me, leaning against it, the light turning on automatically. The warm, soft glow was just enough to highlight the fear remaining in my eyes. I removed the knife, holding it into the air, flicking the blade open. I knew he'd take it away if he found it on me, likely punishing me. That wasn't going to happen. I needed something to protect myself with.

But against who?

I slipped the weapon under a stand of towels, grabbing a washcloth at the same time.

Laughing, I shimmied until the dress eased past my shoulders, falling to the floor. Then I stared at myself in the mirror. All I could see was blood covering everything.

After stepping out of the dress, I tried to kick it away. I never wanted to see it again. Never. The long train had managed to wrap around my legs and within seconds, I was enraged, ripping at the twenty-thousand-dollar Oscar de la Renta designer gown, ready to use the sharp blade.

Then everything started to overwhelm me. As I lowered my head, I could no longer stop tears from falling.

I'd wanted to end the monster's life, but the beast had saved me instead.

* * *

Diego

I raked my hands through my hair, taking long strides toward the bar, waiting until I'd poured a tall scotch before turning my attention to Sergio. "What. The. Fuck. Happened?"

"I already told you. It was an ambush."

"Not good enough, Sergio. I know what it was. It was a goddamn shitshow. We let our guard down. I need to know why and by whom?"

"You know who it is."

"Why don't you tell me."

"Ortiz. They were his men."

I eyed him for a few seconds, still furious I hadn't taken more precautions.

"You're so certain about that?"

He hesitated, finally shaking his head. "I will confirm it, *El Jefe*. The fucker needs to die."

I took a long swig, fisting my other hand. "Soon, Sergio. Soon." Every muscle ached, the anger building to the point the tension had tightened my chest. This was the last goddamn thing I needed. "Who the hell is still at the church?"

"Stone," Sergio sneered. "He managed to clean up some of the debris before the cops arrived."

"Any markings?"

"Not that he noticed. Granted, he's green to this."

Stone had been with the Santos organization for two years.

The two were at odds, which had already annoyed me. "Call him back. I need to know the status of her family now. I don't care whose heads he needs to break." I tipped back the scotch, realizing he was still staring at me.

"Do you want to know about your family?"

His tone was sarcastic, as if he'd caught me in no longer caring what happened to my family. Little did he know my father meant nothing to me. "Yes, Sergio. However, keep in mind that my father knew the risks better than most. I'm certain he was wearing a bulletproof vest just in case."

He thought about what I said and nodded. "You're right. I will find out."

"I need to know as soon as you have any concrete information." I polished off my drink, the light burn from the alcohol doing nothing to soothe the rage inside. After slamming down my glass, I headed for the bathroom, realizing my bride would likely have difficulty removing the stains from her skin. I headed to the small kitchen, searching the cabinets for salt. Finally finding a container, I yanked a glass from another, turning on the faucet. After pouring salt into the glass and filling it with warm water, I grabbed her suitcase, heading for the bathroom. I lowered the case to the floor and rapped my knuckles against the door.

"Just a second." Her soft voice filtered through the closed door.

I waited, the fury given everything that had happened continuing to grow.

"Okay." She held a towel in front of her chest, staring at both of us in the mirror. Her arms were bright red from the scrubbing she'd done.

I slid the case inside, closing the door behind me. Then I crowded her space, the heat shared between us oppressive. "Let me help you."

"I'm fine."

"No, you're not. Soap and water won't be enough." As I grabbed the washcloth, she shuddered in my hold, her body quivering but I knew it wasn't from a chill or fear. The crackling current between us was overwhelming, so much so I found it difficult to breathe. As I took her arm, she fisted her hand, still fighting to keep her voluptuous breasts covered. Her eyes never left me as I poured the water over the worst spots, taking my time to gently rub her already abraded skin.

She said nothing, but her breathing remained scattered, her hot breath steaming up the mirror. When she winced from the salt content, I stopped altogether, lowering my head and brushing my lips across the back of her neck.

Her single moan was sweeter than anything she could say to me. She fell against me, the towel slipping from her hand.

I took a deep breath, angry with myself for being fully aroused, my throbbing cock pressing into her bottom. She dragged her tongue across her lips, never blinking as she studied me. There were so many questions in her eyes as well as worry and hurt.

"Don't," she said, her tone pleading.

After rubbing my knuckles across her shoulder, I backed away, leaving the glass on the counter. As I turned to go, I noticed she'd tossed the towel.

"Wait," she said softly.

"What's wrong?"

"Fuck me."

"What?" What had she just said to me?

"Just fuck me. I need to feel alive again."

I took a deep breath, wanting to devour her. As I turned, the sight of her naked breasts, her hardened nipples took my breath away. I moved closer, trying to keep my control in check. When I wrapped my arms around her, she brushed her fingers across my hand, my cock instantly twitching, already fully aroused. As I pressed my groin against her, she shuddered, her eyelids now half closed.

And I'd never wanted anything more.

I lowered my head, nuzzling against her neck, smiling as she pulled her long hair to the front. As I bit down, she trembled in my hold, grinding her hips against me. I was no longer shocked by the soaring electricity we shared or the burning desire that we'd both had in our eyes. She hated me for who I was and the fact she'd been forced into marrying me, but the longing couldn't be shoved aside.

The moment I pinched her nipples, twisting them painfully, her moans filtered into my ears. Even with the lingering stench of blood, the acrid copper smell filling the space, her sweet fragrance of desire was the only thing I could concentrate on. I licked along her shoulder blade, moving to her ear, nipping her earlobe.

Carina arched her back, easing her arm back to touch my face and the beast dwelling deep within me roared to the surface. I took my time tasting her skin, enjoying the delicious flavor on my tongue.

PIPER STONE

This was time stolen, a horrible tragedy unable to keep our needs contained. I eased away, rolling my fingers down her spine and along the crack of her ass. Every inch of her was beautiful, her curves as perfect as any woman could have. I had a feeling she had no idea how gorgeous she was, always stuck in the shadow of her father.

Tonight, I would show her just how much of a dazzling woman she was.

And this was just the beginning.

As I unfastened my trousers, she took shallow breaths, her lazy eyes staring at me. When my cock sprang free, a slight smile crossed her face. She lifted her head, and I couldn't resist wrapping my fingers around her lovely throat, squeezing until she released a string of husky moans.

Then I cracked my hand against her rounded bottom, a smile curling on my lip as she shivered in my hold. "Are you a bad girl?"

"Yes. Always."

"I guess I'll need to deal with that in the future."

"Mmm… We shall see."

I smacked her several more times, enjoying the heat already building in my fingertips. She undulated her hips, swaying them back and forth and I forced her head back, lowering mine so I could capture her lips. The taste of scotch mixed with her sweet nectar, and I was far too hungry to wait. Yet I brought my hand down several more times before slipping my fingers between her legs, her wetness staining my skin.

30

I allowed the kiss to become a roar of passion as I fingered her, swirling one around her clit then pinching the tender tissue. She mewed into my mouth, darting her tongue inside. Within seconds, I'd dominated hers, my heart racing as I thrust my fingers deep inside.

She rolled onto her toes, tightening her grip on the counter. I couldn't stand to wait any longer to fuck her, the temptation too great.

I kept my grip on her neck as I flexed my fingers open, pumping several more times. Then I shifted my hand to my cock, stroking the base of my shaft several times before slipping my cockhead to her swollen folds.

Then I broke the kiss.

"Just fuck me. Don't be gentle. I won't break."

She could have no idea what her words did to me, the need exploding deep within me. I drove the entire length of my cock inside, tightening my hold until she issued a strangled cry. As her pussy muscles clamped around the thick invasion, I gasped for air, every muscle tenser than before.

"So tight. So damn tight." My muttered words caused her to whimper, jutting her hips back and grinding her bottom against me. I couldn't hold back, thrusting several times, the force driving her against the counter. She didn't care, her eyes glassy from explosive lust.

Nothing could have prepared me for the powerful vibrations coursing through me or the need building to a precipice. I was unable to control my hunger, plunging into her hard and fast, taking everything that now belonged to me. Every sound she made only fueled the fire, igniting embers I'd left dead for far too long.

I pulled all the way out, cracking my hand against her bottom again, adoring her soft cries. I wanted her marked as mine. My needs continued to explode as I thrust like a savage, our bodies molded perfectly together.

As I rolled onto the balls of my feet, a smile crossed her face, the same fire burning in her eyes. I could tell she was close to an orgasm, her brow furrowing as she licked her lush lips. I pounded my cock even more brutally, straining to keep some level of control.

When her breathing changed, her climax close, I shifted the angle again, digging my fingers into her soft skin. After nipping her ear, I whispered exactly what I had planned on doing to her. "I'm going to fuck you for hours, tasting every inch of your sweet skin, your luscious pussy. And after I'd finished, you'll never want another man again."

Her sigh was like sweet music, my mind raging with the kind of thirst that would never be quenched. As an orgasm rolled into her, I pushed us both harder, rocking her body as she let out a slight scream.

"Yes. Yes... Oh, God, yes." Her cry was strangled, her long lashes skimming across her shimmering cheeks. There was no way I could hold it any longer. Her pussy muscles constricted, and my body started to shake. Then as my balls tightened, I closed my eyes, pumping wildly until I erupted deep inside.

She took gasping breaths, continuing to whimper. I crowded her space even more, placing my hands on hers, keeping us together for a full minute.

When I gazed into the mirror one more time, I saw blood in my eyes, thick and coagulated. That's when I realized how furious I was that someone dared try to hurt my wife.

My. Wife.

I repeated the two little words over and over again in my mind. I hadn't wanted her. I hadn't needed a distraction. But I'd had no choice. Seeing the horror in her eyes had broken something in me.

I would hunt down the bastards who did this.

And I'd put a bullet into their brains one by one.

CHAPTER 4

 iego

"Your father was shot. He was transported to the hospital, but he'll make a full recovery. Your mother and sister were unhurt."

Carina blinked several times, nodding and I watched as a single tear slipped past her long lashes. She'd remained quiet the remainder of the trip, nursing a single drink, refusing to look at me. "No thanks to you."

"I will find who did this, Carina."

"Then what?"

"Then they die."

"The way of your world."

"The way of *our* world."

Sighing, a part of me wanted to gather all the men and go hunting, but my bride needed me more. Her attitude had changed again, but it was likely given the volume of shock. I couldn't blame her, although I would need to establish certain rules tonight.

There were men surrounding the property, including Sergio, but the Russian was right in that I could be considered vulnerable in this location. Certain choices would need to be made, and I wasn't in the best state to make them tonight.

As suspected, my father had been wearing a bulletproof vest, which had likely saved his life. My half-brother had been trampled in the mass exodus, but only had scrapes and a twisted ankle. He'd already called, ensuring our safety.

As if I really believed he gave a damn. He wanted to make certain his precious deal hadn't been crushed before it had time to take effect.

Thoughts of fucking her in the airplane rolled into the back of my mind. It had been unexpected, but a sheer pleasure and one that I didn't deserve. I'd dropped the ball, almost getting her killed.

I swirled the liquid in my glass as I studied her. She thought she was so clever, but I'd known her murderous intentions the second she joined my side in front of the altar.

Few people ever surprised me given what I did for a profession. Fewer still would openly challenge a man of my position, let alone intend to commit coldblooded murder in such a public fashion. However, Carina DeMill had not only astounded me, her brazen I-couldn't-care-less attitude had also given me a hard-on the second I'd taken her hand into mine. For a few amazing minutes on the plane, we'd connected unlike we had before. Then she'd turned flippant, distant and cold. Still, I couldn't blame her, including for wanting to kill me. She had every right to be furious with how everything had occurred.

Only she didn't know the full story.

I'd caught a glimpse of the switchblade in Carina's hand, my intended determined to end my life. It had amused me. I'd also become completely aroused. She was supposed to be the dutiful daughter, a woman who wouldn't fight the inevitable, but she'd surprised me not only with her intended action but her beauty and vivaciousness.

While I'd known better than to expect a demure personality given her chosen profession, the fact she'd withdrawn her decision had me curious. Why not act on her need for revenge? The only answer was a simple one.

A single weakness.

She was a powerhouse in business, the two times we'd seen each other immediately prior to our wedding day keeping me aroused for days. I'd wanted to fuck her both times, stripping away her glamorous exterior, thrusting my cock so deep inside she'd scream out my name. But I'd been patient, a hungry man allowing the excitement of his first taste to remain in place.

But tonight, I would claim what rightfully belonged to me. After all, she'd signed a contract.

She had an air of unassuming beauty, nothing like the prima donnas that were so typical in Hollywood. Her skin was flawless, untouched by chemical peels or plastic surgery, her perky nose and high cheekbones dazzling, especially when her sparkling green eyes held venom as they did right now.

Damn it, my cock was aching all over again.

Taking her inside the plane had been a sheer delight. Then I'd seen tears in her eyes. It was no wonder she'd shut down her emotions, returning to loathing me for ruining her life. It was a protection mechanism and one I understood far too well. She'd remained inside the bathroom for another fifteen minutes, leaving the bathroom in fresh clothes, refusing to mention her wedding dress. God, the woman was beautiful.

With every touch, there'd been a distinct current running through both of us that couldn't be denied. I hadn't expected to enjoy the thought of fucking her, let alone the act itself, but that's exactly what I felt, the need to tear away her dress, exposing her voluptuous body almost all I could think about.

But I remained on edge, forced to accept the attempt on my life wouldn't be the last. Too many good people had lost their lives in the massacre, including several politicians and actors. The tragedy had already hit Hollywood hard. It was likely only a short period of time before the authorities would want my statement. I'd handle that when necessary, but tonight belonged to us. To regroup. To get closer.

If that was possible.

Finally alone in my house on the beach after the hour flight in my private plane, I unbuttoned my jacket, watching her stare out the window at the tumultuous ocean waters. Dark waves lapped against the shore, matching the vile mood I'd been in for weeks. At least being alone with my bride would help soothe the rage.

I'd made several phone calls myself, leaving her alone to her new surroundings and I'd found her in the same place almost an hour later.

Our honeymoon was booked for a week later, business more important in the world of the Santos Empire. Now that our families were merged, there was much work to be done, including eliminating certain enemies.

But first, the hunt would begin.

Perhaps I should move her to a different location, although I had a feeling whoever was behind the killing spree had gone to great lengths to locate the various estates owned by the family.

I exhaled at the thought, rolling the cool glass across my forehead then placing it on one of the tables. Then I headed toward the prechilled bottle of champagne. Watching her was like enjoying the sight of a beautiful flower just before its opening. When she'd left the bathroom, she'd pinned her hair, perhaps to keep me from running my fingers through it. But now, she'd removed the hairpins holding the dark curls in place, her thick strands falling close to her waist. All I could think about was bending her over the back of the couch, driving my cock past her swollen folds.

Perhaps I was a bad man for thinking such filthy sin after what we'd been through, but my lovely bride had been right. This was just another part of a monstrous life.

As the cork popped, she visibly jumped but didn't turn around. While she was clearly annoyed with me, she was also uncertain of my intentions. When she glanced in my direction, I was pleasantly surprised to see the first hint of fear. However, she knew that I wouldn't hurt her unless necessary. At least that's what she'd been told. I poured two glasses, leaving them where they were as I slowly removed the bowtie, unbuttoning my shirt and rolling up the sleeves.

When I started to approach, she bristled. We weren't to be married in name only. I'd gone over the contract word for word, my background allowing me to easily decipher the various passages. I would take her tonight per terms of the contract, but I had a feeling the passion we'd shared only two hours before wouldn't be repeated. Perhaps I was wrong. I'd thought about not doing so, but the moment I'd caught a glimpse of her, all I'd thought about was what it would feel like to have Carina in my arms.

Now that I had, I was already insatiable.

I put the glass in front of her, noticing her ragged breathing. But it wasn't from trepidation, only anger. She was one formidable woman, much more so than her father had obviously given her credit for.

"We should have a toast to our marriage."

She slowly lifted her head, darting her eyes back and forth across mine.

"This isn't a celebration, *Diego*. I will never be happy being your wife. Think about all the people who lost their lives because of our unholy union. Being around you disgusts me. This is a business arrangement and nothing more. And I will get back to work tomorrow."

"No, you won't, Carina. Not until I determine who destroyed our wedding."

"As if you care about the wedding."

"Take the glass, Carina." I kept my tone even but authoritative. She would soon learn that there was no way out of the contract or our marriage. That wasn't allowed.

She jerked it from my hand, drinking half then backing away, but not before considering tossing the rest in my face. Then a smile crossed her face just like the one I'd seen seconds before she'd decided not to drive the sharp blade into my carotid artery.

"What happened before was nothing. I want you to know that." While she tried to have conviction in her tone, I could tell by the look of desire on her face that she was angry with herself for how much satisfaction she'd gotten from the moment shared.

"Think what you want, Carina. If that's what you need to do."

"It's the truth."

My defiant little flower. My balls were already tight, aching.

I took a sip of the bubbly, enjoying the perks of my position. "I'm curious about something. Are you still contemplating killing me, perhaps driving a sharp blade straight into my jugular, or is that too personal for you? You can certainly handle a weapon. Perhaps you'd rather shoot me from a distance."

My question seemed to surprise her, and although she hid it well, her eyes betrayed her. "Eventually and I want it messy, which will make my actions *very* personal and extremely enjoyable. However, I will bide my time until it's the right moment and one you least expect. Then I'd drive a stake right through your heart."

God, the woman turned me on more than any other had. It was obvious she felt guilty.

"That's good to know." I took another taste of the champagne then moved closer. "Why don't I give you a chance right now?"

Her armor slipped enough I sensed she was uncertain what she should do.

"Oh, come now, Carina. I know about the knife. You are a very clever girl, but I'm a trained killer. Give it to me." I held out my hand.

She immediately backed away, skirting around me and placing her flute on the table before taking long strides toward the set of stairs. If she thought I was going to allow her to play games tonight, she was dead wrong.

I tossed my glass, enjoying the sound of it shattering against the door then easily snagged her wrist, jerking her around to face me.

She did as I suggested, pressing the blade just under my chin, her body trembling in my hold. As her eyes darted back and forth, the explosion of electricity between us became undeniable. Just like it had been before. "I'm going to jam it into your brain. That's what you deserve."

"For protecting you? Or for going along with the contract?"

As her mouth twisted in frustration, I sensed she was already losing her fight with the strong resolve she'd planned on keeping. "You were forced to protect me. I'm much more valuable alive."

"Is that what you think?"

"That's what I know. My own father sold me off like a possession and that's what you intend on keeping me as. A prized doll on a shelf."

The woman was impressive, more so than I'd given her credit for.

I glanced down, a smile crossing my face. "Do it, Carina. Please, go ahead. If that's what you really need to do in order for you to make peace with yourself, then by all means take out your anger on the one person who can take away the pain and anger you carry around like a cross to bear."

"Bullshit. You're going to destroy my family. I read the terms of the contract. You think you're going to be in charge of our companies and my life. That will never happen."

"I'm curious. Do you really care if your family's corporation or reputation is ruined?" The contract would be considered illegal in a court of law but ironclad in the world of the mafia, the codicils obviously not something she'd agreed to. If what I'd read about her father was true, the man was as much a savage as Xavier Santos, my father. She had every right to be angry, but that couldn't matter.

"Kill my father. I don't care."

Strangely enough, she meant what she said.

"I assure you that one day that will happen. And your mother?"

Her laugh was just as bitter. "Sadly, my once beautiful mother is a shell of herself. Killing her would end the endless years of pain at my father's hand. You'd be doing her a favor."

Interesting. It would seem every family had an ugly secret.

As I drank in her perfume, I had a sense of the reason she'd agreed to the contract in the first place and decided to test it. "And what about Mia? Your beautiful younger sister. Do you not care about her?"

The flash in her eyes allowed me to glance in the few cracks in her armor.

"You fucking bastard. You will never hurt my sister, or I swear you will face a wrath that no God will be able to help you escape." She pressed the tip of the blade into my skin, the pressure enough a single trickle of blood flowed down my neck. Her smile was an indication she was pleased with herself, but her eyes told me that she didn't have what it took to be a killer.

43

"Be careful telling me your weakness, *mi novia*. When you face your enemy, you never play your cards in one hand." I'd heard she was spoiled, but her tenacity had come from being hardened by life spent around her immoral, ruthless father. That could prove to come in handy, but it would mean I'd need to trust her and at this point, I couldn't allow myself to have faith in anyone.

"Don't worry, Diego. I might be your bride but the only weakness I hold is I still have my humanity left. I can't say the same thing about you or what you've done."

I would be curious to find out what she believed I was responsible for. Coercing her father into signing on the dotted line had been easy. He'd been close to bankruptcy and needed an infusion of cash, but the groundwork had already been laid long before I'd arrived in town. Now, Montgomery DeMill's powerful empire was once again liquid, able to continue operating. However, I would hold the reins tightly in my hand.

But not tonight.

Tonight she would learn that going against me on any level wasn't in her best interest.

When she blinked, I knew I was right about her. She hated her father and would do anything in her power to make him pay for the unholy union. The moment was tense, her chest rising and falling as she debated her choice. The chemistry between us was exploding, my need to taste and fuck her increasing tenfold. I wouldn't be able to keep my control for long, but I wanted to allow her a chance to play her hand.

After that, she would belong to me.

Then I would destroy the empire.

"Do it, Carina." She jammed the point against my pulse of life, the look of glee in her eyes telling me what I could expect from her. My cock twitched and I refused to back down, dropping my head until the tip sliced into my skin.

The action surprised her, and I couldn't help but notice her lower lip was trembling. She was full of chutzpa, but she was no killer. Breaking her would be so delicious.

When she lowered her gaze, I took the knife from her hand, tossing it aside. Then I slipped my hand around her neck, pulling her close. "You're a very naughty girl, my beautiful wife. You will learn to obey me. If you do not, there will be harsh consequences."

"I'm not your fucking prisoner. I am a DeMill, a powerful woman."

"You are now Carina Santos, my stunning bride. And I don't consider you my prisoner and won't unless you deem it necessary to do so. You're my wife, but you will do things my way. As far as your work, I'll need your presence to remain, but you will abide by my rules, and I assure you that you will be under my command at all times." The words seemed so foreign to me, the real anger I felt for an entirely different reason. However, this was necessary. One day it would all matter.

"And if I don't?"

"Then you'll learn what brutal punishment is like and I assure you that's not something you want."

As I crushed my mouth over hers, she resisted at first, pummeling her fists against my chest. Then she acquiesced, clenching her fingers around my shirt.

I hadn't anticipated the taste of her would cause my cock to push hard against my trousers, but she'd managed to ignite a fire within me that would be difficult to control. I eased my hand down her back, cupping her rounded bottom and lifting her onto her toes. She undulated her hips, grinding against me in such a way I was ready to rip off her pretty little dress she'd changed into for the rehearsal.

I dominated her tongue, sweeping mine back and forth as she dug her long nails into the back of my neck. The thought of marrying someone I didn't know, forced to pretend for another purpose hadn't appealed to me, but with every passing second, I was learning to accept if not appreciate the perks of being Diego Santos. The lifestyle. The cars. The women. The power. They'd never been a part of my life.

Now I had it all and I planned on taking full advantage.

As the taste of her shifted into my system, her scent of fresh flowers and berries filtered into my nostrils, vile things shot into the back of my mind of what I'd do to her in the coming days, weeks. Either she would become an ally or a prisoner. Either way suited me just fine.

When I broke the kiss, she gasped for air, dragging her tongue across her ruby-stained lips, her eyes imploring. Searching. And I sensed she loathed the way her body responded, the building need that she'd ignored for however long this façade had been in place. But there was an undeniable connection that would be used, nourished.

Her lovely mouth twisted, and she cocked her head, running her fingers down the side of my neck and over my shoulder. "One big man. Powerful. Dominating. Aren't you?" Her words were dripping with innuendos, pushing my buttons to see what I was made of.

"You like it that way, Carina. You hunger for a man to take you. Use you. Fuck you like the little slut you are. You can't deny it."

"Mmm… try me." She pushed gently against me, giving me a full blast of explosive heat and when I eased back on my firm hold, she did exactly as I'd expected.

She cracked her palm across my cheek and broke free, laughing as soon as she did so.

I pressed my fingers against the slight sting on my face, watching as she raced around the other side of the couch.

"Do you really think I give a damn about who or what you are? Do you think I'm that easy, *Diego?*" The way she exaggerated my name was interesting, as if she didn't believe who was standing in front of her.

"What I know is that you've craved a firm hand your entire life. You long to be taken roughly, used and dominated, breaking you down to your most primal base, then remolded into the perfect woman to fulfill my every desire." I took two long strides, amused that she continued moving around the sofa, as if this little game was one she could win.

"Then your arrogance has bested you. I'm not that kind of woman. I take control. I lead. I will never follow behind a man, no matter his true identity or intentions. Trust me, *Diego*. I *will* have my revenge."

And so, the line had been drawn in the sand. I knew what to expect from her. That made stripping away her defenses, taking her when I wanted that much sweeter. "There's something you should know about me, Carina." I took another two long strides, anticipating where she'd go next. "I never lose." When she dared to try to run down the hall-way, I snagged her arm in two seconds, yanking her back with one hand, grabbing the front of her dress with the other. With a single jerk, I ripped the thin material all the way down, exposing her matching pretty pink lace thong and bra underneath. How virginal.

She gasped from shock but the fury in her eyes returned within seconds. As she came at me with everything she had, her fists flying, I ripped another portion of her dress, flinging the remnants to the side. Then I wrapped one hand around her throat, pushing her against the wall, shoving one arm over her head.

"You're adorable when you think you can win," I murmured, lowering my head and nipping her earlobe. She moaned her response, the scent of her feminine wiles floating between us, her eyes glassy from desire.

"Oh, I will win. Be wary of those you think you can control. They are the ones who will wait, calculating the right moment before pouncing like a jaguar."

I couldn't help but laugh, eager to see her try. Maybe I didn't know what I was made of, the Santos blood running thick in my veins. I squeezed her lovely neck until she pursed her lips. Then I used the same hand to brush the backs of my fingers down her side, sliding a single finger under the thin elastic of her thong. She kept the unrelenting smile on her face as I snapped my wrist, freeing her of the lacy confines.

"Now, I think you need to learn a lesson in obedience."

She laughed, the sound like the sweetest concerto I'd ever heard. "You will never break me no matter how hard you try."

"We shall see, my *flor preciosa*. We shall see." She was a precious flower. As I unfastened my belt, her eyes never left mine, myriad emotions rolling across her face, her cheeks now stained with the same luscious color as her lips.

"What are you doing?" she demanded, her tone riddled with defiance.

"Providing what your behavior warrants and what you've been craving. Discipline. I'm going to spank that beautiful bottom of yours. Then I'm going to fuck you like you deserve to be fucked. Rough and raw. And baby, I'm not just going to stop with your pussy. I'm going to claim your tight little asshole."

CHAPTER 5

"$\mathcal{A}$*nd, after all, what is a lie? 'Tis but the truth in masquerade."*

—*Lord Byron*

Carina

As his words resonated, all I could think about was the disguise we were both wearing. Mine had been one of protection, thick armor to keep the wolves at bay. The mask Diego was wearing was for an entirely different reason, one I was determined to discover. But it was apparent that we were both living a lie.

I'd always known there was a thin line between love and hate, but as I stood almost entirely naked in front of a man I didn't know, I was shocked at the truth. There was an even thinner line between rage and passion. My body had betrayed me, hungering for his searing touch while my mind remained firm in the belief that he should die a bloody violent death.

Why hadn't I taken the opportunity to end his life when I'd had it so easily in my fingers at the church? Because something was wrong, as if the earth had tilted on its axis, creating a surreal reflection of the real world. The game plan had changed, and I hadn't been privy to learning what that was. Maybe my curiosity had gotten the better of me, or maybe the electric charge that continued to hum like a diesel engine was to blame.

The man was sickeningly hot, chiseled in every way. His burnished skin and curly dark hair had driven me mad with longing. I'd wanted to run my fingers through his locks, tangling and pulling while he kissed me over and over again. I'd yearned to run the tips of my fingers down his broad chest, tickling his carved abs until I couldn't resist crawling my fingers to his cock.

And now, as he tugged on the thick leather strap, the look on his face carnal, dangerous, I couldn't seem to force my body into trying to escape his clutches. Breathless, I shuddered when the belt was free and he cracked it on the floor, the sound reverberating in my ears.

But I closed my eyes, making a new promise that I would not break. He'd threatened my sister. While vague, merely testing my resolve, he'd made a fatal mistake. She was far too innocent for this world, her sweetness never altered by the brutality of my father's actions. As soon as possible, I was getting her out of Los Angeles, ensuring she never suffered the kind of fate I'd been forced into.

Another shiver coursed through me, my mind incapable of comprehending the massacre as well as the ugliness that I'd asked the man to fuck me. Why? Why in God's name had I done such a crazy, twisted thing? Yes, I'd felt helpless, terrified that my entire family had been wiped out, but to drop to that level was insane and…

And Diego had calmed me, his strength and resolve making me feel safe. The feel of his arms surrounding me had been exhilarating. I'd enjoyed every minute of him fucking me. What did that make me? A traitor if to no one else but myself? I wasn't certain at this point.

"Bad. Bad. Girl. I can't wait to taste every inch of you." Even the way he said the dirty words was scintillating, the husky tone unlike what I'd heard before. He was a man on fire, the burn appearing in the rich purple flecks in his eyes. Was it possible I'd never seen them before? No. I was observant, had learned everything about the bastard to use against him.

"I hate you." And I did, with everything I had inside of me. There was no room for anything else, the rage filling my heart and soul, stealing every scrap of happiness.

"Good. That will make this more delicious." He yanked me by the arm, tossing me over the back edge of the couch, yanking one stiletto off then the other. Then he unhooked my bra, forcing the straps from my arms. "A woman should always be spanked without a single piece of clothing. I am going to enjoy this."

Enjoy? The man was as sadistic as I'd believed. Then why were butterflies churning in my stomach? Why did this arouse me instead of making me sick?

Diego rolled his fingers down my spine before pulling my hair to the side. I heard him take a deep breath as when I moved, determined to get the hell away from him, he pressed down on the small of my back, crowding over me with his full weight.

"I don't think you want to do that, my lovely creature. Your punishment will be that much worse."

"Fuck you," I spouted off, digging my nails into the smooth leather. If I didn't fight him now, I'd fall under his spell, and I couldn't allow that to happen. We weren't friends or lovers. Just two enemies forced to endure each other.

"Soon, baby girl. Soon. Penance first before pleasure. Always. *El placer es un regalo.*"

Pleasure is a gift. If that was the case, gutting him would be a prize.

As soon as he took a step back, I was prepared to bolt but he was faster, bringing the belt down twice without hesitation. Agony blasted through me, sucking my breath from my body. Tears immediately formed in my eyes, but I refused to give in to his tyranny or his control. That would never happen. He could spank me every day, issuing whatever form of punishment he wanted, but he would never be able to break down my defenses.

And he would never steal my heart.

The fact I'd even thought that was ridiculous. He was a monster, a man who killed for a living. Was that any different than my father's world? My father was considered the most powerful man in Hollywood, capable of making or breaking a career in an instant. But he'd taken it too far, his enemies suddenly disappearing. That was exactly what happened under Xavier Santos' reign, an empire he'd just turned over to his son the moment I said 'I do.'

As the crack of his wrist brought a whooshing sound, I clenched my eyes shut, loathing the fact a single tear had managed to escape, trickling down my cheek and dropping ever so slowly to the couch. I had to endure this for a little while, even pretending I was compliant, but that wasn't in my nature.

Diego took another deep breath, daring to caress my already aching bottom. "I do so love the color red on you, Carina. And I will adore the marks I'll place on your sexy little body."

The man was twisted, although the lingering thought that he wasn't the right man remained in my mind. I'd heard about Diego's reputation, his sick need for an entirely different kind of control in the bedroom. Sadistic was a tame word for what women were forced to endure, his reputation suggesting his proclivities were extreme.

As the belt was brought down four times in rapid succession, I couldn't control my body in pain any more than I'd been able to in passion. I kicked out, lurching up from the couch, a strangled whimper escaping.

"You're such a bastard," I hissed.

"Yes, but if you learn to obey my rules and never attempt to end my life again, things will go easier for you." He laughed, the sound penetrating my eardrums. He really believed he could keep me on a leash. He would soon learn what I was made of.

His exhale was exaggerated, and he cracked the thick leather again, smacking me three times across the sit spot, twice on my upper thighs. The anguish was maddening but the fact I was wet, pussy juice trickling past my swollen lips was horrifying.

"Your pussy is glistening, Carina. Are you excited? Does this make you hunger even more?"

"I'm not aroused and never will be."

"Why do you keep lying to yourself?" He slid his hand between my legs, cupping my mound and grinding his palm against my pussy. As he rolled it up and down, I gasped from the amount of pleasure sweeping through me.

He pressed my legs as wide open as possible, his breathing labored as he rolled his thumb around my clit. Within seconds, I could swear I was going to have an orgasm. That just couldn't happen. It wasn't possible.

You want this.

Like hell I did.

You do. Why lie to yourself?

I dropped my head, stars floating in front of my eyes, panting as I did everything I could to keep my body from reacting. When he slipped several fingers past my swollen folds, I almost lost it.

"God, you're so wet and tight. Have you been with anyone else?"

55

"You're horrible."

He removed his hand, immediately cracking the belt against my bottom, the blast of pain entirely different than before. So electric. So arousing. "Answer me."

Oh, my God. What did he think this was? I was a grown woman. I'd had boyfriends before, although not in several years. "Yes. Okay? Is that what you wanted to hear?"

He seemed disappointed in my answer, immediately returning to the spanking, bringing the belt across my heated skin six more times. I was drained already, my mind a blur as tingling sensations danced down the backs of my legs. The horror of what was happening had quickly given way to building excitement. Did I really hunger to have his cock thrust inside again?

Yes. Yes.

Dear God. What was wrong with me?

"Hear me now, my bride. You now belong to me. If a man ever dares to look at you, he will lose his eyes. If he touches you, I'll cut off his hand. And if he dares to fuck you, then you will watch him die by my hands."

His words of possession were strangely erotic, pushing back my defenses to the point I'd never felt so vulnerable in my life. He fisted my hair, pulling my head to an awkward angle, peering down at me with his lust-filled eyes. Then he shoved his slickened fingers into his mouth, licking them clean.

I was repulsed.

Aroused.

Sickened.

Electrified.

I swallowed hard, the mesmerizing moment seemed to stop all time. When he was finished, he tossed the belt, jerking me up from the couch, turning me around then wrapping his arms around me. "You taste divine, but I need more. Much more." He lifted me into his arms as if I weighed nothing. Then he moved toward the grand piano in the corner, positioning me on the edge above the exposed keys, planting each of my feet on either end.

Exhaling, he studied me, the look on his face as if he was going to devour me whole. When he backed away, I eased onto my elbows, watching as he yanked off his shirt, exposing his glorious chest, a portion covered in dark ink. His eyes pierced mine as he unzipped his trousers, kicking off his shoes before lowering the material over his hips.

When he was fully undressed, I was momentarily unable to breathe, my mind a blur from the sight of him. Every muscle was honed to perfection, as if he'd been carved out of some magnificent stone. Even his skin glistened in the dim lighting. A chain remained around his neck, a small piece of metal dangling by a half inch. It was a symbol of something important. I was certain of it. He took several deep breaths, his chest rising and falling, the look on his face growing more intense.

I wanted to run, to keep from hungering the way I did, but it was impossible to ignore the vibrations skipping through me or the need festering deep inside.

He approached, narrowing his eyes as he yanked back the bench and sat down. I wasn't certain what I'd expected but when he began to play the piano, I was shocked. I hadn't known he could play. There were no records anywhere that he was a musician. As he continued, the mournful sound of whatever piece he'd selected echoed in my ears. It was hauntingly beautiful, but so sad, yet it matched the way I'd been feeling for the two weeks since being told my wedding had already been planned.

I couldn't take my eyes off him, my heart racing with every stretch of his long fingers, the deep bass as the piece built to a crescendo. I marveled at his skill, the ease with which he tickled the ivories, and the passion that exuded from every chord. I'd thought of him as nothing but a savage, thirsty for blood and nothing else. This was an entirely different side of him, a way of showing me that he was a complicated man.

Or was this just another part of his game, an attempt to break down my defenses to the point I wouldn't be able to fight him. When he was finished, I leaned back on the cool surface, staring up at the ceiling. Everything about this day had been so unexpected.

Diego yanked my bottom off the edge then brushed the rough pads of his fingers along the insides of my thighs. There was no denying how my body felt with his touch, prickles dancing on every inch of my skin.

"So beautiful," he whispered. "And all mine. I might be the luckiest man in the world." His words were another surprise, killing off some of the desperate need to run.

Maybe he was a master manipulator, capable of breaking down my defenses in several ways.

As he blew across my pussy, I took several shallow breaths.

"You're glistening for me, your sweet pussy lips already swollen." Even his deep voice sent skitters throughout my body. He pressed my legs back, exposing all of me. Then he dipped his head, his eyes never leaving me as he swiped his tongue across my clit.

I placed my hand over my eyes, refusing to watch.

But the controlling man was having none of it.

"Watch me, Carina. Watch as I feast on your honey."

I slowly lowered my hand, rising onto my elbows. My throat was tight, as if icy fingers were cinched around them.

Or a collar.

No, a noose.

Butterflies continued to swarm in my tummy yet when he flicked his tongue back and forth across my clit four times, whimpers slipped past my lips. He was enjoying every moment, growling as if the beast inside of him was prepared to break free. "So delicious."

Why was he doing this to me? Did he think this would win me over? I couldn't seem to stop shuddering as he rolled his tongue up and down. Just the fact I was on top of a sixty-plus-thousand-dollar piano being feasted on was filthy, sinful in a way I hadn't expected.

And to me, it was the most passionate thing that had ever happened.

As he continued, he seemed to know exactly what my body needed, shifting his tongue when I moaned, driving it deep inside every few seconds. He brought me so close to the edge of rapture then pulled away so many times I was panting, ready to beg him to allow me to come.

The sparkle in his eyes indicated he knew exactly what he was doing to me. I bit my lower lip to keep from crying as he thrust two fingers inside, the angle enabling him to slide it across my G-spot. I couldn't see clearly, stars in vibrant colors flashing in front of my eyes.

"Oh. Oh… I…" I tossed my head back and forth, my legs shaking in his hold.

"Do you want to come?"

The question had to be rhetorical. "Yes. God, yes."

He rubbed his lips on one leg then the other before burying his face into my pussy. That was all I could take. As an orgasm swept up from my curled toes, I threw my head all the way back, unable to keep from screaming. I'd never felt so blissful, the pure ecstasy unlike anything I knew existed.

"Mmm…" He refused to stop, licking up and down savagely, every sound he made animalistic.

I writhed in his hold, bucking up from the piano, my feet making thunking noises as they skipped across the keys. The wave of euphoria turned into a second, the climax almost blinding me. I laughed, blinking several times as my body continued to shudder.

He pressed kisses on one leg then the other, finally standing to his full height. He was such a handsome man that it took my breath away. Every move exaggerated, he placed one hand on the piano then the other, leaning over, his strong jaw clenched. "Are you ready?"

The question was one I couldn't answer. I pushed my hands against his chest, kneading his heated skin, tingling as another jolt of current flashed into my system. He was so tall that as he gripped my hips, the tip of his throbbing cock immediately pressed against my slickened folds. Then he impaled me with a single thrust, sucking in his breath as he threw his head back.

"Oh!" My cry was washed out by his strangled exhale and as my muscles stretched, trying to accommodate his wide girth, several filthy images rolled into my mind. I hadn't expected to enjoy this, or want the man on any level, but the dark cravings that had erupted entangled my emotions in a tight web.

His upper lip was curled as he peered down at me, his eyes now dilated. With his fingers digging into the skin on my hips, he pumped in and out methodically, the rhythm generating excessive heat. Seconds later, he was yanking me up and down brutally, almost as if he was taking out his frustration by fucking me like an animal. I was dragged across the surface of the piano, my toes constantly hitting the keys. It seemed strange that there was a melody flowing, just as haunting as the music he'd selected.

The incredible stamina the man had was shocking, his hard fucking continuing, my muscles spasming. As my pussy clenched and released, I remained lightheaded. His muscles had tensed and as he rolled onto the balls of his feet, I was certain he was ready to erupt deep inside.

But he planned on making good on his promise.

With his cock remaining inside, he once again leaned over, brushing his lips across mine. I wrapped my legs around his hips, pulling him in even closer. He shifted his gaze down, a smile crossing his face. "You still believe you're in charge. Don't you, my beautiful bride?"

"You have no idea what I can do."

"I'm very much looking forward to finding out." He captured my mouth, holding our lips in place, opening and closing them before darting his tongue inside. While the intense hunger remained, the moment of tenderness unexpected, I sensed a deeper hunger had been ignited. The fact he was ravaging me was just the beginning. Of what, I doubted I'd learn for days, maybe weeks.

What was his purpose?

My brain was rattled, still consumed by the difference in his eyes. As the kiss continued, I was swept away, swooning like a lovesick girl. I slid my arms around his shoulders, tangling the fingers of one hand in his thick locks just like I'd wanted to. The moment of intimacy was different, even more passionate. Yet as before, his tongue dominated mine as he explored every centimeter of my mouth.

And I did his as well.

His scent rocked me, so full of testosterone, cedarwood, and spices that I was momentarily intoxicated. No man was supposed to be this good looking or have a fragrance that could ignite a thousand fires.

When he finally pulled away, he dragged his tongue across my lips then lifted me completely off the piano, the same wry smile on his face as he carried me toward the bank of doors leading to the expansive deck. After throwing one open, he headed outside, turning sideways until I was allowed to see the churning ocean. While the day had been filled with bright sun, dark clouds had invaded the sky, the wind whipping across the sand as a storm approached. To me it was a sign of what our relationship would be.

Difficult.

Tumultuous.

Passionate.

Dark.

As a single flash of lightning sparked the night sky, he eased me onto my feet, forcing me against the thick steel railing. I trembled in his arms because of the closeness, the over-bearing sweep of emotions that refused to leave me alone. All I'd thought about for days was carving my name in Diego's skin. Instead, he'd seared his in mine with his sizzling touch, his kisses that left me weak in the knees.

At this moment I couldn't stand myself.

"Are you afraid of the dark?" he asked as he nuzzled against my neck.

"Should I be?"

"They say monsters thrive in the hours surrounding midnight, a time when curses are placed."

"You're superstitious?" I asked out of curiosity.

"In my home country of Colombia, there are witches who banish away the demons, providing charms of protection, but at times the demons still prevail. However, I consider the darkness my friend, allowing for unseemly endeavors."

I wasn't certain why he was sharing his thoughts, other than to issue a terse message, a warning that he was a very dangerous man.

"But don't worry, my lovely bride. I can protect you from all the evils of this world." He bit down on my shoulder, his teeth sinking in to the point of pain, but I writhed against him from the pleasure it brought.

He rolled his fingers over my shoulders, slowly allowing them to drift to my hands as he pressed his knee between my legs, pushing them apart.

Another crack of lightning energized the sky, crisscrossing across the horizon in an intense neon blue. I trembled from the power of it as he pressed his cock against my pussy. Then he slipped inside, pushing me hard against the railing.

"You can't protect me, Diego. No one can. And why would you?" It was my honest opinion, although I wasn't certain why I said the words. He would try to do with me what he wanted. I closed my eyes as a rumble of thunder came from the distance.

"Because my family has many enemies."

"So does mine, including the Santos clan."

"You will learn, my bride. One day, you will learn." He picked up his rhythm, although it was more sensual than before, taking his time to enjoy fucking me instead of claiming me as a possession. I arched my back, resting my head against his shoulder, taking deep breaths of the ocean breeze as the wind flowed around us in a tight swirl. The feeling of his heated body against mine was more powerful than before, my heartrate soaring.

When he pulled his cock from my wetness, I gasped for no other reason than I knew what he was going to do. As he pressed the cockhead against my dark hole, my entire body tensed. He pushed the tip inside, allowing me to get used to the thick invasion. The moment he wrapped his hand around my hair, twisting the long curls around his fist, the first drops of rain began to fall.

"Breathe for me, baby," he whispered in my ear then licked the shell as he slipped another inch inside.

I wasn't anticipating his tenderness, the pain not nearly what I'd expected. Still, I gasped as the sensations tore through me. The drops continued to fall, sizzling against my overheated skin. When he was fully seated inside, he issued a husky bellow followed by a series of growls.

"Tight. Hot. Mine."

The three words floated through my mind, increasing my blood pressure. Another crackling bolt of lightning lit up the sky as if fireworks were going off. Panting, the anguish from before began to fade, leaving me with an explosive level of heat that I hadn't anticipated. Every time he brushed his fingers across my skin, the tingling sensations increased.

His breathing had become labored and I sensed he was doing everything he could to hold back. I'd never expected to enjoy the filthy act, but with him, every brutal action drew me further into his darkness.

And I loved it, craved more.

He wrapped his arm around my waist, flicking his finger back and forth across my nipple. I closed my eyes, allowing the wash of need and intense longing to overtake the previous anxiety. I felt safe in his arms, but there was no doubt I was his possession.

"My beautiful creature," he murmured, nuzzling his face into my neck as he twisted my nipple until I cried out in pain.

Then he reared back, gripping my hips, digging his fingers into my skin.

The husky sounds he made kept my mind spiraling, my heart racing. He was nothing but a primal beast claiming what he believed belonged to him.

When he cracked his hand on my bottom several times, another rush of vibrations tore through me. And I heard him whisper the most powerful word of all.

"Mine."

For the next few minutes, he fucked me, claiming what had been sold to him, and another tear slipped past my lashes.

Not from pain.

Not from fear.

From the knowledge that killing him would be more difficult than I'd thought and from the hatred for the girl inside who'd believed her life was her own.

Leaning over, Diego pressed the full weight of his body against me, cupping my breasts. He pulled me against him, the burn of his skin against mine a permanent stain. He pinched my nipples, twisting them between his fingers, and seconds later, he erupted deep inside, filling me with his seed.

As the thunder continued to roll, lightning crisscrossing the sky as rain pelted against our skin, I lifted my face toward the heavens, praying that one day I could find salvation.

But that was only possible after exacting revenge.

CHAPTER 6

 arina

The storm had lasted well into the night, the rumbles of thunder keeping me awake. Or maybe the very demons Diego had talked about had been the reason. Then there was the ugliness surrounding the fact I remained in a huge bed in a house that wasn't mine. While suitcases with my personal effects had been taken unknowingly from my apartment and brought there, there was nothing else familiar.

No old bookshelf that I'd found at a thrift store, painting it funky colors to suit my moods.

No favorite old coffeemaker that I'd had for years.

No pictures of family and friends, vacations and music premieres.

No sense of self-worth or accomplishments.

As beautiful as it was, this wasn't my house and it never would be. There'd been no discussion of where I'd live or if I would maintain my position at the music company where I'd worked my way up from an assistant to vice president all without my father's help. There'd been no talk of anything.

I hadn't read the terms of the contract before signing away my life. I'd been so fearful that the man called the Butcher would carve his initials into my sister's skin as I'd heard he'd done to almost everyone he killed. I remained sick inside at everything that had happened in two short weeks, but I would make the same choice again. Mia wasn't strong enough to handle being married to a drug lord's son. My father had known it was my single weakness.

Now Diego owned a portion of my father's empire, including my beloved music production company. How many tears had I shed turning the company into the force it was today? How many long hours spent? What would the bastard do to it? The whirlwind engagement had left me bitter and hollow, a wonderful place to build on my plan of revenge.

Then everything has been pulled out from under me with a single close-up glance in his eyes. I remained confused, uncertain of what the future would bring. Why hadn't I gone through with my plan?

Because you were mesmerized by how gorgeous he was.

That was bullshit. No, there was something going on that I wasn't party to. Ugh. Why couldn't I put my finger on why?

I was good at figuring out puzzles, even better at knowing when someone was lying.

I also couldn't figure out why I hadn't planned an alternative just in case I'd lost my nerve, even if that meant hiding both Mia and myself somewhere safe for an undetermined length of time. My resolve had simply failed me. After taking a few shallow breaths, I realized his scent lingered everywhere. In the room. On my skin.

As I rolled over, glancing at my husband as he slept, fleeting images of the passion we'd shared continued to cross my mind. He'd been sensual in his method of domination, his hunger knowing no bounds. I'd expected brutality, not unbridled passion, which added to the puzzlement. When he'd finally carried me to bed sometime after two, there'd only been a short lapse before he'd pulled me on top of him, saying nothing in the darkness as he fucked me as if he hadn't touched me before.

I bit my lip, sinful images floating in my mind, my nipples fully aroused. The day had dawned gray, which matched my mood. I walked to the window, peering outside, the ocean still as turbulent as the night before. Two guards appeared in my periphery. I wasn't certain whether to feel protected or even more like a prisoner. It was obvious Diego was concerned I'd try to get away. Where would I go from here? I certainly couldn't go home again, the threat on my sister remaining over my head. Even if I wanted to run far away, the short meeting with the man outside his office building had told me in no uncertain terms what I could expect from him.

He hadn't bothered to remove his sunglasses, just like he'd done the day he'd been outside my father's house, but he didn't need to for me to know he was scrutinizing me, his scoff one of disdain. Then he'd told me what would happen if I dared try to get out of the deal.

"If you think you can run away from the contract or from me, you are dead wrong. There isn't a location on this entire planet where you can hide where I won't find you. And when I do, everyone who was stupid enough to help provide you with assistance will be terminated. After that, I'll enjoy watching you writhe in a steel cage."

I would never forget his laugh, the harsh sound that oozed of control. That had been the moment I'd promised myself that I'd cut the man's heart out with a rusty spoon. Even the sound of his laugh had been different. Or was I just lost in a thick fog? Nothing made any sense at this point.

Exhaling, I realized I'd reached for him and instantly curled my fingers, ice running through my veins. Then I thought about my family, the shock of what had happened fading sometime in the night. The reality was much worse. My sister. She had to be terrified. I needed to talk to her. I had to see her. Would he be human enough to allow me to speak to her? All bets were off.

Who could have done such a horrible thing?

While I was no fool about my father's business, realizing he had connections to several crime syndicates, he'd kept the women in the household in the dark on purpose. Still, I'd caught enough of dozens of conversations to know he wasn't immune from benefitting from greed. Why did I have the feeling we'd never be safe?

As I eased back the covers, I half expected Diego to grab my arm, yanking me back into bed. Maybe he'd handcuff me to the iron posts while he went about business of the day. The anticipation of what I'd face had left a bad taste in my mouth. One night of passion shouldn't mean anything to me. It was his way of unnerving me, reminding me that I was his.

Hate him. Keep hating him. He's your enemy, a monster.

After a few seconds, I was re-energized, my only emotion anger.

I couldn't remain this way any longer. The stench of him had become sickening. After throwing him another look, I gingerly stepped out of bed. I needed time to myself. I needed to regroup to try to fix the heartache.

He didn't grab my arm or try to stop me. As I neared the door to the bathroom, I turned one last time, lingering long enough that my heart started to ache. I'd promised myself so many things, including that I wouldn't cry. As I closed the bathroom door behind me, tears slipped past my lashes, accepting another failure pushing bile into my throat.

The bathroom also had an incredible view of the ocean waters, the morning dawning more tranquil than the night before. I stood in front, watching as the waves lapped against the shoreline. San Diego was one of my favorite cities, although I'd been far too busy over the past three years to make the trip. I was surprised the window was open, allowing me to catch a whiff of the fresh ocean air. As the salt-kissed breeze tickled my skin, I was reminded that I'd had plans this summer, taking Mia and driving up the coast to Oregon, exploring every winery. That obviously wasn't going to happen.

I shifted away, unable to capture the tranquility being by the ocean usually offered, the sense of feeling violated and dirty far more intrusive. As I ran my hand across the granite counter, I caught a glimpse of my reflection and shuddered. Where had the powerful woman gone, the one who took no shit from anyone? My reputation as a harsh leader of the music industry was well known, but I'd turned naïve, shell-shocked musicians into megastars. The woman staring back at me had none of the verve for life.

I turned around to face the shower, no longer surprised at his lush surroundings.

The shower itself was oversized, three rain-style shower-heads attached to thick slabs of marble. Diego was well known for his gluttonous tastes, his expensive sports car collection one of many things he enjoyed flaunting. He'd disgusted me long before being forced into marrying him. I turned the faucet, the water blasting hot almost immediately.

As I eased inside, closing the shower door, I'd never felt so inconsequential in my life. At least I hadn't been forced to endure the reception, shaking hands and faking a smile for hours on end. God. What was wrong with me? I was thankful a slaughter had kept me from faking my happiness. An ugly laugh erupted from my throat. I was either losing my mind or I'd already been indoctrinated into the life of a mafia boss.

Even though Diego and his entire clan had insisted they were nothing but regular businessmen.

The single question Diego had asked me had been followed by my icy glare as the answer.

"Would you have really killed me in front of your beloved sister?"

I smashed my hand against the marble wall twice, the force enough I knew my hand would ache. I didn't care. Gasping for air, I stood directly under the shower, taking rasping breaths. Why were the tears continuing to fall? They wouldn't do any good. I had to stay angry, so much so that I wouldn't allow him to get under my skin.

As the water trickled down my back, hitting my bottom, I burst into laughter. I'd wanted pain, but the sick reminder of what *he'd* done, of what I'd allowed *him* to do to me disgusted me even more than enjoying the sex.

And I had relished every second of the hot, raw, rough sex. Fuck. Fuck.

God. I didn't want to say his name out loud ever again, or even think it. I smashed my hand against the shower three more times until the ache took over, my knuckles bruised and bleeding as I started to sob. The wretched sound was magnified in the damn room, so much so my cries echoed in my ears. Then I felt cool air and jumped.

I'd been so busy smashing my hand I hadn't paid attention to the fact the shower door had opened, a huge, gorgeous man stepping inside.

When I lifted my head, his eyes never blinked as he studied my tearstained face and the blood seeping through my fingers. But he did something that added to the suspicions that had already formed in my mind.

He gently took my hand into his, trying to calm me with words that weren't making any sense. "Sshh… Let me do this. You've hurt yourself." He held my hand under the water as he rubbed the tears away with his thumb, his expression one of concern.

As the blood trickled down the drain, I studied his eyes, the bright light allowing me to see every inch of him. Then as suddenly as I'd wanted to shove him away, I wrapped my arms around him, lifting my head.

There was no other gesture needed. He crushed his mouth over mine, pulling me close. As he spun me around, driving me against the shower wall, I wrapped my legs around him. There was no pretense with this, no admittance that our little coupling would ever work out, but I couldn't ignore the need to be close to someone, the ache inside unanticipated.

Terrifying.

Soul crushing.

This also wasn't romantic by any stretch of the imagination.

He had the same sense of urgency, thrusting his cock deep inside without a thought given to foreplay or conversation. We weren't lovers, just two people hungry for the continuation of passion. The taste of him was as magnificent as it had been the night before, my needs building to the point of frenzy.

As he broke the kiss, I clawed at his arms, the pain in my hand little more than a dull ache. Gasping, I dragged my tongue around my mouth then bit down on his lower lip, both our breathing labored.

He pulled me away, pressing me against the marble again then rolling onto the balls of his feet, driving his cock deeper. Harder. His guttural sounds mixed with husky growls, and I raked my nails all the way down his arms with one hand while clinging to his neck with the other. The force he used was enough to slide me up and down the wall. I lolled my head, water dripping off both of us in strings.

Diego spun me around again, thrusting me under another one of the rain heads. I grabbed the liquid soap, pouring it over his head and body, laughing softly until he started to lather us together. He was slippery, which made the sex that much hotter. I slapped my feet on the shower door to try to steady myself, but he pulled me away and into the corner. When he turned me around, pushing me over at the waist, I did what I could to get out of his hold, but he was too strong, the soap almost forcing both of us to slip.

He impaled me again, holding his position as his cock swelled. "God, you're so tight. So damn wet." His husky voice was little more than a growl, the sound sending vibrations dancing down the back of my legs.

I slapped my hands on the wall, struggling to catch my breath. When he thrust even harder, I was jolted forward, my pussy muscles clenching and releasing several times.

He fucked me long and hard, the sound of skin slapping against skin heard over the moans rushing up from my throat. As he wrapped his hand around my neck, his fingers digging into my skin, I scrambled to try to hold onto anything.

"Uh. Uh. Uh. Uh." I was jarred, the sensations even more intense than the night before. Breathless, my mind was blown by how good it felt to have him inside of me. When he pulled me back, wrapping his arm around my waist and holding me aloft, all I could do was smile.

"I could fuck you for hours," he murmured, using his strong thigh muscles to lift me onto my toes. All I could do was wrap my heels around his thighs, squeezing his arms.

"Then do it," I managed.

He nipped my earlobe and eased us under the water, allowing all three showerheads to wash us clean. As an orgasm swept through me, I leaned my head against his shoulder, my scream strangled.

"Yes. Yes. Yes!"

His hot breath skipped across my face, his growls increasing in volume. "More. Come again for me."

There was something about his voice that I couldn't ignore. As I struggled to breathe, my heart racing, my body obeyed him, and a second incredible orgasm jetted into me. Steam from the shower along with the heat from our bodies created a thick fog and as the soap began to slide down the drain, beads of perspiration trickled down both sides of my face.

Diego cupped my breasts, kneading and squeezing them as he eased me to the shower floor. Then he dragged his tongue up and down my neck, his heated breath creating a wave of goosebumps.

When I started to push away, he yanked me back, pinching and twisting my nipples. "I'm not finished with you yet."

He pushed me against the wall again, thrusting one then my other arm over my head. Once he pressed the tip of his cock against my pussy lips, he intertwined our fingers, pressing the full weight of his body against mine as he plunged deep inside. For the next few minutes, our bodies molded as one, his gyrating hips creating a beautiful wave of friction.

Panting, beads of perspiration continued, his actions becoming more brutal. I could barely breathe, my thinking muddled, but the incredible sensations continued. And the man wouldn't stop, his savage fucking as if he needed to fill me with his seed as much as he needed to breathe. As he held me, I dug my fingers into his palms, shifting my hips back and forth.

When his body started to tense, I closed my eyes, squeezing my muscles. Within seconds, he erupted deep inside, and I felt another splash of warmth, an insane need for even more. His scattered roar filling my eardrums, the scent of his testosterone overpowering everything else. Even after his body stopped shaking, he remained where he was, his chest heaving.

As he turned me around, I opened my eyes, staring into his. And I knew without a shadow of a doubt that my initial instincts had been right.

"What's wrong?" he asked as he lifted my chin with a single finger.

"Who are you?" I darted my eyes back and forth, hoping he would be honest with me.

His brow furrowed, a look of surprise crossing his face. "You know who I am. I'm the man you pledged to remain with for the rest of your life."

"No," I said, shaking my head. "Whoever you are, you're an imposter. You are not Diego Santos. I demand the truth. Who. Are. You?"

In the next few seconds, his gray eyes turned dark, the flecks of purple deepening. Then a smile crossed his face, one of knowing.

And one of revenge.

The man I'd married had taken Diego's place. But for what purposes?

And what did he have planned with me?

* * *

Two months earlier

Dante

I'd known this day was coming, but I'd prayed for a miracle or at least for another period of remission. My mother's life had been rough for as long as I'd become cognizant of everything she'd done for me. Even though she'd struggled with dark sadness and trying to keep a roof over her head, she'd doted on me and had managed to keep a smile on her face. She'd done everything in her power to create happiness for a fatherless boy, holidays and birthdays always special. Now she lay dying in a hospital bed, and I already felt as if my heart was broken.

As I approached her room, the doctor stopped me.

"*Lo siento mucho*, Dante," he said. I knew he was sorry. Everyone was sorry that they hadn't been able to cure a horrible disease.

"*Cuanto tiempo?*" I asked. How long?

"*Horas.*" Hours.

Hours. As soon as I'd gotten the call, I'd asked the judge to delay the trial I was working. At least he'd understood, although I would have walked out if he hadn't. Family was more important than anything else in life.

I nodded, unwilling to waste any additional time. An icy grip had my heart in its clutches, the pain of losing my only real family crushing. As I moved into the room, red roses in my hand, I stood still for a few minutes. She was so frail, her skin almost transparent. She'd tried so hard to keep fighting against the ravages. I admired her for that and so much more.

As I pulled the chair close to the bed, she opened her eyes. There was still a twinkle in them even though she was full of morphine.

"My son," she said in English. She'd made certain I spoke English fluently, often preferring the language. She'd told me it was necessary, and I'd never asked her why.

"I brought you your favorite flowers."

"They are beautiful." In her hand were rosary beads and tears formed in my eyes. She was ready to let go, the pain too significant. I pulled a rose from the arrangement, allowing her to gather a single whiff. She'd once told me that it had been a very long time since she'd gotten roses. After my father had died a hero, she hadn't been able to remarry. I never pressed her, but I knew the heartache had eaten her up inside.

"Just rest, Mama. I'm right here."

"I need to talk to you, my son."

"You're too weak."

"No. You need to listen to me."

"What is it?" I pulled her trembling hand to my face, hating how cold it was. Anger boiled inside as it had for years. How could God allow such an angel to suffer so much?

She suddenly gripped my fingers with more strength than I believed she had. "I lied to you about your father."

"It's okay, Mama. Whatever it is." My mother never lied. But she was a good Catholic, needing to absolve herself of even the smallest sin.

"Listen to me, Dante. This is important." When she coughed, I started to stand, reaching for the call button. "No. Please. You must listen."

"Okay."

"You father is not dead, but he is dead to me."

Whoa. Could she be delusional from the morphine? She squeezed my hand, nodding several times.

"I don't understand, Mama."

"I need to tell you a story. You deserve to have the life you were meant to lead. I never wanted you to find out this way and I am so sorry that I failed you."

What in the hell was she talking about? "I'm listening, Mama."

"What is so urgent, Xavier?" I asked as I entered my husband's study. I noticed he remained at the window, his body tense. When he turned around, I almost didn't recognize him from the fury riding his face. "I thought you were meeting us downstairs. The boys are eager to spend some time together." There was a blackness in his eyes, as if something had died inside of him.

"Did you really think you could get away with betraying me?" While his tone of voice was calm, I sensed a growing rage, his jaw clenched.

I walked closer then stopped, noticing an open file on his desk. "What are you talking about?"

He took four long strides toward me, his swift backhand across my cheek catching me off guard. As I tumbled to the floor, a scream erupting from my throat, he laughed then stood over me. "You are a worthless bitch. A whore."

Tears were already streaming down my face, my mind reeling from his accusations, anguish exploding in my head. I tried to crawl away from him, but he was too fast, yanking me up by my long strands of hair, punching me twice in the face. Then he tossed me aside, hissing under his breath.

Stars floated in front of my eyes, the agony increasing. As I dragged my tongue across my lips, the coppery taste of blood was a reminder of how violent he was, his anger often consuming him. Fighting the pain, I managed to stand, although my body swayed back and forth. "I don't understand. What's wrong?"

He finished making his drink, nodding toward the file on his desk and saying nothing else. My eyes never leaving him, I walked to the desk, peering down at the papers and photographs strewn across the file. My fingers shaking, I pulled one into the air, the agony almost blinding at this point. As I stared in horror, I realized I'd been set up, but by whom? Who would do this kind of thing? "No, Xavier. That's not me."

"That's not you?" he bellowed. "Then who is it?" He laughed bitterly, taking a swig of his drink. "There is no way that photograph could be doctored. You are a loathsome slut, and I should have never married you. What did he give you to betray my organization?"

"This is a lie. I don't know this person."

In a quick move, he tossed the glass against the wall, the sound of it shattering drawing another yelp. As he'd done before, he backhanded me; this time my body pitched against the wall. Then he advanced, wrapping a hand around my throat, squeezing until I couldn't breathe. His eyes were dark, full of evil.

"I'm going to kill you and those bastard sons you have." Laughing, he released his hold, waiting for me to cry for mercy.

"They're your sons too. Do you want their blood on your hands? They are innocent children." I gritted my teeth, wincing as tears flowed past my lashes. He would not hurt my babies. I would kill him first. Then I coughed, the horror of what he'd suggested bringing more pain that anything else he could do to me.

"So what? I'll produce more. Many more. I don't need you."

"Please. You can kill me but not my babies." I wasn't certain if the man had any sense of humanity left. "Please, Xavier. They were innocent babies." When he said nothing, I screamed. "Please." Tears rolled down both cheeks, my chest heaving as I tried to breathe. Why would he do this? Why?

Xavier backed away, his nostrils flaring. Then he turned toward me once again. "You have one other option, my beautiful wife. You can choose."

"What are you talking about?" Please, God. Please save my children. When he laughed, raking his gaze down the length of me, I no longer saw a portion of the man who'd been so happy the day the twins were born. There was nothing left but rage.

"You can choose one of the children, taking him with you, where I will make certain you live in poverty and despair for the rest of your life. The other will remain here with me. He will be my prince, my successor, and a very wealthy man. It's up to you, Fiona. It's your choice to make."

"I curse you, Xavier, for all eternity. You will never know the love of a child again. Heed my words, my husband. You. Will. Suffer."

As my mother finished the story, I sat back, so stunned I couldn't speak, couldn't think clearly, but rage unlike anything I'd ever known erupted from deep within. I took a deep breath, trying to hold my fury.

"Speak to me, my beautiful son. Do you hate me?"

"Hate you, Mama? How could I ever hate you? I am so sorry." Tears streamed down her face. What she'd endured was horrible, repulsive. What the fuck was wrong with that man?

Something broke inside of me, the level of hatred something I hadn't expected. I took a deep breath as the hatred grew.

"I love you, Mama."

"My beautiful, special boy."

I brought her hand to my cheek, a single tear sliding down my face. "I will avenge your pain."

I expected her to dissuade me, to remind me that I'd been raised a God-fearing man, but there would be no compromise, no promises made to a woman that had never deserved the horrible life she'd been forced to endure. "What. Is. My. Father's. Name?"

"Xavier Santos. He is in Los Angeles where you were born. I forged your birth certificate. Your real name is Dante Santos, brother of Diego."

I'd gone by the name of Dante Fernandez my entire life, my law school graduation diploma carrying the fake name.

Out of the corner of my eye, I noticed the only man who'd ever been decent to my mother standing in the doorway, his expression grim.

"My beloved Fiona," he said, drawing her attention.

She reached out to him with her other hand, tears in her eyes. "Emmanuel. Please take care of my son for me. It is my only wish."

"He is my godson, my beautiful love. I will honor your wishes for the rest of my life. And I will help him seek revenge."

My mother placed his hand near mine, wrapping her bony fingers around both. Then she turned her head in my direction. "There is a box hidden beneath the floorboard of my bed at home. You will find the truth and the answers you seek. Be careful, my baby boy. Xavier is a truly evil man."

The bastard had no idea what I was made of or what I would do. As I glanced into Emmanuel's eyes, he nodded out of respect, but I sensed he'd known the story for much longer. He was also a powerful man and if anyone could help me exact the revenge my mother deserved, it was him.

"I love you, Mama. You have always been my true angel," I whispered, her grip slipping on my hand.

"And you are my perfect son. Find your brother. You two were... so close. Let him know his mother never... forgot... him. Diego."

As she slipped away, my heart stopped beating, all sense of humanity lost. I would avenge her death in ways that would destroy my father's empire. Then I would enjoy watching the bastard take his last breath.

CHAPTER 7

Demons.

My mother had always been very private about her past, ignoring certain questions as I grew and after a while, I'd stopped asking. There'd never been a day I hadn't seen extreme sadness in her eyes, but she managed to enjoy the simple things in life. The smell of her favorite flower. The joy in her eyes when she was able to provide the single present I'd coveted. And I would never forget her laughter, although rare. Emmanuel had brought her most of her limited happiness over the years, his warmth and generosity something she often refused, but he'd managed to find ways to bring joy.

I was no fool. I'd known about who and what he was for years. He'd never attempted to hide his identity or the kingdom he'd built from violence and bloodshed. As the leader of a brutal cartel, he should remain my enemy, my work as a prosecuting attorney a direct opposite to his beliefs and actions. But he'd never attempted to sway my beliefs or judge my decision to practice law. He'd been respectful to me as I had been to him. Now he was the only man who could provide the assistance I needed.

It should sicken me what I was thinking. It didn't.

I'd struggled with my emotions, unable to pry off the board under the bed, revealing the steel box underneath. In my mind, I'd wanted to preserve my way of life, pretending that my legacy wasn't built on lies. I wasn't angry with my mother, my admiration for her strength only increasing. And I loved her with all my heart.

Now, as I sat with the box unopened, my glass of scotch placed just beside me, I still found it difficult to face the inevitable. Had my brother been told what had happened? Was he a part of a repulsive continuation of my father's unholy decision? I wasn't certain of anything, except my need for retaliation. If I was honest with myself, I'd have to admit I'd sensed she hadn't told me everything about my father. I'd also sworn a part of me was missing.

Classic separated twin behavior.

My mother had raised me to be a respectful man, following every appropriate rule and law. Now I had to dig deep to find the inner darkness that I knew existed. I swirled the glass, concentrating on the sound the cheap crystal made on the marred wooden surface. Being in my mother's home was bittersweet. After taking a gulp, I knew I had to find the courage to open the box.

So I did.

As I pulled out old photographs, I easily recognized her as a young woman. There was joy on her face, her eyes lit with happiness from being beside two identical children. We were very young, two or three, but the resemblance then was uncanny. When I finally saw a picture of my father, the bile that formed in my throat was suffocating.

He was a large man, muscular and powerful in his stance as he looked over whatever was going on with my mother and her two children. But I could see a darkness in his eyes, as if the hold he had over her and whatever empire he'd built had driven him into believing himself God. Disgust was a heavy weight as I pulled my original birth certificate into my hand. Diego was born three minutes before me, but it was clear that my mother had birthed two sons that day. I carefully laid it aside, finding a few more trinkets of her life, including a few baby toys and a locket that had both her sons' pictures nestled inside.

She'd left with nothing but a bag full of memories. How had she managed to make it, returning to her home country of Chile? I would never know.

At the bottom of the box was a typed letter in an envelope addressed to me. As I peeled away the flap, my muscles tensed. I read over the information twice, the four pages containing much of the same story as well as further identifying just how powerful my father truly was. When I was finished, I awakened my laptop, searching the internet for the missing pieces.

It was easy to find additional information on Xavier and his empire. He'd parlayed his initial holdings into becoming one of the most influential people in Hollywood, his movie production company worth close to a billion. As I flipped through page after page on Google, I developed a better representation of his methods used to build his kingdom.

They were brutal, several people disappearing over the years. My father had been questioned several times by the police but had never been charged with a crime. But there was no doubt the man had blood on his hands. After taking a deep breath, I typed in my brother's name, the reigning prince of my father's empire. He was just as successful, owning several houses and expensive cars, and his reputation as a ladies' man well documented. He was everything I wasn't, his appearance polished by his ten-thousand-dollar suits and expensive haircuts, but there was no doubt he was my identical brother.

I also realized after additional searching that Xavier had remarried several times and that I had a half-brother, although he was much younger. There was no indication how much time Diego had spent with him over the years. There were no pictures of them together. I'd say Diego had no interest in nurturing any brotherly relationship.

What the hell could I do to destroy my father? And how would my twin react? I'd wallowed in anger and sadness, the hours spent with bloodlust in my heart, but I was no killer, nor was I a monster. I was a man of the law, a decent human being. How could I fight a battle with a man who likely had members of law enforcement under his thumb?

I took a deep breath, realizing I'd finished every drop of scotch. Hissing, I rose to my feet, grabbing the bottle from the kitchen counter and pouring another full glass. Today was the day I would get drunk, ignoring the pain and heartache. Tomorrow was my mother's funeral. After that I would make my plans.

I'd always known something was wrong with our little family, the stories my mother told me far too perfect. A strange sense of knowing had finally settled in, the shock now worn off. Now I had to admit certain truths to myself. I had felt as if I was missing something my entire life, as if a part of me had been cut in half, stripped away. As I closed my eyes, taking several deep breaths, I allowed my mind to shift to any memories I had as a child. A few holidays filled with laughter, only a few presents, but it hadn't mattered.

School.

Playgrounds.

A swing made of a rope and an old tire.

A haze developed around my eyes, and I took several deep breaths. Then a blurry image slipped into my mind, shimmering and vanishing only to reappear as if in a different still frame from a movie.

Laughter. A boy. A boy who looked… like… me.

Gasping, I opened my eyes, still able to see the short scene in my mind. My father was there, looking on us as Mother turned us around in a circle, her face beaming.

Then blackness.

Pain tore through me, doubling me over. I couldn't breathe. I couldn't think. Oh, my God. It couldn't be true.

But it was.

I stood, slamming my fist on the table, lifting my arm to toss everything to the floor. Damn the fucking asshole who did this. To hell with being a righteous man. I lifted the bottle, prepared to smash it against the wall.

Then I slowly eased it to the table, closing my eyes briefly before taking purposeful steps toward the old upright piano my mother used to play. She'd loved music, had told me how much she'd loved playing the piano as a young woman. She'd been groomed to become a concert pianist but love had interfered, taking her away from what she'd loved the most.

As a kid, I'd seen the piano in the window of a consignment shop. I rolled my fingers across the keys. They remained in pitch. Laughing bitterly, I sat on the bench, stretching my fingers before lightly placing them on the keyboard. The memory of begging the owner of the shop to allow me to work for him in exchange for the piano was one of my best memories.

I'd managed to surprise her that Christmas, even though my schoolwork had suffered. I'd never seen her so happy. Then she'd insisted she teach me how to play.

As I closed my eyes, the music came to me, the haunting strains of Chopin's Prelude in B Minor, one of her favorite pieces. And while I played, I felt peaceful, no longer filled with the same level of anger that had captured me from the moment she'd told the story.

Minutes later, the sharp knock on the door forced a hard stop. What few people who cared about my sweet mother had already paid their respects. The house was filled with food and drink, knowing that I would spend some time in the home I'd grown up in. However, I wasn't certain I could stand plastering on another fake smile as one of her friends shed tears.

I wasn't surprised Emmanuel was leaning against the door-frame, but there was something entirely different about the look in his eyes than had been at the hospital. They were cold, detached. And dangerous.

"Emmanuel."

"Dante. You play like your mother."

There was no reason to feel uncomfortable, but my music had always been private.

"She was trained, and I am not."

"Some things come naturally," he stated with a glint in his eyes. "I believe it's time we had a conversation."

I allowed him in, although the expression he wore made me tense. He moved toward the kitchen table, glancing down at the material then at my glass.

"We shall have a drink together," he said. "Then we will plan how to handle this. You will not fall into a bottle after this day."

"I mean no disrespect, but I haven't decided what I'm going to do." I grabbed another glass, pouring him a drink.

"None taken, my godson. However, you will need the kind of help only I can provide." The edge in his eyes was unlike anything I'd ever observed around my mother.

"I will listen to you, but I can't make any promises that I can accept your advice."

"Understood."

We both lifted our glasses together, a toast to a woman who'd changed both of us. I often believed her goodness had rubbed off on him, allowing him to experience a part of life that he mostly ignored given his position. Maybe I was fooling myself. Today it would seem he was all business. Perhaps that's what I needed.

"The answer as to what you're going to do is simple. You will take back what belongs to you." Emmanuel tipped his head, never blinking as he looked into my eyes.

"And just how do I do that?" I asked, curious as to his answer.

He turned toward my computer, enlarging the picture of my brother on the screen. Then he laughed, a deep-throated sound that for most would be ominous. But for me, it was comforting.

"There is an easy answer, although not an effortless solution." He kept his hard gaze, his upper lip curling. "You will become your brother."

The suggestion was startling, but not necessarily something that hadn't crossed my mind, although the undertaking was blasphemous. "That will be impossible. We come from two different worlds. He is American. I am not. I could never fool my father or the hundreds of soldiers the Santos Empire employs. They would see right through me." I closed my eyes, allowing the rage to build once again. Could I do it? Was I capable of pretending to be a killer?

Maybe.

"Nothing is impossible, Dante, unless you deem it so."

"Then what do you propose?" I heard the terseness in my voice and sighed.

"With my help, you will become Diego." He moved around me slowly, studying me. My dress. The way I held my body. "You will learn everything there is to know about the man. His likes and dislikes. His mannerisms. His way of speaking. His way of handling business and you will transform yourself. You will eat, sleep, and study the man. You will learn to become something that you're not and in doing so, you will be able to absorb his life."

"And how do I do that with limited information?"

He returned in front of me, his smile cunning. "You will leave that to me. Our paths have never crossed on purpose, Dante. You mother forbid me to either nurture you or convince you to become a man of importance in my organization, which I questioned more than once. However, I honored your mother's wishes because of the way I felt about her. And you. You are the son I never had."

"I won't do anything illegal."

Sighing, he held up his glass, twisting it in the limited light. The look in his eyes was one of disappointment. "You must ask yourself if you really seek revenge or if this madness will end. You need to search your soul, Dante, to know what you are capable of. If the answer is that you will grieve then return to your life, then my idea will be buried with your mother. However, if you know that your heart will never heal until you've embraced your need for retaliation, then you will come to me asking for my assistance. In doing so, there will be no turning back. You will become the man you've fought to prosecute your entire adult life. You will follow my direction without question. Period. You must understand and accept that without reservation because where you would go once making that determination you can never return from."

He allowed his statement to sink in and I nodded, uncertain I could make that decision easily. He polished off his drink then patted me on the shoulder before walking out the door without saying anything else.

And when he did, my entire world seemed to crumble around me.

* * *

"Death is not the greatest loss in life. The greatest loss is what dies inside us while we live."

—*Norman Cousins*

. . .

Three days later

Death.

As I remembered the first time my mother had explained death when speaking about the 'loss' of my heroic father, she'd had stars in her eyes that were easy for an eight-year-old to see. She'd spent at least five minutes describing my father as a hero of his people, dying in order to save several others who otherwise would have died in a horrific fire.

All lies.

However, I was now able to accept that her vision had been the one she'd needed to hold onto, refusing to acknowledge the tragedy that had been her life. After suffering through her funeral on a stormy day, I'd been forced to face the fact I had no feelings left inside, zero emotions. I was neither angry nor sad, just existing from minute to minute. Emmanuel's words had filtered through my mind several times, enough I hadn't slept in three days.

The mere act of closing my eyes had brought visions of the few movie clips I'd found of my brother and father attending movie premieres, treated like an exalted king and his prince. But during the last few hours, the anger had made a return to my system, making it difficult to breathe.

Then it was as if an epiphany had occurred, a light shining over me telling me what I needed to do.

I pulled my truck onto the aggregate driveway, the thick iron gates in front of me no doubt daunting for anyone else

PIPER STONE

who dared enter the world of a man called the dragon. To me, the thick metal posts provided a pathway to salvation, freeing my soul from the chains embedded into the tender tissue. There was no need to provide a name or any form of identification. It was as if the armed guards had anticipated my arrival.

As I parked my vehicle, my attention drawn to the lush grounds and the massive flow of water erupting from the mouths of what appeared to be demons in forged concrete, I sucked in my breath. I'd heeded Emmanuel's words, his advisement that if I chose this path, there would be no turning back. That much I'd taken to heart, resigning my position at the prestigious law firm the day before.

Where I was going would secure my place in hell, but I was resolved to follow the path. It had to be done. I eased out of my truck, buttoning my jacket. Inside the pocket was one of only two weapons I owned, their purchase becoming a necessity after almost losing my life to a monster I'd put away for what I'd thought was life. That had been my first taste of understanding that anyone could be bought for a price. There wasn't a man or woman alive who didn't have a threshold, a barrier where they'd cross the imaginary line from good to evil.

At least in my case, the fact I'd already taken a long stride over the fiery divide hadn't been about greed or power, the reason much more basic.

I didn't hesitate before knocking on the door, holding my head high as I heard footsteps.

When the door was opened, I took a deep breath.

98

"I knew you would come," Emmanuel said.

"It's what I need to do."

"You must have patience. And I will be watching."

Nodding, I lowered my head out of respect. "Understood."

"Then so be it. The moment you set foot inside my house, you will be under my control, following my orders no matter how painful or taxing. Turning you into something you are not will take time, but it will be done. *Te convertiras en un hombre poderoso.*"

You will become a powerful man.

"But only if you're willing to do the work and sacrifice your soul," he added. He tilted his head, his dark eyes scanning mine, the smile on his face one of cunning.

"I will do the work."

"Excellent. Then let us begin. As of now, Dante Fernandez no longer exists. I will be a harsh taskmaster, brutal to the point you will want to kill me. But that is what will be necessary in order to alter your mentality. I will not accept weakness or failure. I will ask you one last time. Is this what you want?"

I took a few seconds, mulling over his proposal in my mind. Then I made the only choice that I knew would help me find salvation. "Yes, with everything inside of me."

The simple act of crossing over his threshold had sealed my fate.

Dante Fernandez was dead. Risen from the ashes of blood and treachery was his replacement.

I was now Diego Santos, brutal heir to an empire of ash and bone.

And soon, it would belong to me.

CHAPTER 8

iego

"Remember, my beautiful son. The only thing in life that matters is family. Not possessions or power, money or influence. They will not define you. They will entrap you."

My mother's warning remained in the back of my mind as I headed to Emmanuel's office. She'd told me that many years before when I'd broken down in tears of because kids had made fun of my tattered clothes.

"Mi importa una mierda lo que quieras. Mantenerlo alli," Emmanuel snarled.

I don't care what you want. Keep him there.

During the last few weeks, I'd been privy to few of the drug lord's business dealings. He was a private man, his compound well guarded with dozens of soldiers, all carrying automatic rifles. He had dozens of employees, his wife and her sisters, along with his nieces and nephews all living behind ten-foot solid concrete walls. There were security cameras everywhere, but that didn't seem to faze anyone living inside the fifteen acres. I'd been amazed at the level of security but no more so than the generous living quarters provided to the men and women working for him. Emmanuel was a man of many surprises.

He was also a true savage.

While I'd been given decent accommodations, they were sparse in comparison. A cot with a thin mattress. A single chest to hold what few clothes I was allowed and one lamp. The bare existence suited me, allowing me to hone both my mental and physical skills. I was stronger. Faster.

Angrier.

I'd witnessed more than one act of violence, required to go with him on several of his 'hunts' as he called them. He'd gauged my reaction each time, providing his words of encouragement as well as punishment depending on my actions.

After taking a deep breath, he tossed me a file, leaning back in his desk and taking another puff of his cigar. As always, he watched my reaction as I took a look at the contents. Almost immediately, my muscles tensed, the same hatred I'd felt just after my mother died resurfacing.

"Additional proof in case what your mother told you wasn't enough," he said, his tone chipper.

"You are certain of this?" I asked as I continued to stare at the information, details that I'd suspected but hadn't wanted to face. It had been almost two months since I'd made the decision to push aside my real identity, becoming my brother. In the long, arduous days spent around my godfather, I'd been put through a series of tests as well as being reshaped into a man I no longer recognized.

Even though Diego and I were identical in most aspects, the differences were enough to undermine my intentions. I took a deep breath, the pain from the welts suffered at Emmanuel's hands no longer increasing the anxiety I'd originally felt. I'd been caged, whipped, scarred, and tattooed, deprived of sleep and food, all to ensure that I could handle my father's brutality.

I'd gained twenty pounds of muscle, but what had hardened more than my body was my blackened heart. No one would ever be allowed to get close ever again.

Inside the file were wedding pictures and a marriage license.

"There is no doubt, Diego." He'd already taken to calling me by my brother's name so there was no chance I'd ignore being addressed in my future life. "You father broke your mother's heart when he made her choose."

"That's the reason I'm here, Emmanuel."

His nostrils flared as he glared at me. He didn't like that I challenged him in any way. I might not have an upbringing of hate and violence, but I'd learned quickly that there was no place for empathy or self-doubt.

"Your father enjoyed allowing his firstborn son to rule, telling him horrible stories about his mother."

Why was he digging the blade of the knife in even deeper? "Also something I know."

"Then you will do what it takes to destroy them both."

I moved closer to his desk, smashing my fist on the surface. "Do you think I'm weak, Godfather Emmanuel?" My tone held an air of discord.

His eyes flared with anger. Then he smiled. "Quite the contrary, Diego. You are strong and resilient. Incidentally, as you might imagine, there are passcodes you need for his social media, computers, and his security systems, most of which the men I employ were able to secure. However, there are undoubtedly certain codes that were not listed in a location that my hackers were able to discover. You will need to ascertain which ones you have access to, perhaps through your method of handling your brother."

A part of me hated being called by my brother's name, but I understood what he was doing. "That I can do. It's time. I'm finished waiting to settle this."

He cocked his head, pulling out another file. "And in case you don't believe what your father is capable of or why it's very important that you shed all concept of your former life, here's additional proof."

The photographs were vivid and graphic, the three victims tortured before they were allowed to die.

"Can you do this if required?" he asked.

I lifted my gaze, controlling my breathing. "I will do whatever is necessary in order to fulfill the promise I made to my mother."

"That is your brother's handiwork, a man called the Butcher." He waited for me to acknowledge what he'd said, as if that would strengthen my hatred of the man. At this point, I was numb, preferring to feel nothing but ice in my veins. I would need utter control in seeing the two men for the first time.

I crumpled the paper, taking a deep breath. "Then my brother must face the same wrath as my father."

"That will make what needs to happen to him that much more palatable."

A part of me wanted my brother killed, but the man needed to suffer as much as my mother had. There was only one way of doing that.

Imprisoning him, which had already been discussed.

"I have no problem with what needs to happen, Emmanuel," I snarled, tossing the wad of paper into the trash.

"I will provide you with four soldiers to take with you when you leave. In addition, I have contacts within the Los Angeles area. Is it still your decision to imprison your brother?"

"Yes," I hissed.

"Very well. Then I have secured a location that will be manned by my soldiers for as long as you deem necessary."

A wry smile crossed my face and I flexed then fisted my hand. "Excellent and much appreciated."

"I assure you that one day you will repay me the favor. You will be given a private flight into a little known airfield. At that point, you will be taken to San Diego, where your brother generally spends the majority of his time. From there, it will be up to you how you handle the situation. While my soldiers will be under your command, please remember that they belong to me."

"What do you get out of all of this?"

His laugh was full of amusement. "You already know me too well. There is a smaller cartel within Los Angeles, truly scum of the earth as far as I'm concerned. However, they have been foolish enough to hijack two of my shipments. It was very costly and unacceptable. They will be handled in accordance to my laws."

His laws.

He certainly had a way of keeping his men in line.

"Understandable."

He stared into my eyes for a full minute, never blinking. "I believe you're almost ready. However, there is one more test for you before you return to your home."

My home. I had no memories of Los Angeles or of my father. I'd read once that twins had an innate ability of reading each other's minds, knowing when the other was in pain or needed help. I'd only felt since that something was missing. Now I couldn't care less. I would enjoy inflicting the same kind of pain my mother had experienced on both him and my father.

"What is the test?" I flexed my hand, the ache in my knuckles also remaining. I'd taken up boxing, which helped relieve some of the anger, the exercise also good for my coordination and stamina.

He eased his feet to the floor the stubbed out his cigar. As he walked to his bookshelf, as I'd seen him do before, he pressed a button under one of the shelves. There were at least a half dozen secret closets throughout the compound. He'd explained that because of his level of power, he would always be challenged, his enemies attempting to end his life on several occasions. The secure facilities were necessary to keep his family safe in case of an attack.

This one held dozens of weapons of all sizes and shapes. He selected a handgun as well as an AK-15, tossing both in my direction before yanking down boxes of ammo. "I need to handle a situation with a dealer who thought it would be wise to try and steal from me. He also murdered one of my men as well as his innocent son." He shoved several magazines across the desk, waiting as I checked and loaded the weapons. He'd been impressed at my knowledge of weapons already.

"Am I to assume I'm coming with you?"

"Yes. I think it will provide firsthand experience as to how business is handled."

"When are we leaving?"

"There's no time like the present."

* * *

While Emmanuel's compound was nestled in seclusion, nothing around for thirty miles, the city he drove to was bustling with activity. Twilight had fallen, bars and restaurants already packed. He'd said nothing more about the person we were going to see, but I had no desire to learn anything about the man. Even though I'd left my life behind, I was focused on one thing, not becoming a soldier for the man in upcoming months.

He parked just outside a building, the warehouse space far removed from the entertainment focus. After tossing his cigar on the ground, he headed for the door, the two soldiers flanking the entrance immediately opening the door then saluting. In the dim light, I could tell they wore no expressions. They were good soldiers and nothing more, following orders as if in the militia.

That's the kind of power Emmanuel wielded. I wanted to be impressed by his focus, drive, and ability to command, but I'd accidentally witnessed a man's murder point blank the second day I'd arrived. I hadn't been prepared. The whipping I'd received at his hands in front of several others had been a stark reminder that emotions were not allowed in this business. Becoming hardened had been easy.

I trailed behind him, scanning the facility. The location was obviously used as a decoy, but I suspected given the stench of blood and shit, that wasn't the first time it had been used for other purposes over the years.

The murderer was tied to a chair, his head dropped to his chest, his breathing labored.

As we approached, the soldiers inside also saluted, all four of them in precision timing. I took a deep breath, remaining quiet as Emmanuel rubbed his chin and studied the man.

"*Parece que temenos un problema porque me has estado robando,*" Emmanuel said with zero inflection. It would seem we have a problem in that you are stealing from me.

When the man said nothing, Emmanuel sucked in his breath then tipped his head to me. My godfather was testing me just as he'd already warned. He'd provided many aspects of training, including proving words of wisdom.

But this test was a final exam.

Emmanuel threw up his hand, shaking his head. "*Para quien estas trabajando?*" Who are you working for?

"*Nadie, Señor Santiago,*" he managed. No one, Mr. Santiago.

There was attitude in the man's voice, as if this was just a game.

"*Si me estas mintiendo, te cortare la lengua,*" Emmanuel hissed. If you are lying to me, I will cut out your tongue.

The asshole was obviously lying, his right foot tapping on the concrete floor, the stench of piss suddenly filling the air. The environment wasn't one I was used to, although life as a prosecutor had taken me to some unwanted locations in search of fearful witnesses. Drug lords were a way of life in several countries, Chile not sparred from the daily violence. However, seeing it from this perspective was entirely different.

Enough so it repulsed me.

The man made the mistake of grinning at him as he lifted his head. "*Vete a la mierda.*"

Fuck you.

"*Asesinaste a un niño inocente,*" I hissed.

You murdered an innocent boy.

The grin remained on his face. Then he spit on the ground. "*Una víctima de la guerra.*"

A casualty of war. The asshole couldn't care less that unnecessary blood was spilled.

"Untie him," Emmanuel told his guards.

After the man was freed, he was jerked to his feet. Then he immediately went into a fighting stance.

Emmanuel turned in my direction. "Provide the justice required for a grieving wife and mother forced to watch her only son slaughtered in front of her eyes." His command was sinister, the look in his eyes as dark as I'd seen.

I took a deep breath, staring at the man. There was no way to avoid his order. While this world was brutal, killing an innocent boy wasn't acceptable. This time I didn't hesitate, immediately issuing several hard punches to the man's face.

He jerked back, weak from his previous beatings. Then he lunged toward me, managing to get in a punch to my gut. My reactions were quick. I backhanded him with enough force he was pummeled against a stack of cargo boxes. He struggled to stand but I was on him, issuing swing after swing.

The man was resilient, providing an undercut to my jaw, my ears ringing as I almost lost my footing. I became a machine, words Emmanuel had said running through my mind.

"Never allow an opponent to get the upper hand. Strike until there is no breath left. If you let your guard down, you will die."

I had no intentions of allowing the murderer to get the advantage. I lunged forward, grabbing him around the throat, smacking his head against the crate several times. Then I cracked my fist into his kidney before issuing a hard kick to his stomach. As he dropped to the ground, I licked blood from my lips, my breathing labored.

"You're not finished yet," Emmanuel stated. Then he turned to face me, a smug look on his face. "Kill him."

I'd been faced with danger several times in my life, street thugs who attempted to steal from me or worse. I'd been beaten the first time because I'd hesitated in following my instincts. I'd outweighed the man by forty pounds, but he'd managed to get the better of me because of that hesitation.

This time I knew better. This time I had no choice.

I took three long strides in the murderer's direction, yanking him to his feet. Then I threw punch after punch, hearing the cracking sound of bones breaking as blood splattered across my face and chest. Then I dumped him on the ground, taking gasping breaths.

One of the soldiers crouched down, feeling for the man's pulse. Then he nodded to Emmanuel, the words he spoke cutting through me like a knife.

"*Él está muerto.*"

He's dead.

I'd passed the final test.

Now I was ready to take on the motherfucker who'd destroyed my mother's life, taking from me what was rightfully mine.

And I would return the favor.

"*Limpiar el desorden,*" he told his men. Clean up the mess.

As we walked outside, I took a deep breath of the humid night air in an attempt to rid my system of the foul odors, the sickness in my stomach from what I'd done.

He flanked my side, staring up at the moon. "The second hardest thing to do is to kill an acquaintance, Diego."

"And the first?"

As he turned his head, his stare was icy. "Taking the life of someone you care about."

"I can imagine."

His words weighed heavily on my mind. Before climbing into the Jeep, he leaned over the metal bar. "There is an alliance that Diego allowed himself to be coerced into, or so it would seem."

"An alliance?"

"Yes, a brotherhood of sorts. Mafia leaders from several regions of the great United States." He laughed. "They are working together to keep certain organizations such as myself out of their territories."

This was the first I'd heard of it. "How do you know this?"

"As I've told you before, I have my sources. At some point, you will be required to attend a meeting with them. They could be a problem for you. It could also prove to provide unlimited information that you will be able to use in the future."

I found it interesting that given everything I knew about Diego, he would allow himself to be pigeonholed into joining an alliance. Although they certainly weren't unheard of, powerful mafia Dons creating a roundtable of sorts to air grievances in order to keep blood from raining on the streets, Diego didn't strike me as the type of man to consider something of that nature. Besides, it was old school, the tradition very rare in the States. "I will handle it."

"As I'm certain you will. Undermining them could be help-ful." As he laughed again, it became obvious he would attempt to use his tutelage to his benefit. While I was grateful for what he'd done, I also had no intention of trusting the man.

I nodded my answer.

"And unfortunately, I also found out something else that will affect your performance."

"That is?"

"Diego is to be married. The woman is of importance but will also become one of your greatest challenges. Use her.

113

Fuck her. Break her. But do not fall in love with her. She could be dangerous to what you're trying to accomplish."

I took a deep breath, holding it for several seconds. I would take the man's house, his cars, his clothes, and his business. Then I would take his wife.

As a smile crossed my face, Emmanuel began to laugh.

And all I could think about was a phrase that had haunted me as a boy.

Forgive me, Father, for I have sinned.

CHAPTER 9

iego

San Diego, a city I'd never been to. While I'd traveled to the States on two occasions, both had been for collecting evidence for a case. I'd flown in under the cover of night, the four soldiers Emmanuel had provided on the same jet. Then I'd been taken to a hotel outside the city, finalizing the last details.

I'd watched my brother from a distance, stalking him, hunting him like the predator I'd become. He was careless in his security, acting as if no one would ever dare touch him. He'd been captured easily, taken without issue.

Now I stood in the shadows, watching the moment of my brother's imprisonment unfold. I'd wanted to be there, to be the one who put a noose around his neck, dragging him away from his posh surroundings. But I'd made the determination that the joy of seeing his shocked face wasn't worth the risk of being seen prior to the change.

The prison Emmanuel had provided was perfect for my needs, the location just outside the city, the location rural and very private. My brother had been bound and gagged, a dark canvas bag put over his head, then dumped in the trunk of one of the soldiers' vehicles. I'd provided the soldiers with strict instructions that the man wasn't to be hurt.

That was unless I handled the task.

Before he'd been taken, I'd realized that my entire personality had been altered, the man I'd once been vanishing. I'd been indoctrinated into a brutal world where second guessing and weakness would mean a death warrant. Until this moment, a part of me had pretended that I could turn off the other side, returning to my normal, happy-go-lucky life. Now I knew that not to be the case.

After tonight, I'd be labeled the same vicious monster my brother had been. The trouble in my mind was that I was no longer certain I cared. The thought of absolute power over money, empires, and life or death was enticing. Maybe that meant I'd been born a bad seed, my father's genes crushing my mother's. I shoved the thought aside and would need to keep it buried if I intended on following through with my plan of action.

As my brother was dragged on his knees into the cinderblock walled room, I took a deep breath and lit up a cigar, the flicking sound of the lighter drawing his attention. I hadn't smoked my entire life, but it was a habit I'd been forced to acquire. I studied him for a few minutes, reminding myself why his imprisonment was necessary.

He would provide me with information when necessary, the means of obtaining it something he wasn't used to.

"Who the fuck is there?" Diego asked, anger still in his voice. That would soon change.

I said nothing, merely taking several puffs of the cigar, allowing him to gather a whiff of his favorite Cuban.

His shirt was ripped from his body, two soldiers shackling his wrists then attaching him to the cinderblock wall. For now, that's where he'd stay. As far as leniency, there would be none for the time being. I would provide what was necessary to keep him alive and nothing else.

"What the fuck is this? Do you know who my father is?" he bellowed, struggling even as the men were attaching the bands of steel.

Father. I clenched my jaw as soon as he asked the question. I flicked an ash then waited until the soldiers left the room, slamming the thick metal door behind them.

"No! You can't keep me here. You will be found. My father will hunt you down like dogs. Then he will gut you. All of you!" Diego yelled for some time, still fighting with the chains.

Sighing, I forced myself to look away, needing another reminder of why I was doing this. There was no doubt my brother was a brutal, savage man, or that he'd ordered the murder of dozens of people, their blood staining his hands. To him, life was worthless. I resisted laughing at the thought. His arrogance came through in everything he did. Every quoted conversation, every time a reporter had caught him on camera. I abhorred men who lorded their stature over others as much as I did vermin who believed they were allowed to be judge and jury.

How many bastards had I prosecuted in my life who'd been just like him? Enough to know there was no redemption for them.

The thought of his last breath didn't bother me in the least. What did was the fact I was starting to enjoy the thought of being the one to take it. After closing my eyes, I allowed visions of my mother's serene face when she'd gone to her heavenly father to enter my mind. Then I remembered everything Emmanuel had shared with me, including the bloody photographs he'd supplied. Nothing I could do would be as disturbing as what I'd seen.

I took another puff and walked closer. That's when he realized someone had remained in the room.

"What the fuck do you want?" he yelled. "Money? Is that what this is about? A fucking ransom?"

Chuckling, I walked closer.

"No, Diego. Your father will not send men to hunt you down, nor do I give a shit about your money, other than how I can use it to destroy your entire family." I was surprised how easy it was for me to lose my accent almost completely. However, I allowed it to remain at this moment, curious as if he recognized who I was.

He lifted his head, his expression full of confusion. "What the hell?"

"Do you not hear the sound of your own voice?"

"Who the fuck are you and what do you want?" His growl was bordering on exasperation.

"What do I want? That's a loaded question. I'll give you an easy answer. Everything."

I took another puff then yanked the hood from his head, taking a step back into the light. I'd prepared myself for my reaction as well as his own. However, all the practice runs in my head, the words of rage and hatred hadn't done the moment justice.

Nor had it prepared me for the reflection of myself staring back at me.

There was nothing more I wanted to do than to drive a blade into his heart. The only reason I didn't had nothing to do with the torture I wanted him to suffer, but with the love my mother had for her lost son. I took a deep breath, studying his facial expressions as he blinked several times, finally huffing as if this was a game.

But I'd seen a moment of real fear in his eyes.

"What the hell is this? Who the fuck are you?" Some of his defiance returned, his nostrils flaring as he struggled once again with the chains.

I debated what I was going to say to him. As I came closer, the slight tic in the corner of his mouth indicated fear as well. Good. I wanted him very afraid of me and what I could do. "What's wrong, Diego? You can't recognize your own twin brother?"

His eyes opened wide as if from a delayed reaction. Then he burst into laughter, which was the wrong thing for the bastard to do.

I backhanded him as rage rushed through every muscle. "I suggest you remember where you are."

"What the hell is this, some kind of joke?"

Everything about the man's arrogance pissed me off. There was such contempt in his reaction that it was pointless to try to get through to him. I took a deep breath, raking my hands through my hair. "Did you ever ask *our* father about our mother?"

"What the hell are you getting at? Do you even know who I am and what my father will do when he hunts you down? Trust me, he will. He'll cut you apart limb by limb, enjoying every shriek of pain as your body betrays you."

I wrapped my hand around his throat, digging my fingers in. A huge part of me wanted to snap his neck, ending the charade then assuming his life without fear of discovery. But I wanted to see him suffer like my mother had more than I cared to admit even to myself. "Our mother was tossed away as if her life didn't matter, forced to choose between her two children which would live in poverty and which would flourish in wealth and power. I was the lucky one."

As I allowed the words to sink in, I sensed he was still living on the belief I was an imposter. I backed away before my rage got the better of me. "Enjoy your new accommodations, Diego, while I enjoy yours."

"You can't be serious."

I tipped my head over my shoulder, allowing a smile to cross my face, the feel of power flowing into my fingers. "I assure you that I'm deadly serious, including enjoying the taste of your beautiful bride." As I opened the door, the sound of the chains being jerked was like sweet music to my ears.

"You'll die for this. You'll die!"

"Entonces nos pudriremos juntos en el infeirno."

Then we'll rot in hell together.

* * *

"Retaliation is related to nature and instinct, not to law. Law, by definition, cannot obey the same rules as nature."

—*Albert Camus*

I'd understood the concept of retaliation my entire life. I'd studied it in philosophy. I'd written about it in college. I'd even embraced the need more than once in my younger life. But never once had it been as all-consuming as it was at this moment. The need filled me with the same kind of fire I'd had when entering law school. To excel. To beat the odds.

To win over everyone else.

However, there was a significant difference in boyhood whims from that which fueled a studious man. Now the need was so intense that it had altered my life forever. I'd crossed the invisible line between right and wrong, never to be allowed to return to the other side. At least not with what I'd done to my own brother, a man I didn't even know.

After selecting a suit, one of dozens hanging in a room-sized walk-in closet, I stood in front of a six-foot mirror, staring at a reflection I no longer recognized. While my features were identical as the man I'd imprisoned, the subtle changes to my appearance had provided an entirely different image staring back at me. My hair had been cut, eliminating the majority of thick curls. The beard I'd once coveted had been removed. In the two months, I'd bulked up in muscle mass, at least enough to fit perfectly into the man's tailored, eight-thousand-dollar suits.

As I grabbed the jacket from the hanger, I hesitated before putting it on. One thing Emmanuel had told me as a kid was that once a man slipped into his jacket, he assumed a persona. He could be anything he wanted to be but was required to accept that person with everything he had. As a young man I hadn't understood what he'd meant. Now I realized that a man's suit jacket disguised the brutal beast underneath.

Chuckling, I eased my arms into the sleeves, fixing the collar and taking a step back before adjusting the tie I'd chosen. It would seem my brother was a clothes whore, something I'd never thought of. I retreated from the closet, heading into the man's bedroom. While I'd been provided with security codes and passwords, most of which I'd already memorized, my brother's phone held a wealth of information, including additional details about offshore accounts even Emmanuel's hackers hadn't discovered. I was surprised at my brother's carelessness, which told me even more about his level of arrogance.

He'd thought he'd become untouchable.

There was a safe in his bedroom as evidenced in several sketches that had been added to an architect's file prior to an authorized renovation. However, I'd found no other information, including how to access it. I moved to the location, a bookshelf located in front. As I pressed my fingers under every shelf, I quickly realized that would make the secret room far too easy to access.

I glanced toward the bed, chuckling softly. Then I moved to the nightstand, feeling under the lip as well as both drawers. Nothing. As I stared at the ornately crafted headrest, a smile crossed my face. Then I felt behind the posts, almost immediately finding a button that could easily be ignored, considered a flaw in the wood and nothing else. As soon as I pressed my finger against it, the bookcase swung out into the room, exposing a door with a keypad. I was surprised facial recognition hadn't been used, which mean the room itself was one he would allow someone else to access. From here I was taking a risk of setting off a security system. However, after studying everything about him, I gathered a sense of what made the man tick.

Including his desire for simplicity. The code would be the same one he used for his phone. I likely had one chance at this, but it was worth the risk. After punching in the code, I half expected one or more of his men to come rushing into the house. Instead, I heard a soft click. As soon as I opened the door, a light came on. What I found inside surprised the hell out of me given the layout of the house.

A panic room had been established as well as a small arsenal. Inside was a single bed, table and chair, a refrigerator, and even a bathroom. There was also a communications system set up on one wall, which I assumed provided a panoramic view of the entire property. How clever. I walked inside, marveling at the design, the walls undoubtedly soundproof. While I'd arrived on a private charter to an unknown airstrip courtesy of Emmanuel, allowed to bring in my own weapons, the choices were infinitely different than what I'd anticipated.

I pulled out a VP9, a weapon I'd become familiar with in my days as an attorney. My brother had excellent tastes, a semi-automatic favored by assassins. After loading it with ammo, I slipped it inside my jacket. Now I had a meeting with my father about the upcoming wedding, which I'd originally planned on canceling. However, Emmanuel had encouraged me that it would provide a secure hold on another empire, which would provide me with a greater ability to ruin both the Santos name as well as the family fortune. It would all depend on what my father had to say.

I had the contract that had already been drawn up and was surprised at the level of detail. My brother had thought of everything, including providing a clear understanding that the woman selected would perform all sexual duties as required. He'd even been descriptive about his expectations.

The man was obviously sadistic as fuck.

As I returned to the main portion of the house, a reflection of the sun caught my eye. I walked toward the massive set of windows, peering out at the ocean. The man lived a life of luxury, something my mother should have been allowed to indulge in. There was a sense of serenity watching the waves tumbling against the shore and for the first time, I allowed myself to embrace the fact that if things had been different, my entire life would have been altered significantly.

Would I have turned into the ruthless brute my brother enjoyed being?

I needed time to absorb the gluttony and power, which is the one thing I didn't have. As I pulled the single item that had belonged to my mother I'd dared bring with me into my fingers, the locket I'd found, the anger I'd initially felt returned.

"You will be avenged." I fisted the necklace, feeling a strange sense of interior burn as I unfastened the clasp, taking it to the panic room for safekeeping. Then I closed the door, allowing the bookshelf to hide the only thing that mattered to me, a memory that would never be forsaken. That was the moment in my mind that Dante Fernandez vanished.

Forever.

In his place another man was born.

And he was a trained killer.

At least the hour and a half long drive was pleasant, allowing me to enjoy both the day and the feel of the powerful Porsche. My brother had good taste in automobiles, several classics located in the garage of his San Diego home. They were just a few of the many luxuries he'd amassed over the years.

I'd spent hours memorizing details about my father's house, the best route traveled by vehicle, as well as everything I could about his lifestyle. In addition, I'd made certain I knew everything there was to know about my father's corporation as well as the partnership Diego had entered into with two other men. While his work as an attorney was vastly different than my own, I had a feeling the change wouldn't be an issue.

However, I'd also taken a crash private course in entertainment law.

None of that bothered me. After I'd mastered the art of entering a courtroom, facing some of the vilest criminals in South America, nothing could.

Except for keeping my hand off my weapon.

That would come later, but only after the man suffered.

As I drove up to the house, I was surprised there were no guards present, although I'd been forced to stop at the gate, lowering the window to allow the camera to highlight my face. I pulled around the circular driveway then took a deep breath.

The meeting should prove to be interesting.

I grabbed the briefcase holding the contract and eased out of the car, scanning the area. That's when I noticed one guard walking the grounds, a semi-automatic in his hand. I made note for future reference.

Then I jogged up the stairs, almost knocking. As I opened the door, I made certain I had a smug look on my face. The layout of the house was exactly as I'd memorized, and I found my father's office easily. I headed inside without knocking, which seemed to surprise the man standing in front of an arched window, the house high on a perch over-looking the valley of sin.

At least that's what I liked to call LA.

He laughed when he saw me, shaking his head. He was puffing on a cigar, his face showing years of alcohol abuse. So much gluttony. My half-brother stood by his side, his face pensive as he studied me.

"Let's get this over with," I said as an introduction. Then I narrowed my eyes as I studied Cartero. "Brother."

He laughed, shaking his head. "It's been a long time since you referred to me in such a familiar term."

"Does that bother you?"

"Should it?" he challenged.

I wasn't happy with the way he was studying me, but I'd confirmed that Cartero had never been close to the real Diego. Perhaps because he knew he would never be considered *El Jefe*.

"You seem eager to get the contract finalized, son. I'm glad to hear you've come to your senses," my father said. It was difficult to think of him that way. I had no memories of the man or of the house I'd spent two years in.

There was a second of hesitation before I walked closer. While the resemblance to the man was only in the color of our eyes, I was instantly grateful both Diego and I had taken after our mother. Time for the show. "On the contrary, Pops. I still have no interest in marrying the woman." I'd seen several pictures of Carina DeMill. While beautiful, in my mind she didn't deserve what she was about to face. I was well aware of the harm it would cause to her life given the codicils in the contract, including turning over partial control of her music empire for me to control.

His face instantly turned red as he moved closer to his desk, stubbing out his cancer stick then slamming his hands on the wooden surface. "I'm sick of your bellyaching. She's beautiful, intelligent, and young enough she will bear as many children as you would like."

"That's not why she's required to become my bride. Is it? It's all about the power grab."

Snorting, he scanned the length of me, still surprised at my attitude. He would need to get used to it. I wasn't playing things his way no matter how my brother had behaved.

"Power is something you've enjoyed acquiring your entire life. Do not tell me you're going soft on me."

Cartero laughed. "I told you he wasn't ready."

"Shut up," my father said, his gaze never leaving me.

"Soft?" I laughed as I unbuttoned my jacket, walking closer. Then I slammed my hands on the desk only two feet away from him, glaring him in the eye. "I have no problem breaking the woman, taking what should already belong to our empire. What I do have a problem with is the timing. There's far too much business to take care of for me to take on additional work managing the DeMill Corporation."

"If you're denying my request, then I'll allow Cartero the privilege of marrying Ms. DeMill." There was a glint in his eyes, but his moment of attempting to keep control enraged me enough I saw a sea of red in my eyes.

When I yanked my weapon into my hand, shoving the barrel against his temple, he moved from surprise to shock.

Cartero moved away, obviously concerned I wouldn't stop with killing our father.

Xavier Santos was a pig, and I couldn't stand being this close to him. He cursed under his breath, almost reaching for his weapon out of instinct. Then a smile crossed his face.

"I thought you would reconsider. Cartero is too young to take the helm of my empire, but if that's what I need to do, then I will. You will fuck this up."

"I have no intention of doing so, but if you threaten me again, I will pull the trigger," I said calmly.

"I see I've done my job in teaching you. Excellent."

The repulsion churned in my stomach. I backed away, shoving the handgun into my pocket. In my mind, the man was already dead.

"He is not fit to lead, Papa," Cartero stated. When Xavier backhanded him, the force enough to drive Cartero into the bookshelf, I sensed he had no more love for the kid than he had for his other two sons. Diego had been necessary in order to keep the power in the family and nothing more.

Blood dripped from Cartero's mouth. He wiped the back of his hand across it then headed for the door, hissing as he passed. Before he left, he issued a warning of his own.

"*Voy a disfrutar matandote, hermano.*" I will enjoy killing you, brother.

I couldn't wait for him to try. While the kid was a victim of violence and anger, he would attempt to make good on his promise, which would leave me with no choice but to end his life.

"You will be in complete control of the DeMill Corporation, Diego. You can hire anyone you want to handle the day-to-day operations. However, if you decide to tear it apart instead, forcing a leveraged buyout, that is perfectly acceptable."

Why did I have the feeling the proposed contract had been forced on Carina's father? That's information I wasn't privy to.

"Imagine the power you will wield once the announcement goes in the paper," he said, lifting an eyebrow as he watched my reaction.

Getting out of the marriage contract wasn't an option. I took a deep breath, easing to my full height. "Yes." When I smiled, he started to laugh.

"Montgomery DeMill is expecting that you'll drop off the contract today. The final details should be in order by Friday for an announcement Saturday. Then the wedding will be expedited."

"It seems you've taken care of all the details."

He moved to his bar, pulling down two brandy snifters. "As I always do. Now, let's have a toast to the future. Then you can drop off the contract personally."

The last thing I wanted to do was engage in pleasantries with the man, but in doing so, I would learn enough about the man to help in taking him down.

I'd passed the first test. Now nothing would stop me from getting what I wanted.

CHAPTER 10

L os Angeles
Carina

There were two things I hated most in life. One was dealing with prima donna musicians who couldn't stand taking career advice from a twenty-four-year-old woman. I especially loved the has-beens who got in my face, acting as if they could use their age, size, or brawn to force me into keeping them signed to the music company I'd taken over two years before. They quickly learned I was a viper, refusing to accept any excuses or bullshit. I gave one warning that a musician's behavior was getting out of hand and that was it.

Then they were out the door, the very clear clauses in every contract providing the power.

However, that often didn't stop their threats of lawsuits or bodily harm. If that didn't work, some of the smarmy assholes had tried to seduce me. That's when things had gotten physical.

And I always won.

The second thing I loathed was coming to my parents' house under most circumstances. I tolerated the holidays, and my younger sister's birthdays, but anything else left me with bile in my throat and a rapid increase in heartburn. It wasn't that I didn't love them. It was simply that they were both oppressive, requiring me to dress a certain way, talk a certain way, be a carbon copy of them. I couldn't swallow any of my father's ancient rules, the same ones he'd grown up following in Italy.

Then there was the issue of my mother. After all the years of being married to a brutal man, she'd become nothing but a puppet. It sickened me that her every move was controlled and had been for as long as I could remember. I'd seen pictures of her at my age, a glamorous movie star, one of the highest paid actresses at the time.

Then she'd met my father and he'd forced her into early retirement.

What bullshit, but she'd been the fool to say 'I do.'

Sighing, I pulled onto the long driveway, determined to avoid speaking to either one of them. Doing so always put me in a nasty mood. I was here to pick up my sister, taking a day off to go shopping, which Mia had been begging me to do for two full months. Why not? It was a beautiful day in

Los Angeles, and I could afford the time. As I rounded the circle, I immediately slowed down.

What in God's name was Diego Santos doing here?

I couldn't stand the pompous prick. I'd faced him inside a courtroom after being sued by at least three of my disgruntled former talents. He was a shark in expensive clothes. We'd sparred to the point both of us had almost landed in contempt of court. There was nothing worse than a man who thought he was God's gift.

And that's exactly how to describe him, but I had other words as well.

The man was a criminal, a bloodthirsty killer. Granted, my father had shifted between the gray areas of criminal activity. I'd known that most of my life, but as far as I knew, my father had never killed a man or woman in cold blood.

I pulled the car into my usual parking space, squeezing the steering wheel before bothering to cut the engine. I'd go upstairs, collect my sister, and get the hell away before either my father or the prick noticed I'd arrived.

As I stepped out onto the aggregate driveway, the front door opened. I stopped short and glared at Diego from a distance. He looked particularly suave in his charcoal suit and crisp white shirt. The man was obviously handling some sort of business with my father. I had to wonder what the hell my father was doing consorting with such scum.

I slapped on a huge smile, adjusting my shades as I walked closer. When Diego heard my approach, he turned to face me. I hated to admit that even though I loathed every inch of him, Diego was undoubtedly the most gorgeous man in LA. He could have been a model or an actor instead of a mobster. Reported to be worth billions, the Santos Syndicate had their claws in much of Hollywood as well as the rest of California, Oregon, and Washington State.

"Well, well. Look what the cat dragged in," I said, half laughing. I sashayed closer, removing my sunglasses.

He kept his on, but I could tell he was staring at me, his chiseled jaw clenched, his breathing ragged.

"Ah. Did that cat get your wittle tongue?" I asked.

Why did he have to look so gorgeous?

He remained silent.

"Hmpf." I moved past him up the three stairs, glancing over my shoulder once. "Nice chatting with you. Asshole."

"What a shame such a beautiful woman has such a caustic mouth. It would appear you need to have that mouth washed out with soap."

"And I'm certain you think you're the man to do it."

Now he walked closer, the challenge on. "I suggest you learn manners, Ms. DeMill." His arrogance was finally bubbling to the surface.

"And I strongly suggest you learn not to be a dick. That would help you in every aspect of your life." I remained where I was, happy as peaches and cream I'd worn my heels. I stood almost eye to eye with the dark and sultry man, his dour expression allowing me to maintain a bright smile. As his masculine scent roared through my system, I had a fleeting feeling of arousal, my nipples tightening. I could swear he noticed immediately, his chin dipping to my breasts. Goddamn the arrogant bastard. He'd used his extreme good looks to win over juries more than once, staring tiger-eyed at each female as if he was going to devour them whole.

I could never fall for such a prick. "Now, if you don't have anything else to say, I suggest you get the hell off my father's property before I call for security. And I assure you, *Diego*, they won't be nice in escorting you off the grounds."

He dared to move even closer, inhaling and holding his breath for a few seconds. When he exhaled, his hot breath created a series of goosebumps dancing along every inch of both arms. How could I be so attracted to such a jerk?

"You have no idea how close we're going to become, my beautiful Carina, but you will soon learn."

Close? He had to be out of his mind. When he dragged his tongue across his lips, I was repulsed, my stomach revolting. But as he backed away, the look on his face full of smugness, a little red flag rose in the back of my mind. What was he cooking up with my father? I reined in my rage, never blinking. Then I blew him a kiss. "I'm looking forward to the challenge."

I watched as he headed to his car, his gait as if he'd just won the lottery. What the hell was going on?

God, I wanted to scratch his eyes out.

If only I could see them behind his dark shades.

When I walked inside, closing the door immediately, I was already laughing. There had to be another lawsuit on the horizon. Groovy. I'd come at him with everything I had.

I headed for the stairs but heard footsteps almost immediately.

"Carina. Please come into my office. I need to see you." My father's voice held an air of urgency.

As I threw him a look, I noticed strain on his face, which was unusual. He was always gloating about a recent win or a takedown of a rival.

"I'm in a hurry, Dad."

"This can't wait. Now, Carina."

I took a deep breath before following him into his office. He closed the door behind me then headed for the small bar hear the massive window.

"A little early to be drinking. Wouldn't you agree?" I asked, barely taking a few steps closer to his desk.

He said nothing as he poured a tall whiskey, gulping almost half. Whatever Diego had said had obviously infuriated him. When he returned to his desk, he slowly lowered the glass before lifting his head and looking into my eyes.

"You are a very important member of this family," he stated, but there was something odd about his choice of words. It had been a long time since he'd paid me a compliment.

"What's the catch, Dad? Why don't you get to whatever it is you need to tell me?" Why was I so antsy?

"Sometimes in life, we must make difficult decisions for the betterment of the entire family. You'll learn that as you begin your married life."

"I don't plan on getting married, Dad. Not my thing." Where was he going with this? When a slight tic appeared in the corner of his mouth, I swallowed hard.

"Often the choices are seen as… unfortunate even if they are necessary."

"Cut to the chase. I have a busy day ahead of me." The edge in my voice was sharp, the volume increasing. He wasn't known for drama so why now?

"Lower your damn voice!" He slammed his fist on the surface, which made me jump. As he raked one hand through his hair, he glared at me with more venom in his eyes than I'd ever seen before. "You are required to follow rules. My rules. Period." He allowed the few words to hang in the air as he studied me.

Now I felt terribly uncomfortable. "Fine, Dad. I understand. What do you need to tell me?"

He took another swallow then slid whatever he had on his desk closer to me, grabbing a pen and doing the same thing. "You'll need to sign this."

"What is it?" I tentatively walked closer, my heart skipping several beats. Was he selling off a part of the business? He'd threatened once before to sell the music production company to an enemy. I'd threatened my own father for the first time in my life when he had.

"A contract."

"For what?" I was losing my patience at this point.

"You are getting married."

"Excuse me?"

"This is non-negotiable."

"Just who am I supposed to be getting married to?" I asked the question through gritted teeth as I jerked the contract into my hands, searching frantically for the details, including the name of the individual I was supposed to marry.

Even though I knew.

A cold shiver slammed into my spine, taking my breath away the second I noticed his name.

Diego Santos.

"You are fucking out of your mind," I snapped, tossing the contract in his direction. "This isn't the nineteen hundreds, and we aren't in Italy, Pops. You're not going to sell me off to the highest bidder. I'm not your goddamn possession." As I backed away, I could barely think straight. How could my father even think I'd go along with this charade?

"You will do this. It will stabilize our corporation."

"What do you mean? We're doing just fine."

"No, we are not. We are drowning in debt."

His admittance shocked me almost as much as what he was proposing. "That's not possible." But somewhere in the back of my mind I knew it was. A significant amount of money had been spent on getting the production company up and running on my insistence. I'd done the research. I'd known it was the right time two years before. I'd grabbed onto the thought and wouldn't let go. Was he blaming me for the loss?

He nodded and for the first time, I sensed he was a broken man, hiding a secret from everyone in the family. He and my mother lived a lavish lifestyle and always had.

A yacht.

Foreign cars.

Expensive villas and vacations.

Diamonds.

Furs.

Jesus Christ. When I thought about how much money had been wasted, I was sick inside, even more so than the thought of marrying such a repulsive man. I tried to clear my mind, but it remained foggy. I wanted to double over and cry, but what good would that do? "So Xavier Santos smelled blood in the water and this is a leveraged buyout. Is he blackmailing you for some horrible proclivity you have hidden in the back of your closet?"

The split second of a dark expression crossing his face told me I was right. Oh, my God.

"Enough!" he bellowed. "You will do this. In doing so, the combined corporation will allow us to become the most powerful movie and music company in the entire world. No one will be able to carve out a piece of the market. No one."

The tension was horrible, the air sucked out of my lungs as icy fingers clawed around my neck. But this couldn't happen. Not this way. "I won't do it, Father, but I will find another way to destroy them." I turned around, heading to the door before he could say anything else.

"Then Mia will be required to marry him."

And there it was, the black hole that he knew I wouldn't allow my baby sister to fall in. I remained where I was, all the anger I'd felt for my father searing every nerve ending, turning my vile thoughts into hatred. As I turned around, I allowed the fact I loathed him to show.

"She's not yet eighteen years old."

"She will be by the date we've selected for the wedding. Of course, she will be required to have a child immediately, so she'll have to put college on hold."

"She's a brilliant musician with a full scholarship to a conservatory in France. That's all she's ever wanted. She did it herself without a penny from you or the trust fund held over her head."

"That will go away." He stared at me and there was no sadness in his eyes, no look of remorse whatsoever. Just the same gloating look I'd seen on Diego's face.

He had me caught in a web. There was no other choice. None.

"He will brutalize her. The man is a freaking sadist." Could I appeal to his sense of decency?

"She will learn to obey and endure," he insisted.

My God. The man was heartless, his hunger for power driving him into making this horrible decision.

I walked closer, picking up the pen in my hand, sliding the contract closer. Then I lifted my head and stared my own father in the eyes. And I made a promise, words I never thought I'd hear myself say.

And I meant every one of them.

"I will do what's required to protect my sister, but I assure you that I will find a way to destroy both you and my... *husband*. Then I'll enjoy ripping out your throats with my. Bare. Fingers."

CHAPTER 11

 *resent day*

Diego

"A fucking circus," I said under my breath as I stared at the television. Sixteen guests dead, only five of the shooters, which wasn't nearly enough.

"You know the FBI are going to be knocking on your door," Sergio said.

I shook my head. "They can knock all they fucking want. What the hell do I have to offer?"

He snickered. While the Santoses weren't new to dealing with several law enforcement agencies, for me, the timing couldn't be worse. The last thing I needed was a microscope shoved up my ass.

The news footage of the carnage, although I knew it had been watered down, was horrific. It had been an absolute bloodbath. I flicked off the screen and rubbed my eyes. The long days were just beginning.

"Are we any closer to finding out the identity of the perpetrator?" I asked casually, which seemed to surprise Sergio.

"No. There were no identifications on any of the dead assholes," he said bluntly. I could tell he'd had a long night, his demeanor surlier than normal.

"Did Stone look for tattoos?"

"Yes. They were cut out recently."

That surprised even me, and I'd seen and heard all aspects of gangs trying to hide their colors. "Fuck. I want to make certain my wife is guarded at all times."

Sergio nodded. "Do you think she was the target?"

I'd thought about little else all night long. "My guess is that we both were."

"That's what I was thinking."

My wife.

How many thoughts had crossed my mind about canceling the wedding altogether? Even now, I wondered if dragging her into this life had been a good decision. I'd almost gotten her killed.

Even if the arrangement had been out of my hands prior to my arrival in the States.

Still… what I was doing could destroy her.

Stop thinking. You made a choice.

I had a difficult time believing Carina was now mine. She wasn't anything like what I'd imagined. She was more. Much more. The way I already felt about her unnerved me, as Emmanuel had warned me about.

The taste of her had been unexpected, her touch searing my skin. And driving my cock into her sweet pussy had sent an explosion of heat and sensations into every muscle. However, her question lingered in the back of my mind, and I knew it was one she wouldn't let go of until she discovered the truth.

I couldn't get the haunted look on her face out of my mind, or the image of the blood covering her wedding dress and hands. I'd called the hospital, learning her father had already been released. The man was a tough bastard. I'd called, Montgomery curt as usual. He'd barely asked about Carina, which pissed me off even more. At least Mia would know her sister was okay. It had been the least I could do.

"The shit from last night isn't the only thing we need to deal with. We may have a problem with a shipment coming in from Colombia," Sergio said as he lifted his eyebrows, curious as to my reaction.

I tipped my head, glaring at him. He was the one man I hadn't been able to read, but I'd realized from minute one I couldn't trust him. He was cold and calculating. Up to this point, there hadn't been any issues with the illegitimate side of our business. But he'd kept me informed of the various shipments we had coming in from various destinations. I found it curious that the one that would create an issue was from Emmanuel's origin of business.

The timing wasn't coincidental.

"How so?" I eased my weapon into my jacket, walking around the desk.

He had a curious look on his face, one I didn't like. "It's my belief one of our informants tipped off the Tijuana pigs." When I stared at him, he smirked, as if he believed I had no understanding of what he was talking about. "The Black Angels?"

"The rumors that Luis Ortiz is in town are true," I stated in a matter-of-fact way. What Emmanuel had said about the Black Angels was proving to be right on the money.

Interesting.

"Let me put two and two together," I said, snarling under my breath.

"That's what I was thinking. Ortiz was behind the massacre."

"A shot across the bow with bloody consequences. He thought he could shake me." Did the low-level asshole actually believe he could take on the Santos Empire? Or had there been something between my brother and the cartel leader I hadn't been made aware of?

The light faded from his eyes, but I could tell he was still uncertain I could rule like Xavier.

"Yes," he growled. "He needs to be handled this time. The fact that your father ignored his earlier chance has proven to be a bad decision."

Ortiz had reared his head months before, but the limited information hadn't provided many details.

"I'm not my father, Sergio. That's something you need to accept. If not, I'm certain I can find another one of my men to replace you." I sensed he didn't take the threat lightly. I watched as he fisted his hand, his gaze icy. The fact remained I'd need to be cautious, handling Ortiz just like Sergio wanted if necessary. But I'd learned during the first year of law school that syndicates often played against each other.

"Yes, *sir*. I am the only man who knows just how savage Ortiz can be."

I'd learned that Sergio had been taken hostage by the man two years before, beaten to the point he'd almost lost his life. He'd remained loyal to my father, refusing to give up anything. For that he'd almost been emboweled. While that should earn him a permanent place in the upper ranks, I didn't trust him.

The power of Mexican cartels had risen significantly over the last few years, LA considered one of their main territories. But Ortiz stood in a class all his own. I'd overheard a conversation Emmanuel had with one of his lieutenants weeks before. Ortiz was attempting to enlarge his territory. It would seem he'd set his sights on the Santos Empire as well as becoming an annoyance to Emmanuel. However, the two men had made a pact years before to keep out of each other's territory, which was one reason Ortiz was determined to take parts of California. Ortiz's soldiers would need to be handled on my watch. "Since the shipment is due in two days, I suggest we have a greeting party for them."

A return shot was needed, or my reputation would take a hit, another thing I didn't need.

"That could start a war."

Why did I have a feeling the man was still testing me? "Are you fucking questioning my orders, Sergio?"

He had the audacity to roll his eyes. "You're different since you married."

"Different?"

"You act as if business no longer matters."

I walked closer, the hatred I felt for the man rising to the surface. Within hesitation, I issued a brutal punch to his chin. "If you dare question me again, you will face something entirely different than the feel of my hand."

He clenched his jaw, glaring at me with a calculated fury in his eyes. "Yes, *Jefe.*"

The term wasn't being used as one of respect.

"Have the soldiers prepared for the shipment arrival. And yes, Sergio. I will be there personally to begin the party." I kept my glare on him for a full thirty seconds. "I have a meeting at my office in LA. Keep my wife locked inside the room. You will need to check on her."

"And if she tries to escape?"

"Then you will what's necessary to make certain she doesn't. However, you will not hurt her. Is that understood?"

As he studied me this time, I could tell he was second guessing his concerns. "Completely."

I headed for the door, turning only when I'd reached the entranceway. "And Sergio. Make certain my brother doesn't gain access to the house. Cartero has proven to be... difficult."

Now he chuckled. "Absolutely, sir." At least I knew there was no love lost there since my father had treated Sergio like a second son.

Sir.

I could get used to the title.

* * *

My blood boiled, my skin prickling from the thought of fucking my lovely bride all over again. While I hadn't been surprised our attraction had been so intense, the fact she'd questioned my identity from the start would prove to be an issue if I didn't handle her questions appropriately. Her tenacity shouldn't have come as a shock given I'd read over the few case files where she'd been representing the very music company I now owned, my clients suing her for wrongful termination.

Or I should say my brother's clients.

From the notes my brother had penned on several documents, it was obvious they'd sparred on every occasion. No wonder the fire in her veins was part acid. That had made the sex that much more enjoyable. Enemies to lovers. The thought kept my cock at full attention.

I'd locked her in the room, telling the man considered the most trustworthy of his dozens of soldiers to keep watch. However, if she mentioned her concerns to Sergio under any circumstances, I would need to be prepared to act quickly. I was no fool to think she'd become compliant on any level but getting her under control was more important than I'd originally believed.

At least with a half dozen men remaining at my house, she should be protected. I doubted Ortiz or anyone else would make another attempt so soon.

As I walked into the conference room of my office, I felt more empowered than I had in a long time. This was my element, keeping an edge while making deals. It didn't matter whether it involved a corporate entity or prosecuting a bloodthirsty criminal facing life or execution, the methods of reaching a deal were always the same.

The person who held all the cards won.

That I was used to, exceling with a ninety-six percent prosecution rate. Today would be no different, only I was ensuring the combined Santos–DeMill Corporation was the one with all the aces.

One of my partners within the firm was also sitting in on the contract signing. I'd read everything there was on Edwardo Rivera. He was a true snake in the water, a man who was well respected in the entertainment field. He was also a known associate of my father's from years ago, which made him dangerous to my situation.

He stared at me as I walked in, giving me a single nod. The parties in question were already seated at the table, both rising to their feet as I closed the door. I'd been late on purpose, increasing their anxiety. They'd believed they could ask for more money than the entire project was worth. That was easy to see. I didn't need to have worked in the industry for years to know they were desperate for money to fund their project since no one else in the industry, including foreign backers would come near them. Their movies either flourished or flopped with no dependency.

They were also trying to strong-arm us, which was a huge mistake on their part. I'd cut the contract funding in half, which they would either take or leave. I honestly didn't give a shit.

"Mr. Waldorf. Mr. Jameson. I'm going to make this quick as I do have other commitments today." I didn't bother sitting, merely taking out two copies of the contract I'd carved up, sliding them across the table. Then I headed for the bar, pouring myself a short whiskey. I wasn't in the habit of drinking in the late afternoon, but appearances were everything in this business.

They needed to know without question that I was in absolute control.

A full three minutes passed. Then I heard one of them laugh.

I glanced at Edwardo and smiled.

"If you think we're going to sign this piece of trash, you're wrong," Waldorf snorted as he shoved it unsigned back in my direction.

"Then it would seem we have nothing else to discuss. Have a nice afternoon. Get out of my building." I casually took a sip, not bothering to turn in their direction.

"Hold on, Bobby," Ruger Jameson told his partner. The once decent actor had fashioned himself to be a movie producer, his success enough to get him into the front door of every movie house. His cocaine habit, fueled by my father's product, was what had earned him a less than favorable reputation. He liked to hurt women when he was high, badly enough he'd been arrested several times. His father a state senator, the kid had skated out without spending a night in jail.

I abhorred men who took out their frustrations on women with violence. Even as the thought raced through my mind, I thought about Carina and the sadistic needs my brother had required being satisfied. Ruger and my brother had been friends, frequenting local, private BDSM clubs together. That made this deal even sweeter in my mind.

"I heard about what happened to you, Mr. Santos. I'm really sorry," he offered.

After shooting him a quick look, I nodded. "You have one minute to decide."

Ruger jerked Bobby to the side, whispering harshly but my keen hearing allowed me to catch every word. They weren't just desperate. They'd waged every dime they both had on the project. I did so enjoy putting a man's balls in a tight vise.

"Fuck him," Bobby hissed.

"Just shut up and take the deal."

Even with Ruger's encouragement, Bobby jerked up from the table, coming at me with his fists clenched. "You're a son of a bitch to go back on your word."

I turned toward him slowly, keeping a smile on my face. "Until a deal is signed on the dotted line, there will always be changes. Especially since I discovered that you haven't paid several of your actors from your last project given your penchant for blow, and the grandiose parties you've had. And I know about the girl who died at one of them."

Bingo.

He knew I had him. I'd simply put the pieces of a puzzle together. While the incident had been shoved under the covers, I'd followed my instinct, the look in his eyes telling me the gamble had paid off.

As soon as he tried to throw a punch, I snapped my hand around his fist, tossing the glass against the cabinet then shoving him against the wall with enough force it shook. Then I wrapped my hand around his throat, digging my thumb into the skin under his chin. The move cut off his air supply completely.

"I suggest you rethink your method of operation, Bobby. If you dare ever try to lay a hand on me again, I will cut your nuts off, shoving them down your throat. Then I'll move to your eyeballs. Are we clear?"

He wheezed but managed to nod. I squeezed for a few seconds before letting him go, watching as he stumbled to the side. Ruger was already on his feet, his eyes full of fear.

"How did you find out?" he asked. His question meant Diego hadn't been invited to the party.

"Does it matter?" I asked casually, selecting another glass.

"No. I'm just… We'll take the deal," Ruger said, his tone full of exasperation.

"I thought you would. Now, sign it and get out of my office."

The two men wasted no time, both eager to get out of my sight. I took several sips of my drink, surprised Edwardo had said nothing.

When he stood, he took a deep breath. "First of all, I'm glad your family survived, including your lovely bride. I guess I should be thankful I had a meeting I couldn't ignore."

A meeting. I looked at him and shook my head. "Yes, I guess you are a lucky man."

"At least more than some. One of the state congressmen lost his life."

"I heard. So did a lot of other good people."

"Is Carina okay?"

I was already tired of the chitchat. "I don't mean to be rude, Edwardo, but I need to get back to her as soon as possible and yes, she's shaken but unhurt. Let's get on with finalizing our business."

"Understood." He studied me briefly before pointing to the signed contract. "The meeting was fascinating, Diego. I must admit, I am very surprised how you handled your friend."

"I learned a long time ago, Edwardo, that there are no such things as friends in this business, only those who want something from you. I'm finished being a team player." I turned my gaze in his direction, watching as he smiled. Another test passed. My partners wouldn't bother me as I used the firm to destroy the Santos Empire.

"Your father did the right thing in turning over his empire to you. It was time for new blood and yours is on fire."

He'd thought me weak. More blood in the water. I made a mental note to keep that in the back of my head.

The man was my father's age, close to retirement himself. He'd enjoyed all the perks of being a member of the firm, all his dirty little secrets just as ugly as my father's. "Expect changes over the next few months."

"As I can imagine. I can see that marriage will be good for you, son."

Son. The man would never be given the opportunity of calling me that again. He'd been the one to destroy all evidence of my mother's existence. He'd been the one to advise my father how to go about destroying her life.

He would be the first one to bleed by my hands.

CHAPTER 12

 arina

Anger swept through me like a tidal wave. I'd been locked into a room like a bad little girl. No phone. No computer. Nothing. Why was he treating me like a child? I couldn't contact my sister, my mother. Nothing. I was sick with worry, angry at the entire world. There wasn't a television in the room. Did the man not care about what was happening outside his little fiefdom?

I was more overwrought than I had been the night before.

The only other thing I'd been able to do was think about why the nagging remained in the back of my mind about his identity. He was obviously Xavier's son. He looked exactly as he had the day I'd run into him at my father's house. Then why couldn't I get the feeling both families were being duped out of my mind?

I wrung my hands as I continued pacing, the feeling of suffocation remaining. I'd been brought nothing but water, the savage soldier checking on me every couple of hours. I'd made a decision that the next time the asshole came into the room, I was going to strike. There had to be a vehicle outside. I would escape.

And just where will you go?

Mia was still in town, which meant she could easily be captured. She had to be terrified. Did my family know I was alive and unhurt? Surely, Diego would have let them know. Right? I had to wait until she was in Paris. Then I'd tell her the truth. Until then, I had to be a good girl. Oh, my God. What was I thinking? I was going to make certain the limited time I spent with Diego would make him so miserable he stayed away from me.

Then I'd initiate a plan of destruction. How could I do it? More important, who could I trust? I had a feeling Diego would bring his people into our company, firing anyone he believed was loyal to my father. Oh, this was such a nightmare. As the anger continued to furrow, I headed toward the door leading to the balcony. I'd thought of jumping but it was high enough I'd break a bone or two. And climbing down wasn't an option. He'd made certain of that.

I was a prisoner in a gilded cage in a world of blood and violence. As I stood in the doorway, the light breeze bringing the scent of the ocean into the room, I could almost believe this was paradise. His scent remained all over me, even though I'd taken another shower. I couldn't rid my mind of images of his naked body, the tattoos covering one arm and part of his chest, or the thick waves in his dark hair. When I closed my eyes, the visions became even more powerful, my pulse increasing.

Why was I attracted to him?

A few seconds later, I heard a noise and had a few seconds to decide what to do. I needed time and space to figure things out. Maybe I'd grab Mia and we'd run away together. Getting away was the only responsible thing to do until I could figure out a plan. As I glanced around the room, I noticed a thick crystal vase on the table sandwiched between two chairs.

There was no time to put on shoes, but at this point I didn't care. I grabbed it, moving behind the door, holding my breath as it was unlocked. As soon as Sergio walked inside, I bashed the vase against his head, the thick glass only cracking even though I'd used all the force my muscles could provide.

At least he dropped like a rock, blood trickling from the gash on his forehead. I pitched it aside, wasting no time before racing out of the room. The man's roar sent a wave of fear through me.

"Damn it, bitch," he hissed, his thick Russian accent sending a wave of shivers down my spine. I could sense he was right behind me.

I flew down the stairs, glancing over my shoulder only once. He had his weapon in his head, already lumbering down the steps.

"Don't worry about it, Sergio. I have her."

The deep voice stopped me cold, the authoritative sound resonating in every cell. I stopped short, gasping for air as I swung my head around to see Diego standing at the bottom of the stairs.

His expression held the same one of amusement, but his eyes were laced with annoyance that quickly shifted into fury.

"I'm sorry, Diego. She jumped me as soon as I got into the room," Sergio snarled, sending another chill through me.

"It would seem my bride doesn't appreciate her accommodations and privileges. I'll take care of that. Remain outside. We have additional business to discuss." There was more of an air of dominance in his tone.

"Yes, sir." As Sergio walked down the stairs, I crowded against the wall, uncertain what to expect.

Only after he'd walked outside, closing the door did Diego move closer.

"It would seem you have an issue with authority," he said quietly, so much so I had to strain in order to hear him.

"I need to talk to my family. You took my phone." I closed my eyes, rubbing my forehead.

"Your family is doing well, sequestered in their estate. I talked with your father and made certain he'd relay the information to Mia. You will be able to talk to them."

"Just not now."

He took a deep breath, his eyes reflecting the same exhaustion I felt. "Soon, Carina."

"Jesus Christ. You're not my master, Diego. In fact, you're nothing to me."

"Your body says otherwise."

The man was leering at me, lust spilling into every vein and muscle.

"No. I can't stand when you touch me." Why was I bothering to lie after the night we'd shared?

Because if I gave into my desires then I was terrified of losing what was left of myself and my independence.

"Keep lying to yourself, Carina. Maybe one day you'll come to believe it."

Of course he could see right through me.

"You are keeping me as a prisoner. I'm not your wife. I'm just another possession. I need to feel whole again, to live my life. You won't allow that."

He cocked his head, his nostrils flaring. "That's because I need to be able to trust you. I also need to keep you safe."

"What do you think I'm going to do? I can't absolve this marriage. I won't risk my sister's life. I can't live in terror. What you don't understand is that I don't trust what my father will do with Mia. He doesn't care about his children. We weren't the sex he wanted."

My words seemed to hit him hard, but I could only tell by the way his nostrils flared.

"What do you want, Carina? You will have your work after we've established new guidelines, and after I've figured out who's targeting us."

A part of me knew he was right. "I just don't like feeling like a caged animal. Certainly, you must be able to understand that."

"And I don't want you to feel that way. What can I do to help you through this?"

"My phone. I'd like to call my sister before she leaves the country. No, I want to be able to see her one last time. I'm certain you won't allow me to fly off to Paris. I need to know she's safe. Did you even bring my phone?"

His laugh pissed me off as well as sent shivers down my spine. He had that kind of effect on me. Then he took a deep breath, studying me intently. What was he searching for?

"I do have it, and I'll take your request under consideration. There's a chance your phone has a tracking device on it."

"A tracking device? My father or someone else?"

"That's a good question," he answered.

"I get it. Then just leave me alone."

"I'm afraid I can't do that." He snapped his hand around my wrist, immediately heading up the stairs.

"Let go of me." I struggled but his hold was too firm. As he dragged me up with him, I did everything I could to fight him. When I managed to slip out of his grasp, he turned around with so much venom in his eyes, I was instantly shocked, thrown off balance. As I started to tumble down the stairs, he wrapped his arm around my waist, pulling me against his chest.

"You will learn not to fight me, my beautiful bride."

I pushed my fists against him, hissing. "Never. You should know that about me by now. I am a DeMill. I will do what it takes to bury you."

He laughed and I was no longer certain my suspicions were true. The sound was the same as I'd heard in the courtroom. Confusion settled in, my mind uncertain of anything at this point. Why was I pushing him so hard?

"It would seem you need to learn what it's like to be a Santos, which is what you are. Your former life no longer exists, and I assure you that the life you spend with me can be made very difficult. Perhaps a taste is in order."

He threw me over his shoulder as if I weighed nothing. Then he marched us both up the stairs, passing by the room I'd been staying in to another all the way down the hall. He'd barely clicked the latch on the door before kicking it in. Then he stormed inside, turning in a full circle while I struggled to see the room where he'd taken me.

It was almost empty, except for a twin bed and a single nightstand. There was no lamp, no dresser, no chair. Just the empty space proving that he could strip me of everything I'd once been, driving me to the point of madness. Well, to hell with him. I was stronger than he had any idea about.

As soon as he eased me onto my feet, I tried to jerk away, but he wasn't ready to let me go. He gripped the back of my neck with one hand, sliding the other down my back, cupping my buttocks through the thin dress.

I managed to slap him across the face, but the force wasn't enough to allow me to get free.

"You shouldn't have attempted to escape. Until you grasp what we're dealing with, I'll do everything in my power to make certain you don't cause yourself harm," he said quietly.

While I understood part of his change in demeanor was to protect me, he was also asserting his control. Or maybe he didn't want me asking questions in an attempt to confirm my suspicions.

"I will find a way to get free of you."

"And do what exactly, Carina? Tell me. You signed the contract yourself."

"I was coerced."

"But it was your choice."

Huffing, the second I tried to rake my nails down the side of his face, he snapped his hand around my forearm, bending it to the point of pain.

"Fuck you," I managed, furious that all I wanted to do was kiss his lips.

"You are such a delightful temptation. Since you already belong to me, that's exactly what I'm going to do."

"Then what?"

"I'm going to allow you to think about fulfilling the terms of your contract, which includes obeying my rules."

"I will not follow them."

"Then you'll be spending a significant amount of time in this barren room. You'll have to earn back your privileges. One. By. One."

The man was infuriating. He really believed that by saying those ugly words that I would change my way of thinking. He had another think coming.

"This is insane," I told him. Why bother? I could tell by the look in his eyes that nothing I said would matter.

His chest rose and fell as he studied me, gauging my reaction. I refused to give him any.

"Maybe you're right, but it's your life and one you agreed to. So, this is where you'll stay until you accept reality."

"The only reality is that I signed a contract with a monster. That doesn't mean I won't find a way to break it," I told him with clear defiance in my voice.

As he slowly smiled, he brought our lips closer together, forcing my head to lift so I would see his eyes clearly. There was such a difference in them than when he'd been inside a courtroom. I couldn't stand the fact I was mesmerized by them, my mind reeling from the possibilities that he was an imposter. What I couldn't understand was anyone going to the lengths he'd gone in order to pass as the real Diego.

"Why are you doing this?" I managed. The only thing I could do was try to break down his resolve, exposing his reason for pretending.

"Marrying the most beautiful woman in LA?"

"No, faking who you are. Is this about gaining power? If so, you'll need to take a number. I won't allow my father to rule my life, nor will I let you control it."

He took a deep breath before capturing my mouth, even as I pushed against him, struggling to breathe let alone create any space between us. The man was too powerful, but not just because of his strength, carved muscles creating a godlike physique. His real power was his way of making me feel wanted, his dark cravings appealing to a woman who'd never had enjoyment from a man. They'd been too terrified of me. Maybe I'd broadcast my self-perceived authority over them, but this man couldn't care less who I was.

There was no way of avoiding the connection, the intensity of the electricity flowing through us unlike anything I'd ever thought existed. I was lost in a sea of passion, every ember ignited to the point of a firestorm raging inside. This was his method of control over me, seducing the woman who'd craved a man's touch.

As he plunged his tongue inside, sweeping it back and forth as he quenched his thirst, I became lightheaded, no longer able to feel my legs. He lifted me onto my toes, grinding his hips against me, the feel of his throbbing cock exciting every part of me. I wanted this man for all the wrong reasons, and he knew it.

The kiss wasn't just a passionate roar. It was an explosion of need, and cravings that would never be satisfied. It was as if I was floating on air, taken to a different realm. When he finally broke the sweet moment of intimacy, he fisted my hair, jerking me into a deep arch before dragging his tongue from one side of my jaw to the other.

Panting, I blinked several times in an effort to focus, but there were too many unwanted stars floating in front of my eyes. How had I allowed myself to fall so hard, so fast for his advances? The man was pretending he gave a damn, but I wouldn't allow myself to fall any further.

Sex was one thing.

Feelings another.

If he thought he could snatch my heart, he would learn I'd grab his first, but on the end of a sharp blade. Still breathless, his husky growls caressed my muscles, the need to have his cock buried deep inside outweighing the hatred I had for him.

He nipped my chin before rolling his lips to my earlobe, sucking on the tender tissue as he continued grinding. Then he backed away, but not before wrapping his fingers around the bodice of my dress. With one quick snap of his hand, he ripped it down the front, yanking it from my body with flair. His hungry eyes took another heated gaze down the length of me, immediately slipping his hand between my legs.

"Where did you think you were going?" he asked, his husky tone dripping with lust.

"Anywhere away from you."

He laughed, the sound sending vibrations down the backs of my legs. "Don't you know by now that you will never get away from me?"

"You wait and see."

He pressed his fingers through the thin lace of my panties, immediately rolling a single tip around my clit. I was shaken, still struggling to breathe as he drove his other fingers past my swollen folds. I was so wet and hot that a flush of embarrassment drifted up both cheeks.

"I can't wait to see you try. Just remember, I'm the hunter and you're my prey."

I half laughed, turning the tables as I ripped the front of his shirt, buttons flying onto the floor. If he thought this was a game, it was one he would lose. I slipped my hand inside, digging my nails into his skin.

That only enticed him even more, the expression on his face turning carnal.

"What is your body saying to you now?" he asked as he raked his teeth across my chin.

I nipped his lower lip, pulling it into my mouth, issuing a growl of my own. As he pumped his fingers inside, my mind cleared enough to enjoy giving him what he hadn't expected, at least so soon.

Acceptance.

"That you're everything I can't stand but the very man I'll use." Need was a relative term. In my mind, I would turn his own ruse into a violent uprising against him.

"Oh, yeah?" He snapped his hand around my throat, cocking his head. "Be careful what you wish for."

"You as well."

He thrust all four fingers inside my pussy, flexing them open, the force keeping me on my tiptoes. I didn't want to give him any satisfaction of knowing how much his touch excited me, but I had no control over my body. Within seconds, I was driven so close to an orgasm that I threw my head back, several moans escaping. As I bucked against him, he gave me what I craved, his hand becoming a powerful tool. There was no way to ignore the blinding pleasure, my moans becoming purrs as he swept me straight into nirvana.

"Do you want to come for me?" he asked.

"Yes."

"Then admit you want me. This."

"Never."

The way his heated breath floated across my skin was breathtaking, sending goosebumps down my stomach. More buttons popped to the floor as I jerked his shirt free of his trousers. Then as I rolled the jacket off his shoulders, I took a good look at his face, memorizing every crease, noticing a slight scar on the corner of his right eye. Had I seen it before? Had I paid enough attention to the gorgeous, pompous man that I'd noticed the slight blemish?

His frustration grew, his chest heaving as he wrapped his fingers around the edge of my thong, ripping it away. Then he yanked off his tie, immediately putting it around my neck. When he tightened it, I glared at him, cupping his groin and stroking his cock.

"You're not in charge any longer, princess," he said as he brushed the backs of his fingers down my cheek.

"Don't underestimate me."

"Oh, I don't plan on it." He shoved his thumb between my lips as he wound the tie around his other hand, keeping me right where he wanted me. "With a single snap of my hand, I could end your life. Does that bother you?"

"No. Because you're not a killer."

His eyes twinkled as he backed me toward the bed. "Then you don't know me very well."

"No, I don't know you at all. Your face is the same. Your voice is the same, but you're not the evil man I've faced inside a courtroom."

"I have many sides, my sweet bride. Only some of which the rest of the world will ever see." When he tossed me onto the covers, he immediately placed his hands on either side of me. "But you'll get it all. Every inch. Every mood. Every need. And you will fulfill my every desire."

He wasted no time shedding the rest of his clothes, narrowing his eyes as he approached again. Then he grabbed the tie, using it to jerk me to my knees as he climbed onto the bed. He slipped the knot into position, adjusting it as he peered down at me. He was so handsome that I wanted to lick every inch of him.

As he cupped my breasts, I traced my finger over the tattoo on his chest, finding it impossible to keep my eyes off him.

A smile curling on his lip, he pinched my nipples between his fingers then dropped his head. I pushed myself into an arc, clinging to his arms as he swirled his tongue around first one nipple then the other before biting down.

"No," I whispered. "I don't believe you."

"Toda realidad tiene un lado oscuro," he said almost breathlessly.

"What does that mean?" His Spanish accent was much heavier as he spoke his native language. While I shouldn't be surprised his father had required his children to learn the language, they'd seemed so Americanized.

"Every reality has a dark side." He bit down on my nipple, swirling his tongue back and forth.

I closed my eyes, the meaning of what he'd said as if he'd tossed out a lure.

Or a clue.

"I morti non raccontano storie," I returned in Italian.

"Mmm... The dead tell no tales. Is that your way of threatening me?" He lifted his head, the grin on his face turning dark.

"You surprise me more and more. You speak Italian."

"And French and Russian as well."

"No, this is wrong. You speak several languages. You play the piano. You're not a sadistic freak. Everyone knows Diego has disgusting tastes." Why was I telling him? As I stared into his eyes, I was pulled into a place of quiet serenity for a few seconds. Then the same level of anger I'd seen before returned with a vengeance. But I'd seen the hint of surprise that meant I was right.

"Is that what you want? For me to hurt you? Is that what you've been expecting?"

His demand surprised me, but the thought disgusted him as well. I was mad with trying to figure out what was going on.

"No. I'm not like that."

"Hmmm... Aren't you?" he whispered. "You know what they say, my beautiful bride. That if it feels wrong then maybe it's exactly what is needed the most."

"Tell me right now who you really are and what you've done to the real Diego, or I'll make certain everyone knows you're an imposter."

As he wrapped his hand around the tie, twisting it until I could no longer breathe, his nostrils flared. He yanked me closer, staring down at me in a way that should terrify me.

"I see this ending one of two ways, my beautiful bride. Either you become compliant and stop asking questions and I will make certain your life and that of your sister's is spent in the lap of luxury." While he loosened his hold slightly, I realized he had no intentions of letting me go.

"And the second choice?"

"I will make you disappear from your world."

"Then the contract will be dissolved." I didn't believe him for a second. But for some crazy reason, his words excited me, the dangerous game we were playing the most intense foreplay I'd ever experienced.

"While that will pose something of a problem for me, I assure you that the Santos family is much more powerful than yours. Will it make what I need to do that much harder? Yes, but I am committed to what needs to be done."

"That means I don't have a choice," I said, issuing a hissing growl.

"No. You don't."

"Whoever you are, you're much worse than the original. I promise you, my husband. I will find out who you are and what you're doing. And when I do, I will watch you burn in the fires of hell."

He tightened the noose once again, fisting my hair with his other hand, his breathing more ragged than before. "Then I'll die a happy man."

CHAPTER 13

iego

There was something about Carina that produced insanity inside of me, a raw, insatiable need to be something that I wasn't, or at least a man I wasn't used to. Maybe it was the way her luminescent green eyes called to me every time she spewed venom from her luscious mouth. Or maybe it was her rebellious attitude, her refusal to understand that she had no choice in what was happening in her life. Or maybe it was because of the way my body reacted every time I was around her. Hell, maybe it was because she was so damn beautiful that I couldn't control my needs even though I'd told myself staying away from her was in my best interest.

As well as hers.

Then she tried to escape, and I'd lost myself all over again. I'd wanted to drag her over my desk, ripping off my belt and spanking her rounded bottom all over again. Then I'd wanted to chain her to the bed.

Now I'd reached an entirely different plateau by threatening her. What the fuck was wrong with me? She'd witnessed a massacre and I was acting like king of the world. The truth was that I remained deeply concerned about what had occurred. She was enough of a spitfire that she'd try to escape again. She hadn't been fully exposed to the world of criminals, pampering and protected in a different way.

Even if her father was just as ruthless as mine.

I could become the killer in order to exact revenge on the two men who deserved to face my wrath, but I would not harm her.

However, I would punish her as necessary until she accepted reality.

Dear God, I needed to consume her.

Taste her.

Fuck her.

Hell, I wanted to do filthy things over and over again, but no one would ever be able to hurt her. She was mine. My possession. My lover. My wife.

Fuck.

I'd fallen into a strange abyss that could become far too obsessive.

Carina was determined to find answers, refusing to believe I was the man she'd faced inside a courtroom. The fact I'd threatened her had surprised me, but I had too much at stake to allow her a single opportunity of telling anyone her beliefs. If that meant keeping her locked inside the house, then so be it. I'd figure out a way to explain her absence.

As I crushed my mouth over hers, the need to drive my cock inside her tight channel became overwhelming. The only thing I wanted more was Xavier's head on a silver platter. That would come soon enough. Tonight I would take what belonged to me all over again. At some point I'd need to become sated, although I had my doubts.

I'd never fashioned myself as a wolf, but as the setting sun cast a dazzling display of colors across the Pacific Ocean, I became the predator. I'd expected her to mean nothing to me, but the moment I'd laid eyes on her, it had stirred something within that refused to be denied.

I kissed her as if she was the only person capable of bringing me back to life. I'd died the same day as my mother, the only spark from the thought of driving my knife into Xavier and fucking her. What did that make me? Maybe I was more like my brother than I wanted to believe.

She kneaded my chest, her fingernails digging in. The moment she scratched all ten fingers down to my abdomen, I broke the kiss, dropping back into a sitting position, forcing her to straddle me. I kept my hand wound around the silk tie, several filthy thoughts about what else I could use it for.

"I will hate you forever," she said, although there wasn't the strong conviction in her voice I'd heard before.

"Then hate me, *hermosa* creature," I whispered as I lifted her hips, sliding the tip of my cock against her slickened pussy. She was a beautiful creature in every way. The scent of her desire was incredible, the sweetest perfume I'd ever had the luxury of breathing. She shuddered in my hold, the soft sounds she made driving me as mad as she'd done before. "But you will remember what I said."

"What are you doing?"

"Anything I want."

This wasn't about tenderness. There would be no romance. When I was finished, the only promise I would make is to allow both her and her sister to live. I hadn't realized how important Mia was to her, but I'd done my research, had overheard the conversation her father and mine had had during the rehearsal.

Mia had been used against her.

I'd come damn close to putting bullets in both their brains and I'd barely known the woman I was supposed to marry. However, I was a keen observer, realizing instantly that Mia had been completely sheltered from her father's world, sent away to school most of her life. The only reason Carina hadn't been provided the same level of protection had been because Montgomery didn't have any male heirs.

As I pulled her all the way down, she threw back her head, her mouth forming a perfect O. "Hate makes for some of the best sex." I yanked her head by the silk reins, forcing her to keep all her attention directed toward me.

She squeezed her pussy muscles, gyrating her body as she bucked against me. "Hate also makes for the sweetest revenge."

Pure loathing and extreme desire were an explosive combination, one I shouldn't risk but one I refused to be denied. "That's something I'll keep in mind." I rolled my fingers down her long back, marveling in the feel of her porcelain skin. With the sun streaming in the window, her skin shimmered and my balls tightened. I wanted nothing more than to fill her with my seed.

The way her long eyelashes skimmed across her cheeks pushed my needs to an entirely different level. I pulled her almost completely off my cock, dragging her down again. And again. My actions were savage, unforgiving.

Every look she gave me was sultry, but I sensed she was fighting her desire. The need to have her, keep her, fuck her was so overwhelming I suddenly couldn't breathe.

I pushed her down, gripping and bending one leg at the knee, shifting my hips and fucking her like a crazed man. She never blinked as she pressed her hands against my chest, darting her eyes back and forth. There was such madness to the way we felt, a strong need that surpassed all rationality. I didn't know her, and she certainly could never know my true identity, but this was the only way I'd be able to cope with the bullshit I'd be forced to handle before ending the nightmare.

I yanked one arm over her head then the other, wrapping one hand around both her wrists, enjoying the look on her face as I thrust deep inside.

Her trembling response delighted me. As she pursed her lips, a slight moan escaping, I slipped my other arm under her legs, pinning her knee against the comforter. Then I fucked her long and hard, using enough force the cot was slammed against the wall.

Her eyes were glassy and as she dragged her tongue across her lips, I remained hunkered over her, slowing down my actions. There was a look of fear in her eyes, as if she'd suddenly realized nothing was as it seemed.

"Do I frighten you, princess?"

"I'm not your princess. I'm nobody's princess." There was such a forlorn sound in her voice that I was taken aback.

"Yes, you are."

"Like Rapunzel begging for release."

Just the feel of her breath as it tickled my skin was enough to ignite another fire. I thrust brutally, trying to control myself. It would seem my animalistic needs were brimming to the surface, eating at my insides. I kept her pinned down as I drove deeper, the sensations overwhelming. Then I crushed her with my full weight, enjoying the feel of her wiggling underneath me. Every curve fit perfectly against my body; everywhere her smooth skin touched mine, the heat was scorching.

Carina tried to free her arms, the flash of light in her eyes indicating she was enjoying our filthy little game.

"Do you want more?" I asked her as I ground her against the bed. When she didn't respond immediately, I thrust several times until she cried out. "Answer me."

"Yes. God, yes."

"Tell me. Tell me what you want, princess."

"Just fuck me."

I reared back, using the tie to drag her with me. As I returned to my knees, I pushed her head down. "Open that beautiful mouth of yours."

She slipped her tongue across my sensitive slit instead, trying to maintain some level of control. I allowed her to play for a few minutes, hissing the moment she slid her tongue all the way down the underside of my cock. When he pulled one of my testicles into her mouth, I threw my head back with a series of growls.

Her mouth was hot as Hades, so wet that I would enjoy every minute of spewing my cum down her throat. I was such a bad man, but I could spend hours in bed with her. The need became overwhelming, and I pushed her head down, keeping my fingers tangled in her long strands. "That's it. Take every inch." I took full control, rocking my hips forward as I fucked her mouth. Every sound she made added gasoline to the flames, my chest tight from how tense my muscles had become.

As the tip hit the back of her throat, I closed my eyes, savoring the feel, even enjoying the slight gagging sound she made. But this still wasn't enough. She'd awakened the beast to the point he would never return to his lair. I pumped several additional times then pushed her completely away, gasping for air.

"What's wrong?" she asked, the sound of her voice coy. "You can't handle me?"

"Mmm…" Laughing, I snagged the tie, jerking her back then shifting her onto all fours. As I wrapped my body over hers, she tried to claw her way free. I kept a firm hold on her neck as I rolled the tip of my cock up and down the crack of her ass. "It's not about being able to handle you, my lovely bride. It's about the method I use in breaking you."

"That will never happen."

"You might be surprised."

I used my knee to press her legs apart, teasing her by swirling my index finger around her clit several times. When I pinched her tender tissue, she exclaimed, her body shuddering against me. There were no other words needed but every time she tried to pull away, I tightened my hold until she lifted her head in exasperation. There was nothing like seeing the shimmer on her skin or the way she moaned from my touch.

My hunger knew no bounds. There was no sense of decency with regard to her, as if I was drowning in lust, never satisfied. I toyed with her for a few more seconds. Then I couldn't take not being inside her tight pussy any longer. I slipped my cock past her swollen folds, leaning back and gripping her hip with one hand. She was so soft to the touch that I wanted nothing more than to take her roughly, driving her to the point of screaming out my name.

I pumped hard and fast, every action becoming more brutal. A dense fog had slipped across my eyes, the waning sun creating a series of shadows. I tried to think of nothing but her, yet the ghosts of a past I hadn't been allowed to experience had formed in the darkest regions of my mind. She'd already become a drug to me, toxic in every way, but there would always be the demons waiting in the darkness, threatening to drag my soul straight to hell.

Together we moved as one, our bodies molding to a perfect fit.

"Oh. Oh…" she moaned, the sound warming the darkness, breaking through the hate and anger.

If only for a few precious seconds.

"Come for me." My command was dark, laced with absolute authority.

She bucked against me, keeping her back arched as I drove into her like a wild man. Every pant she issued, every scattered breath pulled me to the very edge of losing my mind. As her pussy muscles clamped and released, I could tell she was close, so close.

I wrapped my arm around her thigh, flicking my finger back and forth across her clit. That was all she could take. Her body tensed, her moans increasing, and I fucked her even more savagely.

As a climax swept through her, she clawed at the bedding once again. We were nothing but animals, unable to control our actions. Nothing had ever felt this good.

"Yes. Yes. Yes…" One orgasm quickly shifted into a second and I knew I couldn't hold back much longer. Her body finally stopped shaking, but her whimpers only increased in volume.

As the tension continued to mount, I gasped for air. I held her life in my hands, yet I was the one fighting to breathe. Even the sound of skin slapping against skin couldn't soothe the strangled ache that had grasped hold the day I'd set foot in LA. It was as if I was losing all control, no longer certain of who I was. I needed to remind the man inside I'd had a good life before, well respected among my peers, a few friends that I could count on.

But my life as I'd known it had been terminated and far too many people were to blame.

"You were such a bad girl attempting to escape, injuring one of my soldiers. For your punishment, I'm going to fuck you in the ass."

I thrust harder until her cries of exhaustion brought me back to reality. Then I drove the tip of my cock into her tight asshole.

When her body spasmed, excitement tore through me. I wanted to own every inch of her. What the hell was going on with me? I pushed past the tight ring of muscle, forced to take several deep breaths. Only when I was fully seated inside did I exhale, but the tension hadn't eased. Only one thing would allow me to do that.

"Oh, God. Oh…" she whimpered, but she turned her head, licking her soft lips. Just watching the way that she reacted to the hard fucking was invigorating, once again pushing my limits of control.

As her moans intensified, I smacked her bottom several times, the tingling sensations in my fingertips as powerful as anything else. Everything about this moment was sinful, the scent of her intoxicating. I wanted to drink her in for hours, to bask in the glow of our sex. And I longed to cover her with my cum.

She was so tight, her muscles clamping around the thick invasion. I pumped hard and fast, unable to focus. As I finally gave myself permission to erupt deep inside, I realized I'd never felt so damn cold in my life, the chill enough that my orgasm wasn't enough to soothe the beast inside. Maybe nothing could at this point.

As I released my hold on the tie, gently easing it from around her neck, I couldn't stand to remain where I was any longer.

I got off the bed, hating myself for the first time since I'd made the decision to alter my life forever. I grabbed my clothes as well as hers, heading to the door. It was at that moment I was forced to accept the fact I was exactly like the two men I'd sworn to erase.

And I was capable of doing anything.

I closed and locked the door, fisting my hand and pressing it into my mouth. What I needed was a taste of vengeance.

* * *

Carina

What had just happened?

Exhaling, I kept my eyes closed for a few seconds, basking in the afterglow of our wanton, filthy sex.

But that's all it had been. Just sex.

Even if I'd felt a powerful emotion deep within him. Then he'd yanked it back, closing off what little humanity he had inside of him. Why?

The answer wouldn't be easy to find if I managed to do so at all.

He'd saved me, using his body as armor, and I was acting impetuous.

Just like a child.

Still, I had every right to learn more about him.

A cold shiver drifted down my spine as I pulled the sheet over my breasts, staring at the door as the sounds of his footsteps echoed. He'd been entirely different than the first time he'd taken me, his hunger as if he wouldn't be able to survive without fucking me. Then he'd shut down, returning to the anger I'd seen in his eyes at the bottom of the stairs.

Another round of fury returned furrowing deep inside, hatred mixing with confusion. I couldn't handle the yin and yang of his emotions.

Or mine.

I slipped out of bed, yanking the sheet around me then taking long strides to the door. I tried the knob, the door unbudging. No. Why would he do this? Then I pounded on the wooden surface, more exasperated than I'd been before. My anger boiled over and I was beside myself, smacking my fists on the wooden surface. "Let me out of here, Diego, or whatever your fucking name is."

Gasping, I listened for any sounds, my heart racing. He'd done this to prove a point. I continued pounding for several minutes, yelling at the top of my lungs until my voice was harsh. I could swear I sensed his presence. "Are you there? Don't leave me in here."

Why was I doing this to myself? He was a brutal man who would only ever show me tenderness through sex.

I pressed my face against the cool wood, taking several deep breaths. His scent lingered in the room, my skin tainted with it as well. I could still feel his lips against mine, his touch so dominating. He'd been all about control, but I hadn't felt any fear, only excitement from the darkness he dragged out of me when I was with him. Sighing, I turned around, slowly sliding to the floor, pulling my knees against my chest. As I started to rock, I had to accept everything that had happened. There was no other choice, especially if I wanted any kind of life.

But could I tolerate being around him?

Laughing, I tilted my head, staring at the ceiling. A sickness was eroding my mind. I enjoyed being around him. I actually relished every bit of being with the powerful savage. What the hell was going on with my brain?

As I squeezed my knees, the acceptance allowed me to breathe easier. However, I was no pushover. If Diego really thought that he could treat me this way, then I'd best him. I'd gain his trust. I'd give him what he wanted and in return,

I'd obtain my freedom. I allowed a smile to cross my face as I moved to a standing position.

I would become a phoenix rising from the ash, taking back my life. Only then would I find out the truth about who he was and what he wanted.

Only then would I be able to take away everything he held precious.

As I returned to bed, a wry smile crossed my face. I would become the greatest enemy Diego had even experienced, and my method would be foolproof. Maybe my mother had been right all along.

Use your body first, but only after you've developed a foolproof plan of action. No man can resist being seduced by a beautiful woman. Then you can do anything you want with them. We are their greatest weakness.

Yes, Diego would soon learn. As I lay down, pulling the covers over me, I had the first hopeful outlook in a long time.

It would fun manipulating him, using him the way he was using me.

Until I found the truth.

After all, I was tigress in disguise.

Very soon, he would hear me roar.

iego

Anger was the only emotion that felt comfortable at this point in my life. I'd honed it, lived it, breathed it, and created steel-plated armor around myself in doing so. I'd had no reservations in ordering a hit on the Mexican cartel and the informant. There'd been no hesitation, no need to second guess myself. The decision had felt good. Necessary. Just like reminding Sergio had been.

I was beginning to excel at not feeling any other emotion, the only other sensation the continued desire I felt for Carina.

However, I'd heard her cries when standing at the top of the stairs. And for a few seconds, I'd considered returning, scooping her into my arms, continuing our passion. But she needed to learn that there would be no chance for escape, no ability to alter her life without my approval.

The only way to do that was to break down her defenses one by one.

Goddamn the ache building in my system, the need to touch her almost uncontrollable.

"Women can be used as the greatest weapon, but guard and watch them carefully for they'll stop at nothing to destroy you."

The remembrance of Emmanuel's words was a stark reminder.

At this point, she'd need to learn to trust me. That would obviously take some time. My actions had been far too harsh with her, but I was concerned her phone had a tracking device. The Santos family had placed a huge bullseye on our heads with the announcement of the wedding. I'd tasked one of my computer genius employees to sweep it clean.

However, I knew the feisty woman. She'd hold it against me.

As I parked the Jeep near the building housing my brother, I took a deep breath. It had been a few days since I'd come to see him. I would need to determine the end date for the game, but that likely wouldn't be for several additional weeks.

He'd said nothing, staring at me as if he was still certain his own soldiers would rescue him. It was time for him to talk. I needed to learn everything I could about the Mexican cartel from his perspective and what issues he'd experienced, which had allowed Sergio to be captured. However,

I'd need to take every word he said with a grain of salt. He could easily use lies in order to try to destroy my hold on his empire. Still, I couldn't ask the brutal Russian the questions and there was no documentation of their various criminal activities.

My father had employed a loyal accountant who'd easily managed to cook the books, keeping the illegal businesses under the radar. The amount of taxes both the corporation and my father and brother had paid over the years precluded scrutiny from the IRS. No wonder the various FBI investigations had been futile over the years.

However I handled my brother, he would tell me what I wanted to know.

I had no qualms about what it would take to get him to talk. After all, I had no feelings for him whatsoever. He meant nothing to me other than being the only person capable of providing me with what I needed. In the end, I'd send him to Emmanuel where he would remain locked behind prison walls for the rest of his life. Or perhaps there would be hard labor.

As I strode toward the building, I stopped short close to the two guards on duty. It would seem they'd forgotten their manners and the fact they were working for me.

"*Ponganse firmes, imbeciles,*" I barked. Stand at attention, assholes.

When the two of them glanced at each other, I yanked my weapon from behind my back, pointing the barrel against the forehead of the one closest.

"*Olvidar tus modales no es lo mejor para ti.*" I was putting them on notice that their manners wouldn't be accepted any longer. While the first soldier, Arturo opened his eyes wide, both remained quiet. It was the smug look on the other asshole's face that yanked my chain. I smacked the handgun against Gabrio's head then shifted the barrel toward Arturo.

"*Si, señor,*" Arturo said. "We are... sorry, *El Jefe.*"

There was that title again.

"Yeah, so sorry," Gabrio mimicked, but I sensed he was through with following my orders.

"There won't be a second time. Open the door."

While Gabrio continued glaring at me, Arturo reacted instantly, opening the door.

"He has been a problem," he told me.

"How so?"

"He almost managed to get away," Gabrio huffed. "But he was taught a lesson."

When the door was swung open, Arturo flicking on the light, bile formed in my throat. "What the fuck did you do?" My brother was still chained to the wall, his head hung low, his chest barely rising and falling. The difference was that blood and whip marks crisscrossed his chest.

Gabrio grabbed a bucket from inside, tossing water in Diego's direction.

My brother gasped, the agonizing sound ringing in my ears. He immediately started to struggle, but I sensed he was weak.

And the fury continued to increase.

"Leave. Now! You will not touch him again without my permission. Is that understood? *Pedazos de mierda sin valor.*" They were worthless pieces of shit and if I had any other options, I'd put them all down like useless animals.

They both backed away.

"Keys. Give me the goddamn keys and some bottles of water."

"He can drink from the bucket." Gabrio had just tested the last of my patience.

A part of me became unhinged. I threw punch after punch, tossing him against the back wall. He came out snarling, prepared to fight when Arturo grabbed his arm, saying something under his breath. No doubt a warning.

Gabrio wiped his face, spitting blood onto the ground. "You're a crazy motherfucker."

"That I am. Now, get the fuck out. You won't be told again," I snarled.

Arturo was clearly concerned about what I would do, tossing the ring full of keys without hesitation. I moved inside, unable to tell if my brother was still breathing. When I lifted his head, he did his best to open his eyes. They'd beaten him prior to the whipping.

Rage had become my best friend as of late, but I couldn't fly off the handle and kill them. At least not yet. "Diego," I muttered, although in saying his name, my chest tightened. "I apologize. They were not to touch you."

His laugh was bitter.

"What... do... you... fucking... care?"

"You're right. I don't. However, I need information from you, which you will supply, or I will allow them to continue."

His nostrils flared and he managed to spit, the glob hitting me in the face. "You... are... dead."

"All points to the contrary. I am going to unlock the chains. Then you and I are going to have a nice conversation." I wiped it away, taking a deep breath.

"Fuck off."

"Or I could leave you here to rot. The choice is up to you." The anger remained, the sight of him in such an atrocious condition leaving a dull burn inside. I shouldn't care in the least, but the torture he'd endured had been unreasonable. I moved closer then stopped myself.

Fuck. What was I doing? Did I actually give a damn about him? As I unfastened the first shackle, I realized he still had the resolve to try to get away.

"If you try and run, I will make certain you'll only be able to crawl for the rest of your fucking life." I glared at him, waiting until he nodded a single time before moving to the other shackle.

When he was freed, he dropped to the ground, gasping for air as he winced in pain. I was able to see just how badly he'd been worked over, the ugly realization forcing me to look away. Questioning what I was doing now was too little, too late. I'd crossed a line that could never be recrossed.

You lost your soul. Are you going to lose your nerve as well?

I shoved my hands into my pockets, pacing the floor. The stench was nauseating.

He remained crouched on the floor, his back heaving as he tried to catch his breath. In the few weeks of incarceration, he'd lost significant muscle mass, at least ten pounds if not more. If I had to venture a guess, I'd say he was dehydrated. Why should I care? He deserved every minute of suffering.

"Tell me about Luis Ortiz."

Very slowly he lifted his head, managing a smile. "You are weak and can never rule."

I resisted kicking him in the face, preferring to keep the conversation civil.

For now.

"I'll repeat my statement. Do not think you will have a third opportunity. Tell me everything you know about Luis Ortiz."

His eyes were dark pools of hatred and I'd anticipated his move. What I hadn't expected was the level of strength and agility that remained. He lunged toward me, the force pitching me against the wall. Pain tore through my right shoulder from the direct hit. When he wrapped his hands around my throat, I shoved my hands against his chest, able to break the connection.

He toppled back by several feet, almost tripping. Then he came for me again, issuing a hard punch to my jaw. Something snapped inside of me, the rage that I'd attempted to keep pent up rushing to the surface. I threw two jabs, both connecting, a single cracking sound indicating I'd broken his nose.

Undeterred, he hunkered over as he came for me again, managing to get two brutal jabs into my kidneys.

"Umpf," I hissed, taking a deep breath then circling him like a vulture. "Do not continue."

"Or what, you piece of shit? Are you going to use the whip like the monsters guarding me? Maybe you'll shoot me in the knee. I couldn't care less what you do to me."

The fact he was pushing me indicated he had no full understanding of what his life had become. I wasted no time, barreling toward him, throwing one brutal punch after another until the momentum drove us both to the hard concrete floor.

We rolled and pitched, both of us getting in several punches. After slamming his head on the floor, he dropped his arms, the fury remaining in his eyes. Then I noticed something I hadn't expected from the pompous asshole.

Fear.

I had my arm raised, ready to slam my fist against his face several more times. Then I pulled back, crawling off him and stumbling to my feet. My knuckles were bloody, the coppery taste of it filling my mouth. This was getting me nowhere. "You don't seem to understand what's happening." I paced the floor, trying to catch my breath, throwing him glances every few seconds.

"Why don't you tell me." He grinned, as if this was still nothing but a game.

"A massacre occurred at the wedding you and Xavier insisted on."

At least he was shaken by my announcement. "Who?"

"If you mean who was killed, several guests and a few of my best men."

"My men, you fucker." He finally eased to a sitting position, his face pinched.

"As far as who was responsible, I believe it's Ortiz. The question is why? And don't give me bullshit about the limited drug runs. That's accounts for less than fifteen percent of the business. There must be another reason, something more personal."

He grinned as he wiped blood from his lips. "I guess that's something you're going to need to figure out."

"You don't give a damn about Carina, do you?"

My brother seemed surprised by the question. "What our union brings to the table is the only thing that's important. Why are you asking? Does that mean you are enjoying every aspect of pretending to be me?" He laughed, although the sound was bitter.

I was finished with reacting to his brash statements. "She was almost killed, clearly targeted by whoever was responsible. Perhaps he or she didn't want the union to take place."

When he stood on shaky legs, I was momentarily reminded and incensed about the actions I'd taken. Then I shoved it aside.

"Does that mean you said your vows?" he asked, and I wasn't certain if it was out of a sense of curiosity or anger.

"We did." The tension between us was palpable, but in those few seconds, I could tell he didn't care about Carina in the least. He would have enjoyed destroying her.

"Who are you? Tell me. I deserve to know."

All I could do was laugh. He really didn't get it at all. I was almost manic inside, the memories swirling in my mind jabbing into my brain. He needed to know. He should wallow in the understanding of the monstrous world he'd been born into. Had his life been any better than mine? No.

Had he benefitted from being the only twin Father kept?

Yes.

Did that make what I was doing any better than his acts of violence that had earned him such an illustrious title?

Exhaling, I fisted my hand as I stared at him. And when I spoke, my agonized tone held the accent of my culture.

"As far as I'm concerned, you deserve nothing, but I see no reason to keep you in the dark. My name is Dante Fernandez, although I was born Dante Santos, my birthplace Los Angeles. I lived in this country for two years of my life until a monster ripped me away from everything I knew. In other words, I am your twin brother."

The instant silence was deafening.

Then I watched as a series of emotions crossed his face, confusion remaining. I'd waited for, had thought about this moment for months, salivating at the very second when I shattered his entire world. Now that I'd done it, I felt nothing inside except emptiness.

When he lifted his head, he shifted his gaze back and forth, searching my eyes as his own memories began to kick in. "How?"

"How? The how is the easy part. Our father decided that our mother had betrayed him. In what way, I do not know but after beating her, threatening to kill both her and the two children she loved more than anything, he finally gave her a choice. She could live but only by determining which son she would take with her out of the country to live in poverty, which he promised her she would for the rest of her life. The other would be raised in a lush, powerful world, allowed to benefit from being the Santos prince. The why is something she did not share with me before she succumbed after years of battling cancer."

He was stunned but in truth, so was I. How many times had I replayed the moment? How many versions had allowed my anger to refuel, sucking on the fumes as if nothing else would quench the beast's thirst? And how many sleepless nights had I experienced because I'd been raised entirely different than the man standing here today?

After lowering his gaze, his breathing changed, even more ragged than before. "I... I don't remember." His statement held an air of truth, but as I'd experienced in the first moments after hearing the horror story, his confusion was keeping him in a thick fog.

"Don't you? Did you not feel like a part of you was missing your entire life? Did you not ask yourself why there were no pictures of our mother in your house? Or why our father never talked about her? Didn't you give a damn what happened, demanding answers? Don't you remember the music?"

Until that moment, I hadn't fathomed the possibility as a two-year-old I'd remember hearing my mother playing. I cinched my eyes shut, able to catch a single fleeting image of her sitting at a huge black piano while I was... While the two of us were in a contained space filled with toys.

Fuck. I was disoriented for a few seconds, my heart thudding.

"Answer me!"

"I was told she died!" he snapped, fighting to get to his feet, doubling over from the pain as he stumbled toward the wall. He held his stomach as he leaned against the concrete, but I sensed he was remembering more than he was prepared to handle.

As he started to dry heave, I realized how much I hated what I'd become. Nothing would make the situation right. Nothing could bring back the years of heartache she'd endured because she'd had no understanding of why she'd been tossed aside like an animal.

I shook my head, uncertain where the hell to go from here. As I tried to control my breathing, I could feel his angry gaze pinned on me.

"Music. I remember the music." He lifted his head, his look of anguish exactly like the one I'd had after learning of her death. I took a deep breath, shoving aside the sadness.

"So you know, *brother*. She really died the day she had to make an unholy choice, her mind crushed beyond belief, but she never forgot about you. She mourned you, prayed for you, and loved you to her last dying breath." The words hung in the air thick with hatred and sadness. I looked away, raking my hands through my hair, my heart thudding to the point the damn sound was echoing in my ears.

"I was never told I had a brother." He sounded like a beaten man.

"But you knew in your fucking soul. Didn't you?"

"Why didn't you try and figure out what happened before this, Dante? Ask yourself that. If you sensed there was something wrong, why not push harder?" He laughed, his bitterness increasing.

"Because of how much I respected her. She had a horrible life. She deserved peace, not terrible memories."

We remained unblinking as we stared at each other. This was getting me nowhere. I had no sense of peace or accomplishment. I was hollower than before.

"So you want to take my place on the throne. Is that it? Is that all you ever wanted, money and power? Trust me, brother. It's not all it's cracked up to be."

"I never gave a shit about money before and I certainly don't now."

"What do you do in your other life, *brother*?"

"I'm a prosecuting attorney."

A smile slowly spread across his face. Then he laughed. "Perhaps we are related after all. If not for money, then what? What do you hope to gain out of this subterfuge?"

I moved closer, ready to strike him with my fist. What the hell was I doing? While he didn't back down, I was able to witness the same kind of horror in his eyes I'd seen when looking at my own reflection.

A man I no longer recognized.

Exhaling, I wasn't certain I could be completely truthful with the answer. "What I wanted was a family and for my mother not to suffer working three jobs just to be able to put food on the table. I wanted to see her smile more than a few times in my life. Maybe I wanted to feel whole. What I will get is revenge." Why was I bothering to admit the truth? I threw him a look, hatred still wrapped around me like a thick blanket. Fuck. This isn't how I wanted the conversation to go. But the truth had to be set free for him to understand that he'd lived a lie his entire life.

"Then you'll need to get in line. If Ortiz is behind this massacre you mentioned, he will try again."

"Why?"

He shook his head. "He's always had a beef with my father."

At least he admitted it. However, could I believe a word that came out of his mouth?

"Tell me about the shipment."

He hung his head, laughing softly to himself. "My father... our father requires a hold on the drug market, especially given the vultures that scour the streets, killing anyone who stands in their way of gaining territory. He refuses to let go of how he became rich in the first place."

"The Black Angels."

"You've done your homework." He eyed me carefully then looked away. "The shipment was to be used as a lure to bring in Ortiz. The man never leaves his comfortable estate in Costa Rica."

I thought about what he was saying and laughed. "Word on the street is that it's worth much more."

"You catch on fast."

"It could also bring in the authorities." He wasn't being completely honest with me.

"In case you haven't figured out, we own the majority of the Los Angeles police."

"And the DEA?"

He smiled, far too smug for my liking. My brother and father believed they were bigger than the law.

When he said nothing else, I walked toward the door. He needed time to process what I'd told him. Maybe then I could get additional answers.

Then I would do exactly what I'd promised myself and my mother months before.

I'd drive a blade into his heart.

* * *

"Too much sanity may be madness and the maddest of all, to see life as it is and not as it should be."

—*Miguel de Cervantes*

Madness.

It had been used thousands of times in a court of law. I'd prosecuted at least two dozen cases where the monster who'd committed a heinous crime had attempted to use the defense. I'd seen through the mastery of their mask into their blackened eyes, digging until I'd found the truth. Only a single person had ever been allowed to use the insanity defense and win in my courtroom.

A woman.

I'd learned a lot about her, including why she'd succumbed to the darkness that had fed her soul for years. Revenge. She'd harbored anger, allowing it to furrow inside, nurturing it with small acts of violence until she'd been ready to claim the victim she'd hunted then stalked for years. He'd kidnapped her as a young girl, stripping away her innocence. And he'd been allowed to go free.

She'd cut him into pieces, taking her time doing so. Only then had she released him to the demons who'd come to drag him straight to hell.

I would never forget her face, the peace she wore during the entire trial. She hadn't cared what happened to her. Her own death had meant nothing. Her attorney had convinced the jury she needed help, not an injection ending her life.

I'd often wondered what had happened to her, but I'd admired her tenacity, her creativeness in how she'd exacted her own revenge.

Now it felt as if I was no different.

I stood in my office, staring down at the top of my desk, trying to figure out what the hell I'd turned into. I no longer recognized myself in the mirror and it had nothing to do with the expensive wardrobe or the stylish haircut. My eyes no longer held the wonderment of life, the belief in right versus wrong. Everything was blurred and it disgusted me.

As I took several deep breaths, I tried to remember the day surrounding the single image that remained lingering in the back of my mind. A family. Happiness. A brother. Maybe I was fooling myself that I could grasp onto anything of that nature ever again.

There was no sense of peace, no feeling of vindication for what I'd been able to accomplish so far. Just… darkness.

I raked my arm across my desk, sending everything to the floor. My laptop. Files. A half empty glass of whiskey. Nothing mattered. None of it was mine. Then I stood back, unbuttoning and folding my sleeves before walking through the mess, barely hearing the crunching sound my boots made against glass and metal.

Then I headed up the stairs to the locked door at the end of the hall, still lost in a fog of my own creation. As I walked inside, the deathly quiet struck me first. Then the barren surroundings became another stark reminder that Diego and I weren't much different at all. We'd been born with brutal genes created by a monster who had placed no value on life. I'd just managed to live in a pretense that I was a godly man capable of only behaving as a righteous man should.

Then I'd fallen into a void, a hunger for the very power and influence my mother had warned me about. The fact I'd slipped into the monster role far too easily had baffled me at first. Now I was forced to accept the ugly truth.

I was just another beast born of blood and violence who'd managed to hide behind the pretense of the law instead of expensive attire and glittering parties.

There was no way of denying who or what I'd become.

As I stood over Carina, drinking in her sweet fragrance, my stomach churned. Our desire was apparent with every touch, but she despised me and all I stood for.

She was now a part of my world and there was no way of setting back the clock. Her chest rose and fell in a peaceful sleep, oblivious a dark creature hovered over her, a predator who'd already claimed his prey. This wasn't about love or even about obsession. The intrinsic need for her stemmed from something much darker that had furrowed inside of me for years.

Only I hadn't noticed its existence.

Now it was tangled in a web of deceit and lies, and eventually the mortal sin would devour us.

Unless she managed to offer salvation.

I eased back the sheet, revealing her lush body and my mouth watered, my cock immediately hardening. I'd taken her innocence just as the heinous bastard had the woman I'd prosecuted. As I stood over her, hunger mixing with strangling need, I hated myself.

I took several shallow breaths, barely able to contain my desires as I used the tip of a single finger to trace the curve of her face. Then I brushed it down her arm before allowing it to drift to her taut nipple. I closed my eyes briefly, longing for things to be different, but I'd made my choice. Period.

As I gathered her into my arms, I expected her to awaken, but she remained peaceful, her hand drifting against my chest. She felt good in my arms, her scent invigorating. I could take her right here, chaining her to the bed to keep her from lashing out.

I could defile her daily, breaking her down until there was nothing left of the formidable woman who'd done everything in her power to build an empire. Then I could remold her into a woman who would never defy me in any way.

But that's not what I wanted.

I carried her to my bedroom, easing her down, staring at her for a few precious seconds longer before placing the covers around her. Then I moved to the single chair in the room, sitting down in the darkness.

At least I could protect what was mine.

For now.

arina

"Wake up, Carina."

The three little words were hushed, as if a whisper from a ghost. I shifted, feeling warmth and comfort, ignoring the request. Still in a fog, when I stretched, I felt a weight covering me, holding me down. Wait a minute… where was I? As soon as I snapped open my eyes, I gasped, jerking up, fighting whatever was holding me down.

No. No!

I thrashed for a few more seconds until I was able to focus. Then a strange sense of calm swept through me. I wasn't in the stark, cold room any longer. I'd been placed in his bed, covered with a soft comforter, the goose down pillows nesting me from the rest of the ugly world.

As I took a few deep breaths, I realized I was searching for him. My captor. My husband.

My lover.

He was nowhere to be seen, but he'd been here. I sensed it. No, his scent remained saturated into every piece of material, his fragrance tickling my skin. Tiny prickles appeared on my arms as I thought about him. He was so complex, hating me one minute then craving me the next. But wasn't that exactly the way I felt about him?

I wanted to despise him but the more time I spent around him, the less possible that seemed.

A single warm glow of light came from the lamp on the dresser. As I glanced around the room, so many feelings rushed into my system from hatred to confusion but mostly, I missed him, an intense ache building inside. As I rolled over, I thought I heard music. As soon as I sat up, I was certain of it.

I noticed a glass on the table near the upholstered chair. He'd remained on guard. What was he most worried about? His need or his fear I'd run away?

Or perhaps it was because of the demons plaguing his every move.

As the music became louder, echoing throughout the house, I was drawn to the haunted melody, the increasing rise in pitch as he pounded the keys. Shivering, I folded my arms, heading to the bathroom in search of a robe, finding one made of thick terrycloth on the back of the door.

While it was at least two sizes too large, the soft material helped soothe the tremors. There was no locked door to keep me hidden away, no guard standing on the other side. I eased into the hallway, taking careful steps toward the stairwell. There was no reason for my heart to be racing, at least not now, but even a single thought of him affected me more than it should.

I carefully made my way down the stairs, still struck by his selection of music. He was a brilliant pianist, the rise and fall of tempo matching the music perfectly. By the time I drifted to the doorway of the music room, I was in awe of how many emotions the gothic piece had pulled to the surface.

Strings of the full moon drifted through the window, cascading an eerie circle of blue across the Steinway's surface. He'd left the top closed, perhaps to try to keep from awakening me. I remained in the doorway, enthralled by the haunting sound. He was fully into the moment, his head and shoulders drifting back and forth, his muscular arms and long fingers working almost every key.

I'd never seen anyone play with such passion, the beautiful sound more powerful than anything I'd heard before. He was brilliant, so much so I couldn't imagine why he hadn't considered a life of performing in concert halls. As he continued, oblivious to my presence, I couldn't resist walking closer. The wave of vibrations was incredible, both from the pristine acoustics as well as the rapid beating of my heart.

I felt as if my entire body was on fire, my mind a blur of colorful lights. It was hypnotic as well as emotional and tears formed in my eyes.

As I walked closer, I was caught up in the beautiful moment, incapable of separating the joy I felt hearing him play and the anger I wanted to keep close to my heart. When I was within a few inches, he took a deep breath, and I knew he was aware of my interruption.

But he continued playing and I placed my hand on his shoulder, allowing the crackling electricity to flow back and forth between us. My body ached, the need for him the most commanding thing I'd ever felt.

I slipped my hand down to his chest, sliding my fingers under his open shirt as his arms flexed against the crisp white material. Within seconds, I was drowning in his scent, more intoxicated than from the finest champagne or expensive brandy.

The crescendo was building, his entire body moving as he pressed his foot on the pedal, the beautiful echo of the bass chords leaving an imprint on my heart.

When his fingers rolled over the keys in wild abandon, I gasped for air, my mind a whirl of need and desire. I dug my nail of one finger into his skin and slid my other hand down to his thigh. Every muscle in his body was taut, his breathing as rapid as mine. When he played the last chords, the echo remained in the room for several seconds.

Then there was stark silence.

He stretched his long fingers around my arm, pulling my wrist to his mouth, darting his tongue back and forth across my pulsing veins. I remained mesmerized, not realizing I'd been holding my breath until he bit down on my wrist. The sharp cry I issued was from a need to release the joy he'd provided, but almost immediately it was replaced with the kind of burning desire that couldn't be ignored.

His breathing was rapid, his chest rising and falling as he dragged his tongue up the inside of my arm. I couldn't stop tingling, tiny moans slipping past my lips. He allowed me to swipe my fingers across his cock, but I sensed the intimate moments were going to turn into something else entirely.

He was thick, throbbing with the same hunger that continuously swept through me. My nipples ached, fully aroused and as they slid back and forth across the dense material, I was forced to take several shallow breaths.

I pulled my arm away, slowly crawling my fingers along his chest before tangling them in his thick strands of hair. As he leaned his head back, the moonlight drifted across his chiseled features, accentuating the two days of stubble covering his chin. I cupped the side of his face, teasing him by brushing my lips back and forth across his, darting my tongue along the seam of his mouth several times.

He had his eyes closed, his long lashes skimming his cheeks one of the sexiest things I'd ever seen.

Especially in the moonlight.

I was surprised he said nothing, but he didn't need to. I could tell what he wanted by the thick bulge between his legs.

As I finally pressed my lips against his, he curled one arm around my waist, keeping me in place. He darted his tongue inside my mouth, tasting me gently at first, as he would a delicacy. Then the kiss became more urgent, our mouths crushed firmly together as he drank from me.

He tasted of peppermint and scotch, the combination irresistible. I could kiss him for hours, basking in his scent and the fiery touches and nothing else. I couldn't breathe, the sheer madness of need suffocating.

I was the one who pulled away, dragging my tongue across my lips as I backed away.

Diego instantly swung around on the bench, spreading his legs wide open as he allowed his gaze to fall ever so slowly. His expression was more intense than I'd seen, his entire body shifting from his labored breathing.

I adored when he had his sleeves rolled up past his elbows, highlighting his muscular inked forearms. After cocking his head, he beckoned me with a single finger, his upper lip curling.

A part of me wanted to continue teasing him, but he shook his head as if knowing what I was thinking.

"I wouldn't do that if I were you, my princess." The sound of his voice was darker tonight, exactly as the music he'd selected, reeking of savage passion.

Yet I couldn't help myself, keeping my distance so he was unable to grab me. The shadows in the room seemed to ebb and flow, creating an almost ominous feel to the stark room. But I wasn't afraid.

Not of him.

Not of the moment.

Not of the slight tingle of love that was already starting to build, shifting past the lust.

I was crazy but didn't care. I wanted him. All of him.

As soon as I moved to within a few inches, he snatched my arm, forcing me closer. Then he gripped my hips, caressing me through the thick material. When he pressed his head against my stomach, I was surprised at the moment of tenderness. I lifted my hand, hesitant to place it on the top of his head, but somehow, I knew that's what he needed.

To calm the beasts who'd reared their ugly heads. I was taken aback by his actions, wishing it could always be this way. He was entirely different, a man I would have no qualms about spending the rest of my life with. But he was like Jekyll and Hyde, and I couldn't take not knowing which one I'd be forced to deal with.

When he lifted his head, he narrowed his eyes, slowly untying the sash on my robe. The moment he placed his hands on my stomach, I issued a series of moans, his rough fingers searing my skin. He kept his eyes pinned on me as he kneaded my tummy, crawling his fingers upward until he was able to cup my breasts, slowly standing to face me.

The look on his face was carnal, the moonlight accentuating his prowess in a delicate wave of shadows and light. He pinched my nipples, rolling them between his fingers, the harsh pain creating a wave of bliss.

I couldn't stop shaking, lightheaded from his actions. I wanted to jerk off his shirt, basking in his glorious physique but I knew better than to challenge his dominance. As he pinched and twisted, a single growl rose from the deepest portion of his chest. I was enthralled at his movements, swaying back and forth. There was no doubt I would have lost my balance had he not been holding me.

As he narrowed his eyes, he lowered his head, flicking his tongue back and forth across my nipple. The tender tissue was so sensitized that I was forced to take several rapid breaths. Just the way he pulled the hardened bud between his teeth was enough to ignite another series of fires. I gripped his arms, my fingers digging in as he shifted his attention to my other nipple, taking his time laving and sucking, biting down until I cried out in pain.

All time seemed to cease, the quiet in the room exacerbating the ragged beating of my heart as wave after wave of electricity tore through me. As he slipped the robe from my shoulders, allowing the garment to fall, I shuddered, given his full command.

When he fisted my hair with one hand, twisting his fingers in my long locks, I sensed he was losing his control of his needs. Then he cupped my jaw with his other hand, his hold so firm my face ached.

"You are going to please me tonight, Carina." He used his hold to lower me onto my knees in front of him. Then he unfastened his trousers, roughly jerking them down his hips until his cock sprang free. "Open your mouth, my beautiful bride."

Still trembling, I did as he asked, staring up at him with a mixture of awe and a desire so powerful my pussy clenched and released several times.

"Wider."

He jerked back my head, staring down at me, never blinking. There was no doubt how much he enjoyed being in control, making me feel adored even in my vulnerability. Stars floated in front of my eyes from the hint of pain as his fingers dug into my scalp. As he thrust his hips forward, slipping his cock inside, I pressed my hands on his thighs.

He pulled out, thrusting again until I gagged as the tip hit the back of my throat.

"Take all of it, my *flor preciosa.*"

I felt like his precious flower, but one he was going to rip the petals from, deflowering what was left of my innocence. As he plunged several times, I struggled to keep breathing, fighting the gagging urge as the tip was slammed against my throat.

Every part of me was quivering, my pussy so wet I sensed juice trickling down the insides of both thighs. I couldn't deny how much I adored the way he used me, holding back nothing as he sought to fulfill his satisfaction.

I should feel shame or a level of debasement, but my entire body was alive with energy and fire, thirsting to swallow every drop of his sweet cum.

But as he thrust harder, as if he was punishing me, I sensed something had changed inside of him. I caressed his thighs, his muscles tight as he rolled onto the balls of his feet, using the leverage to punish my mouth. He was fighting his demons, exorcising them in one of the only two ways he knew how to do it.

Music and sex.

Rough sex.

And I loved every second of it.

I wanted to scream out for him to use me, fuck me, but in the back of my mind I knew that wouldn't be necessary. He would take what he wanted without reservation, without asking. I was his to fuck and fondle at all hours of the day and night.

As I used my strong jaw muscles to suck, my throat finally accepting the brutal actions, I closed my eyes and savored the moment. I swirled my tongue back and forth, slickening his cock with my saliva, the few drops of pre-cum sparking my senses. His desperate need was increasing, his entire face pinched as he tried to hold back for as long as possible.

"Look at me, Carina." His voice was even more commanding than before.

I did what I was told, noticing the change in his expression.

He pushed deeper, taking me to where I'd never gone before. I sensed it wasn't enough. There was a mixture of emotions on his face. Anger and frustration. Lust and need. I was embroiled in the moment, incapable of thinking about anything else but sucking him.

When I knew he couldn't take it any longer, I clamped my lips around his shaft with enough pressure he let out a strangled moan. Every plunge was savage, sending several small waves of electricity into every muscle.

Then he filled my mouth with his cream, the long strings sliding down the back of my throat. He refused to stop thrusting, fucking my mouth with wild abandon. When he pulled out, he wrapped his hand around the base, growling as he gasped for air.

"Do not close your mouth." His words were full of darkness, his eye glassy as he spewed the remaining drops of his cum onto my tongue. When he let out an intense roar, I dragged my tongue around my mouth, staining my lips with his seed.

And somehow, I knew the moment was far from being over.

* * *

Diego

"*Tu eres mi unica salvacion*," I whispered. And she was my only salvation. Nothing else could calm the anger that had remained since returning. Only her. Her touch.

Her mouth.

Her pussy.

There was no way I could get enough of her. Not tonight. Not ever.

I kept my hold on Carina's hair, dragging her roughly to her feet, then freed my legs from the confines of my pants. She didn't object in any way, her needs as significant as mine. I wanted to defile her in the filthiest of ways. And God help me, I wanted to cover her luscious skin with my marks, providing anyone with a clear indication she belonged to me.

When she tried to move away, I grabbed her arm, pulling her tightly against me. "If you think you're leaving now, you're wrong, my sweet. My needs are far too great tonight." I crushed my mouth over hers, sweeping my tongue inside, tasting my cum. She wiggled in my hold, pressing her palm against my chest. I could drink in her essence all night long, but my filthy desires were getting the better of me.

I had to taste her.

Jerking back, I took several scattered breaths, laughing softly from the look on her face. "What's wrong, baby? Don't you like it rough?"

"You know I do."

"Mmm... Yes, I do. You're one filthy little girl."

She sucked on her lower lip as an answer and my cock was already twitching, building with need all over again.

Her lower lip trembled as I yanked out the piano bench, pushing her down onto the surface, keeping her head hanging over the edge. I craved tasting her, coating my tongue with her sweet nectar. I pulled one of her legs into the air, placing her foot on the keys. There was nothing better than hearing her soft mews as she tickled the ivories.

Maybe tonight she could finally calm the beast.

"Oh…" she moaned, the sound better than any concerto I could ever play.

As I crouched down, she placed her hand over her mouth, tossing her head back and forth. There was no reason for her to stifle her moans, unless she didn't want me to know just how much pleasure I was giving her.

I ran my fingers along the insides of her thighs, teasing her just like she'd done to me, rolling the tip of my index finger around her clit several times. She gasped for air, which pleased me tremendously, but the need building inside of me had already become insatiable. As soon as I pulled the tip of my tongue all the way down her pussy, she bucked up, rocking the bench from the force.

"Oh, yes."

"If you want me to continue, then you need to scream out my name, telling me exactly what you want."

Panting, she chewed on her lower lip before dropping her head. "Lick me. Please. Diego. Lick me."

A series of vibrations collided with my hunger, the electric force tremendous. I buried my head in her sweet pussy, thrusting my tongue past her swollen folds. How could she taste any sweeter than she had only hours before? I allowed myself to become lost in the moment, tossing aside every aspect of anger and concern.

"Yes. Yes," she moaned as she continued to squirm in my hold, her lovely breasts jiggling from the force I used.

I plunged several fingers alongside my tongue, driving deep and hard, savoring every drop of her sweet cream.

"Oh, Diego. More. Yes, please."

The sound of her voice would always drive me insane with need, my mind a blur as the taste of her filled my senses. I licked her ferociously, driving her close to the point of an orgasm then pulling away. I craved her juice trickling down my throat. I needed my face stained with her luscious scent. I continued dragging my tongue up and down like a wild animal.

Carina moaned from my every touch, lifting her bottom from the bench as she flailed in my firm hold. I wasn't letting her go anywhere. Not tonight.

Not ever.

My madness continued and I drove two more fingers inside, rimming her asshole with my thumb. When I plunged it inside, she gasped before allowing a full scream to rush to the surface.

That's the sweet moment she lost control. "Yes. Yes. Yes!"

As she wiggled madly, her long hair brushing the floor, she erupted in my mouth. I couldn't get enough of her, growling as I feasted, driving my tongue as deeply inside as her body would allow. The moment another climax rushed to the surface, I opened my mouth, rolling my lips up and down her sweet pussy, coating my jaw.

Her screams finally died down, yet her body continued to tremble in my hold. I could tell she was exhausted, lolling her head to the side.

"I'm not finished yet, my sweet." I gathered her into my arms and she immediately wrapped her legs around my hips, her arms dangling over my shoulders and her face pressed against my neck. I took long strides toward the bank of windows, able to sense how much she adored the ocean. I cradled her in my arms for another few seconds before easing her onto her feet, my cock already at full attention once again.

When I turned her around to face the ocean, she planted her palms on the glass, spreading her fingers wide open.

I used my knee to open her legs, adoring the way she glanced over her shoulder, the moonlight able to capture the glisten in her eyes. She pursed her lips, her breathing remaining ragged. As I crowded against her, crushing her with the full weight of my body, she laughed softly.

"I'm going to fuck you now." I made the dominating statement, and a single purr escaped her mouth as she blinked.

She arched her back as I slipped my cock between her legs, rubbing the tip back and forth. I couldn't take wasting any additional time, driving the entire length of my cock inside.

The way she threw her head back, gasping for air only added fuel to the already raging fire. I pulled out, slamming into her again, the force pressing her hard against the glass.

"I could fuck you for hours," I murmured.

"Then do."

"Are you challenging me?"

"Could I?"

I nipped her shoulder as I ground my hips, driving my shaft in even deeper. When I grabbed her long strands of hair, yanking her head back at an awkward angle, she let out a series of scattered breaths. Every sound she made turned me on to the point I couldn't think clearly, but there was no denying my intense cravings or the way she made me feel.

As if I could conquer the evil.

As if I could sleep through the night.

As if she was the only person who could alter the ugly course I'd set in motion.

Panting, I fucked her long and hard, rolling onto the balls of my feet, the vibrations skittering through me like a wildfire. Our hot breaths had fogged the glass and I watched in fascination as she dragged her finger through it, creating zigs and zags as she moaned, the lovely sound floating into the air around us.

I let out a series of growls, the husky sound mixing with her sweet voice as my balls began to tighten, my heart racing. Even though I wanted to keep control, to make this last for as long as possible, I couldn't handle the extreme need that was spiraling out of control. I cracked my hand against her bottom twice before digging my fingers into her hips.

She arched her back even more, meeting every hard thrust with one of her own. I gritted my teeth to the point my jaw ached, doing everything I could to hold it.

The moment she squeezed her muscles, I dropped my head, biting down on her long neck. Her cry met with my muffled growls and in those fabulous seconds where all time stopped and I filled her with my seed, I could finally feel a moment of peace rushing into my system.

My need to possess her, keep her, and use her only increased.

But she wasn't just my possession.

She'd already claimed a part of my soul.

iego

"Your brother will be the only man you can trust."

I jerked my head up, certain whoever had muttered the single sentence was standing in front of me. In the early morning light, I could almost swear my mother was standing just off to the right. Exhaling, I shifted back in my chair, doing what I could to control my rapid breathing.

"That's not going to happen," I answered in automatic reflex, laughing bitterly. I'd answered a ghost. Fuck. What was going on with me? Sleep deprivation? Possibly. I hadn't indulged in more than a few hours of sleep since arriving in the States. Trusting my brother hadn't been on the agenda. If he didn't know about my existence, should I give him a pass? Then what?

My laugh turned darker, my thoughts divisive. What I hadn't spent enough time on was going through the corporation's records. I'd confirmed the street value of the shipment arriving at the port was little more than a million dollars, which wasn't large by drug trade standards. Was it worth the risk to lure Ortiz to the States? At least my brother had provided a real truth. There was bad blood between Ortiz and my father. One or both of them had a personal vendetta.

I almost laughed again. Was what I was doing any different?

Unfortunately, returning to LA would be dicey on all fronts. I'd already been contacted by the DEA, which meant they believed the attack had been gang related. They would hound me until I talked with them. It was better to handle the situation head on. My first stop would be a destination of my choosing. And perhaps I could gain some useful information as well.

As far as what I'd learned, tonight's shipment was the only one on record for the year, the various codes used not easy to decipher. Every drug cartel and syndicate used their own language to keep track of business activities while leaving much to the imagination. However, the deterrent was useful against the DEA and other law enforcement agencies. At least I'd become very familiar with certain terms used during my time as a prosecutor. That had allowed me to decode the majority of information.

That would made leaked news more credible on the street. No wonder the informant broke protocol, risking his own life to provide information to Ortiz. A hefty finder's fee was likely involved.

How was it connected to the massacre? That's what I needed to discover.

However, I remained surprised the risk had been deemed acceptable. Even though the forty-three miles encompassing the port wasn't easily manned, I remained irritated as well as convinced the entire situation was a setup of some kind. My brother hadn't mentioned the port police. Having several on the payroll was the only way to get shipments in and out. How long had the plan been in place?

After searching the records for another thirty minutes, I found nothing else I'd consider useful. I'd go with my gut that tonight's event was meant to be a bloodbath all along. Then why was Sergio testing me on the details? More important, who was he working for?

As I fingered the weapon on my desk, spinning it around in a full circle, I put the pieces I knew together in my mind, something I'd been good at since I was a teenager. With Ortiz gone, the Santos reputation would explode, putting the fear of God into the smaller cartels throughout South America.

Interesting. That would leave the Santiago Cartel and the Santos Empire, the others easy to crush like cockroaches.

I closed my eyes for a few seconds, still able to see a faded version of the shadowed image that disturbed me almost as much as the uncertainty about the shipment.

In the vision, my mother had used the term 'only man.' Did that mean the only woman I could trust was my wife? Was she attempting to warn me that I was headed for a cataclysm?

Tonight I'd find out.

The knock on my office door pulled me out of the thick fog. As Stone walked in, Carina's phone in his hand, I wasn't certain whether I'd hoped there was a tracker or not.

"And?" I asked.

"It was clean. Nothing out of the ordinary," Stone said as he placed it on my desk. The kid was an expert at all things technical, including hacking, which offered an opportunity. My gut continued to tell me that someone within my organization was spilling information, the informant merely a cog in the wheel.

"Good to know. I'm tasking you to do another project."

"Of course, Mr. Santos. What do you need?"

"I need you to check several personal bank accounts as well as emails. Is that within your area of expertise?"

Stone grinned. "There isn't a single account or computer I can't break into, sir. It might take a little while, but I can find out anything you want to know."

"Excellent. I'll provide you with a list. And Stone. This is between you and me."

"Of course, Mr. Santos."

If there really was a situation between Xavier and Luis, there was a good chance someone had ignited another fire or there was an ongoing attempted coup.

And something told me that my brother might be innocent in this after all.

* * *

Carina

"You're going to submit to me no matter what I ask of you. Never forget, my beautiful flower, that you belong to me."

I opened my eyes, blinking from the brightness. As soon as I rolled over, I realized just how much my body was aching. Then the incredible memories of the night before trickled into my mind, and I tingled all over.

After biting my lip, I turned my head, realizing Diego wasn't in the room. Then I glanced at the clock. Jesus. It was after ten. I never slept this late. I eased back the covers, uncertain what to expect. He'd been so primal the night before, his emotions and passion as strong as mine, but there remained a wall between us. It wasn't the obvious one that involved the reason for our marriage, but something else that would nag me until I found the answers. If only I could get to a computer. Maybe I'd sweet talk him into allowing me to use his.

I almost laughed. Who was I kidding? He wouldn't allow me enough freedom to discover anything, including his plans for my business. A heavy weight remained on my heart. I had an executive officer and while the man was qualified, he didn't have the same edge or intuition about the artists. At least my departure had been planned, pushing him into the leadership position. However, one way or the other, I'd need to find out if everything was under control. There was so much to lose.

The moment I set foot on the ornate thick rug strategically placed under the bed, a cold shiver trickled all the way down to my toes from the foreboding feeling that everything was going to come crashing down. My mother had once told me that when people lived in glass houses, the exterior would eventually crack, fissures growing every week.

She should know, given her life had been nothing but misery.

I glanced around the room again and found a few surprises.

There was a vase of roses on the table near the window, their rich red color drawing my attention. And he'd placed clothes on the chair. I could see tags still hanging from the dress. I also noticed he'd left water on the nightstand. Why had he tossed me into a prison then turned around and provided a passionate night? Now this? As I walked toward the flowers, their scent filtering into my system, something else caught my eye and I resisted squealing.

My phone.

He'd placed my phone on the table next to the water. Did this mean he trusted me, or was this all a test?

The man continued to confuse the hell out of me. Maybe that was his intent, to keep me on a precipice, and if I fell from it, I'd never recover. Or maybe I was overthinking it. I glanced toward the closed door and bit my lip. Then I wasted no time shifting around the bed, grabbing my phone in my hand. Why was I shaking as I dialed Mia's number? I was doing nothing wrong in talking to my sister.

After the third ring, I was certain the call would go to voice-mail, and I dared not leave a message that would cause alarm.

Then she answered and my stomach flipped.

"Oh, my goodness," Mia exclaimed. "I can't believe you're calling me. I was so worried. Are you okay? Were you hurt?"

"I'm fine. Diego had his men ready to drive us to his plane. I was worried about you and Mother."

"We're both fine. She's shaken up and hasn't left her room."

"And Father?"

She exhaled. "He's angry. He's been talking to the police as well as the FBI. Have you seen the news?"

"Not yet. Diego wanted to shield me from everything."

"I don't blame him. What he did was heroic. You're lucky."

I hadn't been given the opportunity to share with her how everything had happened. If I had to be honest with myself, I'd wanted to protect her, but it wasn't prudent of me to hold back any longer.

"You do know the marriage was arranged. Right?"

"Um. What are you talking about? I thought you had a whirlwind romance."

"Is that what you really thought after all the hateful things you've heard me say about Diego?"

"Opposites attract. All the hot romance novels talk about enemies to lovers. The best sex?" While she laughed, I remained quiet. "You're serious."

"I am. I can't go into details right now, but I need you to do something for me."

"O-kay. You're scaring me."

"No reason to be scared. I'm fine but there are some things I need to find out about and I'm a prisoner in his home."

"That's terrible. Did Father do this?" she asked, her tone shifting into the same anger I continued to feel.

"Yes, but I think he was coerced. Still, that didn't give him the right to destroy my life. I know you're going to have a million questions, but I'll try and figure out a way we can spend some time before you leave. Is that still tomorrow?"

"The day after. Daddy switched the flight. I won't be leaving for a couple days. Just tell me what you need."

"Is it safe for you to get out of the house?"

"I can't go anywhere without a bodyguard."

I was glad she had someone to protect her.

I walked to the door, pressing my ear against it. There was no sound, but I couldn't put it past Diego to have Sergio standing guard behind the door. I quickly walked to the bathroom, partially closing the door. "Do you still have that friend in the FBI?"

"Yeah, Mike and I haven't talked for a couple months, but he's still working for them. Why?"

"Can you get in touch with him?"

"I think so. Tell me what's going on," she insisted.

"I need Mike to find out anything he can about Diego's childhood, and I suspect he's going to need to dig deep, as in try and find information that was shoved under a rock."

"I don't get what you're saying."

I had no clue what I was asking for. His behavioral change was unusual. That was the only thing I had to go on. "Just find out if there's anything weird about his birth, the first couple of years of his life. Any anomalies. And if he took piano lessons."

"Are you sure you're okay?"

"Please. Just do it for me. I'll try and call you later. And do not let Father know what you're doing."

"Okay, sis. I don't know what this is about, but I have a feeling I need to say be careful."

"Don't worry about me and thank you so much." As I ended the call, I prayed I was doing the right thing. After taking a deep breath, I returned to the bedroom, placing the phone back in the same position then grabbing the dress. It was beautiful, exactly my size. What minion had he sent out shopping? Still, it gave me a slight smile.

* * *

I'd half expected Diego would join me in the shower, but I was left alone. When I was dressed, I glanced at my reflection and exhaled. I no longer recognized the girl staring back at me. The one from before had been impetuous, bold, and opinionated. She'd become the bitch she'd thought she needed to be in order to get ahead in a man's world.

The one standing in front of her today had changed significantly. No longer did she feel like the princess her father had allowed her to become. There was no need to stand on a podium accepting an award or to be photographed with the most insanely handsome rockstar. No, the girl was wide eyed with uncertainty, determined yet no longer capable of being foolish in her attempts to gain and keep fame.

I closed my eyes, butterflies swarming in my stomach. The woman I'd become had wanted to kill a man she didn't really know. Now she wasn't certain she could live without him. How was that possible? Or was I just fooling myself, lured by lust and the fire between us into becoming compliant?

The answer wasn't going to be found by holing up in a posh bathroom. As I opened the door, I was prepared for Sergio's nasty banter. No one was there just like the night before. I headed down the stairs, finally hearing Diego's voice.

And he was angry.

"I do not accept incompetence, Sergio. Isn't that something you've learned over the years?" Diego demanded.

"Then what do you want to do?" Sergio barked in return.

"The issue will be handled today. Period. I have a meeting early this afternoon. Have the soldiers at the port by five o'clock."

"Yes, *El Jefe*."

I jumped, hearing one of them slamming something down on a surface, almost giving my attempts at eavesdropping away. I knew all about the use of the port in LA. The rumors about running drugs from various ships had been fodder for the FBI investigations for years. Nothing had ever been found. How they cleverly disguised containers wasn't something I'd asked or cared about until now, but it was obvious a problem had arisen.

"Don't fuck me on this, Sergio. If we start a war, then that's what happens. That massacre is just the beginning, and you know it. I need to force Ortiz's hand with this. If he's responsible for almost getting my beautiful wife killed, I will cut him to ribbons myself."

I closed my eyes, his tone of voice genuine and my heart fluttered a little bit. Even if I was right and he wasn't the real Diego, did I want anyone else to know? I bit my lip, the answer far too easy. A part of me wanted to keep him all to myself.

"Your father will not be happy," Sergio answered.

"And I couldn't care the fuck less. This needs to happen," Diego snarled.

I quickly backed down the hall, sliding into the half bath, watching as Sergio stormed out, cursing in Russian under his breath. I waited for a full minute before walking into the room.

Diego quickly snapped his head in my direction, sucking in his breath, a smile crossing his face. "You're awake."

"You should have gotten me up earlier." His expression of anger quickly shifted to being pleased to see me.

"There was no need."

I walked closer. "What's going on?"

His smile was knowing. "You were listening, my bad little princess?"

"First of all, you should know by now I'd hardly a princess. And second, I was walking down the stairs. How could I not hear what you were saying?"

"It's none of your concern. You've dealt with enough."

"Do you think that as your wife I won't and shouldn't know what's going on in your dangerous world?"

Diego took a deep breath, moving around his desk. He was just as handsome as the night before, today dressed in charcoal slacks and a black shirt. Even today, he had an air of danger enshrouding him, his aura capturing my breath. "There are certain aspects of my business that you don't want to learn about, Carina."

"I'm your wife. Everything you do now affects me. And I'm not going to stop asking."

He chuckled under his breath, allowing his gaze to fall to my feet. When he slowly allowed his eyes to crawl up to the bodice of my dress, he sighed. "I have some difficult business to handle later today. That means we are leaving for Los Angeles in one hour."

"You do remember the movie premiere is tonight." I could tell by a single flash of his eyes that it had either not occurred to him, or he hadn't heard about it.

"It's too risky to go at this point."

"Did you find out more?"

"Unfortunately, nothing concrete. There was no identification on the assailants, and no one had laid claim to the attack."

"How do you live this way, Diego? Will I need to be followed by bodyguards for the rest of my life?" There was something in his eyes that told me he wasn't certain.

"It won't always be this dangerous."

I folded my arms, a slight chill coursing down my spine. "I hope not. If we're going to raise a family, I don't want our children growing up in a prison."

"My beautiful bride, you are entirely different than just this time yesterday."

"As you said, a lot has happened. We are married and nothing is going to change that, but you need to promise me that you'll tell me what's going on and never lie to me."

He tilted his head, studying my eyes. "I can make you that promise."

I wasn't certain whether to believe him or not.

"Pack a bag. We are going away for a few days." As he walked closer, just gathering a single whiff of his aftershave created another series of tingles.

"Does that mean my phone was bugged?"

"No, which is why I gave it back to you."

"But you're still concerned."

There was an instant pained look on his face. Then he masked his emotions, which he hadn't been able to do the night before. "What happened at the wedding was nothing more than a warning."

"What about my business?"

"This is only for a couple of days."

"What are you doing to track them down?"

As he brushed the tips of his fingers down the side of my face, I hated myself for the instant lightheadedness I felt, but he had such a strong effect on me.

"Playing a dangerous game, Carina, and one I want to involve you in as little as possible."

"That's not fair, Diego."

"Maybe not, but it's what I need to do right now."

"I need to see my sister. Maybe you don't understand how important the connection is, but I must see with my own eyes that she's uninjured. Can I meet her for a cup of coffee? Anything?" He had a sudden faraway look in his eyes when I asked the question. What was he hiding behind his gorgeous eyes of steel?

"Do you want her brought here?"

I knew he'd ask me that. "I don't think she'll want to be reminded of the horrible incident. I'm not trying to escape or defy you. I just need a little time. Okay?"

"I do understand, my sweet bride. I'll have Sergio provide you with a driver and it's not an option, Carina. I need you protected. You will stay in a public location."

"What aren't you telling me? Has there been a threat made?"

"Nothing new, but you will always be in danger since you're my wife, a possession considered my weakness."

"I'm not a possession."

He cocked his head, allowing his fingers to trail down my neck to my arm. His touch was light, keeping the tingles dancing across my skin. "No, you're not, but in my enemies' eyes you are."

"How many enemies do you have, Diego?"

"Far too many at this point. However, I'm going to attempt to eliminate at least one of them."

"How? By killing this person?"

He fisted his hand, taking another deep breath. "If necessary."

"I'll ask you one more time. How can you stand this life? Don't you want to be able to enjoy living like a normal human being? A family? Indulging in nights spent by a fire or going out to dinner without having guards watch everyone around you?"

"We don't live in a fantasy world, Carina. Do you not think your father had you watched twenty-four hours a day?"

I hadn't thought about it, at least not for the reason he was suggesting. I was no fool. My father had his own share of enemies. I'd seen people guarding me at times, but not always. Or was I just a fool? "You're powerful enough you can make your life, and now my life, anything you want them to be. You have a profitable movie production company. Why can't you just concentrate on that instead of your illegal activities?"

His laugh sent a rush of anger into my heart. "Don't be foolish. I have just as many enemies within that realm as I do in everything else."

"Then sell it. You have enough money to live however you want. We could go buy an island and live there for the rest of our lives without needing a thing. Just the two of us." Was I really suggesting that?

When he narrowed his eyes, I wasn't certain whether he was going to explode from rage or laugh in my face. The smile he offered was genuine, his eyes lighting up as if the suggestion brought him joy. "That would be... wonderful. But even if I could make that happen, the danger would follow. My family has gone too far down the rabbit hole of success."

I wasn't going to win this argument. "May I call my sister and ask her to meet me?"

He lifted his head, studying me carefully. "Make the call."

When I started to turn around to head out of the room, I heard a slight growl.

"In here, my bride. It's not that I don't trust you, but right now, I need to make certain I know where you are at all times."

I wanted to be angry, but I had the distinct feeling whatever meeting he had later would turn into a bloodbath. Nodding, I dialed her number. "Mia."

"I made contact, but I don't have any information yet."

"I'm glad to talk to you as well. Yes, I'm fine, just anxious after what happened. Are you hurt?"

"What's happening?" she asked. "Oh, he's there."

"Thank God. I was so worried. Are you free for a cup of coffee? Will Daddy let you out of the house? No. We're returning to LA for some business."

"Sure. You're scaring me again."

Exhaling, I nodded in his direction. "That's fantastic. Don't forget to bring the pictures you have of your last concert. You never showed me, and I know how you are. You won't send them to me after you get to France."

"You want me to bring my laptop."

"Oh, please. That would be wonderful. I'm so glad you're okay. You know that little coffee shop just outside of Beverly Hills?"

"I know it. Just tell me when."

"We're leaving in an hour. Let's say two?"

"Okay, but you're going to tell me everything."

I turned to face him. "Of course I will. I'm so excited to see you." As I ended the call, my eyes still locked on the man who'd unearthed deep, dark feelings, I took a deep breath. There was no doubt that whatever was happening later today would alter the course of our future.

Why did I have the terrible feeling the horrible bloodshed would include my husband?

CHAPTER 17

 iego

The Brotherhood.

I'd thought little about the group of men who collectively ruled the world until the night before the meeting with them. There were no notes in my brother's things, no files on the computer providing anything other than a notation about the meeting including the location. The King Harbor Yacht Club in Redondo Beach wasn't exclusive nor was it posh in the terms of every other club my brother belonged to. However, the setting suited my mood, the turbulent waters of the Pacific Ocean churning in the afternoon wind.

I stood on one of the docks, staring at the vast display of colors crisscrossing the sky. My mood had changed vastly over the last twenty-four hours, enough so I'd questioned my motives more than once. However, I was too far into the ruse to alter the course. At least at this point.

Fortunately, I'd been provided the names of the men included, all of whom were powerful in their own right. I'd memorized their backgrounds as well as their faces. All six of us were in charge of the up-and-coming syndicates, positioned to take whatever territories we set our sights on.

Constantine Thorn had recently taken over his father's empire, his hold on casinos and other resorts in several Midwest states predicated on his penchant for violence.

Gabriel Giordano had recently suffered the loss of his older brother, shoving him into the position of Don of the New York Cosa Nostra. He was interesting to me, including how he handled accepting the role in a family he'd never wanted anything to do with. Given his push to eliminate the Russians and Armenians who'd threatened his empire, his acceptance of the life had changed his personality entirely.

Brogan Callahan was Irish through and through, his large extended family in Chicago tight. He was also grieving a brother who'd been on death's door more than once, which would also shove him into the leader position. Where the others in the Brotherhood enjoyed violence and bloodshed, he steered away from all aspects of his family's control over the most powerful people in Chi-town.

Maxim Nikitin was brutal by anyone's standards, his upbringing in Russia removing all aspect of humanity at an early age. He was the nephew of the Pakhan who controlled the southern United States, and they had a direct connection to the Black Angels and to my godfather's regime. He could prove to be useful in eradicating Ortiz.

Although I wasn't certain assistance was needed, I couldn't rule anything out at this point. During my terse conversation with Sergio, he'd been curiously happy to report that Ortiz had flooded LA with his soldiers, likely tipped off about the hit. While there were a number of soldiers employed under my helm, any one of them capable of betraying me, Sergio's behavior continued to bother me.

There was no trust to be had in this business.

The final man in the Brotherhood was just as fascinating. Phoenix Diamondis was Greek, his personality gregarious. His hold on Philadelphia was notorious, his methods of torturing his enemies giving him a savage reputation. It was a direct counter to his love of life and his hunger for beautiful women, who he treated like queens.

By far, the meeting and my continued association with them was the most dangerous undertaking. Not only could they expose my duplicity to members of my empire, but they could also lay the groundwork for full annihilation and takeover if they believed me to be a threat.

I swirled the drink I'd ordered, glancing at my watch. It was almost time. As I walked inside, my thoughts drifted to Carina. After our night of passion, she seemed entirely different, although I sensed she was even more confused about what had transpired between us. So was I. I hadn't set out to care about her, but I found myself needing her more and more.

Her presence overshadowed the darkness, enough so I could almost believe I'd been born to live the lifestyle enjoyed by family members I couldn't care less about. The dichotomy of my feelings was starting to eat away the anger, replacing the dark emotion with nothing but sadness for a past that could never be altered.

Shoving it aside, I headed into the private room positioned directly over the water. I'd never been here before, Googling it moments before I'd left the house. With the yachts positioned in the harbor, it was another ugly reminder that I didn't need at this point. After tonight, I had a feeling the entire situation would escalate. Or maybe I needed it to happen. In the few weeks I'd absorbed a life I'd fought against before all of this, I no longer recognized myself.

What I hadn't planned was a final ending to the brutal game, my only thoughts on destroying my father, brother, and their regime. But doing so would leave me wide open, the smell of blood drawing sharks to infested waters.

I didn't like what I was walking into. At least I'd altered the plan. In doing so, I'd learn whether or not Sergio was loyal to me or to someone else. If to my father, I'd receive a phone call at any time from the insufferable man. If to Ortiz, then tonight would be more like a Wild West shooting. I had to know.

As I headed into the room, I was struck by the amount of testosterone. The five were already there, drinks in their hands. Only one of them bothered to shift their attention in my direction when I walked in.

Maxim.

He studied me with cold eyes, watching my every move. I'd learned Diego had been aloof with anyone he didn't know or care about. So, that's how I'd act.

"Diego," Constantine said in greeting. "I heard about what happened at your wedding. From the sound of it, you're lucky to be alive."

"Gentlemen," I returned. "It was horrific and well planned."

Brogan laughed. "I don't think you've used that term ever."

"That's because we aren't gentlemen," Phoenix said as he laughed, lifting his glass.

"Speak for yourselves," Constantine added. "Have the authorities caught the people responsible?"

"Do you really think that's going to happen?" I asked.

"But you suspect who initiated the attack," Maxim added.

I nodded, even if I wasn't certain of anything. "I'm following leads."

"Is there anything we can do to help?"

As I studied Phoenix, I sensed he was being genuine. "Not at this time. How's your brother, Brogan?" It seemed like an innocuous question to ask.

Exhaling, he took a sip of his drink before answering. "Good days and bad days. But lately, they've been damn good days. If his next scan comes back clean, the doc says he might beat it."

"That's fucking fantastic news," Gabriel stated.

I watched Constantine, the only original member of the Brotherhood left, although Brogan had been invited to join the former college group after a rough game of Lacrosse between their two schools. It was fascinating reading material, although I still couldn't fathom why they'd made an alliance at that age and kept it.

"I wasn't aware until I hear about the attack that you were getting married," Maxim stated, his harsh look continuing.

"The marriage was contract based." My answer made the five of them nod. "Not out of love."

"That doesn't happen in our business, except for men like Constantine and Gabriel."

The two men had found women they cared about, which had left huge targets on their backs. "Love is overrated," I told them.

Constantine eyed me as carefully as Maxim was. "Let's get this started and I'm going to cut to the chase. There's a rumor the Black Angels have plans on taking a bigger piece of the West Coast. True?"

"Yes." My clipped answer seemed to surprise several of them.

"They need to be handled, Diego. They've been an issue for several of us," Maxim offered. "If I had to guess, I'd say you suspect Luis Ortiz as the person who placed the order for the assassination."

I turned my head in his direction. Perhaps they were my best source of information outside of the normal channels. "A distinct possibility and he will be dealt with. A shipment is due in to the port tonight. I have it under good authority a hijack attempt will be made."

Maxim lifted his eyebrows. "You don't have a shipment coming in."

"Oh, I do, but not to that port. I've had it diverted."

"Risky, depending on who's-on-whose payroll," Phoenix muttered. "How many soldiers on your roster?"

"I have three crews, a few others."

Constantine lifted his eyebrows, Brogan laughing. "That's it? Sixty plus men?"

"You seem to forget through my help, we'd discarded a significant portion of our illegitimate businesses." I knew how many crews the cartels ran. Hell, Emmanuel had at least thirty and each one was made up of at least thirty men. There were reported to be at least one hundred thousand employed by worldwide cartels, significantly more than the typical mafia syndicate.

The looks they shared made me bristle.

"That's not enough," Gabriel snarled.

"That's what I have and unless you gentlemen want to drop a few on a private plane and get them to the port by seven tonight, there's nothing I can do. This was set in motion some time ago." I'd thought about asking for Emmanuel's advice, if not his help, but he'd made it clear I was on my own. Besides, his involvement would only raise additional eyebrows.

"It's either your death warrant or a brilliant move," Maxim said, his Russian accent much thicker than Sergio's. I didn't like him, his attitude infuriating the hell out of me. He was searching my eyes, which irritated me even more.

"I like to think of myself as observant and intellectual. If Ortiz wants a fight, then that's what he's going to get. At minimum, the informant who relayed the private information will be dealt with, a message sent."

Constantine tipped his head. "You're playing a game. You have a traitor in your midst."

I took a gulp of my drink as I nodded. I'd never thought of myself as a traitor but that fit far too well. "And traitors aren't acceptable."

"I was serious about my earlier offer. If you need backup, some will be provided for you." While I sensed Constantine's offer was also genuine, I wasn't in the mood for a handout or additional time spent around any of them. It was a risk I couldn't afford to take.

"Thank you, but it would appear you all have issues of your own."

"We should talk about this further," Gabriel demanded, which was another surprise given he hadn't been inducted into the group for more than a couple of months.

"Need I remind you that this isn't a democracy. This is an alliance. There are no votes, no determinations made. This is for information sharing and support only when requested." I struck a nerve with the Russian, but Constantine burst into laughter.

"Have you been rehearsing that, Diego? You've acted as if this group isn't worthy of you for two years. However, that was brilliant. Perhaps it should be our motto."

"You do remember that you were invited into this group as a courtesy," Brogan hissed, his usual happy-go-lucky demeanor fading.

I sucked in my breath then placed my glass down on the table. "Enjoy your refreshments, gentlemen. They're on me." As soon as I started to walk out, Maxim cursed in Russian. Then I felt the barrel of a weapon pressed against the back of my head. I took a deep breath, at least two of the others chuckling.

As I shoved my hands into my pockets, I tilted my head. "Are you really going to shoot me in the back of the head, Russian? If so, that would make you a coward in my eyes as well as many others."

"Put it away, Maxim. Whatever has crawled up your ass over the last few months is starting to piss me off," Constantine snarled.

I heard the soft click of the safety and shook my head as I turned around. "That's a good question. What is your beef, Maxim?"

His nostrils flared. "If Ortiz shows up, kill the son of a bitch for me. Will ya?"

All that for a request? I walked closer, shifting my jacket so he could see my weapon. "And if you put a gun to my head again, you better be prepared to fire it. You won't get another opportunity."

While the others laughed, Maxim kept the same scowl on his face.

"I'd say we have a new and improved Diego. Maybe I should get married. Perhaps that would enrich my mood and my wealth."

As the others laughed, I kept my eyes on Maxim. He was the one to watch. However, I would call on their assistance if necessary.

I left the meeting minutes after and was almost to the parking lot when my phone rang, the number unrecognizable. My gut told me to answer it.

"Diego Santos."

"Mr. Santos. I believe it's time that you and I have a frank conversation."

"And you are?"

"Luis Ortiz. I believe you're looking for me."

* * *

Carina

As soon as I walked into the coffee shop, I breathed a sigh of relief. Up to that point, I hadn't been certain Diego would keep his end of the bargain in letting me go. "Mia. I'm so glad to see you. God. I really was terrified." I grabbed her arms, pulling her to a standing position so I could give her a hug. I'd passed by the man our father had hired to protect her. He and the soldier assigned to watch me were like bouncer bookends. At least I felt certain we would be safe.

For now.

"We both have bodyguards. How interesting." She nodded toward the entrance.

"Vitoro."

"He's pretty sexy."

"He's a brute who carries a knife and a gun just like your guy. But right now, I'm thankful they're watching out for us." I was happy she'd taken a table near the back and as far from others as possible. On the table was her laptop.

"What happened?"

"I honestly don't know. I don't think Diego does either, but he's on edge."

"We all are," she admitted. "Father tried to tell me I wasn't leaving town. I laughed in his face."

"Good for you. You need to get as far away from here as possible."

Frowning, I noticed she was clinging to her laptop.

"Has Mike gotten back to you?"

"No, but he's a busy man. I'm not sure if he was assigned to the attack or not. He wouldn't tell me. But I don't honestly know if he'll be able to do so for a couple days."

I chewed on my lower lip, more nervous than I thought I'd be. A couple of days might be too late, and I wasn't certain why my gut was telling me that. I felt like we were in a pressure cooker and as soon as the timer went off, kaboom.

"You look… different," she said when I was silent.

"How so?"

"Umm… Angry. Worried. Happy. It's weird. Plus, your skin has a shimmer to it."

"Maybe I'm all of the above." She could always make me smile. I reached over, grabbing her hand. "Whatever happens and I do mean whatever, you need to get on that plane and never come back."

"What is going on? Why is everything so dangerous all of a sudden?"

I took a deep breath and closed my eyes, wishing we were in a bar instead of a coffee shop. "The marriage was arranged. I only agreed to it so that you wouldn't have to marry a thug." Now her silence troubled me. When I opened my eyes, I expected to see a look of horror. While my sister was passive in several aspects of her life, anything that troubled me bothered her.

She had a blank look on her face.

"That's what I thought happened, but I knew you and Diego had a spark, so I was hopeful that it was something you also wanted."

I half laughed. "I guess I underestimated you."

"You did. I'm not ten any longer, believing in fairy princesses and the world of magic, sis. We live in a brutal environment, our father's regime no exception."

"And here all this time I thought I was protecting you."

She smiled, pushing a cup of coffee she'd ordered for me closer. "You did a great job. You need to let me worry about you for a little while. What do *you* think is going on?"

I thought about how to answer her. "Have you ever had an experience where you know in your gut that the person you're talking to isn't the same one from before?"

"Now I'm confused. Are we talking about Diego?"

"Yes. He's not the same one that I battled in a courtroom."

Exhaling, her eyes opened wide. "From what I could tell, he looks exactly like the man I've seen in the news. Handsome. Debonair. Dangerous."

"He's entirely different, a softer version. I know I sound insane, but I'm certain of it. I was hoping Mike would find his birth certificate. Pictures. Anything that might corroborate my feelings."

"Honey, are you certain this isn't about just being angry?"

"That's what I thought at first, but he's not the sadist I read about. Not by a long shot. He's passionate and dark, but not brutal, at least with me."

"You're a smart woman, sis. Men can pretend to be anything they want to be."

"I know that." I took a sip of coffee, and the bitter taste gave me an instant stomachache. "I like this version."

She laughed. "I can tell. Maybe you're just reeling from the attack."

"I knew it the moment I looked into his eyes in the cathedral. I was going to kill him that day."

She almost spit out her coffee. "What?"

"I'm serious. I couldn't do it."

"And now you care about him."

"Yeah, I do. Can I see your laptop?"

"Of course. I don't know what you'll find."

I pulled it around to face me then allowed my fingers to start flying. As I started the search, I concentrated on trying to find anything I could about when he was born. The trouble was I had no clue. As I moved from one Google page to another, I became more and more frustrated. I found several photographs, but only going back until he was around ten.

"Did you find anything?" she asked as she leaned over the table.

"Nothing useful. But I don't see any mention of piano lessons."

"Where has he been playing piano?"

"His house in San Diego."

255

"If he owns a piano, doesn't that stand to reason he took lessons at some point?"

I hadn't thought about it that way. "I guess. Maybe. Ugh." I closed the lid, furious with myself for going down a bizarre path. "He's just different than every interaction I had with Diego before. He's intense yet there is such a haunted level of sadness to him that it breaks my heart. He's caring, more so than I would have thought. There were roses on the table when I woke up. And last night, whew is all I can say. The way he plays piano is with all he has. He's just vibrant and alive in everything."

"Allow me to make an observation. While the marriage might have been arranged, perhaps karma had something to do with it."

"What do you mean?"

Mia rolled her eyes. "You're in love with him already."

I opened my mouth to retort but nothing would come out. Maybe I was after all. "But what if he's an imposter?"

"Ask yourself this. If he isn't Diego, then who is he? Did someone have plastic surgery to destroy the Santos Corporation?"

"That's what I was thinking. Now he has an opportunity to dissect two powerful and financially secure companies at the same time."

"Has anything happened with Daddy's business?"

"He's broke, or at least he was, Mia."

"What?"

"That's the reason for the marriage. Xavier dug him out of a hole. Now Diego has control of everything, which means the combined company is undoubtedly one of the wealthiest in the world."

"You're not thinking our father was behind the attack," she said in horror.

"No, but it could be someone who didn't want the marriage taking place. I'm just not certain."

She furrowed her brow. "I don't know what to say. Have you mentioned what you just told me to Diego?"

I laughed and flipped open the laptop again, determined to try one last time. "Let me be blunt. We don't talk. We fuck. A lot."

She coughed and coughed until tears flowed down her face, finally grabbing her napkin then laughing loudly enough several people glanced in our direction. "And that's bad why?"

I gave her a frosty look and typed in Diego's name and tried to think about the date he would have been born. As Google popped up a few entries, I leaned over. "Yes, it's enjoyable, the best I've ever had, but it's like being in bed with a stranger."

"And you thought you knew Diego?" She winked at me, still laughing as her phone rang. "I'm sorry," she said after glancing at the number, frowning when she did. "I'm expecting a call from the conservatory. I'll just be a second."

As she rose from the table, trying to find a quieter location, I continued searching, constantly glancing at Vitoro to see if he was paying attention. Thank God he was too interested in whatever he was paying attention to on his phone. I shifted from one page to the other, finally ready to give up when something caught my eye, headlines from an old *Los Angeles Times* article.

Christening for the sons of Xavier Santos

Sons.

My skin began to crawl, my fingers shaking as I opened the article, scanning it quickly as I held my breath. I flicked my finger on the trackpad, desperate to see if there was a picture.

There was.

As I pulled the perfectly colorful photograph into view, my stomach flipped.

"Um, Carina. You're not going to believe this," Mia said in a soft voice.

Blinking several times, my chest was tight as I magnified the photograph. I lifted my head, my mouth slack.

Her face was white.

"Diego and Dante Santos were christened together."

She slowly lowered into her seat. "He might be Dante Fernandez. If he is, you need to get away from him."

"What?"

As she nodded, I noticed how tightly her hand was wrapped around her phone. Her knuckles were white.

"What else, Mia? What was that call?" When she didn't respond, I grabbed her arm, shaking her.

When she slowly turned her phone around, I narrowed my eyes.

Then terror skated down my spine.

CHAPTER 18

 iego

As I headed into the diner, it struck me how many DEA agents I'd worked with over the years. While they had no jurisdiction to make arrests in Colombia, Chile and Brazil were considered their southern cone. I'd been involved in a half dozen cases over the last few years that had their involvement. The moment I walked through the doors and caught sight of the contact meeting me, I'd realized I'd just headed into the lion's den.

Agent Fletch Walker had worked on a single case I'd prosecuted. He'd also been in attendance for several meetings with my office and theirs, many of them dual efforts between the states and Chile. We'd gotten somewhat personal, which meant he knew my voice inflections as well as my manner of speaking. Fuck. I'd just stepped into quicksand. But there was no backing out now.

Upon my approach, he lifted his head. Then he narrowed his eyes. He'd spent most of his career working in other countries, which is why he'd never made a connection to how much Diego and I looked alike. No wonder he had a look of surprise as he peered up at me. "Diego Santos."

"Yes." I slipped into the booth, maintaining eye contact with him.

"Interesting."

"How so, Agent Walker?" I stared him directly in the eyes. I'd perfected my more Americanized accent over the last few weeks but would need to cut the conversation short.

"You resemble someone I've had contact with on the other side of the law. An admirable man with significant integrity."

"Am I to assume you're certain I have none?"

"I don't think we need to play games, Mr. Santos. I'm well aware of your reputation and your business ethics."

Laughing, I waved the waitress away before she approached. This wasn't a social gathering. "Are you trying to insinuate that the Santos Corporation isn't on the up and up?"

The smirk on his face was one I remembered. "Let's just say you wouldn't have found yourself the victim of an extermination attempt if you didn't float across the lines from time to time."

"Now I'll say interesting. I understand you have some questions."

He continued to eye me carefully, tapping his pen on the small pad he had on the table. "Who do you believe ordered the hit?"

"That's why I'm cooperating with the authorities. I don't have any idea."

"Oh, come now, Diego. You must have some thoughts."

"If you're asking if I have enemies, you already know that answer. I have dozens of them as does Montgomery DeMill."

"Yes, but Mr. DeMill hasn't been linked to drug trafficking."

"And neither has the Santos organization. Now I'll ask you. What have you learned from your initial investigation?"

"As an attorney, you are well aware that I can't supply information for an ongoing case."

I leaned over, which obviously bothered him. "You can, however, provide me with the concrete facts that you've secured."

He narrowed his eyes, shaking his head. "Do you know a man by the name of Dante Fernandez? He's out of South America."

There it was. Confirmation he'd made the connection.

From what I'd learned about my brother's actions over the last year, he hadn't been out of the country, let alone stepping foot in Colombia.

"I don't believe I do. Is there a point to this?"

"Maybe. Maybe not. However, there is recent ongoing investigation regarding Mr. Fernandez, several international authorities searching for his whereabouts, which I find almost impossible to believe." He looked at me curiously, waiting for my reaction. "You see, I know him fairly well. He's a man of integrity."

While I bristled, I refused to show the slight sweep of anxiety. What the hell had flagged the man I'd been before? "Does this have a point?"

Shrugging, he reached for his coffee. "Only in that given you look almost identical; the attack could have been based on mistaken identity."

I laughed, although whatever trumped-up charges had been developed combined with the fact my face had been on national news with the wedding had the possibility of creating confusion. My gut told me my previous identity was being used for a setup, but from which side of the law? I needed to ascertain what the hell he was talking about. Maybe Sergio had been right in that it was time to go into hiding until I managed to determine who'd ordered the assassination.

What was about to go down at the port had just become far too risky, although there was no way to stop the events from unfolding. Fuck. Why did I suddenly feel as if I was in over my head?

"I appreciate the heads up, Agent Walker, but I need to concentrate my concerns as well as my actions on locating the person responsible for the attack on my family. I would assume that's the main reason you are here."

He leaned back, never blinking as he stared at me for a full ten seconds. "You're right. It's just the resemblance is uncanny."

"So you said. What have you learned?"

"It would appear the attack was a gang-style shooting; however, the downed assailants had taken careful measure to hide their identities. Still, it's only a matter of time before we're able to identify them by their fingerprints."

"You know as well as I do that many of the soldiers chosen as footmen for various cartels are selected because they have no proven identity. Their births were never documented or often destroyed even before they pledged their allegiance to whatever organization recruited them."

He laughed, shaking his head. "That sounds like something I heard almost a year ago from a damn good prosecutor in Chile. The man who happens to resemble you. It's funny that he's an attorney as well." Agent Walker looked away, as if debating what he was telling me. He was goading me. "He had his shit together, including capturing the pulse of some of the most violent criminals I've ever fought to eradicate."

The fucker was testing me again, although he was right in that my words reflected my time spent as a prosecutor, not as a trained killer and new leader of the Santos Empire. I gave him a hard look. "You need to find the person responsible for the fucking attack. I don't care which rock you turn over in order to do so, the son of a bitch will pay for what he did. Even if I need to handle the situation myself. Do I make myself clear?"

While I didn't know the man very well, it was easy to tell he was attempting to lead me down a path. Was this about warning the man he'd once believed to be on the right side of the law or hoping I'd make a mistake? Either way it didn't matter. The DEA would quickly learn that no matter which persona I used, I wouldn't allow the atrocity to go without punishment.

"I'm going to give you a piece of advice, Mr. Santos. Take it or leave it, but it's the same thing I'd say to the prosecutor who worked tirelessly to rid the streets of Chile of the vilest criminals. Be careful crossing lines. Often, it's impossible to return to the safety zone."

I allowed a smile to cross my face. "Duly noted."

Another awkward twenty seconds passed.

Sighing, he looked away. "Your family will continue to be of interest to me. I'd be able to provide immunity to anyone providing me with qualified information in order to bring the people who did this to justice."

I gave him a hard look, one that should tell him in no uncertain terms I wasn't interested.

"What can you tell me about the attack?" I asked, leaning back against the booth. I could tell he was disappointed.

"It was well planned, the soldiers ordered to make the hit realizing they could lose their lives."

"Then I'd say in fairness that it wasn't about a hit but a warning."

"That's what several members on the task force believe. You need to be honest with us, Mr. Santos. If you have any knowledge of who could have done this, it would serve in your best interest to tell me. It would also be advisable to lay low for a few days."

"That almost sounds like a threat."

"Just a warning, Mr. Santos. If what I believe is happening is the case, a good man will get caught up in a violent cross-fire. And this time, he won't be on the side of the law. No one will come to his aid."

"As you might suspect, I can take care of myself, but I do appreciate your concern."

I drummed my fingers on the table. At this point, I had no interest in providing my unfounded thoughts. He seemed uncomfortable as hell, which meant he was clearly holding something back. What in God's name was going on behind the scenes?

He removed a card, scribbling a number on the back. "I'm not usually in the habit of helping a member of a violent cartel, but my instincts have never been wrong. Take my number. There are reliable sources that tipped my department about a cargo ship coming into the LA port sometime this week. That wouldn't happen to be yours, now, would it?"

Smirking, I glanced at the card, uncertain I wanted to take it. "The Santos Corporation isn't in the business of trafficking illegal drugs, Agent."

"Be careful, Mr. Santos. You're playing a game that you will not win against the DEA. However, if there are extenuating circumstances, I might be able to help you. That is if you can provide me with decent information."

Laughing, I took the card, although I wasn't certain why. "I assure you, Agent Walker, if I knew anything, you and I wouldn't have had this conversation. If you'll excuse me, I have other business to attend to." I rose from the table. The man was fishing, which could prove to be just as dangerous as the threat against the Santos family.

"One piece of advice, Mr. Santos. My friend is obviously being used in a treacherous game of power and control. For what reason he stepped away from the righteous life he worked so hard to achieve is beyond me. But he has no idea who he's up against or the lengths they will go to in order obtain their goal. I only hope he knows what he's doing."

I took a deep breath, tipping my head over my shoulder. "While I appreciate your thoughts, the doppelganger you described has nothing to do with my life."

"I think that's where you're wrong. In fact, I'm certain of it."

Little about the meeting between us had been about finding the perpetrator. The agent had been sent on purpose to try to confirm recognition. Why? And who'd made the connection? I glanced at the number, memorizing it before tossing it in the trash. The last thing I wanted was to have anyone assume I was working with the DEA.

I took a deep breath before heading out of the diner. There was no doubt the game was starting to unravel. However, now I had to wonder who the real players were.

* * *

I'd found nothing in any news source regarding Dante Fernandez. Either the agent had been toying with me or he knew something that had yet to be made public. Whatever the case, I remained on edge.

The sun was still perched above the ocean water as I arrived at the Port of Los Angeles. This was a typical scenario that I'd been prepared for during those grueling weeks spent in Colombia. From what I'd learned about my crews, they knew exactly what to do during a threat of this nature. The majority had positioned themselves in secure locations, including on the docks, on top of several of the buildings, and throughout the cargo holds. In addition, there were men perched in every parking location, everyone able to have radio contact.

Up to this point, no one from the Black Angels had made an appearance, but we were in position early. My decision to move the shipment had likely been in my best interest. My gut told me the authorities were crawling all over the port. While there was no direct link to the Santos family with regard to the owned warehouses or on the ship's docket, the DEA had decent enough sources they could have discovered the name of the holding company Xavier had established only recently. That was another surprise in itself, which kept several questions running through my mind including why.

Sergio headed toward me and from where I was standing, it was obvious to tell his jaw clenched. When he got to within two feet, he removed his sunglasses.

"And?" I asked as I scanned the docks.

"The switch was handled, but we're going to pay a fine. Neither port is happy with the last-minute decision."

I chuckled. "As if I could give a shit. Are our employees there to accept the cargo?"

"They're there." He looked away, his disdain continuing.

"What's bothering you, Sergio?"

He exhaled, keeping his eye on the water. "I still don't like this."

"What is the word on the street?" I had to figure out if I had a larger leak as well as what Ortiz thought he could gain by contacting me.

"It's quiet, which is also fucking unnerving."

"Where is the informant?"

"He's being brought here. My men found him attempting to flee the city. What do you want to do with him?"

"Set an example."

He eyed me carefully before nodding. "And Ortiz?"

"If he shows up with his troops and causes trouble, then he will be executed. If not, then we'll talk."

His brusque laugh was to be expected. "You've never cared to talk to anyone before. Why now?"

"Because I believe there is another player attempting to move in."

"You're worried about the recent alliance with DeMill?"

"For one thing." I wasn't going to provide any details. There were too many balls in the air, important and very lucrative contracts on the table. If there was any hint of impropriety, then those contracts would disappear. While there'd always been questions regarding the legitimacy of the Santos organization, the fact our movie production company made several people millionaires had allowed directors, artists, and attorneys to look the other way. And my brother's creative methods of offering financing had drawn in the most sought-after material. I had to admit the man had been an excellent attorney, using gray areas to accomplish his tasks.

And his stranglehold on dozens of influential people had allowed the Santos family to destroy their more common enemies. It would seem investing in Hollywood had continued to be fashionable, even if Tinsel Town had taken a hit after the dozens of flops and actors behaving badly over the decades. It had been the perfect place to launder money in the beginning. Now there was little need, although my father had maintained a stronghold on everyone under his thumb at the threat of blackmail, which had enabled him to amass a fortune.

Could a man like Luis Ortiz desire to get into the industry? I doubted it. This was about something much bigger.

As Sergio's phone buzzed, I took a deep breath. Time for the show.

"The traitor is in the warehouse," my soldier said after checking his screen.

"Then it's time to see if we can help the informant talk. What's his name?"

"Juan Delgado."

I noticed a strange inflection in his voice and turned my head. "What's his story?"

"Low-level dealer who ended up VP of another smaller cartel. Two-timing fuckhead. He should never have been trusted. I don't give a shit that he's been providing basic information for years."

"Why the turn?" Sergio was more agitated than usual.

Sergio snorted. "Why do any of them become a traitor? Money. Someone is paying him to snitch."

"Money isn't always the motivator, Sergio. Often, it's about position or threats."

I could tell he was studying me carefully as we headed for the warehouse, two soldiers guarding the entrance. Before walking in, I took another look around the dock. "Any sign of the port patrol?"

"None, but they patrol like clockwork. We have forty-five minutes."

"Enough time. When we're finished, hang his body in the Angels' territory. I want to ensure they know I won't tolerate this kind of behavior."

"You're using your words carefully today, *El Jefe*. That's unlike you."

"Perhaps I'm turning over a new leaf."

While he laughed, he continued to watch me. I headed inside, uncertain what I'd find. Juan was on his knees, blood from being beaten soaking his muscle shirt. When he heard footsteps, he lifted his head and almost immediately he began to blubber.

"I didn't mean to, Mr. Santos. I had no choice. They threatened me. My family. My mother." His accent was broken, his words difficult to decipher. And the wild look in his eyes meant he was desperate.

As I removed the knife I'd brought, his eyes opened wider, his stench assaulted my senses. Even in my position, I'd seen men fall apart under interrogation, some who'd been tortured by whatever cartel they'd hooked themselves up with. I'd also witnessed the effects of retaliation, men's tongues removed in an effort to prevent them from talking. Dragging them from the pits of whatever hell they'd been placed in had been difficult for the Chilean authorities. The fact Juan had been captured so easily disturbed me almost as much as my gut telling me this was nothing but a power grab and had nothing to do with illegal substances.

"Please, *señor*. Please. I only told them about the shipment. Nothing more." His chest was heaving, spittle rolling down his chin.

"Who?" When he didn't answer, I kicked him over, waiting as the two soldiers righted him. "One last time. Who?"

"*Señor* Ortiz."

At least he'd confirmed my beliefs, but I did notice he had difficulty looking me in the eye. "What was the point?"

Now he seemed confused. "I do not understand." His blubbering continued.

"The amount means nothing more than pittance on the street." Why did it seem like Sergio was getting antsy?

"I… I do not know."

As my brother would do, I backhanded Juan. As soon as he slumped, two soldiers grabbed his arms, jerking him back into position once again. This was getting old and of little value. I shoved the point of the knife under his chin.

"What would Ortiz gain out of this?"

"Please, *señor*. I do not know. Soldiers raped my wife in front of me. She was pregnant with our third child. She miscarried. I didn't know what else to do. I swear to God. Please."

Juan had been used as an emissary more than anything. While I should follow through with my original plans, it would serve no purpose but to leave a grieving wife and two orphaned children. I backed away, shoving the knife into my pocket.

"What are you doing?" Sergio growled.

"A change of plans. Where are your wife and children being held?"

"They are prisoners in our home."

The cartels were some of the most brutal in the world. They couldn't care less about the sanctity of women and children and that disgusted me. Inhaling, I shook my head.

One of the soldiers keeping guard bolted inside, immediately heading in my direction. "What is it?" I asked.

"DEA is searching the warehouses," he answered. "They're close."

Sergio hissed. "How the hell did they track us down?"

"That's a very good question." I glanced into his eyes. There'd been no way Walker had been able to follow me. He had been attempting to warn me. My earlier decision to move the shipment was proving to be vital.

"New orders. Secure Juan's family and get them to a safe-house to recuperate," I commanded, shifting my angry gaze from one soldier to another.

"What the fuck?" Sergio snarled.

I turned slowly, cocking my head. He of all people should know what it felt like to be strung up and tortured by a man like Ortiz. "Do not question my orders, Sergio, or I assure you that you'll have difficulty writing your own name ever again." The sound of my phone only further infuriated me. When I pulled it into my hand, I almost laughed.

Ortiz.

If I had to guess, and my instincts were never wrong, the cat and mouse game the asshole was playing would continue. It would also guess he'd realized the DEA were in motion.

"Keep him here until I finish other business." I walked out of the warehouse, glancing at the water. "Ortiz. I expected to see your face."

"Do you think I'm a fool, Santos?" he asked as he laughed. "While you chose to move your shipment, I have eyes and ears everywhere. Did you call the DEA yourself? Are you a snitch now?"

"That's a strange statement coming from a man who uses them regularly."

"Fuck you and whatever game you're playing," he snapped.

"It would seem you're playing a game, gunning important people down in a church."

The man hesitated, which surprised me. "That's not my style."

Exhaling, I refused to turn my back on the entrance to the warehouse. "You can have the shipment, Ortiz. I couldn't care less." Tossing him a bone could prove to force his hand. If I played things the right way. He said nothing for a few seconds.

"I find that curious, Santos. Why the change of heart?'

"My interests lie in other areas. Now I am curious. Why bother contacting me?"

"It would seem your reputation has preceded you. You are stronger than I'd anticipated. However, you should be careful who you place your trust in."

His cryptic message held a specific meaning. "And who are you referring to?"

"Those closest to you. Doesn't everyone have a price?"

"Yes, they do, which is why you're going to release your informant's wife and children."

He laughed. "The little pissant means nothing to me. He merely drew you out of your shell, heir Santos."

What the hell was he referring to? Whatever it was, I didn't like his tone or the sound of it. My reputation? My brother's? Something was off. "I may be the Butcher, but I do not allow harming women and children or using them as bait. You will release them, or you'll find my wrath is much more formidable than you've heard."

He hesitated, which meant he wanted something more out of the conversation. "On one condition."

"I'm not in the habit of making deals with anyone."

"Understood, Santos, but you're also in no position not to hear me out. I want permanent access to the United States, but I find myself embroiled in a busy highway."

"So you need my help."

"I don't usually ask for any assistance, but given you're in the mood to exact revenge, I thought we could work together."

"What are you proposing?"

"An alliance."

His suggestion was interesting. "Go on."

As he proposed the terms of yet another unholy deal, I was only vaguely interested.

Not in working with a piece of slime like Ortiz, but in the information he could provide.

"Once I know the woman and children have been released, you and I will formalize our coalition."

He laughed. "You are much more formidable than I originally gave you credit for. It will be done within the hour."

I ended the call. There was no need for sentiments. As I thought about what should be done, the full realization of how far the betrayal had gone inside the Santos world was beginning to unravel.

I returned to the warehouse, easing my weapon into my hand. As I approached the other soldiers, I made certain each one made eye contact. "Juan, you will provide the address of where your family is being held. Marco, Anton, make certain that occurs and once it does, let me know."

"What are you doing?" Sergio asked.

"Handling business. I do not tolerate traitors." I pressed the barrel of the weapon against Juan's temple.

"Oh, please. Please, *señor*. Do not kill me," he pleaded.

"You've been given a second chance; redemption is not something I provide often. Take your family far away from here and do not return. Do you understand?"

His eyes opened wide as they'd done before, but in them was gratitude. "Yes, *señor*. Thank you. Oh, thank you."

Sergio hissed but kept his mouth shut.

"You can thank me by getting a real job. If I see or hear of you in California, I will hunt you down and I assure you that you will not get off so easily again. Get him out of my sight." I waited as Juan was dragged away before turning toward Sergio. "Get the soldiers out of here. Handle the shipment out of San Diego but put the contents on ice."

"The buyers will be pissed."

"They can wait."

He nodded. "I'll take care of it."

Whether or not Sergio was dirty would be learned soon enough.

I headed toward Stone next. "Have you had time to make the inquiries I requested?"

"Some, sir, but it will take time. Nothing of interest as of yet."

"Keep searching. I also need you to hack into the DEA. Is that within your skillset?"

His eyes lit up like a kid at Christmas. "You bet I can."

"Then find out what they have on a man named Dante Fernandez. If the information I was provided is true, he's a doppelganger the DEA could be using against me."

"Any idea why?"

"None."

"That should be easy unless they've classified it. Then that might take some additional time."

"Until you find answers, that's all you're going to be working on."

At least he was smart enough not to second guess me. As I headed toward the exit, I realized the risk I was taking, but it had to be done. Ortiz had a hidden agenda of his own. That wouldn't be allowed.

After this weekend, things would begin to escalate. I knew exactly who I could trust.

And the realization haunted me.

CHAPTER 19

arina

A monster.

I'd bedded a monster.

The thought sickened me. And to think I was almost falling hard for the man. The pictures had been so graphic, so horrific that I couldn't stand the thought of being in the same room with him. How was I going to fake enjoying going to this premiere?

I couldn't do it. I just couldn't.

I'd paced the floor for over an hour, wringing my hands, unable to get the wretched images out of my mind. How could anyone do that to women and children? I'd thought Diego was a brutal savage, but he was heinous and inhuman. No. Who was who any longer? I wasn't even certain of my own name. I laughed almost maniacally. I was supposed to be getting ready for the premiere and all I could think about was how I'd allowed myself to fall into such a web of deceit. What did Diego want with me?

No, he's not Diego.

Was that really the truth?

Nothing made sense any longer.

It suddenly dawned on me that I couldn't stay here any longer. I knew Vitoro was standing just outside the door of Diego's sleek, modern house high on a cliff overlooking the ocean with at least two others manning the perimeter. Whereas the house in San Diego was comfortable and inviting, this location was stark in comparison, businesslike. It wasn't a place I could consider living.

What was I thinking?

I grabbed my phone and headed for the bedroom where the suitcase I'd brought had been dumped by Vitoro. Before I managed to jog up the stairs, it rang. As I stared at the screen, a series of flutters drifted into my system.

Unknown caller.

Should I answer it? I almost laughed at my sudden hesitation. I'd never acted this way before.

Then you weren't married to a heinous beast.

That was true enough.

"Hello?" I leaned against the stairwell, my heart racing.

"Stop asking questions or Mia will die."

The statement was stark, cold, the voice a deep baritone. And they terrified me. "Who are you?"

I didn't need to look at the screen to know the call had ended, but I did. For a few seconds, I was dragged into a vacuum, trying to process the warning. Ask questions about Diego? Undaunted by fear, I hit 'call.' Almost immediately I heard the beep indicating the call couldn't be completed.

Or that the number had been disconnected. The asshole had used a burner phone. I had to get Mia out of the country. My hand still shaking, I dialed her number, her voicemail connecting almost immediately. No. No. That meant she'd either turned her phone off or something drastic and terrible had happened.

I had to get to her.

How?

I had no method of transportation.

Unless I hijacked one of the vehicles. That's exactly what I would do. But how, without a weapon? I closed my eyes and realized the only way I'd be able to do this was by an element of surprise.

And blunt force.

I scampered down the stairs, searching the rooms for anything heavy and small enough to use. Then I noticed an Academy Award on one of Diego's bookshelves. The irony was far too sweet to ignore. I grabbed it in haste, taking long strides to the front door. Then I eased the door open, peering out.

Vitoro appeared within seconds, narrowing his eyes as he swept his gaze down the length of me. "Is there an issue, Mrs. Santos?"

Hearing my married name gave me another series of chills. I stepped further outside, plastering on a smile. "I was wondering if you're heard from Diego."

"He should be back in a few minutes. Is everything alright inside?"

Exhaling, I shifted my hips, trying to throw him off guard. "Yes, I'm fine. It's just…" I took a hard swing, smashing him against the side of the head. He staggered backward, dropping like a rock. Seeing blood from the gash, I cringed, but it had to be done. I tossed the award aside, dropping to my knees and searching for keys to the SUV. I found them easily enough, scrambling to get to the vehicle before he came to his senses.

Once inside, I couldn't seem to stop shaking, almost dropping the keys before managing to slide the cold piece of metal into the ignition. As the SUV fired up, I took a deep breath, not wasting any time before slamming the gear into drive, skittering around the fountain just seconds before Vitoro began to race after me. The driveway was long and winding, and I floored it, screeching around the curves. I noticed one of the soldiers out of the corner of my eye racing toward me.

Thank God I rounded a corner, preventing him from shooting out one of the tires.

It seemed like minutes instead of seconds that passed, my thudding heartbeat echoing in my ears. As I rounded the last corner, a sense of freedom rushed through me.

Until a car turned onto the driveway and I was forced to slam on my brakes. Oh, no. Diego was driving. He stared at me through his windshield, cocking his head in his usual far too intoxicatingly handsome fashion. I was momentarily at a loss for words. Then I reacted like prey being cornered, flinging open the door to the SUV and fleeing.

I should have known better than to try to get away from him. Within seconds, he snagged my wrist, twirling me backward and against him. When he cupped the back of my head, I gasped, smacking my palms against him.

"It would seem you and a statue had a disagreement," he said casually, as if my attempt to run away was hysterical. How could the man have twinkling eyes when there was so much violence in his past?

"I have to get away from you." Even though I said the words, I was struck by the tenderness in his eyes. As if he had no idea why I'd tried to run. The same burning attraction was there, the same need that had grabbed me by the throat, refusing to let me go. I didn't want what I'd seen to be true. How was it possible? And why had he lied to me the entire time?

"And why do you feel the need at this point?"

"Because you're not who you say you are." I pushed hard against him, doing everything I could to try to get away. "You're hiding secrets."

"Aren't we all?"

"No!"

"Then who am I, Carina? Just who do you really think I am?"

"Dante Santos, firstborn son of Xavier Santos, heir to the empire of the damned." As soon as I issued the words, he took a deep breath, his entire expression changing. It was as if all time stood still for just a few seconds. There was nothing but the sound of my rapidly beating heart. "Where the hell did you get that information?" He asked the question so quietly and devoid of all emotion that I was thrown.

"So, it's true?" I asked, unable to sound demanding. I hadn't really wanted to believe it, fearing that if it was true, the small sense of happiness I'd found with Diego would come crashing down. Now I wasn't certain I could feel anything. However, the pictures sent to Mia would forever haunt me.

"It's complicated, Carina."

"Complicated? Since when do you call assuming someone else's identity complicated? Is the real Diego dead? Did you kill him?" Anger was starting to bubble, but even worse was the heavy heart I felt. When he reached for me, I backed away.

He didn't follow, but he remained studying me, his eyes piercing mine, and I'd never felt so unnerved. When he didn't say anything else, all the intense rollercoaster of emotions I'd felt the last few weeks came crashing down. I was livid and so sad that I couldn't stop tears from forming.

"You know? I thought Diego was a horrible beast, but you're even worse. How could you do that?"

"What are you talking about?"

I lifted my phone, pulling up the pictures Mia had texted me. He hesitated before lowering his gaze. Then he walked closer, jerking the phone from my hand, anger sweeping his face. His entire face was pinched, his breathing ragged. Mike had sent an actual bulletin almost like a most wanted list with Dante's name attached. I still couldn't think clearly.

"There's more," I said, unable to take my eyes off him.

The range of emotions in him was confusing. He was genuinely shocked by the horrible photographs that had been caught by a drone. I couldn't bear to look at them again; the brutality and amount of bloodshed was indescribable.

"Where did you get these?" he asked, more calmly than I thought he would. While I'd questioned myself about telling him anything since the beginning, the man standing in front of me couldn't have slaughtered so many people.

"I asked my sister for help given my suspicions. She has a friend in the FBI who sent those to her. Is that you?"

Diego took a deep breath as he walked closer, lifting my chin with a single finger. "No, Carina. The person in the picture is not me."

"Not you, Diego or not you, Dante? And why would the FBI have it if it wasn't you?"

He closed and rubbed his eyes as he handed me back the phone. "We need to talk."

I had to trust him, but I wasn't certain I could trust myself or my instincts at this point. "Tell me now."

"No. What I have to say needs to be in private."

"We're out in the middle of nowhere. Who do you think is going to hear us?" I shuddered, thinking about the threatening call. "What's going on, Diego? I don't even know what to call you. Why did you lie to me? Why? I just had a phone call. The man threatened to kill my sister." I wiped away the tears, furious at myself for feeling such angst.

His eyes opened wide. "Who called you?" His growl returned, his chest rising and falling. It was the same look I'd seen every time he played my protector.

I wanted to have him hold me, but I couldn't make sense of anything.

"The call was from an unknown sender, but I will never forget his voice. It was ominous."

"How the fuck did he get your number?" he muttered, more to himself. Why did it seem like he knew the identity of the man who'd threatened me?

"He could have gotten it anywhere. I never had to hide my phone number before being involved with you." I couldn't help but laugh, although the sound was ugly, and my heart continued to ache. What was I doing? He would never tell me the truth. Why should he?

"Goddamn. You're going to need to trust me, Carina."

I finally jerked out of his hold, shaking my head. "You're out of your mind. I don't even know who you are, not really. Is this a game? Some kind of crazy twisted mind fuck to eradicate your enemies?"

"As I said, we'll talk once we're in a safe place."

"Is there such a thing?"

"I need to know what you were told."

I debated sharing anything with him but as crazy as it sounded, he was the only person who I thought I could trust. "That if I kept asking questions, Mia would die."

Hissing, he cursed under his breath in Spanish. "I promise you that I will protect her."

"How are you going to do that?"

"Contact her."

"I tried." There was so much exasperation in my voice that I was breathless. "I can't get in touch with her. I'm terrified. She doesn't deserve this."

"Call her again."

He never blinked, but the twitch in the corner of his mouth was out of rage. Nodding, my hand was shaking as I dialed her number.

"Are you okay?" she asked, answering immediately.

"I'm fine. Did anything happen?"

"No, why?"

I glanced at Diego, a cold shiver trickling down my spine. "I was just checking. You're leaving at what time day after tomorrow?"

"I leave around eight for the airport," she told me.

"Eight. Okay. We'll talk before then. Just be careful, Mia. Okay?"

"Have you confronted him?"

There was no denying the way I felt about him, the need that I couldn't ignore. "I'm just about to."

"Do you believe the photographs?"

Her question rang in my ears. "No. He couldn't have done those things. That's not the man I know."

"Please be careful, Carina," she whispered.

"I will." I ended the call, pressing it against my cheek. Did I believe he could perform such horrible atrocities? No. The man who'd protected me, saving my life couldn't have done such terrible things.

"I'll have some of my soldiers ensure she gets to the airport. They'll stay with her," he told me.

It was madness what he needed to do, but I was grateful. "What is going on?"

Before he had a chance to answer, one of the soldiers I'd passed raced down the driveway toward us, stopping short when he noticed Diego had returned.

"I'm sorry, *El Jefe*. She appeared out of nowhere."

"Don't worry about it. Take the SUV back to the house. I'll bring her with me," Diego told him.

"Yes, sir."

I folded my arms, backing away, my stomach in knots. I wasn't going anywhere with him until he confided in me.

Diego shook his head, taking long strides in my direction. "Come, Carina. We have a lot to discuss."

"Just tell me one thing before we leave. Are you Dante Santos?"

He exhaled then nodded. I'd never felt such an odd sense of relief in learning the truth.

"That changes everything," I whispered, my heart in my throat.

"Not the way I feel about you."

"You don't know me at all."

"I know the woman I met outside her father's home. She was spunky and quick to challenge, a girl who caught me off guard to the point I couldn't breathe."

His words were so heartfelt that I lifted my head, studying his eyes. "Really?"

"Yes, really. I wasn't expecting you, Carina." The moment he brushed the tips of his fingers down my arm, several emotions hit me hard. I pressed my hand against his chest, longing to feel his skin against my fingertips. "You were nothing I wanted yet everything I didn't know I needed.

You belong to me, not to the man who had no intention of caring about you."

"Then don't lie to me again," I whispered, realizing that I'd fallen hopelessly in love with him.

Whoever he was.

* * *

He remained almost entirely silent after grabbing a few items, tossing them into his car then giving his soldiers instructions not to follow. He continuously glanced into the rearview mirror, remaining angry from what I'd told him.

"You promise Mia will be safe?" I knew he'd made phone calls, ensuring she would have someone with her at all times, but I was still terrified something would happen to her.

"I promise you on my life that she will remain unharmed."

"Where are we headed?" I asked.

"Somewhere safe."

"I hope you're right."

I noticed his hands were firmly wrapped around the steering wheel, the setting sun highlighting his white knuckles. I sensed he wasn't ready to talk, but I couldn't take the anxiety of not knowing what was really going on.

"If that isn't you in those photographs, is it the real Diego?"

He shifted but said nothing at first. Then he shook his head. "I don't know who it is but someone is out to use me in a war that isn't my own, at least not in the way you're thinking."

"I don't understand what you mean and don't tell me it's complicated. What war?"

"Between my father and a man by the name of Luis Ortiz."

"I've heard of the name. He runs some Mexican cartel. Right?"

"Yes. He's proposed an alliance in order to block other cartels from entering California."

"So all this is about drugs?"

As he shook his head, I noticed he was headed to one of the marinas.

"But your family sells illegal drugs," I continued.

"Xavier Santos made his fortune by selling heroin and cocaine." He parked the car, glancing in the mirror for the sixth time.

That much had been alluded to in newspapers. "Does our marriage have anything to do with what you're doing here or with this war?"

Chuckling, he glanced over at me as he parked the car. "That's something I intend on finding out. We're going to a house I rented in Catalina. Then I'm going to find answers."

"Catalina?"

"A location no one knows about. The boat is chartered, untraceable."

"Do you think whoever threatened me is responsible for the attack at the church?"

"Yes." He was deep in thought, obviously trying to figure out what was going on.

As he climbed out, I noticed his weapon and shuddered.

I was right before. We would never be safe.

He grabbed the two bags, keeping his hand pressed against the small of my back as he guided me toward the waiting yacht. As he led me down the few steps to the main cabin, I couldn't seem to stop shaking.

"I'm going to talk to the captain. Then we'll talk."

Nodding, I watched him leave then moved toward one of the windows, staring out at the ocean. All I could think about was whether our marriage would remain legal. How ridiculous.

Yet I closed my eyes, falling into the memories of how incredible being with him had felt, even if daydreaming wasn't going to change anything.

I sensed his presence not long after, the same quivers that I always felt when he was around tickling my skin. I didn't bother turning around, able to see his reflection in the glistening window. He approached as he usually did, every step he took with practiced determination. Had everything he'd done, every action been just as proficiently trained?

"Was anything real between us?" I placed my hand on the glass, spreading my fingers.

He waited to answer until he was directly behind me. As he moved my long strands aside, I bit my lower lip to keep from making a single noise, unable to keep from moaning as his heated breath skipped across my skin. Then he slowly lowered the strap on my dress, exposing my naked shoulder.

Some part of me knew I should push his fingers away, but the warmth and roar of passion was the reminder I needed that what we'd shared couldn't be faked. Then as he lowered his head, rolling his lips along the nape of my neck, dragging his tongue across my shoulder blade, I couldn't stop from whimpering.

"Everything between us was very real, Carina. And perfect. I didn't intend on falling in love with you."

I cocked my head, my pulse racing. "You're in love with me."

"There is no denying what we share, although it's not safe for you to be around me. However, I won't leave you alone. Never again. You are mine, Carina, whether you want to accept it or not."

His dominance that had angered me from the beginning was just another blanket of warmth, a promise of safety and love that came along rarely in our worlds. Money and power always seemed to get in the way. I reached over my shoulder, brushing my fingers against his face and the slight touch seared my skin. Now I wanted nothing more than to have his hands all over me, singeing every inch.

He bit down on my neck, the hint of pain creating a wave of heat between my legs. My core had been ignited the first time he touched me. Dante.

I turned around, lifting my chin. "Dante. Oh, Dante. Tell me you love me."

The way his eyes flashed gave me a sense of what he was thinking, but there was something even more possessive about his touch, as if he would never let me go. "I love you, Carina."

"Please tell me what happened."

I was terrified to hear the story, knowing that whatever had separated the twins as little boys was traumatic, but I hadn't been prepared for just how much so.

As soon as he finished, a single tear slipped down my cheek. What his mother had been forced to endure was repulsive.

He wiped it away with his thumb, gently easing it into his mouth. The action was sweet yet sensual and I'd been so sad in my life. "I'm so sorry."

"There is much more to the story, and I will tell you everything. That much I promise you, but I need to be certain about what my gut is telling me. You cannot tell anyone what I just told you."

"You're scaring me."

"I'm not trying to, but my intentions have taken a difficult turn. Nothing is what it seems."

While all I wanted to do was pepper him with questions, there were so many things haunting him that I was lost in thoughts, fearful that the glass house we'd both been shoved into would be shattered. I cupped his face, the feel of two-day stubble tickling the ends of my fingers. "Whatever you tell me, I'll understand."

"I doubt it." He lowered his head, his lips only a few centimeters from mine. "You're nothing that I expected, the only thing that matters, but things have gone too far."

"What does that mean?"

"It means what we've shared will be challenged."

"By Diego?"

His deep exhale was just as troubling as the look in his dark eyes. "By many. What I was and what I am now are entirely different. So much so, I'm no longer certain who I am any longer."

"You're a strong, honest man who managed to get himself caught up in a nightmare. Don't lose the man inside, the one who made love to me. The one who allowed me to feel free and beautiful for the first time in my life."

His chest rose and fell as he shifted his gaze up and down. Then he captured my mouth, gripping my face with the kind of pressure that told me just how explosive the situation had become. But I fell into his arms, his warm and passionate hold as I'd done before, fighting the demons clawing at the surface. I refused to give up on what I knew was the best thing that had happened in my life.

He held our lips together for several seconds before slipping his tongue inside. The sweetness of his hold became more possessive as the kiss roared of the excitement we'd always shared. I felt safe in his arms, loved even if I didn't know who he really was. What I did know is that I couldn't imagine spending a minute of my life without him.

I wrapped my arm around his neck, tangling my fingers in his hair, arching my back as soon as he shifted his hand to the back of my neck. His hold was dominating, telling me in no uncertain terms that I belonged to him. I was breathless, my mind spinning, the feel of his hard body pressed against mine shoving aside all the fears.

If only for a few precious minutes.

A growl erupted from deep within his throat, spilling past our lips. He swept his tongue back and forth, drinking in our combined essence. His scent fueled me, pulling me deeper into a madness I never wanted to surface from. Stars floated in front of my eyes, every one of them vibrant in color. As the fear faded into the black realm of reality, the love I felt for him continued to increase. There was no rhyme or reason, just an innate acceptance that I was his. Not just for now, but forever.

He pulled away slightly, nipping my bottom lip before sucking on my tongue. Moans escaped my lips as I ground my hips back and forth, my insane need for him growing. Panting, I pushed away, jerking on his belt, laughing softly as his eyes dilated, shimmering in the last sparkle of fading sun.

He wasted no time, yanking my dress up past my hips, shoving my panties aside. The second he flicked his finger back and forth across my clit, I couldn't stop moaning. I was on fire, the need to have him inside exploding like fire-crackers.

"I want you," I whispered, no longer recognizing my voice.

"I need you. I will take you." His words were like dynamite in my mind, setting off another series of explosions.

I spread my legs, panting as he shoved his finger inside, my pussy muscles immediately clamping around his long digit. I could no longer focus as I struggled with his belt, finally jerking it free then fighting with the zipper. A laugh bubbled to the surface as my breathing became more rapid, every muscle in my body tingling. When I was finally able to free his cock, I threw my head back, issuing a series of husky whimpers.

Growling several times, he dragged his tongue from one side of my jaw to the other, biting down on my lip until I yelped from the slice of pain. I stroked his shaft, rolling my fingers up and down, twisting them until I created friction. Every sound he made was a sweet reward.

"You're my bad girl," he muttered.

"Yes."

"You need to be spanked."

Swallowing, all I could do was nod. The crazy intimacy of what we were doing felt out in the open. I should be embarrassed by our intense needs, but the excitement was too intense.

The look in his eyes was carnal as he took a step away, spinning me around. Then he placed one of my hands on the glass then the other before sliding his fingers around the thin elastic of my thong, snapping his wrist and freeing me of the colorful lace. He held my panties to the side, laughing softly. His reflection allowed me to see everything he did as he brought the wet lace to his nose, drinking in my feminine wiles.

"So wet. So damn hot," he muttered. "Open your mouth, naughty girl."

I did as he commanded and the moment he shoved my panties against my tongue, my legs started to quake. This was filthy and amazing, my hunger only increasing. As he yanked my hips, pulling me backwards, I couldn't stop from moaning.

Then he brought his hand down, the hard cracking sound as his palm connected with my skin tingling every one of my senses.

"I will spank you every day just to remind you that you belong to me."

He smacked both sides several times, allowing a rush of adrenaline to sweep thought every cell. When he delivered six in rapid succession, I was lightheaded. As he brought his hand down four more times, every smack harder than the one before, the force increased the elation. I was skittering toward a surreal moment, my pussy juice already staining the insides of my thighs.

"Are you wet for me?"

"Mmm…"

"Are you hungry to have my cock shoved inside?"

All I could do was nod vigorously. The rocking of the boat added to the beautiful round of passion. He laughed softly then shoved his hand between my legs, pressing his palm into my wetness. I was mad with need, bucking against his hand as he rubbed up and down.

He swirled his fingers around my clit, pinching several times before shoving all four fingers inside. I dropped my head, taking shallow breaths, the pleasure driving me toward an orgasm. Then he backed off, continuing the spanking in earnest, smacking his palm against one side of my bottom then the other. The heat continued to build, the pain morphing into the kind of raw bliss that drove me closer to ecstasy.

"Yes, a spanking every day. And you will never wear panties again. I need to have you hot and wet, ready for me at all times." He cracked his hand down four times then drove his fingers back inside, pumping hard and fast.

Everything became a beautiful blur, the world around us fading into the sunset. I met every hard thrust, rolling onto my toes, unable to keep from climaxing. I threw my head back, my scream muffled, my muscles clamped around the thick invasion. I couldn't stop shaking, a single orgasm morphing into a beautiful wave, leaving my mind in a foggy state.

"Yes. Keep coming." He refused to stop, his actions pushing me to the point I was bucking against him.

Only when I finished shaking did he rub his fingers across my aching bottom. Then without hesitation, he drove the entire length of his cock deep inside.

I threw my head back again, trying to catch my breath as his cock swelled. He yanked the panties from my mouth, tossing them aside, nuzzling his face into my neck.

"I could feast on you for days."

His words added gasoline to the fire. I kept my hand planted on the glass, my heated breath fogging the surface. When he plunged into me again, the force drove me against the wooden rail. I spread my legs as wide open as possible, arching my back. He started fucking me like a crazed man, his hunger never satisfied. The entire room seemed to be spinning, my heart thudding in the same beat he was using to fuck me.

Nothing seemed real any longer, only the two of us mattering. The world could fade away and I wouldn't care. He was a beast, thrusting hard and fast, rolling onto the balls of his feet. The shift in the angle created another series of vibrations dancing down the back of my legs.

"Yes. Yes…" My moans were muffled by his husky growls, the sound unlike any he'd made before.

All I could think about was having his cock inside my mouth, his sweet cum spilling down the back of my throat. I wanted to crawl to him, licking his legs, slathering my tongue across his balls. And I wanted to languish in bed for hours, exploring until we were both finally sated.

If that was even possible.

He refused to stop, his fingers digging into my skin, his grip like a tight vise. As he dragged his tongue down the side of my neck, I couldn't seem to stop moaning. Then his whisper created another firestorm of need. "Now, I fuck you in that tight little ass of yours."

His scattered laugh continued to sizzle every nerve and as he eased his cock from my pussy, I whimpered, licking my dry lips in anticipation. The moment he pressed his cock-head against my dark hole, I pushed hard against the window. I craved the hint of anguish to make me feel alive all over again. I never wanted this to end, even though the thought of facing danger loomed in the back of my mind.

He pressed an inch inside, then another before sliding his arms around me, cupping and squeezing my breasts. His breathing scattered, he lowered his head, pressing kisses against the side of my neck before thrusting the final few inches inside.

The pain was instant, like a bolt of lightning, my muscles clamping down hard. I moaned from the discomfort but within seconds, pleasure exploded from deep within, creating another wave of unfathomable desire. He pinched my nipples through the thin fabric, twisting them painfully as he fucked me.

Every sound he made was guttural, his deep baritone creating wave after wave of vibrations. Then he pounded into me, taking all he wanted, every muscle in his body tense. Panting, I kept my eyes closing, willing the rest of the world away.

We were as one, two people who never should have been together but unable to imagine being apart.

He thrust long and hard, pushing us both to the point of no return. I sensed the moment he couldn't hold back and longer and clamped down on my muscles. As he threw his head back and roared, he erupted deep inside and for once in my life, I felt whole.

I scratched my nails down the window before drawing two hearts. He was everything to me and I would fight to keep us together.

No matter what we had to face.

CHAPTER 20

 iego

Time.

It wasn't in our favor, but for the few minutes we'd both been allowed to leave the madness of what we'd be facing behind, we became even closer. We weren't supposed to be together, but I would never allow anyone to break us apart. Carina had become too special to me.

I wrapped my arms around her, bringing her heated body against mine. There were many obstacles to face, the danger increasing every hour. I could feel it in my bones.

"You need to tell me about Diego."

I brushed her hair from her neck and thought about what I could tell her. "He's alive."

"Does that mean you plan on killing him?" Carina pressed.

"That means he's another victim of our father's vicious plan." As I pulled away, losing the touch of her skin sent a cold shiver through me. I adjusted my clothing, my gaze falling to her torn panties. Being inside of her had felt different, the longing continuing. As the sound of my phone ringing drifted into the room, I tensed. My phone. Everything I was wearing, the wallet I carried, and the phone buzzing in the pocket of my expensive trousers all belonged to my brother.

I watched as she adjusted her dress, walking to the other side of the cabin even before I answered the call. The number popped up as the Brotherhood and I hesitated before answering. "Santos."

"I don't know what the fuck you're in the middle of, but there's a contract on your life."

The accent alone allowed me to know who was calling. "What the hell are you talking about, Maxim?"

"Have you been fucking with Ortiz?"

"I've had a conversation with the man. Why?" I could tell by the tenseness in his tone that he was serious. I kept my eyes peeled on the ocean, my gut telling me the end game was close to playing out.

"Well, apparently, he's not too happy with whatever you talked about. My people tell me you'll be dead by nightfall."

Every muscle constricted. "Trustworthy sources?"

"Would I be calling you otherwise? Whatever the hell you're doing, your entire empire is about to go down. Did you have a shipment docked in San Diego?"

I jerked my weapon into my hand, moving toward the door leading to the deck. Why the hell should I tell the man anything? At this point, I had to learn to trust someone else. "Yeah. Why?"

"It's about to be taken."

That meant one thing. Sergio had betrayed me. "Why are you bothering?"

He snorted. "Because we're a damn brotherhood. Where the fuck are you? You need assistance and I'm the only man who can identify Ortiz's men."

"Where are you going?" Carina asked as I opened the door leading to the deck.

"Stay here. No matter what happens, promise me you will not move." I glared at her, shaking my head.

She shivered visibly but nodded. "Be careful."

Reaching out, I ran my fingers across her shimmering face then headed out the door. "Headed to Catalina."

"I need to talk to you. I'm still in LA."

His command was gruff. "Fine. There's a bar called Vintage near the shore on the east side. I'll meet you there in an hour."

"I'm not sure you have that long."

Laughing, I shifted toward the railing, scanning the horizon. "You underestimate me, Maxim."

"I don't know you, brother. There's one thing I do know for certain. You're not Diego Santos."

"You might be surprised." I noticed boats in the distance and bristled. The way they were churning up the waters, I had no doubt they were speedboats.

"Nothing surprises me."

As the two vessels came closer, I had no doubt they were headed in a collision course. "We may never know. It looks like disaster is headed right for me." I ended the call, shoving the phone in my pocket and holding the weapon in both hands.

"What is happening?"

The sound of Carina's voice horrified me. "Get out of here. Go below and find a place to hide."

"I'm not going anywhere."

"Do it, Carina." The boats had come dangerously close, and I raised my arms, aiming and taking several shots in a row.

"What are you doing?" she exclaimed.

"Get out of here!" All time seemed to stand still as the vessels continued their collision course. I fired off another six shots, the small explosion on one of the boats unable to stop their devastating approach. I had to make a choice. Save her life or attempt to stop them. In a split-second decision, I jammed my weapon into my pocket seconds before sprinting toward her. The vibrations from their high-speed approach could be felt in every muscle in my body. I grabbed her by the arm, yanking her against my body as I lunged toward the edge of the boat.

Just as one of the assassins' boats collided with the yacht, I pitched us both overboard, the explosion of the impact jetting us forward by several yards.

As we plummeted into the water, my fingers slipped from her arm. The blunt force of the water as it smacked against me was powerful, a second explosion rocking me forward until I was spinning under the water, fighting to determine the location of the surface. An explosive boom rocketed below the surface, and I lost all sense of direction. All I could think about was saving her.

I fought my way to the surface, gasping for air as I spun in a full circle. Debris was everywhere, the yacht listing to the side. Frantic, I thrashed through the water, unable to see her. No. This couldn't be happening. I dove under the water, kicking out as I raked my arms through the water. "Carina!"

Everything remained a blur, but I was able to see one of the boats had veered away from the crash site, swerving around to make another pass. The boat that had slammed into the yacht was broken apart, a body floating face down near the broken-apart hull. I swam toward it, rolling him over. The bastard was dead, sacrificing himself like a good little soldier.

"Carina!" My call was muffled by the massive fire. I refused to allow her to die. I'd done this. Her life had been placed in jeopardy because of a vendetta. I lost all sense of myself as I dove under again, the waning light just enough to allow me a few feet under the surface. I was almost out of breath when I noticed her. She was drifting below the surface, heading toward the murky bottom.

Nothing was going to stop me from getting to her. I fought my way through fallen debris, planks of wood and pieces of metal littering the sea. When I finally managed to snag her arm, I was completely out of breath. As I broke through the surface, my lungs on fire, I could tell she was close to death.

"No. No! You will not die on me." I held her in my arms, pumping my fists against her chest, cognizant of the sound of the approaching boat. Within seconds, shots were fired, the automatic rifle peppering shots only a few inches away. I jerked her around a larger piece of debris, still trying to revive her. "Come on, baby. Come back to me." I pinched her nose, breathing into her mouth several times. The goddamn boat was already turning around, ready to make another pass.

While I repeated the lifesaving maneuver, I doubted I'd get a third chance, the speedboat increasing their speed. When she started to cough, I said a silent prayer, now fighting to swim toward the broken yacht.

Another series of shots were fired. Then I heard a series of rumbles coming from the west. Within seconds, I sighted two other boats. Fuck me. We weren't going to survive this.

"Come on, baby. Breathe." The goddamn Coast Guard had to be on their way. When she opened her eyes, I felt a sense of relief. As she coughed up more water, I cupped her face.

Until another series of shots were fired, the bullets coming from two directions. What the hell was going on? As the assassins continued to head in our direction, I was shocked when another burst of bullets stopped their approach cold in the water.

Then there was another massive explosion.

I held Carina against me, thankful she was struggling in my hold.

"What is…" She rubbed her hand against my chest.

"Shush. Don't try and talk." Who the hell was on the other boat? The boat slowed as it approached and within seconds, I could see Maxim.

He pulled closer, already leaning over the edge. "Get over here. We don't have time to lose." His call was more of a snarl, the sneer on his face easy to see.

"Don't," she whimpered, clinging to me, her breathing still labored.

"He's trustworthy." And we didn't have another choice at this point. I swam closer, exhaustion starting to settle in. As he hoisted Carina onboard, I took another look at the carnage. How in the hell had the perpetrator found us? I'd told no one about Catalina or renting with the yacht.

I managed to climb onboard, taking gasping breaths.

Several of his men continued to fire, catching stragglers in the water.

"You were just lucky I was close," Maxim hissed. He yanked me to a standing position then nodded to one of his men standing close by. "I might not be a huge fan of the Brother-hood, but we all took an oath. All of us except for you. You're going to tell me who the fuck you are and what you're doing, or you won't need to worry about Ortiz and his men."

At this point, I had no choice. "I need to make certain my wife is uninjured."

He glanced down at her and released his hold, pushing me away. "You have five minutes. There's a berth below. Then you meet me in the captain's quarters." He cursed in Russian under his breath as he walked away.

Carina took several scattered breaths and when I gathered her into my arms, she cupped my face, her fingers icy cold. "You saved me."

"It's not the first time, my beautiful wife. And I doubt it will be the last." I took one last look before carrying her to the short set of stairs. The attempt on my life wouldn't be the last.

* * *

The brutal punch caught me off guard. As I stumbled backward, rubbing my jaw, I heard him cursing in Russian.

"You fucking traitor," he growled.

"I did what I had to do." As I turned my head, looking into his enraged eyes, the realization that I'd pushed the alliance was evident. Maxim was a wild card, a man who accepted no excuses.

"That's bullshit." He thumped down on the chair, continuing to glare at me.

What the hell was I supposed to say at this point?

Maxim sat back in his seat, his untouched cognac still in his hand, his stare hard and cold. Then he snickered under his breath. "You have balls, Dante Santos. That doesn't make it right."

"As I said, I had no choice." I allowed my voice to deepen, the tone expressing the anger boiling in my system.

"We all have choices. You chose to enter into a lion's den!" he snapped then shook his head. Seconds of tension remained. "I'll give you credit. Most men don't have the resolve to take on a fucking cartel the size of the Santos Empire. Unfortunately, it would seem someone is out to expose your identity. That means you trusted the wrong people."

"I haven't trusted anyone."

"Then why the hard push to end your life?" he asked as he stood, finally taking a gulp of the expensive liquor.

"I don't think this has anything to do with Dante. This is about destroying Diego."

"Who would do that?"

"There are a solid dozen possibilities."

He studied me intently for a few seconds. "Ortiz is no friend of mine. The boat his people hijacked cost me four million dollars. I want that back. So, here's what I'm going to do. I'm going to offer you help in your ridiculous endeavor but if you fuck with me on any level, I'll kill both of you without hesitation."

"Why would you bother?"

"I don't know other than the shit you just told me is too insane not to be true. But you will repay my kindness by giving Ortiz over to me to handle. In addition, if I need a favor, both you and your brother will be there without question. If not, my earlier threat applies. Understood?"

"He's all yours."

He studied me as he'd done before, a snarl curling on his upper lip. "Are you aware of the doctored photographs supposedly taken in Colombia?"

"I'm aware. You did your homework."

"I have eyes and ears everywhere, Dante. That's a necessity in this realm of ours. I simply needed to be shown the photograph to know I was right about my assumptions."

"I assume you've told the Brotherhood?"

Snickering, he lifted his glass. "I don't play politics, Dante. Even if it includes men who I need to trust. We are comrades in a war that will never end, but we will never be friends anymore than you and I will. You deserved an opportunity to tell me the truth. You've done that. Those photographs were meant to draw you out in the open."

"That's what I believe." I was beginning to like the gruff man, although I was no fool. He'd make good on his threat if necessary.

"You think it's the authorities."

"I have certain suspicions."

He swirled the liquid in his glass. "Another dangerous game."

"There are two fortunes at stake."

"Aw, the combined Santos–DeMill Empire. The Santos' brutal power and the powerful DeMill hold on hundreds of wealthy, influential people. The trickledown effect could become an avalanche."

"One that could potentially alter the balance of world power." The question that continued to trouble me was who had the most to gain? Had Diego set the plan in motion prior to my arrival? What had been his intentions? Santiago. With the combined effort, they'd have control of the entire western hemisphere, which would include several additional lucrative ventures.

Jesus Christ. Now I knew what was inside the shipment containers and why there were discrepancies about its worth. My God. My earlier assumption had been right.

"Just remember that my support comes with requirements. However, I will help ensure your wife is protected."

I half laughed, finally downing the cognac. At least she was breathing easier, other than scrapes and cuts, no significant injuries. The Coast Guard and the cops were likely swarming over the accident scene, which was disconcerting but at least there was no direct connection to the Santos name. "Also understood."

"What are your plans?"

"There's one man in my organization who I have no doubt betrayed me. We start there. Then we move to Ortiz."

"What about the shipment? Do you have enough men you can trust?"

"Unfortunately, I don't know them well enough to say with absolute certainty."

He looked away. "If it's DEA, I'm not risking a single man."

"I don't think this has anything to do with the DEA." Although my thoughts returned to the conversation I'd had with Agent Walker. Whatever was on that ship was worth the loss of several lives, maybe more.

"There's an old Russian proverb an old woman told me once after learning I was going to America to live with my uncle. *Nikomu ne doveryay, yesli ne ishchesh' skoreyshey smerti.* Trust no one close to you unless you seek an early death."

"Meaning?"

"It is meant for those in our world, Dante. Violent killers with no conscience."

"Fascinating," I told him, the meaning able to be taken several ways. "I need two phones and weapons. Mine are swimming with the damn sharks." Thank God, I had a photographic memory, at least of the important phone numbers.

Maxim lifted a single eyebrow before moving to a cabinet. He yanked out two cellphones, tossing them to me. "I keep several burners, something you should consider." As he moved to another cabinet, unlocking it, I continued to try to put the pieces together. Ortiz had been playing me, determined to get ahold of the ship. Why? What the hell did Ortiz believe was in the cargo containers?

"You can have the weaponry you need," Maxim stated as he handed me a Beretta as well as a Glock. "She'll be safe with my men."

"Yeah, well, I'll feel better if she's armed."

"What are you doing with the real Diego?"

"Releasing him."

He chuckled. "You must have a goddamn death wish."

"He understands what occurred when we were children."

"You walk like him. You talk like him. But you have no clue about the man himself. Do you want to know how I knew you were an imposter?"

I checked the ammo, slapping the magazine back into position. "Why not?" I noticed the boat was slowing. My guess was we were still in California but far enough removed from the accident there would be adequate cover at least for now.

"When I held the gun to your head, the real Diego would have torn my head off without hesitation. Killing isn't in your blood."

"Things change, Maxim. I was turned into a killer the day my mother died."

As the boat was eased near the large dock, he walked closer. "You mentioned you were trained for two months. By whom?"

"The man I knew as my godfather."

He cocked his head, his eyes narrowing. "That would mean he was heavily involved in the business or was military trained."

I wasn't one hundred percent on board with trusting him, even if he had saved my life. "Perhaps a little of both."

He laughed after polishing off his cognac. "Be careful of secrets and lies, Dante. Haven't you figured out that even those born and bred into the lifestyle can't avoid being bitten by one or the other?"

"That may be true, but there are often times when maintaining secrets is the only way to stay alive."

"You're not certain who your real enemy is."

I shoved the weapon into my jacket, raking my hands through my wet hair. "I'll just say the lifestyle isn't for the faint of heart." I headed to the master cabin, happy to see Carina was sitting up, staring out the windows.

"We almost died. Again," she said quietly.

"But we didn't." I took the phones into my hand, programming both with the respective number.

"Who's doing this?"

"It would seem my assumptions about Ortiz were right."

She slowly turned her head. "Then kill him."

I turned to face her, pulling her hand into mine. As I rubbed my thumb across her palm, she started to shiver. "He will pay for what's he done. I want you to take this phone and I also have a weapon for you."

"Why?"

"Because I need you safe. We're staying at a location owned by a friend of mine."

Carina shook her head several times. "You can't dump me somewhere."

"I assure you that I will never allow you to be dumped anywhere. It's only for a short period of time. Then we won't need to worry any longer."

"You're lying to me."

"I'm not lying, sweet Carina, but I have some things to take care of. You will be safe."

She continued to shiver. "We'll never be safe. Unless you leave the life. Will you after this is over?"

Her question wasn't something I'd thought about. The truth was I doubted I'd have the chance.

I'd either be dead or in prison.

"Stay here until we're ready to go to the safehouse."

She laughed then gripped my arm. "Don't leave me for long."

Leaning over, I kissed her on the forehead. "I have no intentions of it."

"Remember something, Dante. You're not a killer."

I sucked in my breath hearing her comment. I'd crossed the very line Agent Walker had warned me about.

As I walked outside, I pulled the burner phone into my hand, dialing the memorized number. "Agent Walker." I allowed my Spanish accent to return for this particular call.

"Who is this?" he asked.

"This is Dante Fernandez. I believe I have something information that will be value, but I'll only provide it on my terms."

* * *

"Emmanuel Santiago," I told the Russian.

"Santiago is your godfather?" Maxim asked, laughing. "So you were a part of the lifestyle after all."

"My mother refused to allow him to introduce me to his world. He kept his promise."

"You do know who he is."

"I'm no fool, Maxim. I'm certain my godfather saw a huge opportunity by helping me fulfill my need for revenge. Ortiz was already an issue for Diego."

"I'm aware. The Brotherhood does talk. From what I know about Emmanuel, he never does anything for free."

"As if killing Ortiz isn't enough?"

"That's nothing to him."

We'd left Carina with two highly trained officers within his organization at a house far removed from the glitz and glamour of Beverly Hills. He'd supplied a change of clothes as well. "I might not have grown up in the lifestyle, but I prosecuted enough violent assholes to know what Emmanuel is hoping for. He wants to move into LA."

"And you're okay with that?"

I turned my head, chuckling under my breath. "I never said I was going to provide assistance with his endeavor."

"Your mother must have been an amazing woman to have you consider coming up against a man like Santiago. He will not accept betrayal from anyone."

"I'm not betraying him, Maxim, but he'll need to do his own legwork."

"What I don't understand is how is this going to allow you to satisfy the revenge against your father in any way."

"I have certain things in motion."

He threw me a look and laughed. "I'm sure you do. You seem to be just as resourceful as your brother."

I pulled out my phone, dialing Arturo. I had to be careful how I pulled Diego from the compound. By the sixth ring, I knew something was wrong.

"What is it?" Maxim asked.

"It would seem my best laid plans have been compromised from all sides." If that was the case, the odds of survival had just dropped to zero.

ante

Blood was splattered everywhere, the four men guarding Diego dead, the door to the bunker wide open.

And my brother was nowhere to be seen.

There were obvious signs of a struggle, evidence on the concrete floor.

"This was an assassination," Maxim stated with no emotion as he bent down next to one of the fallen soldiers.

"No one knew this place existed." Even as I issued the words, the ugliness of what I could be facing swept through me like a sledgehammer. Was it possible Emmanuel had killed his own men, taking out Diego himself?

What the hell was going on?

I heard a sound and snapped my head in the direction. Seeing movement, I took two long strides, crouching down beside Arturo. "Who did this?"

His eyes fluttered open and as soon as he tried to speak, blood spilled from his mouth. He didn't have long, his body already convulsing.

"Was it Emmanuel?"

He struggled to speak, his eyes opening wide. Then he managed to shake his head.

"Then fucking who? Did you recognize them?"

Arturo shook his head again.

"You're not going to get anything useful, and time is running out," Maxim hissed.

I threw my arm back, hissing under my breath. Arturo reached for my arm, and I lowered my head.

"He… not who…"

As he struggled to speak, I could only make out a few words, but they were enough my blood turned to ice. When his hand slipped away, I realized he was gone. Exhaling, I placed my palm over his eyes, closing his eyelids.

Then I rose to my feet, taking deep breaths.

"What the hell did he say to you?" Maxim demanded.

I slowly turned my head, lifting my gaze from the blood pooled on the floor. "That my entire life was nothing but the first part of a vicious game." I stormed out, the cold chill remaining. I felt no emotion, no sense of anything but the old need for vengeance, only for an entirely different reason.

"We need to finish this before it gets out of hand."

"*La venganza es la recompense mas dulce,*" I said quietly.

Maxim moved in front of me, narrowing his eyes. "Revenge is the sweetest reward," he repeated. "I agree with you, but something else just happened."

"Perhaps, but at least I'll finally learn the whole truth, not what was painted after years of heartache and lies." I grabbed the burner phone, dialing Stone's number. Of all the soldiers on my brother's detail, he was the one least likely to hunger for betrayal. "Stone."

"Mr. Santos. I tried to call you."

Stone's voice held an urgency I hadn't heard before. "My phone was destroyed. You will not use this number unless it's an emergency. Do you understand?"

"Yes, sir. Sergio has been looking for you. He's headed to your father's house. I wanted you to know that."

"Tell me what you found." That could prove to be interesting.

"I don't want to believe it so I doublechecked," he continued.

"Tell me!"

"Yes, sir. I found a large deposit in one of Sergio's accounts."

"The sender?" Every muscle in my back tensed.

"I'm still working on that. Whoever sent it was clever, taking me down a trail from one country to another. I'll get it for you, sir."

I gave Maxim another look, then motioned toward his vehicle. At least I had my answer as to the identity of the asshole who'd provided every detail of my whereabouts. As I climbed into the Jeep, I was already planning Sergio's demise. The man would die slowly. I sensed Stone had more to tell me. "What else?"

"I checked emails, incoming and outgoing as well for everyone in the organization."

"Go on."

"I found correspondence back and forth with Luis Ortiz. Recent details regarding your itinerary with Mrs. Santos."

"Was the correspondence with Sergio?"

"No, sir. That's what bothered me the most."

As he mentioned the name, I closed my eyes. Ortiz had been working directly with a family member to ensure Diego would never take the throne. He'd never had any intention of working with Diego, only allowing him to do a lion's share of the dirty work prior to having him assassinated.

Now I fully understood why the church had been attacked after our vows had been taken.

"Change of plans. I'll leave Ortiz for you to handle later. I'm running out of time."

* * *

Ortiz was nothing more than a two-bit player that had also been used. By midnight, he would be dead either by a bullet from one of Maxim's soldiers or one of the men who were loyal to Sergio. Either way, the world would be a better place with him gone.

When my phone chirped again, red flags surfaced. Noticing Stone was making a second call, I knew there was something terribly wrong. "What is it?"

"I found something else you're not going to like. Your phone was tracked. It's still being tracked, as in actively as we're speaking."

"How the fuck can that happen, especially since it took a bath in the Pacific Ocean?"

"There are some very sophisticated services in use today, the tracker spreading like a virus when the phone is a few feet away. The bad news is I think they figured out I was stalking them."

"Jesus Christ. Get out of your apartment, Stone. Go somewhere. Anywhere until I make contact. Am I clear?"

"Yes, sir."

I didn't waste any additional time, ending the call. "Call your men. They tracked my goddamn phone."

Maxim yanked out his, immediately pressing a single button. "You need to fill me in on what we're facing."

"A shitstorm." I dialed the number for the second burner phone, but I already knew the answer. Carina had been taken.

"What the hell is going on? My soldiers aren't answering." Maxim slammed his hand against the steering wheel.

"They're likely dead. Carina has been taken. And Maxim. You were wrong about me. Now, I am a killer."

There were two things I'd learned in my life that had meant the most to me. The first was that family was more important than money or power, vacations or possessions. My mother had been so good at keeping me grounded, away from drugs and gangs. She'd instilled her values without suffocating the once wild kid that had wanted to take on the world. Then she'd allowed me to become a man, taking pride in her hard work.

The second was that through hard work, anything could be achieved.

I'd carried her tutelage with me throughout my determination to make something better of myself, including raising a family. It had seemed the natural progression in my life, a blessing that would allow for additional joy.

Now I knew that many families had a darker side, one that could ultimately destroy all hope for joy or peace, leaving only broken pieces along the way.

I'd pined away for a father I believed was a hero. Instead, I'd found one who'd wanted to be king of the world. But there was more behind the spiral that had set in motion the destruction of the Santos family, claiming the DeMills along the way.

There were no pieces I could glue back together, no way of strengthening ties that had been ripped apart. There was only the certainty of death because of extreme greed.

I'd always heard that everyone had a price where they'd sell their soul to the devil. I'd fought against the regimes that held people's lives in their hands, ready to crush their bones for a single infraction.

Now I had to face that a course had been set in motion that I couldn't run away from, crossing that very line that could never be crossed again.

I was no different, a true monster.

But before I met my maker, I would do everything in my power to save Carina's life. She didn't deserve what she'd been forced into.

If I had to guess, I'd say I had a fifty-fifty chance of getting out of here alive, but it was the only choice I could make. With not knowing who to trust other than Maxim, I couldn't rely on any of Diego's soldiers.

"I took the liberty of calling in reinforcements," Maxim stated as he pulled the car outside the gates.

"You don't have additional soldiers here."

"Not of my own, but Constantine and Phoenix remained in LA on business. We may stand a chance."

I shook my head as I noticed a single flash of headlights in front of us. "I didn't think I'd like you, Maxim. You turned out to be a good ally."

"Yeah? Well, you need to remember that with whatever you decide to do after this shit is over with." He climbed out of the Jeep, immediately moving to the back.

I took a deep breath, eyeing my father's house as a series of memories crashed into my mind. Why hadn't I suspected the truth all those years ago? I'd felt an emptiness but had attributed it to the loss of a father I'd never known.

But that had been only part of the attempt to keep me in the dark in order to protect me.

Who knew a single act of passion could ignite a flame that slowly turned into an inferno?

After I stepped out onto the pavement, Maxim tossed me an automatic rifle.

"You're going to need this. I assume you know how to shoot." He grinned after making the statement.

"You might be surprised what skills I learned in a short period of time."

"You know what? I don't think I would. You're proven yourself to be a formidable soldier. I would hate to have you as an enemy."

"I'll take that as a compliment," I said as I checked the supply of ammunition, moving toward the duffle bag and grabbing another clip.

"It's the only one I give."

He headed toward two other brothers while I held back, staring at the house that held only part of the answers.

That is if Xavier Santos was still alive.

As Constantine and Phoenix approached, I sensed their anger, and I couldn't blame them.

Constantine threw a hard punch to my jaw, hissing under his breath.

"You defied the sanctity of the Brotherhood," he snarled. "Unacceptable."

"But necessary," I told him.

He glanced at Phoenix then toward the house. "If what I heard is all true, then you had every right to do what you did. However, your brother does not deserve to die because of it."

"I know. He is as much a victim as I've been."

"Then make it right," Phoenix said as he butted his weapon against my chest.

"That's my intention. I have no way of knowing if they're all inside, but I suspect my brother wants this to end. Remember Carina's life is to be spared at all costs. Even if it means my death."

"You love her," Constantine said.

"I do. But she doesn't belong to me."

"You know what they say," Phoenix teased. "Possession is nine tenths of the law."

"Maybe so," I told him. "But she's not a possession."

I didn't wait for any additional banter. Time was of the essence. As I headed toward the house, both hands on the weapon, I anticipated soldiers blocking our entrance. There was no one in sight, but I had no doubt our arrival had been caught on surveillance camera. That's the way I wanted it.

The door was unlocked, the unearthly quiet in the house the first indication a siege was taking place. We moved inside in pairs, two of the six soldiers remaining outside to keep watch.

I walked quietly down the long hallway toward Xavier's office, checking every open door. As soon as I neared the entrance, I gathered a sense of her. My wife. The beautiful woman who'd broken through so many layers, refusing to accept that I was a bad man. Little did she know what I had in mind for ending the charade.

After exhaling, I walked inside, Maxim and the other Brotherhood entering the room behind me. Carina wasn't in the room, but both Diego and Xavier were being guarded by two soldiers apiece, guns pointed at their heads. Sergio stood beside the desk, a blank expression on his face.

"I've been expecting you, Diego." The voice was deep yet entirely different than I'd heard before. As he swung around in his own father's chair, casually holding the weapon in his hand, he offered a smile.

"Cartero."

"My brother, Diego. Oh, wait. Should I call you Dante?" The man was pleased with himself, his smile growing. He rose to his feet, placing his weapon on the table then heading for the bar. "You brought friends with you. How clever of you to determine that it wasn't in your best interest to trust any of Diego's men."

I glanced at my twin, taking a deep breath. He'd been beaten after Emmanuel's soldiers had been killed. He struggled in their hold, glaring at me with hatred.

"You'll never get away with this," Diego hissed.

Cartero barely gave him a glance. "It would seem I already have." He took a few seconds, swirling the liquid in his hand before taking a gulp, closing his eyes as if savoring the sweetest reward.

He had no idea what I was capable of, but he would soon learn. "Where is my wife?" I glanced at Sergio, who stood stoically, staring directly at me.

Why the hell hadn't I killed him when I'd had the chance?

"Well, let's see," he muttered as he moved from the bar, walking around the edge of his desk. "Actually, she's not your wife. You were never married to her. A pity but that will work in my favor. She is lovely. I was thinking of killing her at first. Then I realized the coup de grace would be to marry her instead. Then the entire plan that's been in motion for eighteen months, eighteen freaking months would come full circle!" The last part of the statement had drifted into a shout, his eyes wild. His envy was invoking intense emotions, fucking with his mind.

I would use that to my benefit.

I glanced at Constantine who'd moved further toward the back of the room, the location offering a panoramic view of the room.

"Where is she?" I demanded, tightening my grip on the weapon.

"She put up a good fight when I took her," Sergio said.

"You fucking bastard," I sneered.

"You son of a bitch," Diego hissed. "I trusted you for years. Years! You're fucking working with Ortiz after what he did to you?"

Sergio laughed. "I can forget anything when given power and money."

Cartero laughed, the sound maniacal. "Now. Now. Let's play nice. I should have known you'd catch wind of the ruse that was in motion and try to claim your piece of the pie. I guess I underestimated a two-bit attorney practicing in a third world country. However, I believe my efforts to ruin your reputation had gotten noticed. It would seem you're on the International Most Wanted List."

He'd had the photographs doctored. He'd been the puppet master all along. He'd also orchestrated the attack at the church, making sure he lived.

"Why the hell are you doing this? You're my son!" Xavier snapped, one of the soldiers smacking him in the face with the butt of his gun when he tried to break free.

"I suggest you keep your fucking mouth shut!" Cartero's snarl was ripe with venom. "I'll deal with you last, *Father*. You fucking never wanted me. I was just an afterthought in your precious world that you created. You were never going to let me in. Never!" Now he was close to screaming.

Maxim cursed in Russian, obviously growing antsy.

"That's not true. I love you," Xavier whined.

Sighing, I took the opportunity during Cartero's tirade to assess the situation. With the number of weapons we had on his soldiers, it was possible to take control.

But not without at least one casualty.

Briefly, I thought about how much I'd wanted my father to pay for what he'd done. Now I wanted the truth more than vengeance.

By now, the DEA should be boarding the cargo ship. Then perhaps at some point I'd know if my hunch regarding the containers was correct.

"One last time, Cartero. Where. Is. My. Wife."

He snapped his head in my direction, half laughing. "Fine. You want to see the bitch? I'll get her for you. Sergio, go grab the slut and bring her here."

Sergio laughed. "Maybe I'll have a little fun with her before I do."

His words pissed me off and I almost pulled the trigger. Only when Phoenix narrowed his eyes did I remember this was all just a wretched game.

As Sergio left the room, I could feel the tension rise. "What prompted you to do this, Cartero?" I wanted him even more irate.

"Why? Are you fucking kidding me? I'm the rightful heir to this twisted throne. But you already know that, don't you?"

The fact he was baiting me meant he'd learned the truth months if not years before.

"What are you talking about? I was the firstborn son of Xavier Santos, Diego the second."

"That's not true!" Diego spat, as if at this point it mattered who was born minutes earlier.

"At least that piece of shit is right about one thing." Cartero took another swig of his drink before slamming the glass on the deck. Then he headed for the bookshelf, pulling aside several books and tossing them aside.

"What the fuck are you doing?" Xavier growled.

"What's necessary, Father. The truth needs to be told." Cartero started humming, even swaying in time to the beat of his unusual music. He opened a safe, punching in the codes dramatically. When he pulled out a file, he held it in the air then brought the manila folder to his mouth, pressing his lips against it. "This was all the ammunition I needed, Daddy dearest. You've been a very bad boy this year. Oh, wait. That started thirty plus years ago when you tortured a woman who loved you because of your goddamn pride." As he tossed it onto the desk, Xavier struggled in the soldier's hold.

"I'll kill you!" he screamed, his face turning bright red.

"I'm sorry, Daddy dearest. You won't be given that chance." Cartero whipped out a knife, spinning it in the light. "I'm going to enjoy gutting and cutting you. Then I'll be king of the world. King. King!"

Dear God, the man was deranged. I took a chance and moved closer by a couple of feet, Maxim flanking my side.

Cartero swung his weapon in my direction, wagging the knife. "Tsk. Tsk. I started to call you my brother, but that's not the case. You're nothing to me. However, you did allow me to work in peace, ridding me of Diego's annoying habits. You were never quite like him, Dante. You just didn't cut it as a monster. What a shame."

My anger was increasing, beads of sweat forming across my hairline, but I refused to fall into his damning scheme.

"What in the hell is going on?" Diego snarled.

"It's like I told you, brother. Things aren't as they seem. We were both lied to all those years ago." I glanced in his direction then toward the file. I sensed he followed my gaze, grumbling under his breath.

"Let go of me," Carina whined as she was brought into the room. Seeing her only infuriated me even more. Sergio had roughed her up, but she was a fighter, refusing to allow the son of a bitch's soldiers to break her down.

"Here is the little whore," Sergio snarled.

"*Vy ne otnosites' k zhenshchinam tak*," Maxim hissed.

You don't treat women that way.

"*Ona ne chto inoye, kak shlyukha*," Sergio responded. She's nothing but a slut. As the fucker pushed her toward Cartero, I took a step forward and the asshole pointed his weapon in my direction. "I wouldn't do that, *El Jefe*."

"Come here, my soon to be bride to be," Cartero beckoned with a single finger. He placed the gun on the desk, flashing the knife in the light.

I was shaking from the rage, barely able to see focus given my desire to shed blood.

"I'm already married, your bastard," she snapped then threw me a look, her eyes pleading with me.

Don't worry, baby. Only a few minutes longer.

I only hoped she could sense I would protect her with my life if necessary.

"Technically, no," Cartero said then laughed. "You see, you married Diego Santos in name, but you fucked his brother. How does that make you feel, Diego?"

Diego took a deep breath, narrowing his eyes. "Are you ready to meet your maker?"

"I hardly think that's going to happen. I assure you that you'll be fucked," Cartero cackled as he walked closer to her, running the edge of the knife down her arm.

"Get away from her!" I couldn't stand it any longer.

"Oh, what a pity. You don't like me touching her? She's mine now." When he had the audacity to use the knife, ripping through her top, I'd had enough.

I threw a look at Diego, praying to God that for once the fact we were twins would matter.

Read my mind, brother. It's time.

Diego took a deep breath then all hell seemed to break loose as he jerked away, whipping around and yanking one of the weapons from the soldier's hand, immediately lunging back and taking several shots, catching Sergio between the eyes before I had a chance to fire off a single bullet.

I wasn't certain which of the Brotherhood opened fire, but I knew without a doubt they had the situation under control. I lunged toward Cartero, but he'd already grabbed her around the throat, holding the knife against the side of her neck.

Suddenly, the sound of gunfire ceased, the quiet in the room unnerving. I noticed Xavier was cowering in the corner, paralyzed with fear.

"Let her go and you live," I told him.

Diego rushed to my side, throwing a glance toward the file. "You could never rule the kingdom, Cartero. You didn't have it in you. Your weakness was your greed and jealousy. Trust me, there are safety measures put in place a long time ago preventing you from gaining access to anything."

Carina fought him, struggling with everything she had to get away. And her beautiful, luminescent eyes never left mine.

I smiled, giving her a single nod. My amazing wife would know what to do. As she'd told me more than once. She could take care of herself.

After this, she'd never need to feel that way again.

"Not the diamonds!" Cartero said, his laugh unlike anything I'd ever heard before. The man was losing it.

My hunch had played out. I'd be shocked if there were any drugs in the cargo hold whatsoever.

With his grandstanding, he slowly lowered his weapon. That was all I needed. Without hesitation, I took a single giant stride, knocking the weapons from his hand as Carina jerked away, tumbling to the floor.

Then I smacked Cartero with the rifle, waiting until he went down. As I stood over him, he peered up at me with the first hint of fear in his eyes.

Suddenly, I felt her hand on my arm. "You're not a killer, Dante. That's not you. Don't do it."

I took a deep breath as I looked into her eyes. There was so much love and trust in them that I reminded of who and what I'd been. Emmanuel had done everything in his power to try to create a monster, a man capable of utter violence without a moment of remorse or regret. As my mother's face shifted into my mind, the person I'd been most of my life couldn't be ignored. Exhaling, I backed away, looking every member of the Brotherhood in the eyes.

I'd exacted my vengeance.

As I cupped her face, rubbing my fingers across her beautiful skin, it was a moment of being reborn. Was I a changed man? Yes, no longer capable of seeing the world in simple shades of black and white. However, I would do what was necessary in order to protect my family.

No matter the consequences.

I stepped away, lowering my weapon. "She's right. I'm no killer."

"But I am," Diego snarled and then I heard a single popping sound. He'd taken out his own father.

The silence afterward was deafening. Diego looked directly at me, his chest rising and falling. We were twins, sharing a connection that would only be terminated in death, but his anger was understandable.

I moved toward him, allowing him the opportunity to take out his anger on his own flesh and blood. The agony in his eyes was gut wrenching.

Then he pointed the weapon toward me. "You fucking son of a bitch."

"Whoa!" Constantine hissed as he came closer. "This isn't how we do things."

"Oh, yeah? Tell me, brother. How should it go?" Diego gritted out.

"Don't do it, Santos," Maxim snarled. "You've both had your lives torn apart by lies. This won't do any good."

Brogan moved in between us, snapping his head from Diego back to me. "We are a Brotherhood. All seven of us. Do you hear me?"

The words echoed in my mind. He was right.

Diego took several scattered breaths then lowered his weapon, pushing Brogan aside. Then he threw a hard punch, almost knocking me off my feet. "Do not do that shit again."

I had to smile and when Diego yanked me into a bearhug, I could hear a collective sigh coming from the others. As he backed away, he lifted his eyebrow, nodding toward Cartero. "What do you want to do with him?"

The weight of the question was heavy. At least at first. When I approached Cartero again, I knew exactly what needed to happen. "It's your lucky day, Cartero. I'll allow the police to handle you." I stepped back then Carina rushed into my arms.

"I love you. Oh, my God. I knew you'd come for me. I knew it," she said loudly enough Diego laughed.

"So you got the girl after all," my brother told me. "You're not bad as a replacement for me. But I'll always be the better brother."

"Not a chance in hell," I teased.

I nodded to one of Constantine's men. "Tie the asshole up. He can stew for a while."

As two men moved toward him, I backed away further, yanking Carina even closer. "You're not going anywhere, baby girl."

She cupped both sides of my face, tears in her eyes. "God, I love you. No matter your name."

Constantine laughed. "We'll handle the cleanup. Why don't you get her out of here."

I watched as Diego headed toward the file, yanking it into his hands. As he scanned the file, several emotions crossed his face. Then he lifted his head. "We need to talk, brother."

"I know."

He shook his head. "You have great potential. Rule by my side?"

I glanced into Carina's eyes and shook my head. "I crossed the line but against all belief, I can cross back again. That's what I intend on doing."

"Can we go home?" Carina asked.

I had to laugh. "Dante Fernandez doesn't have a home anywhere in California."

"You can stay at whatever house you want," Diego told me. Seconds later, he moved closer, waiting until I backed away. Then he punched me in the face, the force enough to drive me back by several feet. "But if you ever do that shit again, I'll kill you myself and there won't be a single member of the Brotherhood to stop me."

I rubbed my jaw, able to grin. "Understood."

"Get her out of here. I'll help the Brotherhood fix this."

Nodding, I walked closer. "The shipment has been compromised. I had to offer something to the DEA in exchange for immunity."

"Christ," Phoenix muttered. "You do play hardball."

I tossed him a look. "I had no choice."

"Diamonds, huh?" Diego asked.

"If I had to guess, several million dollars' worth."

He glared at Cartero. "At least the fucker had good taste. I'll handle the fallout."

"You won't have to. I took care of any outstanding situation involving you as well."

As he narrowed his eyes, the same swell of emotions played out in his mind. "We'll need to take a trip together to Colombia."

"Yes, we will. Give it a few days."

Diego glanced at the men of the Brotherhood then nodded respectfully. "I appreciate your help."

"You have an interesting family," Constantine stated. "We need to get our butts in gear. I doubt it'll be long before the Feds arrive."

As I took Carina's hand into mine, I was forced to realize my life would never be the same. However, there would no longer be any demons from the past.

CHAPTER 22

" *E veryone has choices to make; no one has the right to take those choices away from us. Not even out of love."*

—*Cassandra Clare*

Carina

Love wasn't easy. It took work and insecurity, heartache and promises made. It also meant making mistakes and dealing with tragedies, making the choices in life more difficult. However, the choice I'd made in staying with a man I still barely knew was an easy one to make.

I loved Dante Fernandez. He was everything to me. He hadn't just become my protector or the man who'd saved my life on three separate occasions. He'd become my friend and lover, and the only light I wanted to drift to every day.

And I dared anyone to try to tear us apart.

The morning sun was just as beautiful, the ocean waves as they shifted softly against the shore taking my breath away, but the man in the reflection was what stilled my heart.

As Dante brushed his hands over my shoulders, the same shiver I'd felt since the first time he'd touched me nearly shattered my system. In the days since I'd been abducted, taken by a man I barely knew, I'd gone through a sea of emotions from anger to hatred, finally back to the love that had grasped onto my heart with long, sinewy fingers.

"What are you thinking about?" he asked as he nuzzled against my neck.

"How much I'll miss this place." We'd returned to San Diego, to Diego's house, the location where we'd shared intense passion. However, it belonged to a man who'd extended a welcome to both of us after facing a horror of his own. Did I think Diego had deserved to know what it felt like to become the hunted? Yes, but I hadn't shared that with anyone.

Including the love of my life.

"You can go anywhere you want, Carina. You're a free woman."

I was astounded he'd made the offer, but the huge hole in my stomach only grew by another several inches. I turned to face him, tilting my head. "Does that mean you no longer want to be married to me?"

The range of emotions on Dante's face was heartbreaking, the glisten in his eyes something I thought I'd never see.

"Dear God, no, but I refuse to hold you hostage to an unholy contract."

"What if I want to be with the man who awakened my senses?"

His smile could light up a room. "Then I'll need to ask you to marry me."

"Then do it."

He seemed taken aback for a few seconds. "I don't have a ring."

"I don't need diamonds." I laughed after making the statement as I thought about the sheer volume of diamonds Cartero had attempted to bring into the country.

Dante nodded once then dropped to his knees. "Miss Carina DeMill. May I have your hand in marriage? I can't promise to be all that you dreamt of, but I will pledge my eternal love and faith." After kissing my hand, he turned it over, dragging his tongue across my palm. "And a lifetime of disciplining you."

All I could do was shiver, my core heated to an explosive level. "That's all I need. And hot sex. I can't forget about that."

Laughing, he rose to his feet. "Life won't be perfect."

"Who needs perfect when we have each other?"

His eyes still sparkling, he reached into his pocket, removing a necklace. "I wanted to show you this. It's the only thing I brought from my home in Chile."

345

As I took it from his hand, I sensed just how valuable it was to him. Very carefully I opened the latch, not surprised at what I found. The two pictures of little boys almost took my breath away. "Your mother loved you both."

"She always wanted to contact Diego and I think she would have eventually."

"This is lovely."

"It's all I have of her, except for the piano I gave her one year."

"That's how you learned to play."

Laughing, he rubbed his knuckles across my cheek. "She taught me to play. I never had formal lessons."

"Your mother sounds amazing. She did everything in her power to take care of you."

"Yes, she did."

He'd told me about what was in the file, the information something I hoped wouldn't haunt him for the rest of his life. At least he knew his lineage. "She will always be in your heart."

"Just like you will be."

He lowered his head, holding his lips a few centimeters from mine. Then he captured them, drawing me closer as he wrapped his arm around my waist. I was pulled onto my toes, the intensity of my feelings for him deepening. I knew we'd face continued scrutiny, but I didn't care. I was happy that we could finally enjoy our life together.

As he swept his tongue inside, I snatched a portion of his shirt, fisting the material. I wanted him to hold me for hours on end, but he had aspects of his life he'd need to finalize.

And some of them scared me to death.

When he finally pulled away, his pressed his forehead against mine. "You're all mine."

"Always and forever."

He backed away, taking my hand into his. As he led me downstairs, I held my breath. A DEA agent was on his way to the house and neither one of us knew what would happen. While he'd provided details about the cargo ship to the agent, attempting to secure immunity for both himself and Diego, it was entirely possible both men would be arrested. I couldn't stand the thought of that happening. I'd fight the justice system with everything I had if that's what occurred. I'd already put my father on notice that he would help in the fight to keep Dante's freedom, or I would spend time with the press, letting them know exactly what he'd done to me.

Diego was already waiting in the living room, a sly smile crossing his face when we walked in.

"The two lovebirds," he said quietly.

"I'm sorry, Diego. I could never love you." I'd wanted to say the words since we'd entered his house. "You're not my type."

He glanced at Dante as he walked closer. "I can clearly see that, princess. Don't worry. There are no hard feelings.

Besides, you're not my type either but it could have worked between us." When he grinned, I felt more at ease. "After all, he and I do look exactly alike."

"Oh, there are differences," I offered.

Both men laughed until we heard a knock on the door. Almost all of Diego's soldiers had been fired, the few who hadn't remaining outside my brother's home.

Diego glanced in my direction, another grin crossing his face. He'd had several long talks with Dante over the past two days, the time spent getting to know each other easing their pain.

But there would always be memories.

Ones of anger and loss. And ones of sadness.

They could never make up for lost time or what each had been forced to do.

As a man entered the room, I sensed Dante knew him from his past.

"Agent Fletcher Walker, Diego Santos and my fiancée, Carina DeMill." Dante extended his hand, the agent grasping it easily.

"That's right," the agent said. "You're no longer married in the eyes of the law."

"Something we will rectify," Dante said, laughing. "Did my information prove to be helpful?"

Agent Walker sighed as he shifted his gaze from Dante to Diego. "We recovered the largest shipment of blood diamonds ever confiscated. The street value is still being calculated but in the excess of one hundred million dollars. Incidentally, there were no other illegal substances on the ship of any kind. And the diamonds were linked directly to your brother, Cartero."

Both Diego and Dante looked at each other, sly smiles on their faces.

"The debris in the harbor, including the bodies we pulled out, is linked to Luis Ortiz," he added.

"I would assume that means we have full immunity," Dante stated.

The agent shook his head. "Strings are still being pulled and you will need to testify, but no charges are being filed."

"That's good to hear, Agent Walker. Now, we can get back to business." Diego half laughed.

"Yes, you can. As long as it's legal," the agent replied. "Oh, did you hear about the car fire two nights ago?"

I tipped my head, studying Dante. He acted as if he didn't know anything. I was well aware Luis Ortiz had been assassinated just outside a restaurant in Beverly Hills. From what I knew, the conniving son of a bitch had gotten what he deserved.

"Ortiz," Dante offered.

"That's right. It's funny that no one had laid claim to the violent act." The agent had a twinkle in his eyes.

A product of the Brotherhood. That much I had been told.

"No tremendous loss if you ask me. What happens to Cartero?" Dante squeezed my hand before letting it go.

"Oh, he'll be spending quite a few years behind prison bars. He's an interesting man." The agent scratched his jaw. "Oh, and I will offer my condolences on the loss of your father and several of your soldiers."

The fact the men of what Dante had called the Brotherhood had made it look like Cartero had shot his father in cold blood was the only reason the two men were standing here today. While Dante had told me little about the organization, it was clear that without their help, all three of us might not have remained alive.

"Is there anything else you gentlemen need to tell me?" Agent Walker asked.

"I can't think of anything. Can you, brother?" Diego tossed at Dante.

Dante shrugged. "Not that I can think of."

"Uh-huh. Then I guess I'll leave you." Agent Walker headed to the door. Then he stopped short. "Oh, before I forget. I had a very interesting email from someone using the handle of the Dark Knight. Does that ring a bell?"

Both brothers shrugged.

"Hmmm… I found it very interesting he was able to provide dozens of missing pieces of evidence from copies of wire transfers, and emails between Cartero Santos and Luis Ortiz to several other pieces corroborating your innocence. And this Dark Knight managed to snag the real photographs of the massacre that you were depicted in, Dante. As far as I can see, you're free and clear."

"I'm glad to hear that, Agent Walker," Dante told him.

"I'm curious. Are you returning to the law when all this is over?"

Dante chuckled. "First, I'm going to take some time off. Then we'll see."

"I think it would be a good idea." Agent Walker grinned seconds before walking out of the room.

As I turned toward the man I loved, he winked. He'd crossed that line of good versus evil, something I'd feared, but he'd refused to fall into the abyss that I'd been worried about. As Dante approached, he rolled his hands down my arms.

"There's something Diego and I need to do together and I'm not risking your life because of it."

I pressed my head against his chest. "I know you do. Just promise me you'll return safely."

"That much I can promise." He fisted my hair, yanking my head up and lowering his. As he brushed his lips across mine, we both heard Diego's intentional cough.

Dante pulled away, giving him the finger.

"Incidentally, I find myself with an open position in my law firm," Diego said absently.

"How so?" Dante darted his tongue inside my mouth and a heated shiver traveled down my spine.

"Well, it would seem Edwardo and I just didn't see eye to eye on things, including how he handled our mother. Are you interested?"

Dante lifted his head. "I just might be, but I'll think about it."

"You do that," Diego teased.

I'd learned at an early age that love wasn't easy, and it could certainly be blind to the realities of life. In watching my parents, I'd promised myself that I wouldn't care for anyone for fear of losing myself. What I'd found with Dante had been the ability to be myself for the first time in my life.

In truth, I had my parents to thank for being introduced to a man who'd defied the odds in life and with my heart.

And I felt like the luckiest girl in the world.

* * *

Dante

There had to be some old Spanish adage or a superstition about keeping secrets, but none came to mind. In the last few weeks, I'd lost my mother yet gained a brother. Diego and I were different people on one hand, but we were entirely the same on another. He had every right to be angry with what I'd done to him, but we both understood the circumstances of the secrets and lies that had shaped our lives.

I'd learned several valuable lessons in my life, most occurring in the last few months. Often when choices were made, the intention wasn't to harm anyone.

Sadly, far too often leaving skeletons in a closet became destructive, the web of deceit extending like sharp claws.

That was the case with the birth of twins who'd been forced apart at an early age in a violent and brutal world.

There was no adequate way to right the wrongs and the past would remain with haunted and angry memories. But the one thing my mother… our mother would have wanted was to live in the present. That's what we both intended on doing.

Diego and I might never become best friends, but we were certainly brothers and that would remain an important aspect of my life.

As we were led into a massive office, Diego slipped his hands into his pockets. "I hope you know what you're doing," he said quietly.

"So do I."

"This wasn't necessary."

"Wasn't it? Why the change of heart?"

"Because it adds another layer of bullshit to our life, but you're right." He turned his head in my direction. "Are you always going to be the voice of reason?"

"Likely, since you're the hothead of the family."

Chuckling, he lowered his gaze to the file in my hand. We'd come a long way for a confirmation that wasn't really needed, but I had to know if what Cartero had found in

Xavier's things was true. It would eat at me for the rest of my life until I knew for certain.

Fortunately, we didn't need to wait long. As soon as I heard footsteps, I turned around.

As Emmanuel walked into the room, he had a huge smile on his face. "I was hoping I'd have the opportunity to see you. I heard about everything you accomplished, Dante." He eyed Diego carefully as he shook my hand.

"I'm sorry about your men."

"Given the war we wage almost every day, casualties will happen," he said. "At least you managed to survive."

"Yes, your tutelage proved invaluable. Fortunately, you also benefitted given you won't have Luis Ortiz breathing down your neck."

"Yes, that is an added benefit. For that I will forever be appreciative. To what do I owe this honor?" he asked as he moved toward Diego, extending his hand.

Diego hesitated before accepting the gesture. Then Emmanuel headed to his bar.

"What can I offer you gentlemen to drink?"

"Whatever you're having." I slowly turned my head, Diego and I locking eyes. I knew this was harder on him than it was on me. At least I had the benefit of knowing the man to a point. I waited until the drinks were poured and brought to us, Emmanuel settling behind his desk before easing the file onto the surface.

"What's this?" he asked, grabbing it immediately.

"A moment of truth," Diego told him.

We both watched as Emmanuel opened the file, taking at least a full minute to look through the documentation. When he finally lifted his head, he was shocked but within seconds had masked every emotion. Was it genuine or a powerful man's attempt at adding to the extensive ruse both Diego and I had just been through?

He stood slowly, taking his drink and walking to the window. I noticed there were kids playing the courtyard, his grandchildren important to him.

"I fell in love with your mother when she was fifteen years old. Of course, she was too young, and I was already involved in a life of crime. Her father forbid her from seeing me. But we kept in touch. In truth, I couldn't stop thinking about her. I learned she'd been introduced to Xavier Santos out of America, and I was indignant, so angry I almost hunted Xavier down. The marriage between them had already been arranged."

I glanced at Diego, able to tell Emmanuel was being sincere. But could my brother?

Emmanuel took a sip of his drink. "We were in love by that point, sneaking out to spend time, but there was no chance for us to be together. One night, she slipped away, and we met in her favorite place by a stream. We made love that night. Once and never again. Somehow, her father found out and she was locked down in the house, sent to America to wait for the wedding. I didn't see her again until she returned three years later. She never told me that she'd become pregnant while still in Colombia."

"And you couldn't figure it out? Did you not think even once that it was possible?" I asked, although the sound of my voice was demanding.

He turned to face me. "Of course I did. When she wouldn't tell me what happened, I asked her. It took her three years to tell me she'd birthed two children. I wanted to come and take you, Diego, but she refused. She never told me I had two sons."

"Why didn't you marry her? From what Dante told me, she was never happy. There was never anyone else."

"You need to understand that in this world, we abide by honor. Our wives. Our families are everything. I would not do that to my wife or my other children. But I made certain I protected her, even if she refused to take any money from me. She called it blood money. Finally, one day I demanded to see the birth certificates. Now I can see she had them doctored, the timing making it impossible that I could have been your father. But that didn't mean I didn't love you like a son, Dante. I wanted nothing more than to bring you into my world, but as you know, she put her foot down. Your mother was a formidable woman."

I could tell by the faraway look in his eyes how much he loved her. Sighing, I glanced at the liquid inside my glass, uncertain I could swallow a drop. "I'm getting married."

He cocked his head then laughed. "Yes, I understand. You love this woman?"

"With all my heart."

Emmanuel turned his attention to Diego. "And you have no issue with this?"

"She was never mine to love," he said.

"Love is the only redemption we have in this life. That's something for you both to keep in mind." Emmanuel sighed.

"I would like for my children to get to know their grandfather, but I will not destroy what you have with your family," I told him.

"My wife knows. We don't keep secrets. She would be honored to have you in our home any time. You are family." Emmanuel lowered his head. "If only I'd known."

Diego shook his head. "Would that have changed anything?"

Emmanuel gave it some thought. "Yes, because the man you knew as your father never understood the meaning of sacrifice."

I wasn't certain what to expect, but at least the truth was out in the open. Would I allow my children to spend time with him? Yes, but they would never be given the opportunity to accept his lifestyle.

Didn't that make me a hypocrite?

I'd been given a second chance at life, love, and to honor my pledge for finding justice.

This time, I would make certain I didn't fuck it up.

* * *

One month later

Carina

I stood in the small room of the church, glancing at the woman in the beautiful white dress and could no longer recognize her. Gone were the dark circles and frown lines, the anger that had once furrowed her brow on a very similar sunny day. In their place were the effects of shimmering skin and bright eyes, a smile that had a life of its own.

On a fateful day less than three months before, I'd made a promise that I would kill the man I was supposed to marry. On this day, I would make a pledge to spend the rest of my life with him. Perhaps it was cathartic, but I liked to think of it as serendipity.

And love.

If what I'd heard was true, true love would always find a way to dig through the muck. Thank God I hadn't driven the knife into his neck. I laughed softly then noticed my sister's face. "Why do you have a dreamy look in your eyes?" I slipped my hand around the glass of champagne, marveling at the beautiful ruby ring my future husband had insisted on purchasing, the sun casting sparkles across the surface of the mirror. As I took a sip, my mind shifted to all the filthy things Dante had told me he'd do tonight, including tying me to the bed.

I couldn't wait.

"Because I just met my future husband."

Champagne flew out of my mouth and all over the mirror. As soon as I started coughing, she grabbed a handful of tissues. "I'm so sorry. I didn't mean to make you choke."

"Please… please tell me who you're talking about."

"That dreamy Diego. He's just perfect."

There was something taboo about my sister talking about my future brother-in-law, the man who was a carbon copy of my hunk in that manner.

"You are kidding me."

"Nope. And don't tell me that because he's a bad man I can't have him. I adore bad boys." When she growled, I stared at her. My baby sister was all grown up.

"I'm not saying a word, except finish school."

"You're not my mother."

"Thank God I'm not," I said as I laughed. "Just be careful. Diego has done some very terrible things."

"So what? He's going to redeem himself."

"Says who?"

She shrugged then gave me a mischievous look. "That's what he told me last night."

"What do you mean last night?"

"We might have had a late-night snack together."

I glared at her in horror. "Don't you dare tell me any details."

"Hey. I'm a grown woman. I can do what I want to do."

"God help us all." As I glanced into the mirror one last time, all I could do was smile. Dante had returned to the law, although he would need to pass the bar exam in California before he could legally handle any cases. The music company was flourishing. Even my parents were content, the agreement with Santos broken without any repercussions given Diego's involvement. And I'd never been happier.

"Here's your bouquet. Let's get this party started. I have a feeling you want to get to your honeymoon night. It is Paris after all, the city of love. Then what's next, Italy? Spain?"

"Nope. We're staying for your concert tomorrow night."

She blushed and bit her lower lip. "So is Diego."

I rolled my eyes and smoothed down my dress. "Things never change, baby sister. I'm always going to watch out for you."

"I hope you do."

As we walked out together, butterflies tickled my stomach. The small church Dante had found was perfect. No guests or press had been invited, which was exactly what we both wanted.

When the pianist started to tickle the ivories, I thought of Dante and his magical fingers. Then I held my breath and advanced to the entrance of the chapel. Seeing both Dante and Diego standing side by side still amazed me.

The moment both men turned, all I could see was the love in Dante's eyes. Yet Diego had eyes for my sister. Well, stranger things had happened.

I fingered the locket Dante had asked me to wear, knowing his mother was smiling down from heaven. And as I walked closer, several tears slipped past my lashes.

Dante turned to me, just like he'd done before, and suddenly everything else in the world faded away. There was only the two of us in the room.

"My beloved," he whispered as he gathered the tears with his thumb, bringing it to his mouth.

"*Ti amero per sempre*," I whispered, and I would love him forever.

"*Has manchado mi corazon*," he returned. "You've stained my heart."

I'd never believed in fairytales or happy endings. I didn't read romance novels or like chick-lit flicks, but what I did believe in was the sanctity of love.

Just like his mother had.

Just like his father had tried to maintain.

And together Dante and I would honor what had almost destroyed two families. We would create memories that would last a lifetime.

The End

AFTERWORD

Stormy Night Publications would like to thank you for your interest in our books.

If you liked this book (or even if you didn't), we would really appreciate you leaving a review on the site where you purchased it. Reviews provide useful feedback for us and our authors, and this feedback (both positive comments and constructive criticism) allows us to work even harder to make sure we provide the content our customers want to read.

If you would like to check out more books from Stormy Night Publications, if you want to learn more about our company, or if you would like to join our mailing list, please visit our website at:

http://www.stormynightpublications.com

BOOKS OF THE KINGS OF CORRUPTION SERIES

King of Wrath

After a car wreck on an icy winter morning, I had no idea the man who saved my life would turn out to be the heir to a powerful mafia family… let alone that I'd be forced into marrying him.

When this mysterious stranger sought to seduce me, I should have ignored the dark passion he ignited. Instead, I begged him to claim me as he stripped me bare and whipped me with his belt.

He was as savage as I was innocent, but it was only after he made me his that I learned the truth.

He's the head of the New York Cosa Nostra, and I belong to him now…

King of Cruelty

Constantine Thorn has been after me since I saw him kill a man nine years ago, and when he finally caught me he made me an offer I couldn't refuse. Marry him and he will protect me.

Only then did I learn that the man who made me his bride was the same monster I'd feared.

He's a brutal, heartless mafia boss and I wanted to hate the bastard, but with every stinging lash of his belt and every moment of helplessly intense passion, I fell deeper into the dark abyss.

He's the king of cruelty, and now I'm his queen.

BOOKS OF THE SINNERS AND SAINTS SERIES

Beautiful Villain

When I knocked on Kirill Sabatin's door, I didn't know he was the Kozlov Bratva's most feared enforcer. I didn't expect him to be the most terrifyingly sexy man I've ever laid eyes on either...

I told him off for making so much noise in the middle of the night, but if the crack of his palm against my bare bottom didn't wake everyone in the building my screams of climax certainly did.

I shouldn't have let him spank me, let alone seduce me. He's a dangerous man and I could easily end up in way over my head. But the moment I set eyes on those rippling, sweat-slicked muscles I knew I needed that beautiful villain to take me long and hard and savagely right then and there.

And he did.

Now I just have to hope him claiming me doesn't start a mob war...

Beautiful Sinner

When I first screamed his name in shameful surrender, Sevastian Kozlov was the enemy, the heir of a rival family who had just finished spanking me into submission after I dared to defy him.

Though he'd already claimed my body by the time he claimed me as his bride, no matter how desperately I long for his touch I vowed this beautiful sinner would never conquer my heart.

But it wasn't up to me...

Beautiful Seduction

In my late-night hunt for the perfect pastry, I never expected to be the victim of a brutal attack… or for a brooding, blue-eyed stranger to become my savior, tending to my wounds while easing my fears. The electricity exploded between us, turning into a night of incredible passion.

Only later did I learn that Valentin Vincheti is the heir to the New York Italian mafia empire.

Then he came to take me, and this time he wasn't gentle. I shouldn't have surrendered, but with each savage kiss and stinging stroke of his belt his beautiful seduction became more difficult to resist. But when one of his enemies sets his sights on me, will my secrets put our lives at risk?

Beautiful Obsession

After I was left at the altar, I turned what was meant to be the reception into an epic party. But when a handsome stranger asked me to dance, I wasn't prepared for the passion he ignited.

He told me he was a very bad man, but that only made my heart race faster as I lay bare and bound, my dress discarded and my bottom sore from a spanking, waiting for him to ravage me.

It was supposed to be just one night. No strings. Nothing to entangle me in his dangerous world.

But that was before I became his beautiful obsession…

Beautiful Devil

Kostya Baranov is an infamous assassin, a man capable of incredible savagery, but when I witnessed a mafia hit he didn't silence me with a bullet. He decided to make me his instead.

Taken prisoner and forced to obey or feel the sting of his belt, shameful lust for my captor soon wars with fury at what he has done to me… and what he keeps doing to me with every touch.

But though he may be a beautiful devil, it is my own family's secret which may damn us both.

BOOKS OF THE BENEDETTI EMPIRE SERIES

Cruel Prince

Catherine's father conspired to have my father killed, and that debt to the Benedetti family must be settled. Just as he took something from me, I will take something from him.

His daughter.

She will be mine to punish and ravage, but when she suffers it will not be for his sins.

It will be for my pleasure.

She will beg, but it will be for me to claim her in the most shameful ways imaginable.

She will scream, but it will be because she doesn't think she can bear another climax.

But when she surrenders at last, it will not be to her captor.

It will be to her husband.

Ruthless Prince

Alexandra is a senator's daughter, used to mingling in the company of the rich and powerful, but tonight she will learn that there are men who play by different rules.

Men like me.

I could romance her. I could seduce her and then carry her gently to my bed.

But that can wait. Tonight I'm going to wring one ruthless climax after another from her quivering body with her bottom burning from my belt and her throat sore from screaming.

She will know she is mine before she even knows she is my bride.

Savage Prince

Gillian's father may be a powerful Irish mob boss, but he owes a blood debt to my family, and when I came to collect I didn't ask permission before taking his daughter as payment.

It was not up to him… or to her.

I will make her my bride, but I am not the kind of man who will wait until our wedding night to bare her and claim what belongs to me. She will walk down the aisle wet, well-used, and sore.

Her dress will hide the marks from my belt that taught her the consequences of disobeying her husband, but nothing will hide her blushes as her arousal drips down her thighs with each step.

By the time she says her vows she will already be mine.

BOOKS OF THE MERCILESS KINGS SERIES

King's Captive

Emily Porter saw me kill a man who betrayed my family and she helped put me behind bars. But someone with my connections doesn't stay in prison long, and she is about to learn the hard way that there is a price to pay for crossing the boss of the King dynasty. A very, very painful price...

She's going to cry for me as I blister that beautiful bottom, then she's going to scream for me as I ravage her over and over again, taking her in the most shameful ways she can imagine. But leaving her well-punished and well-used is just the beginning of what I have in store for Emily.

I'm going to make her my bride, and then I'm going to make her mine completely.

King's Hostage

When my life was threatened, Michael King didn't just take matters into his own hands.

He took me.

When he carried me off it was partly to protect me, but mostly it was because he wanted me.

I didn't choose to go with him, but it wasn't up to me. That's why I'm naked, wet, and sore in an opulent Swiss chalet with my bottom still burning from the belt of the infuriatingly sexy mafia boss who brought me here, punished me when I fought him, and then savagely made me his.

We'll return when things are safe in New Orleans, but I won't be going back to my old home.

I belong to him now, and he plans to keep me.

King's Possession

Her father had to be taught what happens when you cross a King, but that isn't why Genevieve Rossi is sore, well-used, and waiting for me to claim her in the only way I haven't already.

She's sore because she thought she could embarrass me in public without being punished.

She's well-used because after I spanked her I wanted more, and I take what I want.

She's waiting for me in my bed because she's my bride, and tonight is our wedding night.

I'm not going to be gentle with her, but when she wakes up tomorrow morning wet and blushing her cheeks won't be crimson because of the shameful things I did to her naked, quivering body.

It will be because she begged for all of them.

King's Toy

Vincenzo King thought I knew something about a man who betrayed him, but that isn't why I'm on my way to New Orleans well-used and sore with my backside still burning from his belt.

When he bared and punished me maybe it was just business, but what came after was not.

It was savage, it was shameful, and it was very, very personal.

I'm his toy now, and not the kind you keep in its box on the shelf.

He's going to play rough with me.

He's going to get me all wet and dirty.

Then he's going to do it all again tomorrow.

King's Demands

Julieta Morales hoped to escape an unwanted marriage, but the moment she got into my car her fate was sealed. She will have a husband, but it won't be the cartel boss her father chose for her.

It will be me.

But I'm not the kind of man who takes his bride gently amid rose petals on her wedding night. She'll learn to satisfy her King's demands with her bottom burning and her hair held in my fist.

She'll promise obedience when she speaks her vows, but she'll be mastered long before then.

King's Temptation

I didn't think I needed Dimitri Kristoff's protection, but it wasn't up to me. With a kingpin from a rival family coming after me, he took charge, took off his belt, and then took what he wanted.

He knows I'm not used to doing as I'm told. He just doesn't care.

The stripes seared across my bare bottom left me sore and sorry, but it was what came after that truly left me shaken. The princess of the King family shouldn't be on her knees for anyone, let alone this Bratva brute who has decided to claim for himself what he was meant to safeguard.

Nobody gave me to him, but I'm his anyway.

Now he's going to make sure I know it.

BOOKS OF THE MAFIA MASTERS SERIES

His as Payment

Caroline Hargrove thinks she is mine because her father owed me a debt, but that isn't why she is sitting in my car beside me with her bottom sore inside and out. She's wet, well-used, and coming with me whether she likes it or not because I decided I want her, and I take what I want.

As a senator's daughter, she probably thought no man would dare lay a hand on her, let alone spank her thoroughly and then claim her beautiful body in the most shameful ways possible.

She was wrong. Very, very wrong. She's going to be mastered, and I won't be gentle about it.

Taken as Collateral

Francesca Alessandro was just meant to be collateral, held captive as a warning to her father, but then she tried to fight me. She ended up sore and soaked as I taught her a lesson with my belt and then screaming with every savage climax as I taught her to obey in a much more shameful way.

She's mine now. Mine to keep. Mine to protect. Mine to use as hard and as often as I please.

Forced to Cooperate

Willow Church is not the first person who tried to put a bullet in me. She's just the first I let live. Now she will pay the price in the most shameful way imaginable. The stripes from my belt will teach her to obey, but what happens to her sore, red bottom after that will teach the real lesson.

She will be used mercilessly, over and over, and every brutal climax will remind her of the humiliating truth: she never even had a chance against me. Her body always knew its master.

Claimed as Revenge

Valencia Rivera became mine the moment her father broke the agreement he made with me. She thought she had a say in the matter, but my belt across her beautiful bottom taught her otherwise and a night spent screaming her surrender into the sheets left her in no doubt she belongs to me.

Using her hard and often will not be all it takes to tame her properly, but it will be a good start...

Made to Beg

Sierra Fox showed up at my door to ask for my protection, and I gave it to her... for a price. She belongs to me now, and I'm going to use her beautiful body as thoroughly as I please. The only thing for her to decide is how sore her cute little bottom will be when I'm through claiming her.

She came to me begging for help, but as her moans and screams grow louder with every brutal climax, we both know it won't be long before she begs me for something far more shameful.

BOOKS OF THE EDGE OF DARKNESS SERIES

Dark Stranger

On a dark, rainy night, I received a phone call. I shouldn't have answered it... but I did.

The things he says he'll do to me are far from sweet, this man I know only by his voice.

They're so filthy I blush crimson just hearing them... and yet still I answer, my panties always soaked the moment the phone rings. But this isn't going to end when I decide it's gone too far...

I can tell him to leave me alone, but I know it won't keep him away. He's coming for me, and when he does he's going to make me his in all the rough, shameful ways he promised he would.

And I'll be wet and ready for him... whether I want to be or not.

Dark Predator

She thinks I'm seducing her, but this isn't romance. It's something much more shameful.

Eden tried to leave the mafia behind, but someone far more dangerous has set his sights on her.

Me.

She was meant to be my revenge against an old enemy, but I decided to make her mine instead.

She'll moan as my belt lashes her quivering bottom and writhe as I claim her in the filthiest of ways, but that's just the beginning. When I'm done, it won't be just her body that belongs to me.

I'll own her heart and soul too.

BOOKS OF THE DARK OVERTURE SERIES

Indecent Invitation

I shouldn't be here.

My clothes shouldn't be scattered around the room, my bottom shouldn't be sore, and I certainly shouldn't be screaming into the sheets as a ruthless tycoon takes everything he wants from me.

I shouldn't even know Houston Powers at all, but I was in a bad spot and I was made an offer.

A shameful, indecent offer I couldn't refuse.

I was desperate, I needed the money, and I didn't have a choice. Not a real one, anyway.

I'm here because I signed a contract, but I'm his because he made me his.

Illicit Proposition

I should have known better.

His proposition was shameful. So shameful I threw my drink in his face when I heard it.

Then I saw the look in his eyes, and I knew I'd made a mistake.

I fought as he bared me and begged as he spanked me, but it didn't matter. All I could do was moan, scream, and climax helplessly for him as he took everything he wanted from me.

By the time I signed the contract, I was already his.

Unseemly Entanglement

I was warned about Frederick Duvall. I was told he was dangerous. But I never suspected that meeting the billionaire advertising mogul to discuss a business proposition would end with me bent over a table with my dress up and my panties down for a shameful lesson in obedience.

That should have been it. I should have told him what he could do with his offer and his money.

But I didn't.

I could say it was because two million dollars is a lot of cash, but as I stand before him naked, bound, and awaiting the sting of his cane for daring to displease him, I know that's not the truth.

I'm not here because he pays me. I'm here because he owns me.

BOOKS OF THE CLUB DARKNESS SERIES

Bent to His Will

Even the most powerful men in the world know better than to cross me, but Autumn Sutherland thought she could spy on me in my own club and get away with it. Now she must be punished.

She tried to expose me, so she will be exposed. Bare, bound, and helplessly on display, she'll beg for mercy as my strap lashes her quivering bottom and my crop leaves its burning welts on her most intimate spots. Then she'll scream my name as she takes every inch of me, long and hard.

When I am done with her, she won't just be sore and shamefully broken. She will be mine.

Broken by His Hand

Sophia Russo tried to keep away from me, but just thinking about what I would do to her left her panties drenched. She tried to hide it, but I didn't let her. I tore those soaked panties off, spanked her bare little bottom until she had no doubt who owns her, and then took her long and hard.

She begged and screamed as she came for me over and over, but she didn't learn her lesson…

She didn't just come back for more. She thought she could disobey me and get away with it.

This time I'm not just going to punish her. I'm going to break her.

Bound by His Command

Willow danced for the rich and powerful at the world's most exclusive club… until tonight.

Tonight I told her she belongs to me now, and no other man will touch her again.

Tonight I ripped her soaked panties from her beautiful body and taught her to obey with my belt.

Tonight I took her as mine, and I won't be giving her up.

MORE MAFIA AND BILLIONAIRE ROMANCES BY PIPER STONE

Caught

If you're forced to come to an arrangement with someone as dangerous as Jagger Calduchi, it means he's about to take what he wants, and you'll give it to him… even if it's your body.

I got caught snooping where I didn't belong, and Jagger made me an offer I couldn't refuse. A week with him where his rules are the only rules, or his bought and paid for cops take me to jail.

He's going to punish me, train me, and master me completely. When he's used me so shamefully I blush just to think about it, maybe he'll let me go home… or maybe he'll decide to keep me.

Ruthless

Treating a mobster shot by a rival's goons isn't really my forte, but when a man is powerful enough to have a whole wing of a hospital cleared out for his protection, you do as you're told.

To make matters worse, this isn't first time I've met Giovanni Calduchi. It turns out my newest patient is the stern, sexy brute who all but dragged me back to his hotel room a couple of nights ago so he could use my body as he pleased, then showed up at my house the next day, stripped me bare, and spanked me until I was begging him to take me even more roughly and shamefully.

Now, with his enemies likely to be coming after me in order to get to him, all I can do is hope he's as good at keeping me safe as he is at keeping me blushing, sore, and thoroughly satisfied.

Dangerous

I knew Erik Chenault was dangerous the moment I saw him. Everything about him should have warned me away, from the scar on his face to the fact that mobsters call him Blade. But I was drawn like a moth to a flame, and I ended up burnt... and blushing, sore, and thoroughly used.

Now he's taken it upon himself to protect me from men like the ones we both tried to leave in our past. He's going to make me his whether I like it or not... but I think I'm going to like it.

Prey

Within moments of setting eyes on Sophia Waters, I was certain of two things. She was going to learn what happens to bad girls who cheat at cards, and I was going to be the one to teach her.

But there was one thing I didn't know as I reddened that cute little bottom and then took her long and hard and oh so shamefully: I wasn't the only one who didn't come here for a game of cards.

I came to kill a man. It turns out she came to protect him.

Nobody keeps me from my target, but I'm in no rush. Not when I'm enjoying this game of cat and mouse so much. I'll even let her catch me one day, and as she screams my name with each brutal climax she'll finally realize the truth. She was never the hunter. She was always the prey.

Given

Stephanie Michaelson was given to me, and she is mine. The sooner she learns that, the less often her cute little bottom will end up well-punished and sore as she is reminded of her place.

But even as she promises obedience with tears running down her cheeks, I know it isn't the sting of my belt that will truly tame her. It is what comes next that will leave her in no doubt she belongs to me. That part will be long, hard, and shameful... and I will make her beg for all of it.

Dangerous Stranger

I came to Spain hoping to start a new life away from dangerous men, but then I met Rafael Santiago. Now I'm not just caught up in the affairs of a mafia boss, I'm being forced into his car.

When I saw something I shouldn't have, Rafael took me captive, stripped me bare, and punished me until he felt certain I'd told him everything I knew about his organization… which was nothing at all. Then he offered me his protection in return for the right to use me as he pleases.

Now that I belong to him, his plans for me are more shameful than I could have ever imagined.

Indebted

After her father stole from me, I could have left Alessandra Toro in jail for a crime she didn't commit. But I have plans for her. A deal with the judge—the kind only a man like me can arrange—made her my captive, and she will pay her father's debt with her beautiful body.

She will try to run, of course, but it won't be the law that comes after her. It will be me.

The sting of my belt across her quivering bare bottom will teach Alessandra the price of defiance, but it is the far more shameful penance that follows which will truly tame her.

Taken

When Winter O'Brien was given to me, she thought she had a say in the matter. She was wrong.

She is my bride. Mine to claim, mine to punish, and mine to use as shamefully as I please. The sting of my belt on her bare bottom will teach her to obey, but obedience is just the beginning.

I will demand so much more.

Bratva's Captive

I told Chloe Kingstrom that getting close to me would be dangerous, and she should keep her distance. The moment she disobeyed and followed me into that bar, she became mine.

Now my enemies are after her, but it's not what they would do to her she should worry about.

It's what I'm going to do to her.

My belt across her bare backside will teach her obedience, but what comes after will be different.

She's going to blush, beg, and scream with every climax as she's ravaged more thoroughly than she can imagine. Then I'm going to flip her over and claim her in an even more shameful way.

If she's a good girl, I might even let her enjoy it.

Hunted

Hope Gracen was just another target to be tracked down… until I caught her.

When I discovered I'd been lied to, I carried her off.

She'll tell me the truth with her bottom still burning from my belt, but that isn't why she's here.

I took her to protect her. I'm keeping her because she's mine.

Theirs as Payment

Until mere moments ago, I was a doctor heading home after my shift at the hospital. But that was before I was forced into the back seat of an SUV, then bared and spanked for trying to escape.

Now I'm just leverage for the Cabello brothers to use against my father, but it isn't the thought of being held hostage by these brutes that has my heart racing and my whole body quivering.

It is the way they're looking at me…

Like they're about to tear my clothes off and take turns mounting me like wild beasts.

Like they're going to share me, using me in ways more shameful than I can even imagine.

Like they own me.

Ruthless Acquisition

I knew the shameful stakes when I bet against these bastards. I just didn't expect to lose.

Now they've come to collect their winnings.

But they aren't just planning to take a belt to my bare bottom for trying to run and then claim everything they're owed from my naked, helpless body as I blush, beg, and scream for them.

They've acquired me, and they plan to keep me.

Bound by Contract

I knew I was in trouble the moment Gregory Steele called me into his office, but I wasn't expecting to end up stripped bare and bent over his desk for a painful lesson from his belt.

Taking a little bit of money here and there might have gone unnoticed in another organization, but stealing from one of the most powerful mafia bosses on the West Coast has consequences.

It doesn't matter why I did it. The only thing that matters now is what he's going to do to me.

I have no doubt he will use me shamefully, but he didn't make me sign that contract just to show me off with my cheeks blushing and my bottom sore under the scandalous outfit he chose for me.

Now that I'm his, he plans to keep me.

Dangerous Addiction

I went looking for a man working with my enemies. When I found only her instead, I should have just left her alone... or maybe taken what I wanted from her and then left... but I didn't.

I couldn't.

So I carried her off to keep for myself.

She didn't make it easy for me, and that earned her a lesson in obedience. A shameful one.

But as her bare bottom reddens under my punishing hand I can see her arousal dripping down her quivering thighs, and no matter how much she squirms and sobs and begs we both know exactly what she needs, and we both know as soon as this spanking is over I'm going to give it to her.

Hard.

Auction House

When I went undercover to investigate a series of murders with links to Steele Franklin's auction house operation, I expected to be sold for the humiliating use of one of his fellow billionaires.

But he wanted me for himself.

No contract. No agreed upon terms. No say in the matter at all except whether to surrender to his shameful demands without a fight or make him strip me bare and spank me into submission first.

I chose the second option, but as one devastating climax after another is forced from my naked, quivering body, what scares me isn't the thought of him keeping me locked up in a cage forever.

It's knowing he won't need to.

Interrogated

As Liam McGinty's belt lashes my bare backside, it isn't the burning sting or the humiliating awareness that my body's surrender is on full display for this ruthless mobster that shocks me.

It's the fact that this isn't a scene from one of my books.

I almost can't process the fact that I'm really riding in the back of a luxury SUV belonging to the most powerful Irish mafia boss in New York—the man I've written so much about—with my cheeks blushing, my bottom sore inside and out, and my arousal soaking the seat beneath me.

But whether I can process it or not, I'm his captive now.

Maybe he'll let me go when he's gotten the answers he needs and he's used me as he pleases.

Or maybe he'll keep me…

Vow of Seduction

Alexander Durante, Brogan Lancaster, and Daniel Norwood are powerful, dangerous men, but that won't keep them safe from me. Not after they let my brother take the fall for their crimes.

I spent years preparing for my chance at revenge. But things didn't go as planned…

Now I'm naked, bound, and helpless, waiting to be used and punished as these brutes see fit, and yet what's on my mind isn't how to escape all of the shameful things they're going to do to me.

It's whether I even want to…

Brutal Heir

When I went to an author convention, I didn't expect to find myself enjoying a rooftop meal with the sexiest cover model in the business, let alone screaming his name in bed later that night.

I didn't plan to be targeted by assassins, rushed to a helicopter under cover of armed men, and then spirited away to his home country with my bottom still burning from a spanking either, but it turns out there are some really important things I didn't know about Diavolo Montoya…

Like the fact that he's the heir to a notorious crime syndicate.

I should hate him, but even as his prisoner our connection is too intense to ignore, and I'm beginning to realize that what began as a moment of passion is going to end with me as his.

Forever.

Bed of Thorns

Hardened by years spent in prison for a crime he didn't commit, Edmond Montego is no longer the gentle man I remember. When he came for me, he didn't just take me for the very first time.

He claimed my virgin body with a savagery that left me screaming… and he made me beg for it.

I should have run when I had the chance, but with every lash of his belt, every passionate kiss, and every brutal climax, I fell more and more under his spell.

But he has a dark secret, and if we're not careful, we'll lose everything… including our lives.

BOOKS OF THE MISSOULA BAD BOYS
SERIES

Phoenix

As a single dad, a battle-scarred Marine, and a smokejumper, my life was complicated enough. Then Wren Tillman showed up in town, full of sass and all but begging for my belt, and what began as a passionate night after I rescued her from a snowstorm quickly became much more.

Her father plans to marry her off for his own gain, but I've claimed her, and I plan to keep her.

She can fight it if she wants, but in her heart she knows she's already mine.

BOOKS OF THE MONTANA BAD BOYS SERIES

Hawk

He's a big, angry Marine, and I'm going to be sore when he's done with me.

Hawk Travers is not a man to be trifled with. I learned that lesson in the hardest way possible, first with a painful, humiliating public spanking and then much more shamefully in private.

She came looking for trouble. She got a taste of my belt instead.

Bryce Myers pushed me too far and she ended up with her bottom welted. But as satisfying as it is to hear this feisty little reporter scream my name as I put her in her place, I get the feeling she isn't going to stop snooping around no matter how well-used and sore I leave her cute backside.

She's gotten herself in way over her head, but she's mine now, and I protect what's mine.

Scorpion

He didn't ask if I like it rough. It wasn't up to me.

I thought I could get away with pissing off a big, tough Marine. I ended up with my face planted in the sheets, my burning bottom raised high, and my hair held tightly in his fist as he took me long and hard and taught me the kind of shameful lesson only a man like Scorpion could teach.

She was begging for a taste of my belt. She got much more than that.

Getting so tipsy she thought she could be sassy with me in my own bar earned Caroline a spanking, but it was trying to make off with my truck that sealed the deal. She'll feel my belt across her bare backside, then she'll scream my name as she takes every single inch of me.

This naughty girl needs to be put in her place, and I'm going to enjoy every moment of it.

Mustang

I tried to tell him how to run his ranch. Then he took off his belt.

When I heard a rumor about his ranch, I confronted Mustang about it. I thought I could go toe to toe with the big, tough former Marine, but I ended up blushing, sore, and very thoroughly used.

I told her it was going to hurt. I meant it.

Danni Brexton is a hot little number with a sharp tongue and a chip on her shoulder. She's the kind of trouble that needs to be ridden hard and put away wet, but only after a taste of my belt.

It will take more than just a firm hand and a burning bottom to tame this sassy spitfire, but I plan to keep her safe, sound, and screaming my name in bed whether she likes it or not. By the time I'm through with her, there won't be a shadow of a doubt in her mind that she belongs to me.

Nash

When he caught me on his property, he didn't call the police. He just took off his belt.

Nash caught me breaking into his shed while on the run from the mob, and when he demanded answers and obedience I gave him neither. Then he took off his belt and taught me in the most shameful way possible what happens to naughty girls who play games with a big, rough Marine.

She's mine to protect. That doesn't mean I'm going to be gentle with her.

Michelle doesn't just need a place to hide out. She needs a man who will bare her bottom and spank her until she is sore and sobbing whenever she puts herself at risk with reckless defiance, then shove her face into the sheets and make her scream his name with every savage climax.

She'll get all of that from me, and much, much more.

Austin

I offered this brute a ride. I ended up the one being ridden.

The first time I saw Austin, he was hitchhiking. I stopped to give him a lift, but I didn't end up taking this big, rough former Marine wherever he was heading. He was far too busy taking me.

She thought she was in charge. Then I took off my belt.

When Francesca Montgomery pulled up beside me, I didn't know who she was, but I knew what she needed and I gave it to her. Long, hard, and thoroughly, until she was screaming my name as she climaxed over and over with her quivering bare bottom still sporting the marks from my belt.

But someone wants to hurt her, and when someone tries to hurt what's mine, I take it personally.

Debt of Honor

Isabella Adams is a brilliant scientist, but her latest discovery has made her a target of Russian assassins. I've been assigned to protect her, and when her reckless behavior puts her in danger she'll learn in the most shameful of ways what it means to be under the command of a Marine.

She can beg and plead as my belt lashes her bare backside, but the only mercy she'll receive is the chance to scream as she climaxes over and over with her well-spanked bottom still burning.

As my past returns to haunt me, it'll take every skill I've mastered to keep her alive.

She may be a national treasure, but she belongs to me now.

Debt of Loyalty

After she was kidnapped in broad daylight, I was hired to bring Willow Cavanaugh home, but as the daughter of a wealthy family she's used to getting what she wants rather than taking orders.

Too bad.

She'll do as she's told or she'll earn herself a stern, shameful reminder of who is in charge, but it will take more than just a well-spanked bare bottom to truly tame this feisty little rich girl.

She'll learn her place over my knee, but it's in my bed that I'll make her mine.

Debt of Sacrifice

When she witnessed a murder, it put Greer McDuff on a brutal cartel's radar... and on mine.

As a former Navy SEAL now serving with the elite Eagle Force, my assignment is to protect her by any means necessary. If that requires a stern reminder of who is in charge with her bottom bare over my knee and then an even more shameful lesson in my bed, then that's what she'll get.

There's just one problem.

The only place I know I can keep her safe is the ranch I left behind and vowed never to return.

BOOKS OF THE DANGEROUS BUSINESS SERIES

Persuasion

Her father stole something from the mob and they hired me to get it back, but that's not the real reason Giliana Worthington is locked naked in a cage with her bottom well-used and sore.

I brought her here so I could take my time punishing her, mastering her, and ravaging her helpless, quivering body over and over again as she screams and moans and begs for more.

I didn't take her as a hostage. I took her because she is mine.

Bad Men

I thought I could run away from the marriage the mafia arranged for me, but I ended up held prisoner in a foreign country by someone far more dangerous than the man I tried to escape.

Then Jack and Diego came for me.

They didn't ask if I wanted to be theirs. They just took me.

I ran, but they caught me, stripped me bare, and punished me in the most shameful way possible.

Now they're going to share me, and they're not going to be gentle about it.

BOOKS OF THE ALPHA DYNASTY SERIES

Unchained Beast

As the firstborn of the Dupree family, I have spent my life building the wealth and power of our mafia empire while keeping our dark secret hidden and my savage hunger at bay. But the beast within me cannot be chained forever, and I must claim a mate before I lose control completely…

That is why Coraline LeBlanc is mine.

When I mount and ravage her, it won't be because I want her. It will be because I need her.

But that doesn't mean I won't enjoy stripping her bare and spanking her until she surrenders, then making her beg and scream with every desperate climax as I take what belongs to me.

The beast will claim her, but I will keep her.

Savage Brute

It wasn't his mafia birthright that made Dax Dupree a monster. Years behind bars and a brutal war with a rival organization made him hard as steel, but the beast he can barely control was always there, and without a mate to mark and claim it would soon take hold of him completely.

I didn't know that when he showed up at my bar after closing and spanked me until I was wet and shamefully ready for him to mount and ravage me, or even when I woke the next morning with my throat sore from screaming and his seed still drying on my thighs. But I know it now.

Because I'm his mate.

Ruthless Monster

When Esme Rawlings looks at me, she sees many things. A ruthless mob boss. A key witness to the latest murder in an ongoing turf war. A guardian angel who saved her from a hitman's bullet.

But when I look at her, I see just one thing.

My mate.

She can investigate me as thoroughly as she feels necessary, prying into every aspect of my family's vast mafia empire, but the only truth she really needs to know about me she will learn tonight with her bare bottom burning and her protests drowned out by her screams of climax.

I take what belongs to me.

Ravenous Predator

Suzette Barker thought she could steal from the most powerful mafia boss in Philadelphia. My belt across her naked backside taught her otherwise, but as tears run down her cheeks and her arousal glistens on her bare thighs, there is something more important she will understand soon.

Kneeling at my feet and demonstrating her remorseful surrender in the most shameful way possible won't bring an end to this, nor will her screams of climax as I take her long and hard. She'll be coming with me and I'll be mounting and savagely rutting her as often as I please.

Not just because she owes me.

Because she's my mate.

Merciless Savage

Christoff Dupree doesn't strike me as the kind of man who woos a woman gently, so when I saw the flowers on my kitchen table I knew it wasn't just a gesture of appreciation for saving his life.

This ruthless mafia boss wasn't seducing me. Those roses mean that I belong to him now.

That I'm his to spank into shameful submission before he mounts me and claims me savagely.

That I'm his mate.

BOOKS OF THE ALPHA BEASTS SERIES

King's Mate

Her scent drew me to her, but something deeper and more powerful told me she was mine. Something that would not be denied. Something that demanded I claim her then and there.

I took her the way a beast takes his mate. Roughly. Savagely. Without mercy or remorse.

She will run, and when she does she will be punished, but it is not me that she fears. Every quivering, desperate climax reminds her that her body knows its master, and that terrifies her.

She knows I am not a gentle king, and she will scream for me as she learns her place.

Beast's Claim

Raven is not one of my kind, but the moment I caught her scent I knew she belonged to me.

She is my mate, and when I claim her it will not be gentle. She can fight me, but her pleas for mercy as she is punished will soon give way to screams of climax as she is mounted and rutted.

By the time I am finished with her, the evidence of her body's surrender will be mingled with my seed as it drips down her bare thighs. But she will be more than just sore and utterly spent.

She will be mine.

Alpha's Mate

I didn't ask Nicolina to be my mate. It was not up to her. An alpha takes what belongs to him.

She will plead for mercy as she is bared and punished for daring to run from me, but her screams as she is claimed and rutted will be those of helpless climax as her body surrenders to its master.

She is mine, and I'm going to make sure she knows it.

Claimed by the Beasts

Though she has done her best to run from it, Scarlet Dumane cannot escape what is in store for her. She has known for years that she is destined to belong not just to one savage beast, but to three, and now the time has come for her to be claimed. Soon her mates will own every inch of her beautiful body, and she will be shared and used as roughly and as often as they please.

Scarlet hid from the disturbing truth about herself, her family, and her town for as long as she could, but now her grandmother's death has finally brought her back home to the bayous of Louisiana and at last she must face her fate, no matter how shameful and terrifying.

She will be a queen, but her mates will be her masters, and defiance will be thoroughly punished. Yet even when she is stripped bare and spanked until she is sobbing, her need for them only grows, and every blush, moan, and quivering climax binds her to them more tightly. But with enemies lurking in the shadows, can she trust her mates to protect her from both man and beast?

Millionaire Daddy

Dominick Asbury is not just a handsome millionaire whose deep voice makes Jenna's tummy flutter whenever they are together, nor is he merely the first man bold enough to strip her bare and spank her hard and thoroughly whenever she has been naughty. He is much more than that.

He is her daddy.

He is the one who punishes her when she's been a bad girl, and he is the one who takes her in his arms afterwards and brings her to one climax after another until she is utterly spent and satisfied.

But something shady is going on behind the scenes at Dominick's company, and when Jenna draws the wrong conclusion from a poorly written article about him and creates an embarrassing public scene, will she end up not only costing them both their jobs but losing her daddy as well?

Conquering Their Mate

For years the Cenzans have cast a menacing eye on Earth, but it still came as a shock to be captured, stripped bare, and claimed as a mate by their leader and his most trusted warriors.

It infuriates me to be punished for the slightest defiance and forced to submit to these alien brutes, but as I'm led naked through the corridors of their ship, my well-punished bare bottom and my helpless arousal both fully on display, I cannot help wondering how long it will be until I'm kneeling at the feet of my mates and begging them take me as shamefully as they please.

Captured and Kept

Since her career was knocked off track in retaliation for her efforts to expose a sinister plot by high-ranking government officials, reporter Danielle Carver has been stuck writing puff pieces in a small town in Oregon. Desperate for a serious story, she sets out to investigate the rumors she's been hearing about mysterious men living in the mountains nearby. But when she secretly follows them back to their remote cabin, the ruggedly handsome beasts don't take kindly to her snooping around, and Dani soon finds herself stripped bare for a painful, humiliating spanking.

Their rough dominance arouses her deeply, and before long she is blushing crimson as they take turns using her beautiful body as thoroughly and shamefully as they please. But when Dani uncovers the true reason for their presence in the area, will more than just her career be at risk?

Taming His Brat

It's been years since Cooper Dawson left her small Texas hometown, but after her stubborn defiance gets her fired from two jobs in a row, she knows something definitely needs to change. What she doesn't expect, however, is for her sharp tongue and arrogant attitude to land her over the knee of a stern, ruggedly sexy cowboy for a painful, embarrassing, and very public spanking.

Rex Sullivan cannot deny being smitten by Cooper, and the fact that she is in desperate need of his belt across her bare backside only makes the war-hardened ex-Marine more determined to tame the beautiful, fiery redhead. It isn't long before she's screaming his name as he shows her just how hard and roughly a cowboy can ride a headstrong filly. But Rex and Cooper both have secrets, and when the demons of their past rear their ugly heads, will their romance be torn apart?

Capturing Their Mate

I thought the Cenzan invaders could never find me here, but I was wrong. Three of the alien brutes came to take me, and before I ever set foot aboard their ship I had already been stripped bare, spanked thoroughly, and claimed more shamefully then I would have ever thought possible.

They have decided that a public example must be made of me, and I will be punished and used in the most humiliating ways imaginable as a warning to anyone who might dare to defy them. But I am no ordinary breeder, and the secrets hidden in my past could change their world… or end it.

Rogue

Tracking down cyborgs is my job, but this time I'm the one being hunted. This rogue machine has spent most of his life locked up, and now that he's on the loose he has plans for me…

He isn't just going to strip me, punish me, and use me. He will take me longer and harder than any human ever could, claiming me so thoroughly that I will be left in no doubt who owns me.

No matter how shamefully I beg and plead, my body will be ravaged again and again with pleasure so intense it terrifies me to even imagine, because that is what he was built to do.

Roughneck

When I took a job on an oil rig to escape my scheming stepfather's efforts to set me up with one of his business cronies, I knew I'd be working with rugged men. What I didn't expect is to find myself bent over a desk, my cheeks soaked with tears and my bare thighs wet for a very different reason, as my well-punished bottom is thoroughly used by a stern, infuriatingly sexy roughneck.

Even though I should have known better than to get sassy with a firm-handed cowboy, let alone a tough-as-nails former Marine, there's no denying that learning the hard way was every bit as hot as it was shameful. But a sore, welted backside is just the start of his plans for me, and no matter how much I blush to admit it, I know I'm going to take everything he gives me and beg for more.

Hunting Their Mate

As far as I'm concerned, the Cenzans will always be the enemy, and there can be no peace while they remain on our planet. I planned to make them pay for invading our world, but I was hunted down and captured by two of their warriors with the help of a battle-hardened former Marine. Now I'm the one who is going to pay, as the three of them punish me, shame me, and share me.

Though the thought of a fellow human taking the side of these alien brutes enrages me, that is far from the worst of it. With every searing stroke of the strap that lands across my bare bottom, with every savage thrust as I am claimed over and over, and with every screaming climax, it is made more clear that it is my own quivering, thoroughly used body which has truly betrayed me.

Primitive

I was sent to this world to help build a new Earth, but I was shocked by what I found here. The men of this planet are not just primitive savages. They are predators, and I am now their prey...

The government lied to all of us. Not all of the creatures who hunted and captured me are aliens. Some of them were human once, specimens transformed in labs into little more than feral beasts.

I fought, but I was thrown over a shoulder and carried off. I ran, but I was caught and punished. Now they are going to claim me, share me, and use me so roughly that when the last screaming climax has been wrung from my naked, helpless body, I wonder if I'll still know my own name.

Harvest

The Centurions conquered Earth long before I was born, but they did not come for our land or our resources. They came for mates, women deemed suitable for breeding. Women like me.

Three of the alien brutes decided to claim me, and when I defied them, they made a public example of me, punishing me so thoroughly and shamefully I might never stop blushing.

But now, as my virgin body is used in every way possible, I'm not sure I want them to stop...

Torched

I work alongside firefighters, so I know how to handle musclebound roughnecks, but Blaise Tompkins is in a league of his own. The night we met, I threw a glass of wine in his face, then ended up shoved against the wall with my panties on the floor and my arousal dripping down my thighs, screaming out climax after shameful climax with my well-punished bottom still burning.

I've got a series of arsons to get to the bottom of, and finding out that the infuriatingly sexy brute who spanked me like a naughty little girl will be helping me with the investigation seemed like the last thing I needed, until somebody hurled a rock through my window in an effort to scare me away from the case. Now having a big, strong man around doesn't seem like such a bad idea...

Fertile

The men who hunt me were always brutes, but now lust makes them barely more than beasts.

When they catch me, I know what comes next.

I will fight, but my need to be bred is just as strong as theirs is to breed. When they strip me, punish me, and use me the way I'm meant to be used, my screams will be the screams of climax.

Hostage

I knew going after one of the most powerful mafia bosses in the world would be dangerous, but I didn't anticipate being dragged from my apartment already sore, sorry, and shamefully used.

My captors don't just plan to teach me a lesson and then let me go. They plan to share me, punish me, and claim me so ruthlessly I'll be screaming my submission into the sheets long before they're through with me. They took me as a hostage, but they'll keep me as theirs.

Defiled

I was born to rule, but for her sake I am banished, forced to wander the Earth among mortals. Her virgin body will pay the price for my protection, and it will be a shameful price indeed.

Stripped, punished, and ravaged over and over, she will scream with every savage climax.

She will be defiled, but before I am done with her she will beg to be mine.

Kept

On the run from corrupt men determined to silence me, I sought refuge in his cabin. I ate his food, drank his whiskey, and slept in his bed. But then the big bad bear came home and I learned the hard way that sometimes Goldilocks ends up with her cute little bottom well-used and sore.

He stripped me, spanked me, and ravaged me in the most shameful way possible, but then this rugged brute did something no one else ever has before. He made it clear he plans to keep me…

Auctioned

Twenty years ago the Malzeons saved us when we were at the brink of self-annihilation, but there was a price for their intervention. They demanded humans as servants… and as pets.

Only criminals were supposed to be offered to the aliens for their use, but when I defied Earth's government, asking questions that no one else would dare to ask, I was sold to them at auction.

I was bought by two of their most powerful commanders, rivals who nonetheless plan to share me. I am their property now, and they intend to tame me, train me, and enjoy me thoroughly.

But I have information they need, a secret guarded so zealously that discovering it cost me my freedom, and if they do not act quickly enough both of our worlds will soon be in grave danger.

Hard Ride

When I snuck into Montana Cobalt's house, I was looking for help learning to ride like him, but what I got was his belt across my bare backside. Then with tears still running down my cheeks and arousal dripping onto my thighs, the big brute taught me a much more shameful lesson.

Montana has agreed to train me, but not just for the rodeo. He's going to break me in and put me through my paces, and then he's going to show me what it means to be ridden rough and dirty.

Carnal

For centuries my kind have hidden our feral nature, our brute strength, and our carnal instincts. But this human female is my mate, and nothing will keep me from claiming and ravaging her.

She is mine to tame and protect, and if my belt doesn't teach her to obey then she'll learn in a much more shameful fashion. Either way, her surrender will be as complete as it is inevitable.

Bounty

After I went undercover to take down a mob boss and ended up betrayed, framed, and on the run, Harper Rollins tried to bring me in. But instead of collecting a bounty, she earned herself a hard spanking and then an even rougher lesson that left her cute bottom sore in a very different way.

She's not one to give up without a fight, but that's fine by me. It just means I'll have plenty more chances to welt her beautiful backside and then make her scream her surrender into the sheets.

Beast

Primitive, irresistible need compelled him to claim me, but it was more than mere instinct that drove this alien beast to punish me for my defiance and then ravage me thoroughly and savagely. Every screaming climax was a brand marking me as his, ensuring I never forget who I belong to.

He's strong enough to take what he wants from me, but that's not why I surrendered so easily as he stripped me bare, pushed me up against the wall, and made me his so roughly and shamefully.

It wasn't fear that forced me to submit. It was need.

Gladiator

Xander didn't just win me in the arena. The alien brute claimed me there too, with my punished bottom still burning and my screams of climax almost drowned out by the roar of the crowd.

Almost…

Victory earned him freedom and the right to take me as his mate, but making me truly his will mean more than just spanking me into shameful surrender and then rutting me like a wild beast. Before he carries me off as his prize, the dark truth that brought me here must be exposed at last.

Big Rig

Alexis Harding is used to telling men exactly what she thinks, but she's never had a roughneck like me as a boss before. On my rig, I make the rules and sassy little girls get stripped bare, bent over my desk, and taught their place, first with my belt and then in a much more shameful way.

She'll be sore and sorry long before I'm done with her, but the arousal glistening on her thighs reveals the truth she would rather keep hidden. She needs it rough, and that's how she'll get it.

Warriors

I knew this was a primitive planet when I landed, but nothing could have prepared me for the rough beasts who inhabit it. The sting of their prince's firm hand on my bare bottom taught me my place in his world, but it was what came after that truly demonstrated his mastery over me.

This alien brute has granted me his protection and his help with my mission, but the price was my total submission to both his shameful demands and those of his second in command as well.

But it isn't the savage way they make use of my quivering body that terrifies me the most. What leaves me trembling is the thought that I may never leave this place… because I won't want to.

Owned

With a ruthless, corrupt billionaire after me, Crockett, Dylan, and Wade are just the men I need. Rough men who know how to keep a woman safe… and how to make her scream their names.

But the Hell's Fury MC doesn't do charity work, and their help will come at a price.

A shameful price…

They aren't just going to bare me, punish me, and then do whatever they want with me.

They're going to make me beg for it.

Seized

Delaney Archer got herself mixed up with someone who crossed us, and now she's going to find out just how roughly and shamefully three bad men like us can make use of her beautiful body.

She can plead for mercy, but it won't stop us from stripping her bare and spanking her until she's sore, sobbing, and soaking wet. Our feisty little captive is going to take everything we give her, and she'll be screaming our names with every savage climax long before we're done with her.

Cruel Masters

I thought I understood the risks of going undercover to report on billionaires flaunting their power, but these men didn't send lawyers after me. They're going to deal with me themselves.

Now I'm naked aboard their private plane, my backside already burning from one of their belts, and these three infuriatingly sexy bastards have only just gotten started teaching me my place.

I'm not just going to be punished, shamed, and shared. I'm going to be mastered.

Hard Men

My father's will left his company to me, but the three roughnecks who ran it for him have other ideas. They're owed a debt and they mean to collect on it, but it's not money these brutes want.

It's me.

In return for protection from my father's enemies, I will be theirs to share. But these are hard men, and they don't just intend to punish my defiance and use me as shamefully as they please.

They plan to master me completely.

Rough Ride

As I hear the leather slide through the loops of his pants, I know what comes next. Jake Travers is going to blister my backside. Then he's going to ride me the way only a rodeo champion can.

Plenty of men who thought they could put me in my place have learned the hard way that I was more than they could handle, and when Jake showed up I was sure he would be no different.

I was wrong.

When I pushed him, he bared and spanked me in front of a bar full of people.

I should have let it go at that, but I couldn't.

That's why he's taking off his belt…

Primal Instinct

Ruger Jameson can buy anything he wants, but that's not the reason I'm his to use as he pleases.

He's a former Army Ranger accustomed to having his orders followed, but that's not why I obey him.

He saved my life after our plane crashed, but I'm not on my knees just to thank him properly.

I'm his because my body knows its master.

I do as I'm told because he blisters my bare backside every time I dare to do otherwise.

I'm at his feet because I belong to him and I plan to show it in the most shameful way possible.

Captor

I was supposed to be safe from the lottery. Set apart for a man who would treat me with dignity.

But as I'm probed and examined in the most intimate, shameful ways imaginable while the hulking alien king who just spanked me looks on approvingly, I know one thing for certain.

This brute didn't end up with me by chance. He wanted me, so he found a way to take me.

He'll savor every blush as I stand bare and on display for him, every plea for mercy as he punishes my defiance, and every quivering climax as he slowly masters my virgin body.

I'll be his before he even claims me.

Rough and Dirty

Wrecking my cheating ex's truck with a bat might have made me feel better… if the one I went after had actually belonged to him, instead of to the burly roughneck currently taking off his belt.

Now I'm bent over in a parking lot with my bottom burning as this ruggedly sexy bastard and his two equally brutish friends take turns reddening my ass, and I can tell they're just getting started.

That thought shouldn't excite me, and I certainly shouldn't be imagining all the shameful things these men might do to me. But what I should or shouldn't be thinking doesn't matter anyway.

They can see the arousal glistening on my thighs, and they know I need it rough and dirty…

His to Take

When Zadok Vakan caught me trying to escape his planet with priceless stolen technology, he didn't have me sent to the mines. He made sure I was stripped bare and sold at auction instead.

Then he bought me for himself.

Even as he punishes me for the slightest hint of defiance and then claims me like a beast, indulging every filthy desire his savage nature can conceive, I swear I'll never surrender.

But it doesn't matter.

I'm already his, and we both know it.

Tyrant

When I accepted a lucrative marketing position at his vineyard, Montgomery Wolfe made the terms of my employment clear right from the start. Follow his rules or face the consequences.

That's why I'm bent over his desk, doing my best to hate him as his belt lashes my bare bottom.

I shouldn't give in to this tyrant. I shouldn't yield to his shameful demands.

Yet I can't resist the passion he sets ablaze with every word, every touch, and every brutally possessive kiss, and I know before long my body will surrender to even his darkest needs…

Filthy Rogue

Losing my job to a woman who slept her way to the top was bad enough, and that was before my car broke down as I drove cross country to start over. Having to be rescued by an infuriatingly sexy biker who promptly bared and spanked me for sassing him was just icing on the cake.

After sharing a passionate night, I might have made a teensy mistake in taking cash from his wallet in order to pay the auto mechanic, but I hadn't thought I'd ever see him again...

Then on the first day at my new job, guess who swaggered in with payback on his mind?

He's living proof that the universe really is out to get me... and he's my new boss.

ABOUT PIPER STONE

Amazon Top 150 Internationally Best-Selling Author, Kindle Unlimited All Star Piper Stone writes in several genres. From her worlds of dark mafia, cowboys, and marines to contemporary reverse harem, shifter romance, and science fiction, she attempts to delight readers with a foray into darkness, sensuality, suspense, and always a romantic HEA. When she's not writing, you can find her sipping merlot while she enjoys spending time with her three Golden Retrievers (Indiana Jones, Magnum PI, and Remington Steele) and a husband who relishes creating fabulous food.

Dangerous is Delicious.

* * *

You can find her at:

Website: https://piperstonebooks.com/

Newsletter: https://piperstonebooks.com/newsletter/

Facebook: https://www.facebook.com/authorpiperstone/

Twitter: http://twitter.com/piperstone01

Instagram: http://www.instagram.com/authorpiperstone/

Amazon: http://amazon.com/author/piperstone

BookBub: http://bookbub.com/authors/piper-stone

TikTok: https://www.tiktok.com/@piperstoneauthor

Email: piperstonecreations@gmail.com

Made in the USA
Middletown, DE
22 March 2023

27389024R00239